The Island of Cundeamor

The Island of Cundeamor

By René Vázquez Díaz

Translated from the Spanish
By David E. Davis

Latin American Literary Review Press
Series: Discoveries
2000

FIL

The Latin American Literary Review Press publishes Latin American creative writing under the series title *Discoveries*, and critical works under the series title *Explorations*.

Library of Congress Cataloging-in-Publication Data

Vázquez Díaz, René
　　[Isla del Cundeamor. English]
　　The island of Cundeamor / by René Vázquez Díaz; translated from the Spanish by David E. Davis.
　　　　p.cm.
　　ISBN 1-891270-04-4
　　　　I.Davis, David E. II Title.

PQ7390.V37 I18513 2000
863--dc21　　　　　　　　　　　　　　　　　　99-089224

Cover design by Merja Vázquez-Díaz.
Courtesy of Alfaguara.

Latin American Literary Review Press
121 Edgewood Avenue
Pittsburgh, PA 15218

Acknowledgment

This project is supported in part
by a grant from the
the Pennsylvania Council on the Arts,
a state agency funded by
the Commonwealth of Pennsylvania.

PENNSYLVANIA
COUNCIL
ON THE
ARTS

Genesis, 4-8

Cain said to Abel, his brother:
Let us go out to the field."

What is that which is outside in man?
Lezama Lima

They said I wouldn't come, but here I am!
Benny Moré

- One -

Somebody was singing in the streets of Miami Beach and Betty Boop, oddly enough, awoke without feeling the slightest bit alone. Her gaze traveled around the semi-darkness of the room and she realized she still had another hour, one whole hour, a blessed hour, before the alarm would go off. She then realized she had slept all night in her false eyelashes.

"Just like an old woman," and her voice was deep, her breath rank and resentful.

And who in the sleepy streets of Miami Beach could be singing at this hour?

"A loud, melancholy voice," said Betty Boop, yawning.

Betty often woke up in the middle of the night, knotted with fear and with a foul taste in her mouth. Choruses of throaty voices would intrude on her dreams to sing out sad news, which was invariably about two topics: Fuñío and Cuba. These were also the two things she would most like to erase from her being for good, but they clung to the fuzzy roots of her soul, coming unleashed at night, rising up like dirty bubbles in the reservoir of her conscience: Fuñío had been found dead; a people's uprising was underway in Cuba; Fuñío had come back; Cuba had sunk into the ocean. Sometimes, just before waking up, she would see a white-gloved hand beckoning her from the darkness. As if feeble-minded, she would obediently approach. The gloved hand would then wave toward a corner where she and Fuñío were lying embraced in a decomposing heap, their absent child looking on vindictively from a window. Other times, she would see a palm grove lashed and twisted by violent winds, and then see herself, stark naked, all alone and crying, running among the palms and their endless rows of trees, assaulted from the stormy skies by thousands of mangy buzzards that fall upon her, devouring her eyes, her breasts, and, this being the stuff of dreams, her toes as well.

But it wasn't a nightmare that awoke her this time, nor the telephone delivering the fateful news about Fuñío that she incessantly waited for; rather it was an *a cappella* melody that noodled sweetly in the damp plush of the early morning. Something between a lullaby and jazz, and Betty Boop felt grateful for that voice in the dawn.

She felt the foul taste in her mouth and the greasy sweat of living in a godforsaken one room apartment without air conditioning. Her itching body made her think about the crime she would commit that day, and she didn't feel afraid. The crucial day had begun with a favorable sign. Before going to work, Betty liked to have enough time to shower and put on perfume, talcum powder and makeup without feeling rushed. She would also water the plants while talking to them, and set out breakfast for Fuñío (when he was at home), managing to bear for yet one more day in her life the hopelessness of having to suffer from a discouragement and having been born under a bad sign. Standing nude before the mirror, she would take stock of the despicable triumphs of age (of maturity, she corrected herself) on her belly and neck, her thighs and face. Especially on her belly, now lapsing into a roll of embarrassing flab (not too thick yet), which if something wasn't done to arrest it, would soon hang over her pubic thicket. But Betty, not without feeling delight, would also take stock of aging's great defeat (maturity's, that is) in its treacherous siege of her breasts and ass and thighs, still caressable, and her beautiful arms and regal demeanor.

Sitting up in bed, she looked down at Fuñío's pillow.

"Wouldn't it be better if they had just found him dead on some street corner?"

Betty made the sign of the cross and added:

"Good Lord!" and she pulled the sheet over her, acrid with sweat. "Almighty God who is everywhere: the only thing I ask of you is that he die a painless death."

She heard the voice in the street again, tender and vigorous, a woman's voice. There was a kind of languid cheerfulness in the tune and Betty paid closer attention to it. As with anything in English, she didn't bother to listen to the words, but instead concentrated on the melody, whose time turned sharp, then riffed into warm, almost pious cadences. The syncopation was now coming through the open blinds more clearly, diluted in the brackish swelter of Miami Beach.

> *Papa says it's too much for me*
> *To try to go to school*

And look for everything, too.
In the summer I do everything.
Oh, I do every, everything.

A radiant voice. Oh, life! To wake up on that ill-fated day of her existence to the beat of that song.

All the washing, cooking and mending.
The children. I don't mind, oh, I don't mind.
Mama taught us all to work
Before she died.
Oh god, before she died.

Her pink robe, made out of static-cling acrylic, had some little flowers on it that used to be yellow, and some lace at the hem, now fraying, which gave her the look of a lazy, slovenly teen. The robe, damp with her sweat, was now plastered against her breasts, which were surprisingly round and attractive, despite the onset of age, or maturity. Betty sighed, grabbed her breasts and exclaimed: This is one Cuban woman proud of her tits!

But the sweat disgusted her.

The sweat from every day. What mystery was behind the Miami brand of sweat that made it so filthy? It was the sweat of exile, polluted, intoxicated, stress-filled and repugnant. Because in Cuba you sweated in a more pleasant, relaxed, decorous and civilized fashion. Only blacks had that funk in Cuba, those poor people (Betty made a gesture of compassion), though it wasn't the climate's doing; rather it was ignorance, since they weren't versed in the ways of bathing or using powders, perfumes and deodorants to turn everything that was balmy, virginal and incorrupt about their island sweat into sweet smells. Because in Cuba, reflected Betty Boop, sweat came out of the body like spring water; indeed, like mineral water. Or maybe men in Cuba, drunk with lust and prolonged ecstasy and fury, didn't lick the sweat off their females. How could they not insatiably lick it all off, if that sweat was a beautiful island sweat scented by the winds! On the other hand, Americans were quite well-organized and rich, adept at filling the skies of Latin America with jets laden with bombs, but incapable of sweating like human beings. Disgusting, thought Betty Boop, to leave that dream island behind to come to Miami and have to break out in its sweat. Now, as she probed deeper, wouldn't Fidel, in collusion with Communism, have twisted around the Cuban tradition of sweating rich? Because wouldn't the Russians -so continued Betty's morning mental digressions- all suffer, Gorbachov included, as well as Lenin in his Tomb, from a chronic stink?

"Now you really have to get up," Betty said firmly.

But she didn't budge.

Without opening her eyes to imagine the itinerary, she followed with masochistic cruelty the beads of sweat sliding down her belly until they disappeared, viscously, into the steam of her bushy pubes. It was the worst sweat imaginable: it wasn't just Miami sweat, but August sweat. And not just that: it was the sweat of twin uncertainties, of the stabbing she would commit within a couple of hours, and of not knowing how or when Fuñío would turn up. Would they deliver him to her dead, maybe flattened by some car, or lying mortally roughed-up in the middle of some ruthless street? Dear Fuñío! Maybe the poor dear was murdered by one of the trillions of degenerates teeming in the streets of Miami.

But what was most horrific was the thought that they would turn him over to her drowned to death. All bloated, purple, fat as a pig and decomposing after spending several days in a marshy bend of the Miami River, or snagged in some brush in Indian Creek! Would she have to go down to the morgue and ID him?

"May God help you, Fuñío," Betty Boop pleaded.

Betty and Fuñío lived in a one room apartment. The kitchen was a little corner without a lot of dignity, but it was functional enough. The apartment had a bath with cold and hot water, which was indispensable since Betty showered several times a day. The place's simplicity could only be compared to its cleanliness and tidiness, which bordered on the unhealthy. The fastidious order of all the objects lent the place a touch of misery. On the walls hung little painted ceramic or porcelain figures: pudgy, pirouetting ballerinas; flaking greyhounds and tigers; faded, weeping clowns; and kittens with forlorn faces. In a gilt-framed painting, newlyweds Betty and Fuñío smiled out from the haze of time lost. There were also flowerpots and plants and vases with artificial, plastic and Chinese paper flowers, all without even a speck of dust on their tiny petals.

Behind the door was the suitcase crammed with clothes and other important articles that Fuñío, whose senility had been driving him prematurely mad for more than two years now, had readied for his immediate return to Cuba as soon as the Castro regime (at long last!) collapsed. But despite the fact that neither Communism nor the Berlin Wall is around anymore, and even though neither the "socialist field" nor the former Union of Soviet Socialist Republics any longer exists, Fidel Castro has stayed in power by virtue of a sinister miracle. When the USSR dissolved like a lump of sugar in the water of Perestroika, Fuñío furiously tossed a bunch of junk into a suitcase, put on a tie he had kept since 1962 and shouted:

"It's finally time to go home once and for all, *coño*! Now that Fidel is fucked!"

But the fall of Castro took longer than Fuñío's health could hold out for. So the suitcase, all alone and longing, stayed there packed and ready to go behind the door, all the while Fuñío grew more and more sclerotic and mad. He would have long spells where he couldn't remember his name, address, wife, or where he was. Sometimes he would be convinced that he had spent all day working in Luyanó; other times he would be breakfasting in a little place over at the Paseo del Prado and then see a bus mishap out on the Malecón.

"Please, honey, you've got to come back to reality," Betty would plead. "Look: we're not in Havana. This is Miami."

"What the fuck are you talking about?" Fuñío would reply. "I just got back from walking up the Malecón from the Hotel Nacional to the Prado, and then all along San Lázaro over to the University! Bullshit. Miami, everyone here's obsessed with Miami."

Curiously, the one thing Fuñío never forgot was his nationality. For now, at least, the moths of senility hadn't taken that from him.

"I'm Cuban, goddammit," he would shout out anywhere, anytime, and without prompting. "And you have to show me respect because we Cubans got the biggest balls of all!"

While saying this, Fuñío would grab his diminished virility with both hands.

Luckily Betty had made him wear a calamine tag around his neck (she would have liked for it to be gold, but they weren't well-off enough to afford those kinds of luxuries; plus, someone would have snatched it right off him). The tag had his first name, last name, date of birth, address and telephone number. Thanks to this tag, the police would find him time and time again, like a stray dog, in the most unusual places. Sometimes they would call for Betty to come down and pick him up; other times they'd drop him off in a squad car. Once, Fuñío even made it over to Disney World. They found him there, lying in his own piss and shit, sound asleep, right inside the palace of the wicked queen from Snow White. Another time they fished him out of one of the busiest and fanciest fountains in downtown Coconut Grove, soaking wet, trembling and stinking of old shit in his pants. In his dementia and confusion, Fuñío roared, gesturing wildly:

"Get your hands off me, or this will mean war!"

And while the security guards were trying to dredge him out, Fuñío swore at them:

"My cock puts all you little Americans' pricks to shame!"

Waiting for the police to arrive, the security guards tried to calm him down, but Fuñío berated them:

"Because we Cubans, with Fidel in charge, have had twenty presidents in This Country with their heads up their shitters."

And as they were hauling him away:

"Cuba *sí*, Yankees go home! *Viva* Fucking Cuba!"

Fuñío's tirades terrorized and confused Betty Boop, because they were an accurate barometer of her husband's dementia. It was incomprehensible that Fuñío, who from the very beginning was Castro's staunchest enemy, would run the risk of publicly praising Castro and the Revolution. Then one time he created a huge scene and almost got lynched for it. That happened at the Plaza de la Cubanidad, over on Flagler and 17th Street. Without anyone starting anything with him first, Fuñió horned in on a group of old Cubans prattling on sentimentally about the destiny of the Fatherland; they had been gathered under the Martí sign hanging over the Plaza that read: "Palm trees are girlfriends that await us..."

"You bunch of shiteaters!" Fuñío boldly insulted them. "You can stop choking on your pipe dreams, *coño*, Castro is eternal! Fuck you all! Thanks to those stupid ass, worthless, asskissing Yankees, you'll never ever be able to return to beautiful little Cuba again!"

Those old guys grabbed poor Fuñío by his neck and smacked him around, spat in his face, and landed a shower of blows to the head and body as they shouted:

"Give this sorry infiltrating piece of crap an ass kicking!"

"Scum, *gusanos*, Batistas!" Fuñío hollered in defense before they clocked his mouth shut.

The offended old men turned Fuñío into waste pulp: flattened and scrapheap-bound. Then the worst happened. Fuñío suddenly began crapping in a torrent, and the whipped-up throng, repulsed, let go of him just as quickly, dropping the poor old guy to the pavement. Fuñío was thoroughly drenched from the waist down in his own diarrhea, and from the waist up in blood from a blow to the head. Then somebody called an ambulance.

"Help him out, men," one of the tormentors suggested sensitively, "this guy's nuttier than a fruitcake."

They returned Betty's husband, covered with medical gauze. That beating had confined Fuñío to home for some time; she cured him with lots of love, reading from the same scriptures as always, telling him to relax, stay at home with God and rest, and stop defying his self-esteem in exile by defending a revolution that had caused them both so much pain.

"Me defend Castro? Me? ME? ME?" And then he would thunder invectives against the Revolution.

Until one day, now more than three months ago, when Betty returned from work to find Fuñío gone. From that point on she hadn't heard a thing. It was as if exile had swallowed him up.

In Cuba, Betty had been happy with Fuñío. They lived in a little small farm town near Villalona, in a beautiful rambling house bounded by *franchipanis*, royal palms, bougainvillea and orange groves. Back in those delicious times they enjoyed an economic situation that made them worthy of everyone's respect, and the sizeable age difference between her and Fuñío wasn't felt as much. Every year they would go into Havana for a few days, stay at the Hotel Nacional, and imitate the life of the rich.

"We enjoyed ourselves splendidly," Betty Boop said while in bed, "but always thanks to me, because Fuñío didn't know how to have fun."

Around that time Fidel emerged messiah-like from the hills with his string of bearded followers, and everything went to hell.

"Even the kids wanted to get involved in all that."

Betty thought about her son, her only son, her spoiled little son, Fuñío's heir, the little man of the house, his father and mother's whole life.

He hadn't yet turned twelve when they sent him to the United States, all by himself. In the first years of the revolution it was rumored that Castro was going to revoke Paternal Authority from all parents on the island, especially from the bourgeoisie, those blights from the past, and ship the children off en masse "to Russia." And there they would indoctrinate, brainwash, and turn them into Marxist-Leninist machines. The powerful North American propaganda machines wildly inflated the balloon of that nonsense and a general panic quickly spread across the island. Prisoners of insecurity and hysteria, thousands and thousands of families, if unable to get visas for all members of the family, were forced to send their kids to the United States as a last ditch measure, to spare them from that terrible fate of the indoctrination laboratories of Siberia and Moscow. The North American government encouraged and facilitated the exodus of these lonely children, and one of the first exiled youngsters was the son of Fuñío and Betty Boop. At first, he was interned at a camp; after a few months he was taken in by an American family from Tampa who, according to the governmental assistance plan, received a monthly pittance to look after the temporary orphan. The child spent two and half years in the bosom of that foreign family.

"I've always thought," Betty said with resignation, "that when we reunited, the boy was already on the road to ruin. If our boy hadn't slipped up, we'd now be living in dignity with his help, just like lots of other families."

"But exile drove him mad. Mad! Or at least the ungrateful kid pretended to be crazy."

In the last ten years, Betty hadn't had a single shred of news as to her son's whereabouts. The last time he came to see them, he cursed out Fuñío, called Betty a bitch and threw a wad of bills out the window to humiliate them both. Poor Fuñío almost tossed himself out the window to catch the money. As far as they knew, the boy didn't have permanent residency and, when not committed to a mental hospital, dedicated himself to a life of crime and delinquency. To make matters worse, somebody had started a rumor that the boy "was communist", and that he had traveled to Cuba several times in some kind of "Antonio Maceo Brigade," or something along those lines, voluntarily cutting down sugar cane and fetching communists' dirty *malangas*, which would confirm the version of his dementia (schizophrenia), along with his perversity, since this latter rumor had plunged Fuñío into the paroxysm of despair. It was later found out that it was all a lie and that the boy had never been in Cuba with the Antonio Maceo Brigade, but that even so, in his madness, he had told everyone that story of what he had done.

"If he'd just stayed in Miami, in his element, he would have grown up to be an upstanding, hard-working, anti-Communist Cuban like his father," Betty said. "But he blamed us for his suffering at having to live apart from us, because it seems that the family from Tampa mistreated him. When he turned sixteen he went "schizo," said the doctors, and then came the mental institution, the running away, jail, the life of crime. "Bullshit," Fuñío would say bitterly, "crazy my ass, he's a bad seed." Our poor boy went to Chicago and then to New York, and the cold there perverted him.

"Yes," Betty affirmed, "he who loses his Cuban reflexes here becomes lost and goes to seed."

For them, exile had been a painful road to ruin. In Cuba, Fuñío had been a bookkeeper. He kept the books of several clothing stores in the area and handled part of the accounting for a sugar plantation.

"We had it easy," Betty sighed, "above all me, since I didn't have to work. I had two maids and we were the cream, the crème de la crème, the *mamey* apple ice cream about town."

Betty felt a slight itching in her pubes. She was about to get up to finish her shower and go to work, but she stayed in bed. She lightly scratched at her moist down and pricked her ears. The melodious voice had stopped and the noise from the traffic motoring down Collins Avenue, was growing louder.

Strictly speaking that is—Betty Boop summed up as if trying to better understand her situation—, Fuñío's professional preparation would have given us a bright future in this country. But he got stupid, started feeling inferior, lost all confidence in himself, until he himself was erased from existence. He was afraid of English and never managed to learn it. And after that tired old spiel about how "that" took months, how "that one" would fall at any moment, and how in order to survive in this city, you had to, you have to have guts, have to fight tooth and nail. Here you had to, and have to have balls made of steel. On the one hand were the fighters and hustlers who made money; on the other, the opportunists and people with connections.

For years, while Betty tried to get by, working wherever she could, in the tomato plant, in some grocery store, in a restaurant, every day Fuñío would splash on cologne, slick back his hair with brilliantine, take walks down Calle Ocho standing tall, strolling along with the air of a gentleman. But he would always return home gloomy and sullen. What really troubled him was the disrespect of the lower class people he would run across. Not even when he went to Coral Gables (to pretend he was buying expensive items in Miracle Mile) was he shown any consideration. Nobody would greet him with reverence, nobody would approach him and ask for a favor, nobody ever said to him:

"Good afternoon, *Don* Fuñío."

"Fucking *gusanos*!" he would mutter when he got home. "They deserve millions of Fidels and Communisms! Bunch of disrespectful sons of bitches."

Betty slowly shed her static-cling rose robe. She was soaking wet and it was only then she realized she had slept with the fan off. She scrambled to turn it on, exposing her naked body to the flow of velvety air. She closed her eyes sensuously, lifting her hair with both hands and letting the cottony air refresh her flawlessly shaven armpits. Then she tenderly lifted her large and heavy breasts with their nipples, which were perky, like a teen's. She rolled over slowly. The fan caressed the nape of her neck and her sticky white backside. She looked toward the blinds, since the melody from the street was again sharp and diaphanous, as if the voice were coming from inside the room. Betty began to focus on the words:

> *Light brown is the best color of all.*
> *It's just pretty...*
> *Light Brown. So pretty.*
> *I'd rather be any color but black.*
> *It is nasty looking.*
> *Light brown is the best color of all.*

The verses kept repeating, without any clear order. The repetition of words, and sometimes even syllables, created a suggestive rhythm. When the alarm clock rang, she was still being charmed, bewitched by the breeze from the fan fondling her, and by that morningtime song.

—Shit! —Betty Boop yelped.

That alarm clock could roust a whole platoon. Fuñío had bought it at Sears about ten years ago and it already looked like a museum piece. As the alarm sounded, Betty turned into a robot: she quickly got out of bed and, with precise movements, made it up, watered the *pelargonias* in the window, the *areceas* in the flowerpots in the "living room" (it was all the same tiny space) and, lastly, the vicars that bookended the chest of drawers.

Suddenly she remembered the atrocity she was going to commit and said:

"So long forever, my dear flowers, should the long arm of the law nab me."

She slipped out of her panties and, after sniffing them like a curious dog, tossed them into the dirty clothes basket. Then she brushed her teeth. She made some coffee for breakfast and put two slices of bread into the toaster. Then she stepped into the shower. First she lathered up ferociously, as if doing battle against an inaccessible uncleanness, scrubbing away at her parts—most of all her buttocks, since it produced a stinging pleasure—with a loofa. Then she moved onto the stage of deliciousness, the slow, delightful massage, enjoying, eyes closed, each slip of soap. She spread the suds along the folds and bulges of her body and then, with the hand shower, washed them away, trying to get the jets to fondle her as crudely as the little breeze from the fan. She knew she didn't have time for that pleasure, but it was if the water had won her over with its gentle lasciviousness.

After she toweled off, she put on perfume and talcum powder. She dried her hair with a hairdryer she always passed repeatedly over her pubic area, top to bottom, bottom to top, and behind. It was a screaming and burning vapor that stirred her most intimate openings, riffling her black foresty fluff like a well-trained tropical hurricane.

After combing her hair, she ate breakfast. After breakfast, she brushed her teeth again and then looked at herself in the mirror. She was ugly. Mistreated by existence and undeservedly so. She forced herself to locate, with exactitude, just which part of her face was concealing the hatred since she needed it to feed her aggressiveness. But there was no hate in those beautiful black eyes. Nor in her mouth, still well-formed. There was no resentment in the furrows of her forehead. There was no rancor in her haughty shoulders, nor in her ears.

"Maybe it's not hate I feel," Betty Boop said.

No. Not a single drop of hate darkened her face. She then crinkled it up, looking hateful, just to see if some kind of virulence stood out. Nothing doing. She made an irascible face. Nothing. The face of a gossip. Nothing. The face of a traitor. Nothing. Of a murderer... That's it, a killer...She thought long and hard about Burruchaga and turned sideways, looking at herself out of the corner of her eye, coldly and treacherously, as if she was looking at him. But she still kept thinking it was utterly hopeless.

Betty left the bathroom without having found that hatred in her, and that worried her.

She dressed. She picked out a blouse with different shades of yellow, and a blue skirt. When she looked at herself in the mirror, she realized something:

"Yellow and blue!" she exclaimed. "That combination shows conformity. We can't have that."

Betty blindly believed in the hidden meaning of colors. She changed from the blue skirt into a black one.

"Yellow and black. Sorrow."

She put on two gold chains with medallions of the Virgin of Charity and Saint Barbara. When they arrested her (once she committed the crime, she had no any intention of fleeing) the police, who would probably be Cubans, would treat her with kid gloves for wearing those two holy saints around her neck.

She made herself up sparingly. The lack of money wouldn't let her purchase quality cosmetics and that was hard for her. Betty wasn't one of those women who slapped on just any old product from some dime store. Lancôme, Saint Laurent, Helena Rubenstein, Revlon, Clinique, Pierre Cardin...

She heard the voice in the street again and stuck her head out the window. First she looked over at Ocean Drive; in the speck of beach she saw several old people, surely some of the few Jews still living in hotels nearby, on their way to Ocean Park to do calisthenics, or to the ocean to take a quick dip in the virgin morning water. The sun was coming up, flaming in its enormous roundness, promising a reverberating day. A white cruise ship, perhaps on its way to the Bahamas, floated in the void. Betty looked down and finally saw the woman who'd been singing.

"My God, it's Bag Lady!

She was looking at a fat and ageless Negro woman. Her hair was a snarl of kinks, dyed and faded by wind, sun, and dirt. She was sitting placidly on the sidewalk, near the trash cans out in back of the motel at the corner. "Maybe she slept there," Betty thought, "or maybe she stopped panhandling to eat breakfast." The woman was surrounded by the bags she always took everywhere, dragging them around in a shopping cart, or hanging them from her voluminous body with colored strings. Sometimes Betty would see her shambling off to Miami Beach, without looking up at anyone or asking for anything, talking to herself. Inscrutably alone in the world, Bag Lady always went about her way upright and with forehead held high, as if her destiny as a bum would affect the rest of humanity and not her, as if no atrocity could breach her madness. She was eating candy, or maybe a sandwich, washing it down with a Coke in a plastic bottle, and Betty felt sorry for her:

"Oh, poor thing," she said, truly moved. "Drinking Coke at this ungodly hour."

Bag Lady stopped eating and starting her singing again:

> *I just hate white people.*
> *Don't like them at all.*
> *Oh, I just hate white people.*
> *I'm like my auntie.*
> *She hates them, too.*

The sight of Big Lady filled Betty with strength and a spirit of contradiction. She felt an urge to defy the world. Action, what she needed now was action. She remembered the note she had written from the night before, whipped up in a fit of nerves, of desperation and anger. She found it under the flower pot of Chinese paper *hortensias*. They were a few lines that looked as though they had been scribbled in spurts.

> *If Funío turns up dead:*
> *1. Return to Cuba in spite of Castro.*
> *2. Drop out of this world and become a panhandler.*
> *3. Bust balls, and to hell with it all.*
> *Note! Whether Funío turns up or not, I'm going to kill Burruchaga.*

She reread the note and was deeply surprised. The handwriting was chaotic, like chicken scratch, but the message was quite clear; there was a presence of will and mental coherence in those plans, practically dictated as posthumous. She read the note aloud and, curiously, the only thing she didn't remember writing was that part about "in spite of Castro." She must have written that automatically. She crossed it out. She took the pencil and, following the possibility of returning to Cuba, added something new:

> *Sell everything I own and live in a little hotel on Ocean Drive, like a Jew.*
> *When I run out of money: alternatives 2 and 3 will go into effect.*

She felt satisfied and even though she realized she was running behind schedule and would get to work late, she still had two things to do that could not be put off: to cleanse her place spiritually, in case she did return, and if she didn't, to leave it purified; and to pray to the saints at her altar.

She put fresh water in a bowl. She added white wine, seven drops of Perfume of Seven Males, six more drops of anise, a cinnamon clove, a yellow *immortelle* (which she kept in the refrigerator since they didn't have them in flowerpots and it had to be something that looked as much like a fresh *immortelle* as possible); and, lastly, nine kernels of corn that had remained at the venerable feet of Saint Barbara for days. She grabbed the bowl and did a running liturgy through the little room, sprinkling liquid in the corners, mumbling: "With the same fervent devotion that sprinkles this home, may my hopes for happiness and prosperity come true. May these drops serve to protect my home. May all hostile vibrations, hostile influences and negative tendencies now be banished from my house. May all evil spirits between these walls be vanquished."

She repeated this final part nine times.

When the spiritual cleansing ritual had been concluded, she felt a tingling buzz of anguish run through her. She would usually feel anxiety before going to work; just like when as a child she was about to start a new grade after vacation, or when it was exam time: worry and fear. Maybe it was out of a hateful love that inspired Burruchaga and because she hadn't been born to sell herself as a waitress, to be everyone else's servant, just so this fruit hustler could get rich at her expense.

"Who knows whether today will be the last day of my life as I know it. Anyway, I have to pray now. Then I have to get out of here and let God take care of the rest."

On the tiny altar, situated on a ledge near the window, a small statue of Saint Lazarus and another of Saint Barbara watched over a Virgin of Charity, whose face, if one were to scrutinize it, bore a surprising likeness to Betty Boop's. Maybe it was because of her big eyes and fake eyelashes and her expression of seductive innocence. Unfortunately, the Miami sun poked through the cracks of the window, fading the virgin's face in such a way that it looked as though she were stricken with vitiligo. Saint Barbara's skin, on the other hand, remained intact, that cinnamon skin of a *mestiza* saint accustomed to the rigors of the tropical climate. But Betty's Saint Barbara had a spaced-out look, with an expression that fluctuated between dimness and idiocy. The humble artisan who had molded and painted her face, Betty thought, must have been drunk when he drew her eyes, especially with that slobbering mouth of a retard. Or maybe the poor guy was under the gun, since the more saints he painted, the more he got paid. And the Virgin of Charity, in reality, had come out a little cross-eyed. But you could hardly tell, thanks to the wonderful majesty of her infinite tenderness. On the other hand, St. Lazarus' innumerable pustules, rotting sores, bloody gashes and fetid scars had been painted with admirable realism. The problem with the St. Lazarus on Betty's altar seemed to be that small head of his, which was overrun by an ignoble and distrustful baldness. This greatly pained Betty, who venerated Lazarus and, by gazing at him during prolonged prayer sessions, knew him down to the most minute detail of his face, whose expression of unmistakable slyness didn't quite jibe with the pious saintliness of his crutches, or with the comically stupid expression of the pretty little dogs licking at the carrion of his sores. Betty had reproached Fuñío: that was the danger (and shame) of buying these saints second-hand, since all of them had been purchased at a thrift store on Washington Avenue.

Despite their deformations, Betty was happy to have the protection and divine care of the saints close to her; she spoiled them, she was deeply loyal to them and made them offerings and oaths. They rewarded her faith by shielding her from life's slings and arrows.

Betty kneeled and prayed:

"My glorious saints, patrons of my existence, objects of my faith and witnesses to my humility; you, saints full of care, clairvoyance and mercy, celestial custodians of my failed, dead-end life: illuminate and set me on the right path, as it twists and turns without ever taking me anywhere; orient me in the crossroads and help me to find Fuñío, even if he is dead. Help me on this decisive day, this day of aggressive action and biblical vengeance. Remember that I prefer jail a thousand times to going on welfare and asking for handouts. My honor as a well-bred female couldn't bear that, nor would my pride as an indomitable Cuban. Lastly, I ask that in the supreme moment of the stabbing I shall commit, that you, blessed Saint Barbara, steady my hand so it will not weaken before that son of a bitch Burruchaga. Amen."

Before leaving, Betty went to the kitchen and took out all her knives from the drawer. She inspected them one by one, and a feeling of fright numbed the tips of her fingers. A tumultuous scrabbling of scorpions and vermin registered on the inside of her thighs and down her backside. The blades of fine and long steel slicing through entrails, slashing intestines and veins, blood splashing all over her hand, the floor, her clothes. To her, all knives seemed excessively savage, irreal, and suddenly she stopped *seeing* them. In a fit of chaotic spasms, she began testing them against the kitchen shelving. She regained control of herself. No, none of the knives could be concealed under her clothes. She went to the bathroom and picked up Fuñío's straight edge razor. It was a barber's razor with a shiny, sharp blade, its handle made of tortoiseshell; the thing was ancient, since Fuñío liked to shave himself "just the way his barber used to do back in Cuba." Standing in front of the mirror, Betty opened the straight edge and lightly pulled it across her neck. Right there…that's where the large veins, gouting with fresh blood, throbbed. That's where you had to jerk the knife across. She snapped the knife closed and concealed it in her bra, pressing it snugly against her left breast, since that was the one—Betty had a very exact notion of her breasts' density and volume—that was slightly smaller.

Besides, that's where she could pull it out with her right hand.

And finally Betty, head held high, sallied forth into the sun-splashed streets of Miami Beach.

Guarapito and a waiter on Ocean Drive...

"I'll say it again: it was her and I'm telling you with these very hands of mine I served them at least five daiquiris over there, at that table in the corner."

"You sure you're not confusing her with somebody else?"

"It was her. Make no mistake."

"Impossible. That girl's happier than a turtle in the sun."

"It was her."

"It couldn't have been; that girl is, and always has been, a respectable woman, a homebody."

"Then she must be very content and respectable when she's at home. When she's not there she's quite the horn dog, and cunning."

"Cunning?"

"With these ears that have heard everything in life, I listened to her tell the man she was with: 'I like you more than him, a thousand times more than him; I swear, the guy's unbearable. You talk to him, and he looks at you but he doesn't listen, he doesn't hear you, you're of no interest to him, he isn't from the kingdom of this world, he's always off in some other place, he doesn't exist. Take me home with you, I want to go to bed with you.'"

"Hey, cut the crap...Look, what you're telling me here is very, very serious. That girl is like a sister to me."

"Lots of people have depraved sisters. I've seen everything in life."

"There's no way, no way!"

You're so dense, Guarapito...I could pick her out from a million girls. I've seen her here lots of times here with all you guys, including Aunt Ulalume, Nicotiano, yourself and that shady Finn. You can be rest assured that the girl I saw here with another man was her, her and not somebody else."

"That's enough, my friend, enough."

"And of course they were always making out and pawing each other over at that corner table..."

"That's enough, thanks."

"...because I saw them with these eyes that have seen everything in life."

- Two -

I spent that whole night awake tossing and turning, my eyes gleaming in the darkness.

"I hope this all ends soon," I repeated every time I looked at the clock. "It can be as sad as it has to be, but just no bloodshed. And let this get resolved before the end of tomorrow."

With dark circles under my eyes and with the gait of a sleep-walker, I rose before the sun did. My mouth tasted like rotten flower petals.

"I hope she tells him the truth," I muttered to myself in the front yard.

The sun was gaining altitude; like me, it was also rung with circles, and seemed to be snagged in the marine layer out beyond the bay, behind the hotels of Miami Beach. What a frightful night. I took in the scented air of the silent sea and my flowers. In the vegetation, the receding shadows and still sparse light played hide-and-seek. As I walked by, the crickets interrupted their serenade. The Island of Cundeamor was asleep.

As I did every morning, I went outside to feel the crisp massage of the dewy grass, cut short by Cororioco, against the soles of my bare feet. I didn't bother to bathe or comb my hair, or even have coffee. I was wearing the bright silk house robe that Hetkinen had brought me back from Hawaii. My husband had spent time there on one of his investigations for the Crabb Company, and he brought the robe back as a present. On that case they were spying on a young woman, the daughter of a prominent family of exiled Cubans. Her father, a well-heeled politician and businessman, suspected that the girl was having an affair with a Mexican. To the father of that rich, wealthy Cuban girl, the little Mexican was unacceptable. He was penniless, and had all the somatic characteristics of a member of Montezuma's court. Oh, the horror! To think: his little Cuban girl rolling around in the hay with some half-breed. The brood was profoundly repulsed. But the girl practiced her mestizism with all the deftness of a spy, and it was hard to catch her with her hands in the Mexican dough. When the girl got it in her head to vacation in Hawaii, the father suspected she wouldn't be going alone, so he contracted the good Hetkinen and the Crabb Company Investigation employees to document the eventual Cuban-Mexican transgression in Waikiki, and to let his wayward daughter know that everything in this world can be found out. Hetkinen and the boys solved similar cases from time to time. They were open-and-shut cases, fairly low-risk, even though they turned out to be exceedingly lucrative.

So, thanks to that erotic-detective snoop job, I got the beautiful silk house robe I was wearing that morning.

But the silk robe felt incomplete to me; it was one single color, a haughty and nostalgic turkish blue, but it lacked contrast. That's why I gave it to Maribarbola, who gave it to Bartolo, who then gave it to a mulatto friend of his, a guy who came here off the Mariel boat lift and who was a painter and also a bit of a crook, so he could decorate it with all artistic freedom. The result was a slightly erotic, radiant and monumental Saint Barbara that majestically stretched from the back of my neck down to my heels. We immediately christened her Saint Barbara of Waikiki.

If I waggled my bottom, Saint Barbara of Waikiki shook her hips. If I moved my shoulders, her tits would jiggle. If I leaned forward, she would look up to Heaven.

Trying not to think about Mireya, and with the lethargic shuffle of someone who hasn't slept, I went over to my avocado trees. Every morning I weighed the avocados dangling in front of me. I talked to them and pinched them with painstaking delight. They weren't ripe quite yet, but they were visibly and deliciously swollen. I stepped into the dark foliage and delicately probed the furrows of the gourds. I gauged their density, hardness and weight. If somebody who didn't know me had witnessed the fondling, they would have thought I was obscenely feeling up my avocados. And maybe they'd be right, since I did so with a solicitude that verged on sexual pleasure.

"Earth's green balls," I murmured to myself.

I heard noises. They were coming from my nephew's studio and I began to walk slowly in that direction, passing through the trees. Nicotiano's studio was an enormous shed with a saddle roof, large windows and a modern system of cranes that let him move his blocks of stone and sculptures, many of which were the size of monuments, any way he wanted. The trucks that hauled in the supply of rocks would enter from the street and come all the way up inside the studio to be unloaded by the cranes. The spacious studio was set amid the thicket of my vegetation: the huge *jaguey* trees with their skeins of skyborn roots, veritable curtains of whips-to-be; streams of bougainvillea; climbing *jabillas* with their latticework of branches and green-yellow leaves; mangos and papaya plants; bamboo shoots with their cabalistic vertical structure, as if they were concealing sacred mysteries deep inside. In order to feel alive, I have always needed the exuding, tangled and profuse presence of that island vegetation, perfect in its savage disorder, and the uniqueness of its faint and obscene odors, both repugnant and appetizing, like the crotch of a dirty goddess who inseminates herself. Back in Cuba the people of Havana always made me feel ashamed, as they were so far removed from the oniony tang of resin, the earth's nameless perfumes, and the miracles of photosynthesis. Those Cubans in exile who ended up in the cold of New Jersey or Madrid, where humans do nothing (without realizing it) except become sterilized while ensconced (or imprisoned) in the solitude of their apartments, made me feel ashamed.

Just as I thought: Nicotiano was in his studio, sculpting.

He had spent the whole night working. Like it was nothing, as if the ground beneath him wasn't about to crack open. Is it possible he doesn't even notice the storm that's about to hit?

Sometimes whole weeks would go by and Nicotiano wouldn't come out of that shed. He would rise before dawn, eat something for breakfast, and start toiling away. And there he would chisel, hew, drill, and polish rock in the constant company of Cocorioco until noon. If Cocorioco didn't remind him to eat, he would forget. During breaks, he would dive into the pool and swim like a captive whale, from one end to the other; this intense swimming was his idea of a break. When you saw him swimming slowly and deliberately, relishing each stroke, it was because he was exhausted or quite pleased with his handiwork. It was not unusual for him to work several nights in a row, as if hypnotized; according to Cocorioco he would barely utter a word. Thanks to a complex network of suppliers, Hetkinen and I made sure that he always had a sufficient quantity of stone blocks at his disposal. Above all, granite, alabaster and marble. With the help of Mireya, I was also the one who marketed his sculptures, in coordination with Mr. Doublestein. Given the strange nature of the sculptures (the motif was always the same: crabs), it was a difficult yet inspiring job, made even more difficult by Nicotiano's reluctance to appear in public, *live*, as the author of his sculptures. Due to the pseudo-anonymity of the artist, it was a tremendously profitable business. Between Doublestein and me, we were able to fetch some very good prices for my nephew's crustaceans. During those periods of creativity in particular, his sculptures would provide an income even greater than the Crabb Company.

Cocorioco, who was the occasional gardener, sometimes would catch Nicotiano's fanaticism and then eat at normal hours either, or tend to the garden, and the yard would go to pot.

"Cocorioco," I admonished, "the grass is in a state of rebellion. Besides, you look haggard and gaunt. Leave Nicotiano alone and get back to a normal life!"

"Flowers, stuff your flowers!" the good man replied. "Can't you see we're finishing up a huge marble Rosa Aurora crab? There'll be plenty of time for food and other nonsense later."

I never did like it that they became so unsociable and distant, even sinister, when immersed in their work. You couldn't even strike up a normal conversation; the crab-like shapes evolving from the stones cast a spell on them, turning them into strangers. Cocorioco, who in all respects was curtly affable, turned laconic and even a little aggressive, as if he were the depository of some supernatural secret. However, when the Crabb Company had some urgent personnel need, say, for a particularly dangerous mission, or one that required multiple stakeouts, Nicotiano left his studio without a fight and followed Hetkinen's orders. I always felt that these interruptions were good for him. Cocorioco would then tend to the garden and revert to his jovial and sweet self, though God himself would never be able to rid him of a certain degree of unsociability.

During periods of normality, when Nicotiano didn't feel the compulsive need to sculpt, and when the 'crabbery' in the shed took on a more human rhythm, he was a delight to be around. He took part in after-dinner conversations, went on walks with me, or both of us would sit and read together, drinking rum under the pergola or out by the pool. It was in those lapses of normality that his relationship with Mireya seemed to become more loving than ever. They would take the yacht, our marvelous Villalona, and head out to fish in the Florida Keys, sail through the Gulf waters, or discover some patch of deserted isle in the Bahamas.

I stopped just outside the studio. I felt like talking to Nicotiano, but I was afraid that my worry would give me away. I had to hide what I knew from him, but at the same time the desire to spill everything was wringing my tongue like a wet rag. Just what was I going to reveal? Suspicions, clues, rumors? No. Until I had concrete and irrefutable proof, nobody was going to tell my nephew a thing.

Suddenly, Kafka came through the *areca* tree.

My dear Kafka, silent as an eagle's feather, strong and agile as a lion, cunning as a secret agent. Loyal guardian of our house, commander-in-chief of our pack of guard dogs.

Our other dogs were Gotero and Montavar, both of a submissive breed and with an unpredictable ferociousness. Their mission consisted of responding by ferociously barking at certain stimuli they were quite familiar with. They were also scrupulously adept at pursuing, hounding and delivering mortal bites whenever ordered to do so. Among Kafka's duties was to keep them in check and to give them orders when necessary. Gotero was an expert at detection, even at long distances, of foreign elements, as well as all types of narcotics, explosives and poisons. Montavar handled the Crabb Company's dirty work. Every order given to this dog was top secret; everything he did had to be kept mum, so much so that I didn't even know what he was doing, and that's why now I can't even say what it was he did. For their absolute submission and attention to the job at hand, Gotero and Montavar and their services were held in high esteem by the Crabb Company.

But Kafka was a different breed.

Vigilant and reflective, taciturn and distinguished, Kafka spread his canine humanity throughout every nook and cranny in the house. A sense of responsibility shone through his huge sad eyes, and my affection for him can only be compared to what I felt for Nicotiano. Even though it wasn't apparent, Kafka was really quite a dangerous creature: a dog with a lot of feline qualities. Could there be a more dangerous mix? A wolf-puma hybrid. His aggression was fierce. But what was most impressive about him was that he knew just when and how to act. Once when chasing a baseball, the McIntire's youngest son unwisely scaled the *cundeamor*-covered fence that separated us from the outside world. Freezing the boy with their barking, Montavar and Gotero were about to take him down. Kafka, thanks to his absolute authority and ability to discern, luckily saved the boy's life.

Kafka was now at my side, calm and awake in the early morning.

I decided not to go into the studio. The sun was beginning to push the morning forward, revealing shades of green in the overlapping palm fronds, making the dew glisten on the canopy branches. But

I got the sad sensation that minutes that day were going to last months. I checked on my mangos. Every day they were growing more and more flushed and sweet-smelling. Mangos are quite profitable. In addition to the exquisiteness of the fruits, with their *aguardiente* and honey, the rinds of the mango are used in cooking to cure bronchitis. Next I went over to the kingdom of my papaya trees. What a resonant and playful name! Papaya, papayita, papayona. Whose mouth wouldn't water when pronouncing those words? Papaya, that pulpy proud flesh, the most obscene of delicacies.

"Isn't that right, my dear papayitas? Look how tasty they are, Kafka; they look like teens, tall, underfed, baring their green, bare tits. And if you split the fruits open, what comes out of those tits are the little black seeds, all sweaty and lubricated in a tempting pulp."

Kafka followed me around, wearing an expression that was perhaps even a little sly, as if admiring the colors of the Saint Barbara of Waikiki, the orange-violet, green yellow and some other blood red incandesces, now stained with dew. And her eyes: beguiling, emitting an unhealthy power. The ocean sun was now having its way with the sky and Saint Barbara of Waikiki.

"He gave Mireya everything here in this house: comfort, care, consideration and absolute confidence. But I won't let passion carry me away. Tell me, Kafka, since you're calm and clairvoyant, even in moments of greatest stress: who can say what goes on between a couple? Nobody, my boy, nobody. There are mechanisms of attraction and rejection, of repugnance and sweetness at work. It's power and impotence, it's loving and not loving in the same bed, at the same table, between the same four eyes, two tongues and four hands, they're rites and expectations that the years turn routine. But look at these tomatoes, Kafka. Cocorioco isn't tending to them anymore. They're growing thanks to God's will. The most delicious ones are these small ones. Unsweetened tomatoes. So sweet. In Cuba they're even sweeter, almost like *morello* cherries. The Spanish, who learned to eat tomatoes from the Aztecs, attributed aphrodisiac properties to the tomato. I also attribute these properties to them. Note that the French call tomatoes *pomme d'amour.*"

I walked over to the garage to see if Mireya's car was there. It wasn't; I'm sure she didn't sleep here. And Nicotiano didn't even notice. I went over to the fence that was covered with *cundeamor*, separating us from the reality of Miami's dream, to greet Gotero and Montavar. Their mission was to stick together at the fence and wrought-iron gate at the main entrance. Sometimes Kafka took them out to patrol our strip of coast, the pier where the Villalona was docked, and the lush vegetation of the patio. Kafka was the only one authorized to go inside the house and bathe in the pool. As for everything else, his powers were plenipotentiary.

"How is Nicotiano towards Mireya?" I asked Kafka. "Callous, unfair, a bore? And in the realm of sex? Everything is so complex, Kafka; when all is said and done, we don't know anything, and it's no wonder that the proverb holds true that nothing gets between husband and wife...You have to season and sweeten sex so it doesn't become boring. And even a certain level of perversion must exist between the couple; otherwise, sex becomes bureaucratized. You can tell by the way a couple fights or belches if they've been carnally satisfied.

Next to the gate was a sign that read:

DANGER!
BEWARE OF OUR DOGS' OPINIONS

Two rows of royal palms flanked the entrance road to the house. I studied them with a kind of melancholy and they seemed to me to be graceful in the soft morning breeze. A flock of tiny birds nibbled on the little red *cundeamor* seeds.

"Birds are the fish of the air."

At that moment that it occurred to me to look over at the McIntire house, and when I did I saw a man standing on the terrace, aiming at me with a rifle. Like an idiot, I stood there looking at him, trying to recognize the man who in a couple of seconds would probably open fire on me. But what left me frozen wasn't the fear, but curiosity at first, and then indignation.

"Son of a bitch!" I shouted, and I crouched down, disappearing from my aggressor's field of vision.

I stayed there frozen, and for an instant I had an urge to throw a rock at him, or to a let out with a Bronx cheer. That ridiculous McIntire!

Our houses, or better said, the yards of our houses were separated by a street that overlooked the sea. Our fence was six feet or so high, and overrun with tangles of bougainvillea, bellflowers, jasmines, *cundeamors* and other wild thickets that climbed everywhere, even up the posts of the street lighting. Crouched down, with Kafka tense by my side, I saw McIntire moving around with the rifle slung over his shoulder. He again got into shooting position, scanning for me with what had to be a scope. I don't know why I got the impression he was drunk.

"Kafka: Go and tell Maribarbola what's happening. Quick!"

The animal took off like a whistle. What McIntire was holding, I thought, was a machine gun, or something similar. I then stood suddenly, pretending I hadn't even noticed the threat. He aimed at me and, pretending I was picking *cundeamors* near the fence, I crouched back down.

"Poor McIntire," I thought. All the steps that beast had taken to get us to leave the Island of Cundeamor. He was envious of us because we had more money than he did, because our house was bigger than his, because we had a more comfortable, luxurious, and seaworthy yacht than he did. The Cuban flag I always had hoisted up a flagpole higher than the American flag that rippled out on his patio bothered him, and I'm sure he moaned and groaned:

"Those fucking Cubans have taken over our city, there's no area, however exclusive, that isn't infected by that riffraff."

"Yes," he knew I was making fun of him, "we turned the Island of Cundeamor into a new Saguesera, with its domino games in the shade of the *flamboyones* and the drunk houses among the coconut palms.

"The last Anglo to leave," McIntire would say, "take the American flag with him."

Life's ironies! Miami's ironies, I should say; now we were not the ones who in some way were threatening McIntire's existence, but the Cuban American Transaction, who wanted all of us to just disappear from the Island of Cundeamor.

To provoke McIntire, I ducked down again, as if doing gymnastics. I was now convinced he was quite drunk, and although he could have fired at me, he wouldn't have hit me, I stuck my forearm in my crotch area quite vulgarly, my fist closed as if it were an erect penis, and I muttered:

"Fire away if you've got a pair, McIntirito."

But what I saw was how the man quickly retreated from the roof, stumbling about rifle and all, panic-seized as if a pack of demons were chasing after him.

What had happened was that Kafka pulled Maribarbola away from the gym, a well-equipped place at the back of the patio, near the bay water, where he was doing his morning workout, and brought him up to speed. Maribarbola moved quickly, spotted McIntire on his parapet with his rifle, snapped some pictures with his powerful telephoto lens and immediately stationed himself on our roof with a grenade launcher. Meanwhile, Kafka rousted Sikitrake, who was sleeping with one of his lovers, from bed. Sikitrake then got up in a call to action, carrying his trusty AK-47. He followed Kafka to the studio and added Nicotiano to the defense of the national territory, but when the sculptor made it up to the roof armed with an AR-15, McIntire, terrified by Maribarbola's grenade launcher, had now beaten a sloppy retreat from his unusual field of battle.

"Silly old man," I said, laughing uncontrollably.

We gave Kafka a treat.

According to Hetkinen, Maribarbola and Sikitrake were the top men at the Crabb Company. Nobody could beat Maribarbola in marksmanship with handguns and in personal defense. He was a fearsome karate expert and every fiber in his body was marked by the super-soft flexibility of his velvety, precise and, when necessary, lethal movements. He was tall and his limbs were framed in long and powerful muscles; he had the gaze of a lynx and could disarm a man armed with a machete, bare-handed. His mid-air flips were awe-inspiring. He could flank, go forward or backwards with rare agility. Like that he could leap high and deliver a savage kick to his opponent. Just for fun he would jump and knock down whatever mangos he wanted, with an ankle blow. In addition, Maribarbola was the Crabb Company's photographer. He always carried around a stainless steel Colt Python .357 Magnum. It was a frightening weapon that measured more than nine inches in length, from handle to the end of the barrel.

Sikitrake was a very good-looking *mulatto*, clever and iron-willed, sweet when it came to dealing with people, and very principled. He came from Guanabocoa, and was the son of a humble family. Sikitrake had fought in Angola, where he won two or three medals for courage under fire. On his way back to Cuba, the poor guy had a streak of bad luck. In a fight over the ever delicate matter of skirts, a man pulled a knife on him and Sikitrake killed him with a chop. Homicide. From then on, his destiny grew more clouded. In prison, he was taunted by a loud-mouthed guard and Sikitrake smashed his nose. After that he tried to rehabilitate himself. In prison they gave him special treatment, perhaps in recognition of his good human nature and for services rendered in combat. But misfortune never comes alone. During the first leave they gave him, the brother of the man he had killed decided to take the law into his own hands. Sikitrake tried to avert a new disaster, but wasn't able to. He had to kill the guy in self-defense, this time with a steel bar. That night he stole a motor boat, headed north and didn't stop until he ran aground at a beach at Key West. Sikitrake was a specialist in all kinds of heavy artillery and knew a lot about explosives and military radio communication. He was the best long-range shooter in the outfit, even better than Hetkinen himself. For me, Sikitrake was like another son, and I've always asked myself how a young man so upright and noble, such a champion of justice, could be caught up in such an unlucky avalanche of bloody events. He once sketched out the answer, despite the fact that he refused to talk about himself, above all about the Angolan war:

"When I went back to Africa, Aunt Ula, I was another man. I came out of the killing fields and I had killed. For the first time in my life I found myself face-to-face with the dilemma of killing or being killed, vanquish or be vanquished, and many of my closest friends were cut down by mortar shells or bullets. When my cousin was driving a supply truck in long caravan, the UNITA ambushed him, killing him. When I returned to Cuba I found myself in a state of great psychological instability. I refused to work. A bachelor, no wife, no kids to think about, I just hit the bottle and screwed around. I wanted to forget and get back my lost time. Lots of others were able to handle it better than me, I suppose maybe they had a greater degree of maturity; they went back and reentered society without any big traumas. I had bad luck. When I snatched that boat to exile, I did it blindly, not knowing for certain why. It was a way out, something new and unexpected opened up before me, a place where I could begin again. Right from scratch."

We met out to the pergola for breakfast. Maribarbola was developing the pictures of the bellicose McIntire.

"Could it be that McDonald's lost his mind?" Cocorioco asked sarcastically.

The breeze off the sea felt warm and sticky and promised a stifling day. On a bed of crushed ice, the breakfast fruits radiated their wonders: oranges, papayas and mangos, melons and pineapples and small red slices of *mamey*. The ones who didn't eat were Sikitrake and myself. Cocorioco and Nicotiano barely ate; the only thing they had was coffee and a cheese sandwich. They were probably thinking about their crabs, and I felt a burning desire for them to just leave and go straight to work.

That's when Hetkinen showed up.

Finally. From the moment he entered, I knew the news about Mireya would be grim and that all the gossip, speculation, prejudice and jokes about her were true, just by glancing at his expression. I stopped eating.

Hetkinen was a man of few words. Maybe it was that quality that let our marriage last so long. I never would have been able to stand living with a bragging, swaggering and brawling Cuban like Guarapito, for example. Hetkinen gave me a kiss and let his Finnish peasant carapace sag in a chair next to me.

"Maribarbola already informed me about McIntire's idiocy," my husband said. "We'll wait for Mari to bring the pictures. I think we have to treat this as a serious matter."

"McDonalds is growing *guayabas* on his roof," Cocorioco said.

"The man's name is McIntire," Nicotiano clarified.

Cocorioco shot back, "I don't care if his name is McNamara or McAsshole. They're all named McDonalds to me.

"Cocorioco," I said, "lately I've noticed you're looking a little haggard, exhausted even, with really hideous rings under your eyes. What's wrong, are you sick?"

"My teeth hurt."

"Let me look at your mouth. Let's see, open wide."

"Over my dead body. My mouth is mine and nobody looks at it."

"Cocorioco! You should go to the dentist's."

"I don't feel like it."

"You would rather be in pain than go to the dentist?"

"My mouth is mine and nobody tells me what to do."

"Cocorioco, don't be so belligerent."

"I've also noticed you've been looking a little run-down," Nicotiano told him.

"Take care of your own mouths," the old man responded acridly, "and let mine be."

"I think we should charge McIntire," Sikitrake said.

"Is Mireya still asleep?" Nicotiano asked, and I swallowed a large piece of mango.

"I saw her take the car out early," I lied, coughing, since to some extent a cough can cover up a lie.

For several weeks now, at my request, Hetkinen had put the men on heavy surveillance, watching Mireya's every move, and that day they gave me the results. It had been a painful mission. These kinds of "investigations"—infidelities, disappearances, shady behavior—were the everyday grist of the Crabb Company, but to penetrate the innermost secrets of Mireya, whom Hetkinen loved as much as I did, made him feel a little dirty. Because Mireya had humanized Nicotiano; we all knew that. She was like a flower on the Island of Cundeamor, the most radiant, the most beautiful. Her kindness elevated us all, her affection and her considerate attitude made her beloved company.

If the grotesque McIntire incident, more worthy of mockery than fear, hadn't happened, that breakfast would have been more sordid than the Crabb Company story. And I think it was anyway, at least for me. Now all that was missing was for Maribarbola to show up with the pictures. All four of them. The ones of McIntire putting on that queer little show out on the roof, and the ones of Mireya...

I also felt dirty. To have ordered such snooping against my Mireya! But doubt is stronger than all the poisons.

Nicotiano hadn't returned from his crabs and unable to wait any longer, I launched back into Cocorioco to see if I could drive him crazy:

"Cocorioco, I'm going to make an urgent appointment for you to see a dentist. I don't plan on waiting for you to develop neuralgia. Nobody on the Island of Cundeamor has the right to go around with a chronic toothache. So this afternoon you're going to the dentist and..."

"Nag, nag, nag, Aunt Ula. I'm not going to any tooth butcher; the only thing they know how to do is make a mint at the expense of other people's pain."

"You're just afraid," Sikitrake interjected.

"Nobody asked you, young man."

Cocorioco stood, visibly irritated, which was what I wanted. I studied him. He was a hearty septuagenarian, of a small build, packed in flesh that was still tough, but now a little worse for wear, maybe from overwork. Sometimes Cocorioco would wear his belt without running it through the loops in his pants, which made his pants droop, about to slide right off him. It didn't matter whether he wore work clothes or formal wear. It made him look like a peasant, or a poor kid. I also noticed that he had lost a lot of weight. Was he bothered by his hole-riddled teeth, or was he really sick? His pants looked big on him, that's all. And for god's sake, they didn't even eat; neither he or Nicotiano looked after their stomachs, which is, as Cervantes put it so well, the office where all of the body's business was resolved.

"Show me your teeth, Coco." Sikitrake proposed benevolently. "Once in Angola, right in the heat of battle, I pulled a friend's tooth with a pair of pliers."

"Well then you and your dear pliers can go to Angola and pull teeth," the old man shot back and added, speaking to Nicotiano, "I'm going to the studio."

"Don't you want to see the pictures of McDonalds in action?" Nicotiano asked.

"I don't give a crap. If I can't even stand the sight of him in real life, why the hell would I want to see pictures of him?"

And he left.

Nicotiano started laughing and caught up to him. He threw his arm around his good friend and they both walked into the trees. We all breathed a sigh of relief.

Hetkinen was sweating profusely and was gazing absently into the dark greenness of the mangos. A heavy silence enveloped us. The sun lighted up, as if from inside, the leaves of the climbing plants on the pergola. The fruits of the *cundeamor* seemed lighter at this time of day, taking on an orange, almost phosphorescent shade. I peered into the baroque structure of the climbing plants and saw a universe of dead insects and tiny spiders in their webs, little birds flitting by, and a rugged landscape of knotted stalks, dry scrub, small jungles and furry stumps, leaves like bangs, or the hair of a sleeping woman. The fruits of the *esparto* grass hung down in places like tits; in other places like tumid cocks, engorged with pulp and fiber.

"Here comes Maribarbola," Sikitrake mumbled.

I felt sleepy and smelly. It was already mid-morning, and I hadn't even brushed my teeth. The Saint Barbara of Waikiki on my back was covered in sweat.

"Here are the snapshots," Maribarbola said.

"Let's begin with McIntire," Hetkinen proposed.

Kafka lay down at my side. Maybe he picked up on my sullen mood. Hetkinen looked through the pictures, frowning.

"This looks bad, Sikitrake," he finally said. "See: it's an Israeli Galil."

"A sniper's rifle," he said. "For long distance hits."

"Exactly. The scope must be a Nimrod."

"And the clip holds 25 bullets. Professional gear."

"I doubt McIntire has a permit for that kind of firepower," Hitkinen said. "Ula, this is more serious than you think."

"Bah," I objected. "It's just the American's crazy theatrics."

"Maybe," Hetkinen said, and his gaze rested on the tumid cocks of the *esparto* grass. "Maybe that drunk McIntire decided to give us a scare. But this could also be the work of somebody who wants to get rid of us..."

"Somebody gave the Galil to McIntire," Maribarbola reasoned, "and squeezed him in hopes of not just flashing us the weapon, but of getting him to pull the trigger.

"Like the Transaction, right?"

"A great way to get rid of two at once: McIntire as a murderer, and us, so we couldn't keep living here on the Island of Cundeamor without Aunt Ulalume. You're the target, Ula."

"It all seems too sinister, embellished, fantastic and contrived. All I see is one of McIntire's annoyances; he's a bully and an inveterate alcoholic. His aiming at me was pure coincidence."

"In my line of work, there are no coincidences," Hetki declared sententiously.

"Well, he who wants war shall get war!" I began to vent and Kafka got to his feet. "On this island we can live together peacefully, now even more than ever since we're being threatened by a greater power. But don't come to me with little rifles and crap. If you don't like your neighbors, then move!"

"Calm down, Ula."

"I don't feel good. Now, please tell me what you've found out about Mireya's supposed adultery."

Suddenly, Kafka darted off to the front gate; a few seconds later the guard dogs were barking infernally. Maribarbola and Sikitrake went to check it out.

"It's the police," Siki said upon returning.

It was two squad cars and several men wearing bulletproof vests, armed to do battle against an army. The leader was an acquaintance of Hetkinen. A fat, stocky, sun-beaten Cuban who had the look of a smoked ox, but with a uniform, revolver and glasses. His teeth flashed an exquisite white as he spoke:

"What's going on here, Hetkinen? McIntire swears that you all threatened him with a bazooka."

My husband didn't move a muscle or say a word. The dogs were barking.

Me and Hetkinen...

"I'm sorry, Ula, but everything points to Mireya..."

"Let's wait until we get some proof."

"I want to prepare you for the worst. People aren't always what they seem."

"Nothing or nobody is ever what they seem."

"I know this is going to be very painful."

"Let's talk about something else, then. In the meantime, look for undeniable proof. Pictures. I want pictures."

"The Cuban American Transaction keeps maneuvering to uproot us from the Island of Cundeamor."

"Sons of bitches. They want to turn it into an empire of hotels and *casinos, since they're illegal in Florida. But they aren't going to scare us off."*

"There's practically nobody left on the island. Everybody's left their houses, more or less against their will. The Montes de Oca, the Andersons, the Pérez Díaz, the Smiths..."

"Yeah, Maribarbola already mentioned that. We're the last of the few remaining. But I am not leaving this island."

"The Transaction works in mysterious ways. They cut off your credit, threaten, pressure you, make strange offers."

"All that's left is us and the McIntires."

"It's too bad McIntire is so mean. If we got along, we could work together and defend each other."

"He's prejudiced. To him, we're a bunch of fucking spics."

"If McIntire leaves, we'll be alone."

"Better alone than in bad company."

"Ula, shouldn't we start getting used to the idea that...this island is lost?"

"Never! To give up this island that's part of my life, just so the Transaction can prostitute it, would be like living in exile all over again."

"It's very hard to defend an island when you're the only one."

"When you're the only one left on the island you want to defend, you have to use all your balls to root yourself in what is yours."

"We have balls."

"I'm willing to defend the Island of Cundeamor with all of our weapons."

"The Transaction knows this. They don't dare push us too hard. They can't manipulate any bank since we don't have any debts to pay, and we don't need to take out any loans. It would be hard for them to create financial difficulties for us. What they can do is start putting up their hotels or condominiums or whatever they're planning to do, and make our life miserable. The island will never be the same."

"Nothing. They'll have to shoot us, like they did to the macao."

"I don't know what a macao *is."*

"Ask the boys to explain it to you."

The Transaction is dirty, Ula. They'll try to harm us one way or the other. But they won't deal with the Crabb Company just any which way. They're aware of this, they know we can be an astute and dangerous enemy."

"And deep down they're cowards. Hetki...If Mireya leaves the Island of Cundeamor..."

"It's the natural consequence of her acts."

"What will you do, Hetki? I'm afraid of Nicotiano."

"Aside from Mireya and his crabs, that boy has no life of his own. Whenever she leaves him...Well, for now, let's get back to the objective: without Mireya, you alone won't be able to take on the burden of the Crabb Company office work and promoting his sculptures. Look for a substitute, but you'll have to make a good choice. We can't afford to open the doors of this house to just anyone."

"You should focus on finding a trustworthy element; for me, you should find a girl who, in addition to doing good work, would be capable of being my friend."

"In any case, nobody could replace Mireya."

"Who knows, Hitkinen. Who knows."

- Three -

Rather than walking to the bus stop on Washington Avenue to go downtown, Betty proceeded down Ocean Drive, hoping to catch sight of the Bag Lady up close, even if for just for an instant. The ocean exhaled a light breeze that was still somewhat fresh, and Betty hoarded the freshness as much as she could by opening her blouse. A little too much maybe, given the straight edge razor she was concealing in her bra. Out on the hotel terraces, retired seniors languidly baked in the sun like plucked roosters; most of the seniors were third-rate Jews, since the ones with the most buying power sunned further north, North Ocean Park, Bal Harbour, or Sunny Isle.

In the shade of a coconut palm that had been primped for tourists, Betty found the panhandler sitting alone on a bench facing the sea. Overcome with a sharp emotion, she approached her. That extravagant, dirty figure, utterly exposed to the dangers of the street and Miami's nocturnal elements, inspired a strange fascination in Betty. Could she be crazy? Would she be able to carry on a normal conversation with her? For Betty, a light-skinned Cuban from Miami, approaching that black panhandler meant crossing a prohibited line. Deep down inside that gave her some satisfaction.

"If she's not crazy, she must be an extraordinarily brave woman. If she is crazy, she must have her own reasons. I just hope she's not dangerous."

The bum, accustomed to having all five senses on constant alert, heard Betty approaching and whirled around. Betty Boop tolerated her sour look and proceeded even closer, sitting down on the edge of the bench. Bag Lady looked her up and down with a vibe that Betty felt was scornful, though not too aggressive. The panhandler sighed with indifference and went back to looking out at the sea.

"I've approached you," Betty said, getting right to the point, "because I heard you singing this morning and I like it, and I'd like to be your friend."

The woman didn't respond. She didn't even bother to look at her. "Don't think it's because I feel sorry for you or anything like that," Betty made clear. "I've already felt too much self pity. What I need now is *action*. And a friend who won't prejudge or judge me. I was a refined lady, you know? From the Cuban high life. Now I'm a lowly waitress. Everyone has betrayed me: Fidel Castro, Kennedy, my lovers. Fuñío misled me with his weakness; exile sweet-talked me with its dreams of riches, its politics and scams. I've given away money, like a sucker, to every organization proclaiming the disaster of the Revolution (here Betty started ticking off with her fingers): the Rosa Blanca, crooks; Alfa 66, degenerates; The Sentinels of Freedom, sons of bitches; the Cuban Representation in Exile, hucksters; the Cuban Nationalist Movement, shameless bastards; the Committee Against Peaceful Coexistence, mercenaries; the Cuban Power, frauds; the Association of Veterans of the Bay of Pigs, pigs; the Secret Anticommunist Army, liars; the Patriotic Coincidence, slum lords; the Secret Cuban Government, knaves; the Democratic Platform, cons; the National Cuban American Foundation, scam artists; the Liberal Union, they make me want to vomit..."

Bag Lady suddenly looked at her and Betty shut up. The black woman had a penetrating, disturbing look, and she was pretty. But she stank. She stank horribly. She had a sickly sweet reek of rank mud about her, the stench of a trash dump in the sun. "She has to be completely mad," Betty thought, "if she can stand that stink."

"You talk," Bag Lady said, "like a woman who's lost her mind."

The bum again suddenly looked away from Betty.

"My country men make me SICK," Betty Boop said, making an awful face.

"Why are you telling me all this? I don't really care about the political quarrels y'all Cubans have. If you can't agree on anything in Cuba, or here either, why is that our fault?"

"I'm bitter, Lady Bag. This country has turned my people into hyenas."

"This place was already full of hyenas, long before ya'll got here, Cuban woman."

"I'm fed up with this life and being a loser! Here no one cares about what you are, just what you have."

"Here you are what you have. I, for example, am these bags and the color of my skin."

Bag Lady looked straight ahead, and Betty felt a little stupid. Just a little.

"You speak," the indigent said, "like a woman who's really a little lost girl. But it's clear you've really suffered."

Then the indigent woman started singing:

> *White people look bad to me.*
> *Most of them are red white people*
> *With all of them wrinkles 'round their neck.*
> *Well, it looks rusty and nasty to me.*

Betty then caught the melody of the last verse and, in an emotional rhythm that seemed to get the Bag Lady excited, repeated:

> *It looks rusty and nasty to me,*
> *Nasty to me, rusty to me...*

And the panhandler:

> *Rusty and nasty to me, to me, to meeee...*

And they joined in song. The black woman stressed the second voice, forging a vigorous harmony, while the white woman shored up the syncopations by repeating the same part over and over. Using Betty's rich voice as a base, the panhandler embellished with ease, her voice rising and falling, spiraling in brief crossings.

> *Nasty to me, it looks rusty to meeeee...*

At that point they both cut off the melody and started laughing. They were covered with thick, shiny beads of sweat. For the first time in her life, and despite the smell of the homeless woman, Betty wasn't repulsed by the Miami sweat.

"I'm Cuban," Betty said, and signaled to a point beyond the shimmering sand.

"I'm American," the black woman said and added kind of wistfully, "and proud of it."

"My name is Betty Barroso. B.B. That's why they call me Betty Boop. Funny nickname, isn't it? I would have liked to have been named Brigitte Bardo, for example. But what can you do?"

"My name is Bag Lady."

Defying that subhuman stench, Betty got closer and whispered: "I want to be your friend."

"We got nothing in common. You best keep on keeping on, Mrs. Cuban."

"I'm totally alone in the universe; more alone than you are, just so you know. This is your place. You were born here, don't forget. I don't even have that to fall back on."

"Nobody forced you to come here. Look for another shoulder to cry on, Mrs. White Cuban. Everyone's born where they can."

"You're wrong if you think I'm racist like most Cubans here."

"I couldn't care less. It was great knowing and singing with you. You sure do it well. Now, goodbye."

The white woman softened:

"C'mon, don't be silly, Lady Bag; let's shake hands and be friends. I want to tell you things, can't you see I'm depressed, distressed, that I'm profoundly unhappy?" Betty said all of this with her hand outstretched to the woman.

"Get yourself a head shrinker. Go back to your country. Keep going your own way. Get into politics. Vote Republican. Kill somebody. Off yourself."

"Let's shake hands and be friends. Come on, Lady bag, don't make me beg. There's always time in this life to kill someone."

"My name isn't Lady Bag."

"And mine isn't Betty Boop."

"Fine," the black woman said sternly, and the white woman squeezed her hand.

"That's odd," Betty thought, "her hands are soft," and she said:

"The man I loved most in my life was a mulatto, practically black. I was a little girl from a small town who married a guy who was almost rich. It was Fuñío, my husband, the one who made me a lady of society. I fell in love with the postman because Fuñío represented security, well-being and lineage, while the mulatto postman represented passion, pleasure and explosiveness."

"Such are the destructions of love," the homeless woman said gravely.

"I've never been able to subsist without that destruction."

"You're an unbearably superficial and coy woman."

"I know, I know. The problem is that they killed my postman."

Betty covered her mouth, as if afraid to continue. The homeless woman remained respectfully quiet.

"Oh," she finally said in a whisper, "now I get it. Every love affair needs an innocent victim."

"You don't know how I cried. How upset I got, how I tore out, how I yanked out my hair and bit my tongue until my mouth was completely filled with blood. Life sucked me dry, shit, it left me a widow, and with a husband. What could be more horrifying than having the love of your life murdered? Nothing, because you can't cry for him, you can't dress him in his coffin or bury him, or grieve for him. If your husband dies, no big deal: they bury him and the dead to the hole, the clever to the roll. But if your lover dies, what do you call that? There's not even a word for that! I squealed like a pig being butchered. I had to pretend I was having ovary pains, just so Fuñío wouldn't catch on."

"I've never been married," Bag Lady rasped.

"If you've never had a husband, and you've come this far, then don't ever get one. This is coming from a woman of experience. The unresolved dilemma in my life is that I see so clearly just how insolent and tyrannical men are, but I still can't live without them, because I like to make them crazy for me, and it ticks me off me when they mess up my plans. I guess I'm guy crazy."

The homeless woman started laughing.

"What a nice laugh you have," Betty said smiling. "What are you laughing at?"

"At you. You're a really strange white woman. Who killed your mailman?"

"Honey! He has no name in the annals of History. He became a revolutionary. It was that tragic year 1957 and in Cuba there was a tyrant named Batista. My mailman conspired to overthrow him and somebody squealed on him. The rural police filled him full of bullets."

The two women remained silent. Far off, near the sea line, two police zipped past on those three wheelers, with thick tires like the feet of flat-bottomed beasts, that sometimes patrol Miami Beach. Betty interrupted the silence:

"I remember he would recite these verses to me:"

> *Hasta morir, te amaré*
> *Porque mi pecho es tan puro*
> *Como la flor de café*

"Sounds nice, but I don't understand Spanish."

Betty became deeply moved as she recited those short verses. A tear ran down her cheek and she made a gesture to suppress her crying.

> *Quiéreme, trigueña mía,*
> *Y hasta el postrimero día*
> *No dudes que fiel te seré;*
> *Tú serás mi poesía*
> *Y yo tu flor de café*

"Don't be so sentimental."

"It's just that my son," Betty was now sweating unpleasantly and sobbing with her face buried in her hands, "my son who detests me, who doesn't want anything to do with me, he's not Fuñío's son...he's the mailman's son!"

There was again a long silence, which was crushing with the heat, and full of sounds from cars from both close and far away.

"And he came out half-mulatto, with thick lips and kinks, the little bastard was so pretty, and in Cuba that wouldn't have been so terrible, but here they've always treated him like a *mestizo*, a half-breed; poor thing, it all started when he came to this country all by himself. No wonder he hates us so much."

Betty raised her weepy eyes in the direction of the white cruise ships pulling away in the distance of the glittering sea, heading to Bimini, Puerto Rico, Nassau, or going to Hell.

The homeless woman then said:

"I was born in Mobile..."

"That's so great!" Betty exclaimed, wiping away her tears. "That's where the Alabama River ends, isn't it? And that green bay, stunning. Fuñío and I spent a weekend in Mobile a long, long time ago, when we were still young and had dreams. The whole weekend cost us seventy bucks, with hotel and free drinks in the afternoon."

"My youngest brother's name," Bag Lady continued, "was Joe. One night with two other boys, he assaulted an old white couple who lived all alone. They wanted to steal their collection of antique guns. Everybody knew about the weapons, since there was a report on them on the news."

As she was saying this, the powerful sun emerged from behind the touristically shaggy coconut palm, and Bag Lady took a white picture hat out of one of her bags. With the gesture of a snobby madam, she put it on. The hat was a little scrunched up and decorated with a wide, flaming red band. She then slipped on a pair of green neon-colored glasses.

"The weapons," Bag Lady continued, "were from back when death was still romantic and beautiful. Among all the other stuff in the museum, there was a Winchester rifle from 1866 and a Smith & Wesson from 1880. It was the boys' dream to get their hands on them toys. So they went through a window, all drunk and high on marijuana to give them courage, and armed with huge knives 'to give them old timers a scare.' But the old guy was crafty and waited with a gun. He killed one of the boys in the act. My brother, in the struggle to get away, cut off the woman's head."

Betty took out a handkerchief and dried her face.

"Five years later, my little brother died in the electric chair."

The black woman paused. Betty had now covered her mouth with both hands, as if she couldn't bear the stench or as if afraid of saying something stupid.

"For those five years I visited him every weekend. Until that last weekend, I held out hope that they'd commute his sentence. All in vain. A 2,100 volt electric shock. But according to the newspapers, my brother didn't die right away. The doctor had to go into the execution chamber several times and order another electrocution. They say 'human error' was at fault: there are bodies that just refuse to die. But it wasn't that. After several jolts, Joe's heart still kept beating. The doctor was beside himself, and so was the warden: how embarrassing, the condemned man wouldn't die. 'The human factor' was that they put on the electrodes wrong. According to the newspapers, there was this god-awful stench of burnt, overdone flesh in the death chamber. Some witness described Joe's agony as 'shocking and prolonged'."

Betty didn't dare utter a word; Bag Lady pulled out a yellowing news clipping, carefully folded up, and showed it to her. Betty read a few lines, confused: *86% of all executions have been carried out on blacks who have killed whites. Since 1976, no white person has been executed for killing a black.*

"But we shouldn't get too upset about it," the black woman said, "or lose hope, or bother to rebel. After all, we live in the richest country on Earth, in the only superpower left on the planet. Besides, the time for huge catastrophes hasn't come yet."

"It's already come for me," Betty Boop assured.

"Don't be surprised, don't be frightened if one day you get up and see that the ocean has receded from Miami Beach," Bag Lady replied, "to the extent that we could walk across all the algae and coral and reach all the islands in the ocean, even that former country of yours, or don't be startled if one day you find that there aren't any people in the streets, and after wandering around all over the place, you come across huge piles of rotting corpses, stacked higher than those coconut trees. Don't be taken aback if one day you see the streets packed with a slow and solemn procession of hundreds of thousands people with limps, missing limbs, only one eye, folk who are cripples, mongoloids, handicapped and all kinds of wounded people being followed by another throng of people dying of AIDS, or folk with tuberculosis spitting up blood, homeless people, malnourished children covered in vomit and diarrhea, bony old senile people dragging themselves along, teenage prostitutes with pyorrhea, blennoragia, and acne, and bringing up the rear, an immense procession of epileptics frothing at the mouth looked after by legions of priests in leather, flogging them, and blacks missing their heads, don't worry, all of this is normal, it's part of the world's reality and means that the worst is yet to come. BUT..." Here the bum paused rhetorically and adjusted her glasses. "BUT...if one day you go to the grocery store and see that there's no Coke, and then you go around to all the stores, kiosks, restaurants and bars and you can't find even one bottle of Coke, then you best make the sign of the cross and resign yourself to dying a prolonged and shocking death, since that will be the definitive sign that the total destruction of the Western world is imminent, a tragedy of cosmic dimensions, the devastating and final cataclysm of Judeo-Christian civilization and, consequently, of all of humanity."

Betty Boop was puzzled. Bag Lady, a little engrossed, was now fanning herself rhythmically with her hat. Betty thought that the black woman was effectively crazy, but that her dementia was benign and hallucinatory, with a tinge of rebellion to confront the intransigence of destiny, which made Betty fall in love with her madness. "If she's got termites in her roof," Betty thought, "then I'm a friend of those termites; if she's got a screw loose, then I'm made out of the same metal." Because, Betty continued to reflect, who the hell wouldn't lose it if her little brother is condemned to death and then electrocuted six times, leaving him burnt to a crisp? Bag Lady, simply put, was the most extraordinary woman she had ever met in her life. And she thought: "Bag Lady is the bad breath of the American Dream."

She tried to imagine Ocean Drive with those pilgrimages of cripples and syphilitics, young mothers with scabies and children, no longer in school, racked with hemorrhages and oozing eyes. Isn't that what the black woman had said? Praise the Lord! The part about the priests with whips, trailed by long lines of headless blacks seemed especially funny to her, since, even as she looked out at the ocean, she could clearly picture the saggy, bruised and bloodied asses of the priests and their little dicks, shriveled up from so much celibacy. And in front of her she imagined, moving up Ocean Drive towards the North, the quiet multitudes of epileptics also solemnly accompanied by long files of decapitated blacks, many of whom were buck-naked, erect and hung like horses, some of them playing drums or dancing as they fired into the air with huge pistols. Shit, it was true: all of this was nothing compared to what would happen if there was no Coke anywhere…'a tragedy of cosmic dimensions.'"

Bag Lady suddenly began laughing, and Betty Boop did, too. The harder the black woman laughed, the more the white woman howled herself hoarse. A couple of underfed, tan and wrinkled Jewish women walked past them and they also smiled, having caught that unhealthy happiness. When they had both calmed down, Bag Lady said:

"It's important to laugh. The ones who don't have their mouths deformed. And their souls!

When she said this, Betty observed how the homeless woman cast a quick glance over her glasses and made a strange movement under the bags she had in her lap. With a voice that terrified Betty, the black woman said:

"I've got a six-shot Colt King Cobra Magnum double action, short barrel aimed right at you. If you move, I'll fill your chest full of holes."

It was the voice of a murderer. Betty remained silent.

"You're going to kill your friend?" she finally sputtered, and she felt ashamed, not out of fear but out of surprise.

"Fuck you," Bag Lady said furiously, "you fucking traitor. Looky here!"

And with one quick movement of her left hand, she snatched Fuñío's razor blade from Betty's bra.

"Oh girl, you frightened me!" Betty exclaimed, relieved and panting.

"You were going to use that, weren't you? Confess, you bitch!"

"Yes, of course I'm going to use it, but not on you, never on you, on Burruchaga. Today I'm going to cut off Burruchaga's head."

"Who's Burruchaga?"

"The owner of the restaurant I work at, my ex-lover."

"You going to kill him?"

"Exactly. To settle a score. Another victim of love."

"Ah."

"I have it all perfectly planned. I go to work and tell him:

'Burruchaga, I have to speak with you.' And when he comes up to me, smack! I give him one, two, three, four, five, six, seven slashes across the neck. And then blood red."

"You're stupid," the bum said with bald objectivity, "that's murder one."

The white woman looked out at the sea and stepped proudly onto the bench.

"I couldn't care less," she replied. "Let them put me in that stupid chair. They'll have to electrocute me hundreds of times."

"Listen good and don't be such a braggart, *Cubana*: right after the first slash, a gush of blood will cover your arms, dress, face and hair. Besides, that action has all kinds of aggravating circumstances you can't even begin to imagine: malicious intent, malice aforethought, premeditation, planning a crime. All that's left is previous offenses and cover of darkness."

"Well fine, I'll wait to do it at night. The restaurant's open until one in the morning."

"Suit yourself. They won't strap you into the electric chair."

"But if everything goes okay, can we see each other tonight?"

"Those things *never* go well, *Cubana*."

"We all have the right to hold our dignity high, very high. Nobody puts me down."

"Everybody always has the right to put anyone down whenever they have the means to do so."

If the black woman hadn't stunk so nauseatingly bad, Betty would have given her a hug. That's why it seemed incredible to picture herself hugging the woman affectionately.

"Here's your knife. Good luck, whitey."

"Do you know what the color of your hat band means?"

"No," the bum said irritated, "but I do know you'll rot in jail. Murder One!"

"Passion," Betty said, passionately. "The color of the band on your hat means *passion*!"

"May God help you, *Cubana*."

Mireya and her Lover...

"I don't know Nicotiano very well..."
"I don't, either; after thirteen years, I still don't know who he is."
"Sometimes I'm surprised you like me so much."

"And why's that?"

"Because I'm really just a ...I don't know, compared to him, he's a creator, an artist...I'm just a...I don't know, a kind of pencil pusher."

"You're a very charming pencil pusher."

"But he's an extraordinary man, lots of people admire him and...to be honest, I do, too. At least from afar he seems like a good person. Besides, in the future his sculptures..."

"I've about had my fill of his sculptures."

"You're an enchanting woman."

"He's had my head shoved in the mud for thirteen years. He forced me to live a strange way of life. Who am I? I feel uprooted, I don't know whether I belong to Cuban culture or American culture. Because on the Island of Cundeamor you live in a kind of limbo. We're in Miami but at the same time we're nowhere."

"It's because the Island of Cundeamor doesn't exist."

"But I do exist, you know? And for you to really believe you exist, that your part of life and not...I don't know, part of a novel, or a memory, you have to have existential coordinates, you have to have contact with everyday life and have an active part in a social environment. Before I found you I didn't know what to do. I wasn't even aware that I needed an escape valve, a refuge, a change, to escape...I'm not Cuban anymore but I'm not American either, because they haven't let me put down roots in this culture. Aunt Ulalume, Cocorioco, Nicotiano...they live in a false Cuba, they live in a mirage. And nothing matters to Nicotiano: we never go to the movies, we don't see any concerts, we don't go the theater, we don't have a single friend besides those knaves from the Crabb Company, who are noble people, I can't deny that, but that's not enough. It's not enough for me! To him the most important things are his crabs, everything's more important than me...If Fidel said this or that in Havana, if over there this or that book was published, that Fulano the painter has an exhibit on in Mexico City...Nicotiano barely knows where he lives, I swear, he doesn't even remember when his birthday is, not to mention mine! I have never...ever...in these thirteen years...celebrated my birthday...nobody's ever thrown me even a little party, nobody's given me a flower. Not even once have they made me felt that I mean something to them, you know? And it's not Aunt Ula, because to tell you the truth she's wanted to throw a party for me several times, only Nicotiano never showed any enthusiasm and...that's a first, since you know how we Cubans usually...But I'm boring you."

"I don't know what to tell you, Mireya, I'm not a shrink... Come *on, give me a hug.*

"*I feel safe with you.*"

"*Take off your blouse. Come on, let's go to bed.*"

"*Whatever you want. Do whatever you want to me.*"

- Four -

"Look, Mr. Hetkinen," the cop said, gazing out at the cloudscape rather than looking him in the eye. This was something that Hetkinen detested in general, but since he was dealing with a cop, it made him feel scornful. "The Crabb Company has our full respect and attention, but this bit about threatening your neighbors with a bazooka is dangerously insane."

"With a what?" I asked.

"The Crabb Company doesn't have a permit for a bazooka," the official responded. "Mr. McIntire is accusing you all of…"

"Just a minute," Hetkinen interrupted, "McIntire's accusing us? The unmitigated nerve of that guy. Show him the pictures, Mari."

Maribarbola stuck out his long arm, solid with muscles as thick as vegetables, like fleshy asparagus:

"Here."

The dogs kept up their infernal barking (nobody told them to shut up, just so the police would feel uptight), except Kafka, who followed the operation, tense and silent.

"Hmmmm," the cop said as he passed the pictures to his partner, also a Cuban, who then said:

"Well, well… McIntire sure knows how to cast a stone and hide the hand."

"The Crabb Company has permits for all weapons," Hetki said from his seat, "and they are used exclusively in their honest, decent, dangerous and socially useful work. Nevertheless, it would behoove you to find out whether or not McIntire has a permit to aim at my wife with a Galil Sniper. That's attempted murder, with premeditation, intent to harm and malice aforethought. If you seize his gun, you'll find it's got a Nimrod 6x40 scope.

"And that ain't for killing roaches," Sikitrake tossed in.

I noticed by the cops' little glances that my breasts were rather pronounced from the sweat, especially my large dark nipples, and I crossed my arms to appear more presentable.

"What I want is peace and quiet on the Island of Cundeamor, right?" The cop amiably stretched out his arm; on his wrist gleamed a gold bracelet, which must have weighed as much as the revolver on his belt. Hetkinen stuck out his hand.

"Can I take the pictures?" the officer asked.

"Of course," my husband assented. "And tell McIntire that we're willing to forget this altercation. But if he keeps screwing with us, he's going to get some very unpleasant news from our lawyers."

The officer shook his head with worry. They left and then Montaver and Gotero stopped their barking.

"Who is that guy?" I asked.

"The cop? Johnny Rodriguez."

With the sun almost at its zenith, the chlorified atmosphere of the pergola had turned cloying and greasy. Not even a breeze stirred the leaves. The lianas sweated little drops of an obscene milk. The mangos, avocados, güiras and esparto looked like they were about to burst. The little flowers of the cundeamor were exhausted. A couple of lustrous, filthy flies skulked about the remains of the breakfast, and Saint Barbara from Waikiki was enervated, half-conscious. The detoxifying air of the sea was what we needed, but it hadn't come.

"Now I want," I said, squinting, "for you all to give me as full a report as possible. What have you turned up on Mireya?"

"You do the talking, Sikitrake," Maribarbola asked, wanting to get it over with quickly.

Sikitrake said:

"Aunt Ula, I think we all would have given the best of this world just to avoid having to reveal the evidence that…"

"Cut to the chase!" I demanded.

"In accordance with your wishes, we set aside a lot of important jobs. For example, two transports of funds we should have escorted, and a timely security service at a convention in Atlanta, all to spend full time tracking every one of Mireya's movements. The result of the report is that Mireya has a lover, with whom she is having sexual relations highly…shall we say…"

"Let's hear it."

"Active"

"Active…," I repeated.

"These relations," Sikitrake continued, "are carried out in 1)

Mireya's car, or in her lover's car; 2) in various motels in Miami Beach, Coconut Grove and Calle Ocho. The latter two are dirt cheap, real dives; the one they use the most is called The Eden and it's on 2nd Ave.; 4) in the Tower and Trail movie theaters, and even in that dump, Parrot Jungle."

"What else?"

All of this was having the effect of a laxative on me. Overhead and all around us was a flapping of birds. They were hummingbirds coming to nibble on the *cundeamores*. Like the ones in Cuba. I never found out where they came from, if they were imaginary, native, or if they got here by crossing the Florida Strait.

"Your turn, Maribarbola," Siki said.

"Mireya and her lover lead an almost normal life, like girlfriend and boyfriend, or newlyweds. They go out everywhere without the slightest discretion or effort to conceal anything. To the movies, to nightclubs, to the beach, to restaurants like Versalles or La Carreta."

"Wanton disregard," muttered Sikitrake.

"Please leave out the value judgements," Hetkinen interjected. "Let's stick objectively to the report."

"Mireya knows the guy's family and sometimes visits them."

"Who's her lover?"

"I was getting to that; he's a downward mobile YUCCA."

"What's that?"

"A Young Up Coming Cuban American," Hetkinen explained.

"Let's stop dancing around it. Aunt Ula: Mireya's lover is the director of the Galería South, at the beach."

Maribarbola and Sikitrake exchanged meaningful looks. Hetkinen remained undaunted.

The hummingbirds couldn't be heard now. Just the screech-thunder of the airplanes skimming overhead in their descent to Miami International Airport.

"If memory serves me correctly, Nicotiano even brought that man to the Island of Cundeamor once."

"That's right. There's no bigger mistake than bringing a cynical, unscrupulous guy into your own house."

"We have to keep this from Nicotiano at all costs; as far as I know, he thinks highly of that gallery owner."

"Because Nicotiano is slow, he doesn't pick up on the little glances."

"The guy doesn't have a previous record," Maribarbola continued, "and he doesn't do drugs, not even cocaine. But he is divorced and has a couple of kids around. He's in his forties, but he looks younger, and he doesn't carry a weapon..."

"Make it short, please," I asked with a kind of weakness in my voice.

"He doesn't have any huge debts. He drives a nice car, you can tell he wants to get his life in order, wants a little stability..."

"Like Mireya," I interjected.

"The only thing Mireya wants is dick," Sikitrake blurted out, crassly.

"Watch your mouth!"

I'm sorry, Aunt Ula. You wanted to know all this. Now just listen, please."

Maribarbola finished:

"From a legal standpoint, the guy is not a danger to Mireya's safety. I stress that, since that's the information you wanted on the matter."

Without looking at me, Sikitrake, pained, then said:

"It would seem that you want to protect Mireya, even in her adultery."

An airplane passed close overheard and left an oppressive silence. A weak breeze was now blowing over the Island of Cundeamor. My voice was like a trickle of water slipping over a rock:

"Do they get along well?"

"You ordered us not to make value judgements," Sikitrake said.

"Please..."

"He's a nice, good-looking guy. When he talks, he sounds like some B-Mexican movie star advertising gum and candy with a little grin. As far as getting on, they adore each other."

"How," I asked, immediately regretting having done so, "do you explain Mireya's going about so blatantly with her lover...maybe she wants Nicotiano to find out."

"There's only one explanation: she does what she does because she's got no shame, and excuse the value judgement."

"Mireya knows," Maribarbola said, "that Nicotiano has virtually no friends in Miami and doesn't even go out for a beer. His universe is his studio and sculptures, the Island of Cundeamor, Mireya herself...Maybe she thinks her husband's isolation gives her a kind of protection."

Maribarbola, impatient, then pulled out a stack of pictures and said:

"Here's the graphic testimony, Aunt Ula."

"I don't think you should see the pictures," Hitke said.

"Let her see them," Siki grunted, "so she'll be immune."

I suddenly thought I could make out among the *malangas*, far off, a familiar little figure that disappeared vertiginously among the *heliconias*. It appeared again among the *vicarias*, jumped over the *mariposas* without so much as grazing them to scale, like a streak of white felt, the highest part of the frangipani. I now understood why the hummingbirds had grown quiet: Marx had returned from his travels.

"Before I see those pictures, I want to ask something."

"Go right ahead."

"The motives," I said, just to see what they would say. Nobody suspected the reasons better than me.

"What motives?"

"Mireya's motives for what she's done."

"As you will see, Aunt Ula," Sikitrake argued, "we're not planning to prosecute. We limit ourselves to the actual facts of an event. That's it."

"Don't tell me you don't have any recordings. Conversations. Incriminating words..."

"We have tons. You want to listen to some of it?"

"I don't know. At some point, something must have come out, something that can be interpreted as a cause...an explanation..."

"To her, Nicotiano is a past chapter in her life. There are reams upon reams of crap about how worthless Nicotiano is."

"Don't listen to the recordings, Aunt Ula. Spare yourself that bitter drink."

Marx, with his intrusive movements, made his presence known at the pergola. With one little jump, he plopped down between my thighs, right on top of the pictures. I pushed him aside, gently, and began looking at them. Marx pretended he was sleeping. He reeked of the big city, the ocean and mountains, and he looked sated.

The pictures had been taken with Maribarbola's usual professionalism. Mireya, looking joyful, was seen holding the man's hand. At the beach, kissing in the waves, perhaps in mutual masturbation, or frolicking on the sand. Going into a restaurant, Mireya looking at him with the eyes of a girl in love, as he caressed her cheek. In other pictures she was naked and sweating, her hair tussled, her eyes half-closed, her mouth open in a lusty gesture and her lips practically covered with slobber while masturbating her lover with both hands (one hand gripping his penis, the other his testicles) inside a room in which you could tell a television was turned on. All the pictures were shot through half-open blinds. The sequence was complete: her lips closer and closer to his dick, whose thickness screamed that it was being stimulated with great generosity. I thumbed through several shots, seeing them without looking at them, his penis practically shoved into the mouth of ecstatic Mireya, whose eyes were closed, the man and his hands grappling with her hair and certainly pushing her head down so she would suck harder. Then Mireya on all fours, her thighs and back glistening with sweat in the light flittering through the blinds, her buttocks, which I never imagined to be as so round and lustily full in a girl so skinny, were thrust upward.

I looked away and tried to fill my lungs with air so I could go on. Mireya's body seemed so much more perfect in those positions than what she most likely was in reality; she was quite tan, but not her breasts, they were white, shiny, just like her buttocks, but very small, I already knew that. The man was penetrating her, gripping her thighs, her hips, the fleshy whiteness of her buttocks with the force of a man who, would surely plunge into an abyss if he were to let go.

Maribarbola, Hetkinen and Sikitrake kept silent and now several strong rays of sunlight were shining through the climbing vines, striking me right on the head. It was a heat like the lard of a roasting pig. I didn't move, though the skin on the back of my neck was burning, and my scalp was sweating grease. I heard the smack of somebody jumping into the pool, Marx's ears twitched and, leaping up, he disappeared among the *lianas* of the *tibisí*. Saint Barbara of Waikiki was now vomiting on my back, and I could feel my own rank breath. Mireya was mounted astride the invisible penis of the man, who was sucking her tits. "Nicotiano is swimming in the pool, Aunt Ula," I heard, distantly and like an echo; it was Maribarbola's voice: "Give me the pictures in case he comes…" Another plane passed overhead with its whistle-thunder and Saint Barbara disintegration under the sun's heat, and the fragrance of the climbing vines, and the grass coagulating into soggy sap, were all turning my stomach.

"Aunt Ula, what's wrong…"

"Damn, look how pale you are!"

"It's all that bitch's fault," Sikitrake grumbled, taking the pictures away from me, and that was the last thing I remember.

"Aunt Ula! Something's wrong with her!"

Maribarbola and Siki fanned me with the photos, trying to get me to come to. An explosion of sickness that sent me into a whirlpool of crap.

"I have to throw up, please, take me to the bathroom."

"Destroy all of them!" I ordered as they took me through the path of flowers towards the inside of the house. "Everything, the report, the pictures, the negatives, the recordings, everything! I don't want any evidence."

I threw up in three strong streams, almost relishing it. Maribarbola fixed me a very strong cup of lime tea, and I calmed down. Hetkinen had prepared some *mojitos*, but not for me. From the large windows, the view of the bay was splendid. Oblivious to the approaching storm, Nicotiano and Cocorioco frolicked in the pool.

"Aunt Ula," Sikitrake ventured to provoke me, "Mireya's acted like a whore."

I looked at him sternly. When you're nervous, lime tea produces an effect of tense serenity.

"I know very well what a whore is. Don't go giving me lectures."

"But all that's missing is to for that guy to stick it to her in the damn Orange Bowl, cheered on by thousands of fans!"

That said, Sikitrake retreated somewhat, perhaps embarrassed by his strong emotion.

"Hetkinen," I said, "do Bartolo and Guarapito also know everything?"

"Relax; they weren't part of the investigations. They focused on other jobs and don't know anything. Unless they hear something through the grapevine."

"Which wouldn't surprise me," Sikitrake said dryly.

I responded:

"As a single man, Sikitrake, have you ever seduced a married woman?"

"Sorry, Aunt Ula, but you don't need to seduce married woman who have *that proclivity*. All by themselves they'll nibble on you, warm you up, and then eat you. Especially when they're drunk, so afterwards they can feel sorry for themselves and wash away their dirty deeds, claiming 'they didn't know what they were doing.' Women can be experts in forgetting all about the details of their behavior...when it's convenient for them. And just so you know, Aunt Ula: married women (at least the ones I've slept with), always, at some point, talk bad about their husbands. And they act like they themselves were worthless."

"So," I simplified: "all married woman who have lovers are pigs."

"Mireya's acted like an easy single woman."

"Mireya is single," Maribarbola discretely slipped in. "Remember that Nicotiano never wanted to get married, not by the Church, or by anyone else."

"Guarapito, for example, is married," I replied, "and is always caught up in some mess with other women. And nobody's ever called Guarapito a pig, or a whore.

"Forgive me, Aunt Ula; I would give my life for you…But shit, your defending Mireya…there is such a thing as improper behavior."

"I understand what you're saying, Sikitrake, but nobody is going denigrate her in front of me, as long as I'm alive."

"But she has been allowed to disgrace Nicotiano!"

"Calm down, Sikitrake. There may be extenuating circumstances. Mireya is not a pervert. I'm sure she's going through a very painful time."

"Painful? Are you blind, Aunt Ula? Reckless abandon, happiness is what she felt when she was with that guy."

"We can't force her to love Nicotiano forever. When she met him she was just a young girl."

"What you and I most detest is betrayal. If she'd just been honest, if she'd told him to his face: 'Nicotiano, it's over. I love another man…'"

"She doesn't dare. She's insecure. Maybe she's tired of Nicotiano, but at the same time she still loves him…Look, Sikitrake," I added somewhat wearily, "relationships between humans beings, above all love relationships, aren't supposed to be eternal. Everything changes and deteriorates. I know for a fact that Mireya was sincere during all those years she loved Nicotiano. It was genuine, positive for him and for her. We don't have any right to forget about all of her previous behavior because of what she's done now. We can't overlook her merits and cover them up with abuse. Her love for my nephew was as real as her rejection of him is now. The death of feelings is as indisputable as the death of the body. Her love ended and that is that. Mireya, my Mireya, she's not a contemptible person because she stopped loving Nicotiano, my Nicotiano."

Hetkinen and Maribarbola maintained a discreet silence. Sikitrake collapsed onto the sofa, not in defeat, but exhaustion.

"Aunt Ula," he said wearily, "there's no cure for your way of thinking."

"It's love that has no cure, my son."

"What hurts me the most," Sikitrake said in the same apathetic tone, "is that Nicotiano has blown golden opportunities with very beautiful women. That I know for a fact. And you too, Maribarbola! Despite how ugly, slow and unpleasant he can be, I don't know why women throw themselves at Nicotiano."

"And I didn't know my nephew was unpleasant."

"Nicotiano's a pain, Aunt Ula. He's difficult and maybe even a manic depressive. There's his shyness, his irritating naiveté and he's always off daydreaming about something. But he's never short of attractive women. He could've had them if he'd lifted one finger. Since he's so oblivious to what's going on in the real world, he sometimes seems actually profound, and that captivates women. But he ignores them. He would almost always say 'Mireya's enough for me.' 'If I started sleeping with other women, how can I keep loving Mireya?' Guarapito would howl with laughter and make dirty jokes about Nicotiano. And now look, just look at what Mireya's done to him! What really kills me is that if there's a man who didn't deserve this, it's Nicotiano."

Sikitrake and Hetkinen left. As soon as I was alone with Maribarbola, I hugged him. Hard. Very hard.

"Take a bath, Aunt Ula, you smell bad."

I told him no. That I wouldn't bathe until I felt better. It was a form of self-mortification. When you suffer, it's best to punish yourself. The body's misery tends to combat the misery of one's sentimental state.

"Aunt Ula...the truth is..."

"I know, I know! Sikitrake's right on a couple of points. But I am, too. And so's Mireya, for that matter. That's the dilemma."

"You're sad. Aunt Ula, you're hard on yourself and you know it's not worth it. Mireya hasn't died; she left."

Those words were just what I needed: *Mireya hasn't died; she left*, since they formulated exactly what I was feeling: Mireya wasn't dead, no, but at the same time she had already begun to die. That was worse than a biological death.

I began to cry. Noiselessly, without sobbing.

I don't like for people to see me crying. Since it's the only thing that consoles me in unbearably painful situations, I put a lot of emotion into it and end up looking hideous, with my wrinkles spreading and sagging even more, and my swollen eyelids looking like tomatoes.

"You don't want Mireya to leave us," Maribarbola stated.

"But there's nothing we can do about it, my son, there's nothing we can do about it."

But Maribarbola could see me cry. And not just cry. He had the privilege of seeing me naked, and dirty, and I'm sure some day he'll even close the eyes of my corpse.

We found Maribarbola abandoned in the street when we were living in Los Angeles. This was when we had first gone into exile. Nicotiano, still a young boy, was working at a 24-hour hamburger joint. He had the night shift, from 5:00 p.m. to 8:00 a.m. the next day. The manager was a Cuban who paid him slave's wages, and my nephew, who always had determination and a great diligent spirit towards life, handed his wages over to me. Such were the early days of our stay in this country. We worked our fingers to the bone, though we had some money socked away. Quite a bit of money. But back then I was caught up in the frenetic activity of unmentionable dealings. Fortunately, I didn't have to allow my nephew to tolerate that brutal exploitation for very long; with determination, not too many scruples, with a little bit of imagination and a whole lot of balls, we scraped by and forever left behind that tortuous period in which immigrants learn all about hardship and financial straits.

But early one morning at five o'clock, a boy in rags showed up all alone at the restaurant. One of his ears had been hit and was swollen and full of pus. He wanted a hamburger and a little carton of milk, but when he counted out the coins with his grubby little fingers, he saw that he was short. The restaurant was located in East Los Angeles, an area especially sordid with violence and poverty. The boy picked up his coins one by one to go on his way, but Nicotiano wouldn't let him leave. He fixed him up with a delicious breakfast of ham, cheese, eggs, orange juice and milk. The young boy didn't want to believe that all that attention was really for him, just for him, and that the sumptuous breakfast was a stranger's handout. But he began to greedily scarf it down, like a small bruised cat afraid that the big ones would come back and snatch away his prized booty. A kitten. That was the first impression Nicotiano had of the boy as he watched him wolfing down his food. An abandoned street cat, stray and hungry. Since it was early for the restaurant's daily avalanche of breakfast customers, Nicotiano started a conversation with the boy.

"What's your name?"

"Maribarbola."

"That's a strange name."

"A rich old man from Beverly Hills gave it to me. He gave me a lift in his limo and said 'Maribarbolita'. He was a good old man. He never did anything to hurt me. Later he didn't want to see me any more, but the name stuck. Now I don't remember what my name used to be."

"Where are you from?"

"I was born in Mexico, but I don't know where, or when," he answered, trying to smile, his mouth stuffed with food.

"You live around here?"

"No, I don't have any one place to live. Can I leave you this change as payment? I'll bring you the rest tomorrow. Or later on, or maybe tonight. Or would you like it if I paid you a different way? If you want, I can pay you inside there, in the bathroom, or if not, behind the counter."

Nicotiano, who always had little imagination for the dirty things in life, didn't get it and started laughing.

"No, my treat, son. You don't have to pay me anything. Hey, are you in school? You need to know how to read and write, so you can learn lots of new things. What do you live on?" he asked like an idiot, "begging?"

"Well," the boy responded, stuffing the breakfast leftovers into his pocket, "right now I'm not living on anything. Until a little while ago I lived on truckers, but not so much anymore. I don't like living on truckers because sometimes they treat me bad."

"Truckers?"

At this point, my nephew's candor turned so painful that if I had been present, I would have smacked his mouth shut. The boy, with brutal candor, explained:

"I lived by sucking trucker dick. At first it was difficult, but I learned because they made me. You have to stick it all the way into your mouth, until you practically choke, and suck as hard as you can. When the truckers come, you have to swallow their jizz because if you don't, you get hit. Cum tastes like shit, only it's white. And sometimes the truckers don't pay up. When you ask for the money, they hit you, push you and throw you out of the truck, kicking you. And almost all of them want to fuck me. I don't like that because it's so painful. It burns and makes me bleed, and afterwards I can't take a shit without it hurting, and sometimes they don't even pay me. So even if I go hungry, I don't want them to fuck me anymore. But if you want, I can suck your dick behind the counter, you're a nice man who's given me breakfast...Don't be so serious, sir, sucking dick is fast and doesn't hurt me. I can pay for the breakfast that way."

All the while the boy was talking, Nicotiano's legs grew more and more wobbly. There was absolutely no relation between the sweetness of the boy's voice and what he was saying. Nicotiano's hands were sweating, his heart practically rose up to his tonsils, and he clutched at the counter like somebody who just peered into an abyss.

Nicotiano was incapable of uttering a single word. His mind was blocked by conflicting thoughts, dizzying associations and violent reasonings that could not continue or fit into any rational solution. His mind was suddenly the intersection of a street jammed with cars, ambulances and police cars in the wake of an accident.

"Well, it doesn't matter to me," the small boy said, misinterpreting Nicotiano's queasy silence; Nicotiano's eyes were reddening, his gaze fixed on the boy and his teeth clenched, like he was going to hurt him. "Well, don't get so angry, if you want to fuck me then go ahead, but be careful when you stick it in me. Please, put it in real slow. How about behind the counter?"

Standing before the startled little boy, Nicotiano grabbed his own face with both hands, as if to yank it off and throw it to the ground and stomp all over it. It was if he were ashamed of being a man and not a lizard, a snail, an ameoba. And then he let out several deaf screams that were more like gasps, as if he didn't have any air in his lungs and was going to asphyxiate himself; his fingers were practically digging into his eyes, a gesture under his hands as if he were burned, and more gasps, he looked crazed, or like an epileptic about to have a seizure. The boy, completely terrorized, saw that the young man was crying, but then he took off, fear-crazed, disappearing among the shadows of the first fumes of the early morning streets.

Nicotiano stayed there in the hamburger joint like an ocelot locked in a small cage.

These eyes that will eat the worms in this foreign land have witnessed many cruel things. But that story left me, just as it did my nephew, a combination of dynamite and crushed poison weed.

The following morning, at five a.m., I was waiting there in the restaurant. But he didn't show up. I waited for him every morning for three weeks, until finally he came back. So without asking anyone's permission, I brought him home to live with us, and I adopted him my own way, without any papers or going through any legal proceedings. In the end, a child who had been savagely mistreated and condemned to submission and servitude needed a legal existence. What the boy needed was affection, economic security, and lots of respect.

Little by little, he adapted. I was a mother to him; Nicotiano became his brother. Then, after struggling to scrape together enough money, we moved from Los Angeles to Spain and, in a place near Malaga, we bought a restaurant. We lived there for six years; with the increase of tourism (that was the time of the first wave of Swedes, Germans and English) we made a little money. Back then I sold

Nicotiano's first crabs, in Madrid. Then an art dealer from Barcelona ordered thirty alabaster crabs, which raked in considerable earnings. Until we decided to come back to the United States, that time to Miami, and immediately purchased the house on The Island of Cundeamor.

The telephone rang.

It was Hetkinen, from his car. Mireya was on her way back.

"She's driving like a madwoman," he added. "She's drunk, or distraught."

I hurried out to the front yard. I wanted to see Mireya when she arrived. What would the poor girl do? Keep pretending?

I grabbed my longest hose and began watering the flower pots out under the pergola. My little forests of basil, like green-combed afros; the marjorams and lemon balms, just so I could wait for Mireya while getting my thoughts in order.

But time passed and she didn't arrive. Kafka was dozing among the weeds. Curled up next to him was Marx, dreaming his irresponsible dream.

Hitkenen and Sikitrake...

"Hetkinen, maybe McIntire's Galil Sniper is..."

"Is a gift from Cuban American Transaction."

"What do you think?"

"I wouldn't doubt it. To intimidate us."

"But how could they have gotten McIntire to turn on us? Could they have paid him?"

"Who knows if they sent him the rifle through the mail. Keep in mind that McIntire's grudge against us isn't new. But even though we aren't going to be caught off guard, I don't think it's worth wasting time investigating that. McIntire is a sad lush."

"And a racist to boot."

"He looks down on Latinos. He especially hates you Cubans."

"He's envious of us. Like so many other Anglos."

"It's a shame they're going to lose the Island of Cundeamor."

"How far is Aunt Ula willing to go?"

"She's willing to sink into the ocean before she'd give up the island to Transaction. And she keeps talking about a macao, *which I'm not sure what that is. She says: 'They're going to have to burn us out, like a* macao.'"

"Ah! The macao *is a kind of small mollusk. It lives in Cuban*

waters, inside a little snail that acts as its host shell. Nicotiano's got lots of sculptures of macaos *that are amazing. Especially the alabaster ones. The thing is, there's no way to coax the* macao *out of the snail, not even by pounding it out. It defends itself by clinging to piers and docks, sticking to them, you have to burn them out, and when you finally do get it out of its shell, it's already dead."*

"God help me if I ever have Cuban enemies."

"C'mon, Hetkinen, there's no need to exaggerate. You Finns aren't easy enemies."

"Come to think of it, we too can be quite formidable enemies."

"Lots of small nations that have had to come out in the world and meld their nationality with another great and dominant nation are like that...Hetkinen, you ever belong to the Finnish secret police?"

"I don't like to talk about it."

"C'mon, Hetki, can't we trust each other?"

"I was part of a special covert unit of State Security."

"I can imagine the training they must have given you, and the atrocities you must have committed against the Russians.

"What times those were, Sikitrake. The Russians were a formidable enemy, too."

"It seems like a lie to live without the Cold War."

"For us Finns, the Cold War was always pretty hot."

"For us Cubans, too."

"You took part in the Angolan war, Sikitrake..."

"I'd rather not talk about that, Hetkinen, but you already know that I don't regret it."

"I envy each little white South African soldier you cut down."

"Hetkinen, I prefer not to talk about that; I lost two cousins in Angola...Hey, don't you think Aunt Ulalume's exaggerating the value of the Island of Cundeamor?"

"If you don't exaggerate the value of what you're defending, the enemy realizes that you won't exaggerate your resistance either. And then you've lost everything."

- Five -

*T*he El Regreso Restaurant was cramped, crowded, festive and dark. It looked like a sliver of jail which a creative eye, using light and décor, had turned into a cozy place. You could say lots of bad things about El Regreso, though in spite of its defects it was a pleasant place to sit down and have a meal. It wasn't clean or dirty; it wasn't first or third-rate. Sure, maybe a gleaming roach scurried under the shoe of a dinner guest, or set out on a disgusting pilgrimage along the walls, taking cover behind one of the numerous landscapes of Cuban countryside which, with their cloying air of tall and idealized royal palms bathed in the island twilight, lent El Regreso both a touch of emotion and creole kitsch. But invariably one of the nice waitresses would exterminate the roach without thinking twice. Because, in addition to the food, the charm of El Regreso lay in its waitresses, hand-picked by Burruchaga.

The outside façade of the restaurant was its position as a Cuban café, with a little display window and assortment of *boniatillos*, cakes, chocolate shavings, sponge cakes, dairy ice cream and other creole desserts, all of them so illogically sweet that only a purebred Cuban, or an American with the calling of an obese person, would try them. El Regreso also had a fine selection of national cigars, rolled in Tampa, as well as in Honduras and the Dominican Republic.

The bar at El Regreso was long, stretching to the very back of the room, which opened up into a smaller room filled with about ten tables. Each table was set with paper place mats, with the National Shield of Cuba printed in the top right corner: that pointed shield in all of its glory, with the solitary star stamped in the haughty and somewhat soft red of the Phrygian cap. The blazing sun over the islands, half-sunken in the eternal sea, its rays lighting up the firmament of the Patria and the world. The solid rod key to the doors of a symbolic gulf. Our flag's white and blue stripes. Two green hills like the chaste breasts of a young woman sleeping a *siesta*, dreaming that between her breasts lies a slim, fully erect royal palm. Surrounding the curves of the pointed arch, a laurel branch and a holy branch. Displaying our flag in all of its colors on a place mat was no small task for a modest little restaurant like El Regreso. Below the shield was the following inscription, written both in Spanish and English: Our venerable National Shield was designed by *Don* Miguel Teurbe Tolón, under the supervison of the glorious Annexionist General, Narciso López.

Burruchaga didn't skimp when it came to this kind of display, in order to preserve the most healthy and pure nationalistic spirit in his customers, all victims of that "atrocious exile that International Communism imposed on every decent Cuban," as Burruchaga was wont to say.

The kitchen area of El Regreso was dank and greasy, the ventilation defective and the equipment aging, inconvenient and crude. The bad state of the kitchen contrasted with the high degree of professionalism of the cooks, whose food was varied, imaginative and of an acceptable quality. The prices, according to Burruchaga's ads, were "the most patriotic in exile." The menu was composed of a mix of truly Cuban dishes, other dishes of an imaginary Cubanism, and the rest being Burruchaga's own invention; there was also the American fare, which of course was the most indigestible, fetid and bland of anything they sold.

In El Regreso you could eat fried yucca or *salcochada* bathed in its golden creole pork lard *mojo*, garlic and sour orange. There was *boliche*, a beef grilled in a tangy marinade packed with laurel.There was no shortage of grilled suckling pig, which Burruchaga sold in huge quantities for all types of parties, weddings, birthdays and anniversaries, always with helpings of white rice and black beans and fried ripe plantains. In El Regreso, the vegetable stew was thick and sweet-smelling.

But what really set Burruchaga's restaurant above your run-of-the-mill place was the variety of dishes that were egg-based, and were consequently cheap and quite appetizing. Their names were catchy, not at all objective from a gastronomic point of view, but they were sonorous, even poetic: Cuban Eggs Smothered in Onions, Havana-style Eggs in a Volante car, Turtle Eggs in their Sauce, Eggs of Nostalgia with Parsley and Bacon, Charming Malaga Woman Eggs, Eggs as Green as Palm Trees, Eggs from Oriente Province, and to top it off, even Eggs of Our Former Homeland, which was a ham omelet loaded with garlic.

Other dishes were as succulent as their names were eccentric. For example, Cuban Yam without a Necktie, Baire's Shout Yucca, Hurricane Flora Sweet Potatoes, Fufú of Reddish Plantain, Cristal Mountain Arum, or Liberty Bridge Quimbombó.

The staff of The Regreso was exclusively female, except for the cooks and the busboys. Burruchaga had a very strict notion of what gastronomic service was and his slogan was that nobody eats with more enjoyment than a diner served by the feminine hand. Correct or not, El Regreso was an extremely lucrative business. Lucrative, of course, for Burruchaga, but not for his employees, all of whom were underpaid. Without their tips, the waitresses' wages were pathetic. And no one could approach Burruchaga with demands for raises or other necessary guarantees such as paid vacations, maternity leave, and all that union bullshit, which were holdovers from a socialist past (communistoid, Burruchaga would say), now dead and buried in the trash heap of History.

The waitresses' uniforms evoked the Cuban flag: blue skirt, red sash around the waist, and white blouse. The getup gave them the comical air of high school girls, except for their sweat- and grease- and ketchup-stained blouses. The sashes they had were faded (it was Burruchaga's responsibility to buy them new ones) in such a way that it made you think of a Cuban flag come down in the world.

"Burruchaga wants us to wear uniforms," the waitresses gossiped, "but he won't open his wallet so we can have enough of them to change everyday."

In that regard, Betty Boop was profoundly unsupportive of her co-workers.

"Pure pretexts!" she would argue, to justify their being a bunch of pigs.

They would, however, invariably see her going around well-dressed; in the small locker each one had in the back of the store, Betty always kept several blouses and skirts impeccably ironed and spotless, their patriotic colors radiant and pure. Four Yale padlocks, the stoutest kind, protected her belongings; and since Betty's waitress outfit always looked fresh, tongues wagged with resentful force:

"Betty's his favorite," the other's grumbled.

"Burruchaga's always buying her clothes."

"Yeah, but when we go home, she stays here sucking him off."

"Honey, don't be such a pig!"

"Please, she's the pig."

"I don't know how that bitch's teeth don't fall out."

"He's going to give her throat AIDS."

"One time I got here early and caught them in the act."

"No way!"

"What were they doing, honey?"

"Burruchaga was sticking it to her right there, against the counter. He was giving it to her practically up to her back teeth, as far as I could tell."

"How can she not be Burruchaga's golden girl!"

"Golden old girl, you might say."

"The waitress of love, as the song goes."

"That's why she acts like however she likes. She comes late and doesn't even lift a finger...

"She thinks this is Cuba, where you don't have to work, but you still get paid.

"All you have to do is see how that shameless bitch farts through the back of her neck, and how she looks at us like she's some princess."

"Burruchaga gives her that special tune-up."

"You know, dear, I don't even think it's that; that good-for-nothing sells herself cheap. Since Burruchaga's such a tightwad."

"I don't know what it is he sees in her."

"Nothing, dear, it's just that nobody pays any attention to that bitch."

"Truth be told, you have to be crazy to suck him off."

"She does it out of charity, that's all."

"Haven't you noticed how she's the only one, so blatantly at least, to take huge amounts of food home with her, while we have to steal a piece of steak here, a couple of shrimp there, and have to be afraid when doing it?"

"It's so mommy can take it home to that loony husband she has."

"And what if Betty was in love with Burruchaga for real? Sometimes, I've caught her looking at him all starry-eyed."

"Oh, honey, you're so naive....In This Country, nothing is done for love."

Unfortunately, many of those rumors were true. With the exception of a few warnings and passing scandals—more fit for a couple than for a working relationship—Burruchaga allowed Betty to get away with quite a bit. She was a shirker and irritatingly undisciplined; she would take leisurely breaks with a lemon-papaya smoothie, or leave whenever she felt like it, pushing her job off on her coworkers, or frequenting the nearby stores to look at clothes, or to get 'some fresh air.' Moreover, she was arrogant and a loudmouth and acted like she was the First Lady of El Regreso. It was also true that Betty nursed Fuñío with food that she took from El Regreso, shamelessly and with Burruchaga's tacit indulgence. Nevertheless, it was a lie that Burruchaga gave her money or bought her clothes, and the worst, the truly tragic part, was that for some time now Betty Boop's throne in El Regreso had dissolved like a lump of sugar in water.

Burruchaga had frozen her out; he almost never spoke to her. If Betty took her usual liberties, he would insult her crudely. Twice he threatened to fire her. One of those times Betty answered arrogantly and he slapped her in front of everyone, much to the glee of the waitresses and Betty Boop's despair. A little bit of hot blood seeped out of her lip and her heart.

Humiliated, smoldering in a whirlwind of fire and smoke deep inside, she didn't show up to work for three days.

"When will Missy Absent be back," wagged forked tongues.

"Betty Boop's reign is over."

"Poor thing. That's really got to hurt. At that age…"

Betty hoped Burruchaga would reconsider, come to realize what she represented to him, and call her, all sweet and sorry, to ask her nicely to return to El Regreso. But nothing.

"He treats me like garbage," Betty Boop, seized with anxiety, would say to herself.

It was then that she realized her sad and utter solitude in the world. Who could she tell her troubles to? Who could she pour her heart out to? Not one friend to confide in! To not have a true friend with whom to commiserate was the worst of all disgraces. Missing that gave her the true picture of how abandoned she was. To look for a little spiritual company sent her to the saints of her altar, but it wasn't the same, it was never the same as having a flesh-and-blood friend. In her depression she remembered better times, when there was still hope of having a wonderful life in exile. She thought of me, a friend with whom she had worked a couple of unforgettable months in a night club, the best bartender Betty had ever seen in her life. How we had come to know one another so well in just a few weeks! But that pleasant and cultured woman (also rich, Betty always suspected) moved on to Los Angeles with her little nephew, never to return to Miami.

It never occurred to Betty that her relationship with Burruchaga was very important. While he was hers, she never could gauge what he meant to her. Now that she was about to lose him, her chest filled with a burning molasses of nostalgia and rancor that pushed her to the edge of hysteria. Because Burruchaga (she now understood) could be heartless and exploitative, and maybe even a crook, but with her, in their most intimate moments, he was possessive and devoted, bossy and gentle, shameless and tender. He was hers, Betty's, and she was crazy to have dropped him. And even that bit about being a tightwad and opportunist…How else than by running a tight ship could you make a fortune in Miami? And through hard work, dammit, because nobody could accuse Burruchaga of being a layabout. Besides, he was a man who had a family to take care of, a wife and four kids, two of whom were still small. And cheap…he would be with others; but many times he had shown Betty Boop his generous streak, like when Fuñío had to have a vesicle operated on, or when she broke a tooth on a chicken bone: who had taken care of the hospital and dentist bills but Burruchaga? He even got her a dental crown (very expensive) you couldn't tell was any different from her other teeth! But those were idyllic and delightful times, long before things soured between them. That's why Betty Boop asked herself, without shaking the slightest, if she shouldn't 'off' the woman who was to blame for everything.

With the flood of Nicaraguan refugees who arrived in Miami, fleeing not Somoza but the Sandinistas, a lanky, big-assed woman showed up at El Regreso with long eyelashes and lips (thick, almost negroid) always painted. Little by little she displaced Betty from the center of Burruchaga's attention and affection. Nica (as she was called) ended up being an impregnable enemy. Her long silences, her languid way of looking at you, her attractive youthfulness when compared to Betty, made her mysterious, as if she held within her skin a different voluptuousness. Burruchaga ended up falling madly for the Nicaraguan woman.

Betty's rival (such was her story to make herself important) had lost her husband (one of Somoza's ex-lieutenants) in the war against the Sandinista Front. In Miami, that was already a considerable merit. At first, the waitresses in El Regreso treated Nica with that ridiculous Cuban disdain for anyone they feel is inferior to them. In the end, Nica was only an underdeveloped Central American. But as soon as they realized she was dethroning Betty, and that Burruchaga was paying more attention to her with each passing day, their disdain for Nica turned into a complex game of hostility and exclusion, perhaps driven by that nationalism that lurks in the subconscious of every Cuban and makes them prone to the strangest excesses. Despite all her defects, Betty was, above all, Cuban. And the weapons of slander turned on the intruder:

"Nica jacks off Burruchaga in the kitchen."

"And look at her husband, a fine-looking young man who picks her up in a green Toyota."

"At least Betty has a husband who's older than the Malecon and who's nuttier than a fruitcake. The poor thing just needed to take hot meals home for her Fuñío."

"You could really see how she let herself get seduced by Burruchaga."

"Necessity is the mother of all vices."

"I like Nica about as much as I like a kick in the ass."

"She's a dead mosquito."

"Shouldn't we send an anonymous note to Burruchaga's wife, telling her that right here in El Regreso there's a little Somozan that lets Burruchaga have her every day?"

"That'd do no good; besides, I don't water down blood with foreign life."

"You've got that right, honey. Everyone bears their own cross."

Betty entered El Regreso that day with a whirlwind of ideas in her head, with an arrogance about her and with an assured walk. She avoided the looks of her co-workers, donned her uniform and, in the bathroom, made sure she was carrying the blade in a position where she could whip it out and use it in a flash. She then headed right for Burruchaga's little office, a small, dark room with grease-stained walls, located next to the kitchen. Her intention was to decapitate him right there, without any warning, while he was reviewing his damn accounts or checking the price of chilies or sea breams over the phone.

But there was suddenly a hitch in the plan that made her nervous: Burruchaga wasn't there. He had gone out and left a little note on the office door: he didn't know when he'd be back.

Betty kept her nerve and didn't let the setback get her down. She focused on her Saint Barbara and tried to rid her mind of the Bag Lady's words: Murder One.

There weren't too many customers. It was that relative calm, of running fire, before the hustle and bustle of lunch. Then the people would arrive at once, jostling about, rushing to get back to work. Betty saw that the odious Nica was waitressing in the little room and, to avoid her defiant and triumphant presence, stayed behind and tended bar. Clotilde Gandía was there. She was a young fat girl from Pinar del Río who had braids almost three feet long, and a gut about a foot and a half in diameter. Clotilde spent all her time furtively scarfing down food, as if eating in secret were a treacherous act that would cost her life. Clotilde Gandía would eat under the counter and in the service area, in the corners and in the kitchen, careful not to let Burruchaga, or Nica, see her, since she was the only one who tattled on everything. When Betty got there, fat Clotilde was ferociously gobbling down a piece of ham the size of a dictionary.

"Oh, Betty!" She cried out, practically choking, "When Burruchaga returns, something awful is going to happen to you. When he saw that you were late, he blew up and said he was going to fire you without giving you your last month's pay; that if you thought you were the boss of El Regreso you were sorely mistaken and that here you have to pull your load or you're gone. He said at least ten times today that he was going to can you."

Betty closed her eyes and in a flash she made a superhuman effort to summon, like she had in the mirror, enough strength to tolerate her disgrace. She asked herself: *Who are you, Betty Boop, where are you, who were you three weeks ago, two years ago, a dozen years ago,* and she couldn't come up with anything, she was nothing. In that very long instant, she didn't feel hate, or find out who she was, or why she was there with Clotilde Gandía, who now, as if performing some kind of circus trick, had swallowed the whole dictionary.

"Do you feel bad, Betty?" Clotilde said sweetly. "C'mon, eat something, have a mamey shake with lots of milk to help you feel better. And try this ham, it's exquisite, c'mon dummy, go ahead, have some now that Nica the Nark is busy in there."

"Murder One," Betty Boop whispered.

"What was that?" Clotilde answered.

"I don't care," Betty corrected herself.

And she was overcome with a kind of apathy. Leaning against the bar, she was only worried about the disagreeable sensation of weightlessness she had in her hands, since she was afraid that she wouldn't have enough strength to grab the knife. Her hands felt as light as clouds.

"Hello, sweetie, how arrrre you?"

It was *Don* Pirolo Gutiérrez, who had sat down at the bar planning to eat, but above all expecting to have a good time with Betty.

"Hello, tough girl of my dreams," the old man insisted when he noticed Betty was somewhere off in the clouds, "Don't you love your little Pirolo anymore?"

But Betty didn't react. She wasn't really looking off somewhere since she was, ever so clearly seeing, the void within. Betty didn't realize it, but her she was as pale as a cadaver. *Don* Pirolo immediately noticed that something bad was wrong with 'the waitress of his heart,' as he liked to call her.

"Betty, what's wrong, dear girl?" he inquired in another, an almost paternal tone.

Betty then returned to reality. She sighed and propped both elbows on the counter. 'Nothing, nothing, I just feel dizzy,' she thought, and believed she also said it, but she didn't say anything and *Don* Pirolo grew even more worried:

"Betty, are you well, sweetness?"

"Yes, yes, excuse me, Pirolo," she finally said, "I don't know, it was like a fainting spell."

"You're such a dreamer, Betty..."

The unexpected presence of the old man made Betty feel a little more reanimated, almost thankful that *Don* Pirolo was suddenly there, in front of her, with his roguishness, his friendship and kindness. He was, without a doubt, a sign of good luck.

"What can I get for you, honey?"

It was a ceremony of innocent sweet-talk that would be repeated, always in different terms, every time *Don* Pirola came to El Regreso.

"Whatever you want, my little wallflower bud."

Don Pirolo was a well-preened old man, the life of the party, who in the Havana of Yesteryear he had been an employee of ITT, that is, of its powerful branch in Cuba, the Cuban Telephone Company that had a monopoly on communications there. In Miami, on the other hand, *Don* Pirolo had made his mark as a car salesman, par for the course in exile. He started off selling used jalopies with the help of his son, who was a good mechanic, and by the time of his retirement father and son were owners of one the of the most successful businesses in Saguesera: Cotorro Motors.

Despite not knowing him other than as a regular at the restaurant, Betty loved Pirolo greatly, perhaps for being everything Fuñío wasn't: *Don* Pirolo was an entrepreneur and, consequently, a victor in exile; in addition, he was spry and a flirt, and surely a womanizer when he still had the ability to pull it off. Despite his old age, *Don* Pirolo still had a sharp mind and didn't mince words.

Now *Don* Pirolo, opening his hand in the air with the gesture of one who is fondling a very ample breast, said:

"Show me something with a little meat on it, girl."

Betty slyly hoisted her bust in such a way that *Don* Pirolo's hand, which was still fondling the enormous ethereal tit, came very close to her pair, very real, but without being able to so much as brush up against them.

"I give you Plantains of Temptation," the waitress proffered.

"I shall obediently eat anything you put in my mouth, diva."

Don Pirolo's theatricality sometimes made Betty crack up in such a way that she wasn't able to continue with the repartee of the art of seduction. For the two of them it was all a game, yes, but a very important game that gave them the security that they were still alive.

On that fateful day for Betty, *Don* Pirolo wore a light blue, short-sleeved shirt and a wide acrylic, rose neon colored tie, and a coffee and cream-colored checkered jacket that played off the shirt. *Don* Pirolo had the air of a stuffed tropical bird about him with that distinguished attire, and Betty felt like really showing him her tits. 'That stinks,' Betty thought, full of mercy, 'may *Don* Pirolo have his fill of my tits in his last days; in any case, it won't be long before he'll be in the bosom of the Miami's hospitable earth.'

But she didn't say what came to her mind, but instead said:

"Oh, Pirola, anything you eat will always taste like me."

The old man, absolutely slayed by self-assurance, looked like he was going to fall into a trance:

"Oh, what kind of female is this, mama mia, give birth to me again, Mommy, so I can be young again and marry Betty Boop!"

Betty finally served him a beer, which is what Pirolo usually had, and said to him seriously:

"Look, Papi: eat some Peas from the Archipelago, a good meal of Exile Stew and finish it off with dessert of *Boniatillo* with Crazy Head a la Bayamesa. What do you think?"

"Is the stew thick, mami?"

"Potent, Papi, with *malanga*, corn, potatoes, chunks of pork and beef."

"With the works."

"With those works, you'll still be able to pitch a battle in any bed."

"In yours too, Betty?"

She gave him a voluptuous wink and turned her back to take away the food. But just then, Burruchaga entered the restaurant.

Betty looked at him askance, and a complete paralysis overtook her: a numbness of will, a softening between her legs and a sudden stiffness in her knees. Again, the dangerous weightlessness of her hands. She heard the grunts, the little moans, and the loving words Burruchaga would usually whisper when he was inside her. She relived the way he had of swiftly caressing her face, like a gust, when he passed next to her in the restaurant, with nobody noticing.

"I still love him…," Betty said and she clutched the knife. Another wave of sickness. She was going to kill a man. Murder One. She leaned against the bar. She widened her stance trying to locate stability. Burruchaga approached her, irate and inexorably. 'Fucking traitor,' Betty thought to goad her anger, "I'm going to cut you up.'

"Betty!" Burruchaga said, muffling his scream so he wouldn't be heard too much, "Come to my office, I want to have a word with you."

And the cards were dealt. The hostilities were now out in the open. All that was left was to get into the final skirmish.

"Don't you touch me, you fucking faggot!"

Taken by surprise, Burruchaga was stricken with a moment of intense puzzlement. Betty had screamed with such force that many of the guests had turned and look at them. The 'fucking faggot' part had left Burruchaga stunned. But only for a quick moment:

"I want you out of this restaurant right this minute, Betty Boop, and don't you ever come back, you got that? Who the fuck you think you are? I've had enough of your loafing around and your coming in late. Enough already! You're fired. And shut that filthy mouth of yours, I don't want no trouble in El Regreso."

And he made a move of turning his back, but he couldn't. Because Betty pulled out the blade, unclasped it with a dexterity that left her quite surprised amid all the tension of the murder, and cried out:

"Don't you fucking move; if you take one step I'll cut your head off!" Suddenly, Betty's voice had become thick and terrifying, like a witch's in a cave, but at the same time it was deplorably foul, like some street-corner whore.

When Piolo saw the blade so close to Burruchaga's face, he lost his voice and somebody from one of the tables yelled: 'She's going to kill him, she's going to kill him!'

"I'll go on my own accord, just so you know!" Betty went on before giving him the first slash, stretching out those dizzying seconds that now seemed like weeks. "And I'm going because you're a disgusting buggerer, you got all that? A buggerer who spends his life doing nasty things to little Mario in the kitchen! Because you're a fag too, Burruchaga!"

Of all who were there, the one who was most surprised by what was going on was Betty Boop. That offense, totally unfair and untrue, had come out of her mouth at the last minute, without her thinking about it at all, as if somebody had magically put the words on her tongue and the tongue alone that did the job without her having anything to do with it. Little Mario was the young boy who washed the dishes, poor thing, a noble and servile young man who was a fag but who had never done anything with Burruchaga, who had employed him in El Regreso only because Mariolito was a relative of a relative. Betty still held the razor high. After that clever public 'revelation' it would practically be impossible to wash away the affront and restore Burruchaga's prestige and manliness. Betty's revenge had been malicious and atrocious, even though she hadn't yet administered the first slash across her ex-lover's neck. Now all that was left was for Betty to cut his face and aortic vein and dash out of there like an angel of death.

Meanwhile, *Don* Pirolo looked as though the *malangas*, corn and beef chunks he hadn't yet eaten were all going to come out of his eyes and ears.

"I want all of you to know!" Betty Boop insisted as if delivering the final blow. "Mariolito sucks that man's dick in the kitchen! I, who you see standing right in this very place, caught them in this disgusting act and that's why he's getting rid of me!"

As she said this, Betty unwisely let down her guard and Burruchaga rushed her, smacked her face, and the razor dropped to the floor (Help!, somebody called out; Help!, somebody else screamed) and now two customers were behind the bar to stop Burruchaga from killing that poor woman with everyone watching, even though she deserved it. Amid the ruckus and shrieking of Clotilde Gandía, who let out with a couple of screams loud enough to stop a psychopath dead in his tracks, Betty grabbed a plastic bottle filled with ketchup and, squeezing hard, covered the face of her dearly-hated ex-lover with ketchup. The brawl was so quick and thundering that many thought that the razor had done its job and that Burruchaga was running away covered in blood.

"Get her out of her, or I'll kill her, goddammit, I'll kill her!" Burruchaga yelled, writhing in agony.

Betty left El Regreso with the help of *Don* Pirolo, a young customer who took pity on her, and fat little Clotilde, who was always loyal. Moved by Betty's bravery, amid all her screaming, Clotilde had taken advantage of the commotion to scarf down a half dozen Eggs Green As Palm Trees.

Betty's face was slightly swollen and hurt, but she was happy to leave El Regreso, now thrown into total chaos and with Burruchaga sullied forever.

Defiant, and without shedding a single tear, Betty left in search of her new destiny in the Miami dream.

Nicotiano and Santiago, an old friend who has nothing to do with this book...

"Who's there?"

"Open the door, Santiago."

"Who is it, I said?"

"It's Nicotiano, I was in the area and thought I'd stop by."

"Ah, Nicotiano. Come in, my son, you've come at a good time."

"Why'd you answer the door with a pistol in your hand, Santiago?"

"Because I'm counting money."

"But the floor's covered in hundred dollar bills!"

"It's the damn fan, scattering everything all over the place."

"When are you going to get an air conditioner, Santiago? Or a nice house?"

"When I return to Cuba. I'm going to build a big house in Villalona with balconies facing the northeasterly winds and a dock of my own for my boats."

"Look at that pile of bills on the table, Santiago. I didn't know you made so much money."

"Come on, help me count it. But first go to the refrigerator and fix us two drinks, one for me loaded with rum, crushed ice, tonic, triple sec and a dash of lime juice."

"Santiago..., a fortune in cash seems strange in an apartment like this, so modest, even cramped."

"I'm not interested in living well here, but in Villalona, when I return."

"Look at all these bills flying around; wait, let me get the ones that have blown under the sofa."

"It's the damn fan."

"You never age, Santiago. Your beard, though, does get whiter every time I see you."

"And my soul more gray, my son."

"Only Aunt Ulalume, Cocorioco and you call me 'son'. Are all the bills hundreds?"

"No; pay attention when you put the rolls together, because some of the bills are tens, and it's a tremendous pain to organize them in groups of two thousand. The little bastards are trying to trick me. The rubber bands are over there."

"Cheers. To your house in Villalona."

"As you can see, I'm almost a rich man. I don't lift a finger for

anyone."

"*I don't dare ask you how can make so much money.*"

"*How did I make it? Smuggling drugs to Miami through Cuba.*"

"*What? Drug trafficking through Cuba?*"

"*That's what I said. You know I know the Cuban Keys like the back of my hand. I used to pick up merchandise in Cuban territory.*"

"*Did the Cuban authorities know about it?*"

"*I imagine they did and with the cover of the Department of the Interior, Border Patrol Service, the Marines of the Revolutionary War, Customs, State Security and even the Holy Ghost.*"

"*I never imagined...*"

"*To each his own; you keep making your crabs...*"

"*Here are four rolls of two thousand dollars.*"

"*Put them here, inside this suitcase, with the others.*"

"*But Santiago...Cuba has always rejected any implication of drug trafficking...*"

"*The drunk says one thing, the winemaker says another. Look, son, everything's history now, but that's the way it was: there was a secret outfit in Cuba, the MC, intelligence specialists whose mission was to get around the blockade between This Country and ours. You got it?*"

"*Here are two more rolls.*"

"*This Country's embargo against Cuba is illegal and criminal, right? Well then, the way to get around the embargo can't be any less illegal or criminal, either.*"

"*An eye for an eye, a tooth for a tooth.*"

"*Exactly, my son. So we would just waltz right into Cuba with our boats, all kinds of goods whose sale had been banned to our compatriots there: electronic equipment, necessary medicines, Western-made weapons, advanced technical materials for Cuban hospitals. Here we brought in Cuban cigars, art objects...In all, it was a constant shuffling back and forth: patriots from there and the non-patriots from here. And we handled ourselves very well. I'm sure Hitkinen knows more than a few things about these matters.*"

"*But what about the drugs?*"

"*Oh, my son, here the LAW OF TRADE WITH THE ENEMY has since 1963 prohibited any kind of transaction with Cuba. So, to bring in Cuban tobacco is almost as bad as bringing in Colombian cocaine since, according to that famous law, doing business with Cuba is like conspiring against the government in Washington.*"

"*Sure, now I see. Why don't you start dealing hard drugs, then?*"

"*Ecolequa. And we reached an agreement with the MC, whose officials went into that business, apparently without informing their superiors. And that, my son, is how the smuggling of goods began: Colombian airplanes loaded with cocaine landed nicely at the military airport at Verdaero, and the traffickers, true rogues, spent the night as if it was nothing in Santa María del Mar, or right there in Havana. We would then enter Cuban waters in our swift boats and make the pick-up. Lots of times we were protected by Cuban war ships and I myself have spent many a night in chalets belonging to the Department of the Interior of the Socialist Republic of Cuba. But the party soon ended. Cuban authorities found out what the MC was doing and they shot the guilty parties, one of whom was a close friend of Fidel and a Hero of the Republic.*"

"*Don't worry about it; besides this Colt, I have a shotgun somewhere around here...But what's really important is that I have to ask you for a favor.*"

"*Whatever you say, Santiago.*"

"*I want Ulalume to be in charge of all this shit.*"

"*All of what shit?*"

"*All this money. Let her put it in stocks, or do whatever she wants to do with it; we could even return to Cuba. You know I have absolute faith in your aunt.*"

"*She has this illusion of investing over there...I think in the hotel business.*"

"*Good idea. What Cuba needs are investments from decent Cubans like ourselves. Take her the money right now.*

"*I think the most sensible thing would be to call Maribarbola and Guarapito, as a security measure, to transport the money. There are dozens of miles to cover, Santiago.*

"*It's the product of my exile. Hey, Nicotiano, how's Mireya doing?*"

"*Fine, just fine. Super pretty and in great health. I love her more and more every day.*"

Six

Kafka was sleeping among the *areca* palms, while Marx, spoiled and off in his own world, scrupulously and pedantically cleaned his paws. I was watering my herbarium when I saw Mireya's car pull up and suddenly I realized that the apparent peace of the Island of Cundeamor was no longer worth anything, that the basil and the scented clover could dry up and die, that the marjorams and the lemon balm could go to hell, that the mint and lavender had no scent, that the sage and the rosemary, lime, *vetiver*, the *artemisas* and the garden cress could undergo calcination or grow, if they felt like it, downward and rot in the blackness of the earth. Mireya was worth something. Mireya was life. Not only my nephew's life, but also mine.

And Mireya was leaving us.

A wave of sickness suddenly hit me, and my breasts weighed like sacks of concrete.

Mireya sat in her Chevrolet for a while, having second thoughts, or as if it was hard for her to get out. Without daring to breathe, I spied on her from the among weeds. She took out her little mirror from her purse and made herself up a bit, probably to hide the fact that she had been crying. She then muttered something, which I knew for a fact came out:

"I hate him."

And right after that:

"Why am I crying? Since when did he cry for me? Why do I have to stoop to this level and cry for that spoiled brat who's denied me my life?"

And then:

"You smell like another man, Mireya. You've had another man's cock inside you: in your cunt, in your mouth, and in your mind. That makes you more attractive and more insolent, more liberated and a master of your destiny."

She got out of the car and said:

"You smell like another semen, another saliva, another sweat, another sheet, another pillow, another man."

And she went on as if reciting a litany or uttering a threat.

"You smell like another deodorant and shampoo, another toothpaste and aftershave; you smell like other wines, other breakfasts and other promises and sweet nothings, because your words also carry his odor." She sniffed at her fingers nervously, and then the palms of her hands.

"You reek of another's sex, somebody else, another man, shit, I'm another woman."

As I was watering the plants, I began to hum, overdoing it so she would pick up on my presence, that little song that goes:

> *Aturdido y abrumado*
> *Por la duda de los celos*
> *Se ve triste en la cantina*
> *A un bohemio ya sin fe...*

I thought Mireya was moving away from me like a thief running from the police, but I was wrong. And I was grateful for that mistake.

Mireya hesitated a bit, but she approached me. I tried to make it look as though butter wouldn't melt in my mouth and pretended I didn't see her. I turned away from her. I let the Saint Barbara of Waikiki be the one, for now, who would face her. My voice got louder as I threw myself into the song, gently wiggling my waist while watering the lemon balm:

> *...con los nervios destrozados*
> *y llorando sin remedio*
> *como un loco atormentado*
> *por la ingrata que se fue...*

Mireya was only a few steps behind me, but she didn't interrupt me, nor did she continue on her way. I kept pretending I didn't know she was there...

> *...nada remedias con llanto*
> *nada remedias con vino,*
> *al contrario la recuerda*
> *mucho más tu corazón...*

At this point the melody was affecting my voice so much and I put so much energy into my interpretation that Saint Barbara began to shake all over, and you couldn't tell if I was singing as a joke, or if what I was feeling was like something touching a sensitive fiber deep down inside:

> *Una noche, como un loco,*
> *Mordió la copa de vino*
> *Y le hizo un cortante filo*
> *Que su boca destrozó*
> *Y la sangre que brotaba*
> *Confundióse con el vino...*

I clearly heard Mireya moving behind me, maybe her nose was wheezing or she sneezed, I don't know, the sound of the hose caressed the little basil leaves, exacerbated her perfume and accompanied my singing:

> *Y en la cantina este grito*
> *A todos estremeció:*
> *'No te apures, compañero,*
> *si me destrozó la boca,*
> *no te apures, que es que quiero*
> *con el filo de esta copa*
> *borrar la huella de un beso*
> *traicionero que me dio...'*

"Aunt Ula, stop singing that!"

"Oh, Mireya, what a fright you gave me!"

"It's disgustingly hot."

She said that as she gazed off somewhere else, maybe to where the dog and cat were dozing, because she added:

"I see that troublemaker Marx came back. You were worried about him. Were you afraid that something bad had happened to him?"

"Tom cats always spend the night carousing around, looking for female cats. Guarapito says he's even seen him walking around in Sagüesera."

"One day some car's going to kill him."

"It's a risk he runs. But he's loyal. See how he comes back to the place where people love him."

Mireya looked down.

"Sometimes it's the females," I went on, "that come from far away looking for him. There's nothing more frightening than a jealous female cat. Have you ever seen one, Mireya? They don't let danger stop them when it comes to satisfying themselves...They lift their asses, spread them, suffer from the cats that penetrate them. I go out to the yard, at night, just to listen to their plaintive moans, that painful need of cats in heat. In general it seems that in matters of love, cats are helpless."

"In matters of love, we're all helpless."

I didn't respond. She said:

"The smell of those herbs is so thick. It's almost making me dizzy."

"Look at the sagebrush," and I improvised: "in the Middle Ages, witches used it to ward off demons. Those who know say that cooking sagebrush is good when menstruation is disrupted by frights, wetness, loss of taste, sudden chills, unbearable emotions, unfair nightmares and poor blood circulation."

"And lavender?"

"You can see how poorly it grows: due to the excess humidity and heat. But it fights back and, thanks to my efforts, it survives. Lavender baths alleviate nervous excitement."

"Oh, Aunt Ula... I'm going to miss you so," she said suddenly, and she gave me a hug.

"Look, this is vetiver. There's a song that goes: *With this herb... you'll get married!* And that one's lemon balm, which is soothing for when we are consumed with distress, and that little tree is the famous *amansaguapo*, which in Havana they call *Cambia voz*, whose virtues are mysterious..."

As I was going on about that nonsense, Mireya got down all fours and indiscriminately began pulling up leaves.

"A bath," she said panting, "I'm going to take a bath with these herbs..."

"But Mireya, don't mix them, wait, each herb has its own property..."

"Don't give me any advice, Aunt Ula! I don't need it. I don't want it. I'm free, I do what I please and I don't have to account to anyone for anything. I'm sick and tired of being treated like a kid, like a piece of something without any consistency or free will. No more advice!"

And she went into the house as if chased by a lion. As she was drawing the bath, she fixed herself a rather eye-popping glass of rum and ice and, as she downed it, coughed and felt the shaking in her hands ease.

"I'm going to get just drunk enough…"

She got into the bathtub. The water exuded a heady aroma. She clutched at her breasts and closed her eyes. The herbs turned her on and made her recall another mouth, another tongue that wasn't Nicotiano's hated mouth.

When she went back down to the patio, with the resolute steps of a woman who knows what she wants, she felt unyielding, clean, perfumed, desirable down to the most intimate folds of her body. Her hair, jet black and iridescent, hung over her shoulders in a waterfall of still damp curls. She was wearing a crimson skirt, sandals of the same color and, higher up, she wore a white bikini top. Her burnished tone, warmly satin-sheened on her skin, contrasted seductively with the whiteness of her bikini top. Skirting the pool, she stopped. In a hammock, hanging between two mango trees was Cocorioco, who was taking a siesta. What would her ex-"companion's" servile assistant care? Kafka was swimming in the pool with a lot of technique and parsimony, from one end to the other, with movements of a three-year-old tourist. She wouldn't miss Kafka either. Another life, another life…

She went into Nicotiano's studio. The heat wasn't as stifling inside as it was outside. The ocean breezes came through the tall northeast windows and pleasantly fanned the room. Mireya's gaze swept across the tools, cranes, marble and granite monoliths. A completely strange sensation overwhelmed her. What did she have to do with all that? The crabs, some of which were partially emerging from stone, seemed more repulsive then ever to her. Indecipherable, useless. There was something human in them, yes, they were dazzling, yet at the same time disgusting. To her at least, they didn't say anything; they signified nothing more than utter shit. Nicotiano could have sculpted anything else, kids pissing, dolphins skipping, naked women. But no. He had that morbidity, always that obsessive expression of his sick and destructive personality. To leave that man forever would be a net gain! This is what Mireya was thinking and she then called out to him in a very firm voice. But there was no response. She stepped inside the studio a little further and was certain that she would find herself in there alone for the last time.

Nicotiano wasn't there. She closed her eyes and opened them again, enjoying the majestic solitude of those mysterious figures. (they did have a majestic quality that made them imposing; there was no denying that). Something terrible must have happened to Nicotiano, some festering wound in his soul for him to dedicate his whole life giving shape to those gloomy monsters. She then remembered the names of Cuban marble, brought as contraband by Hetkinen from the Isla de Pinos: Orchid Sierra, Countryside Mulata, Green Mountain. She had it on good authority that the Crabb Company, with Cuban authorities, had been smuggling in electronics, medicine, even weapons to skirt the North American Commercial Embargo. Now this all felt like ancient history, old stories, bullshit, a lie even. In general, all of the Island of Cundeamor was developing without her really taking part.

"Everything ends one day," she murmured; "even children die. Why wouldn't love die too?"

Just as she started to go back outside, Nicotiano suddenly appeared from the hiding place from which he was spying on her, a lobster with huge claws, and he grabbed her from behind. Mireya felt his strong arms and hands clutching her breasts, his tongue sucking at the back of her neck and ears. Mireya's bikini jumped up and her breasts, bare and sweet-smelling, lightly stained by the little bites of the *other* man, jiggled, and Nicotiano fondled her breasts with little pinches that made them swell. Nicotiano took off her skirt, and with his hand avidly groped that tangled and black, recently washed sex, which he thought belonged to him. She closed her eyes and yielded to his caresses. 'I'll let him, I don't care,' she thought. Without a word, he lifted her off her feet and lovingly set her down on a work table.

"Suck my breasts, Nicotiano," she demanded, barely conscious of what she was saying or just thinking. "Suck them like a man, lick them like a child…"

He obeyed as if he had heard what she had thought or maybe said, and he sucked and sucked without stopping his caressing of her sex, until time stopped flowing and those nipples grew hard in his mouth, and then he moved down to the center of the woman who was sitting astride.

He made love to her with his tongue, hard and then soft, stopping and then rotating and running upwards, until he finally penetrated her for real. And he kissed her deeply, in such a way that Mireya took all of the flavors of her own sex in her mouth. It all gave Mireya a delight and a horror and she did nothing to avoid it. 'My God,' she thought, 'what am I doing,' but she spread her legs even more and received the pounding from her man, who was no longer pressing against her body, and she savored him savoring her, he punished her punishing herself and if that strong tang that came in and out of her was or was not affection, she didn't care any longer. 'Dear God,' she thought, 'I'm going to come, I'm going to come,' and she began to moan with her eyes squeezed shut. Mireya then came and came as if she were going to tenderly and violently rend herself right down the middle and from deep inside and he still kept slipping and hitting, doing to her whatever he felt like, until the last shriek, until the last spasm and then he kept kissing her, on her overexcited breasts, in her armpits with little kisses and tongue, lots of tongue, on her burning mouth that was now someone else's.

In the end they were both like milkshakes sitting in their dregs, and Mireya enjoyed that lethargy until she opened her eyes and met Nicotiano's. A naïve man. 'Poor Nicotiano,' she thought, but she immediately rejected the idea angrily. *Who the fuck has ever said poor Mireya?*

"Get off me, Nicotiano," she said, "let me up."

And she leapt up, pushing him away.

He started talking about the full-scale launch of his works 'which Aunt Ula is putting together with Doublestein.' He said he wasn't interested, that openings and interviews were a nuisance, but there a grain of truth in the argument that fame raised prices, and the idea was to earn a lot of money, get credit and invest in Cuba, hotels or whatever. Then he said something about Cuban people getting it from both sides, from the United States financial embargo, as well as the dogmatism of the Communist Party and Fidel. But now the country was open to investment 'and since Aunt Ula wants to return one day...'

"Cut it out!" she cried.

"What's wrong, Mireya?"

"Shit, I'm sick of it, I've had it up to here with the blah, blah, blah about Cuba, Cuba, Cuba! I don't give a crap about any of it, and just so you know...I can't stand you anymore, Nicotiano, you don't mean anything to me anymore. I'm leaving this house forever, I'm leaving you and that's it."

Nicotiano's mouth was hanging open and the look on his face was more idiotic than usual, Mireya thought scornfully. And she kept speaking, caught up in her nervousness and rancor: "But we won't even have to get a divorce. You've got to be kidding! Marry Nicotiano. Never. He never wanted to marry his dear Mireya, show up in the social pages of *The Herald* or the *Latin Americas Newspaper*...That nonsense? Never...But it just so happens that Mireya would indeed have wanted to marry, just like any other young woman, in a white dress covered in lace and a bouquet of flowers. Yes, you heard it here,

I would have liked it tacky and common like that. We don't have kids, either; first, because the great patriot refused to have kids in exile. 'Exile doesn't have a future,' the great sculptor would say, 'it only has a past...' No kids in this morally corrupt city of Miami, no kids who would be second-class citizens, neither Cuban nor American, bastards, worthless. And then, when my desperation made you give in to having a child, there was my goddamn sterility...And the interminable, humiliating gynecological exams...But my sterility, my true sterility has been you, Nicotiano, you dried me up, you took it out on me...and you, not me, have reaped all of life's fruits!"

Nicotiano mumbled something she refused to hear. "For years you had me like some sort of appendage to you, like a painting hanging on the wall. You had your crabs, you had your adventures with the Crabb Company and, on the other hand, your goddamned fishing trips, readying the yacht, taking us out to sea, running away from ourselves, to be more of an island than we already are, sailing in the Villalona like a float among the waves. That never gave me any pleasure at all, you never asked me what my true needs were."

"I don't understand anything, Mireya..."

"Shut up, dammit. Because you always had a subtle knack for getting people to feel stupid in your presence. You were always the most brilliant, attractive, interesting, unique, extraordinary, exceptional. Nobody ever heard what I was saying. My ideas were always vulgar, futile, vapid. But if Nicotiano opened his mouth, everyone listened. But for fucking, yes...Oh, the genius needed an ass at his disposal to satisfy himself, the lunatic artist, sexual pursuer for extended periods when he did nothing else but fuck me at all hours, without asking me whether or not I had any desire to. But afterwards you would disappear for weeks into that cave of crabs, not even remembering me! Your irreal existence makes me sick, Nicotiano, because you don't exist, you aren't a flesh and blood man and I want to plant myself firmly in existence. I want to have a normal life, here and now. I want to have a man at my side, one who isn't an unbearable neurotic like you, you never sleep dammit, find yourself a damn nut house! If I even breathe next to you, you'll wake up and then, to top it off, I have to watch over your sleep. It has to be utterly dark, and the silence has to be sacred. You are a bloodsucking bat! Thirteen years of putting up with you and I've had enough. Thirteen years of watching TV in secret, because the supreme genius despises TV and his dear aunt applauds him."

Sweating profusely, Nicotiano wasn't able to understand his emotions, and unable to think clearly at all. Mireya was in a kind of trance, her cheeks flushed and her eyes bulging from her face.

"I'm in love with another man, just so you know. Another man who knows how to flirt for real and knows how to court a woman. A man who's come into my life like a burst of energy and freshness, a man interested in me, just for me and who likes me for what I am, exactly as I am, and who's made me feel important, attractive…And I've eaten with him in restaurants, and I've told him all about my misfortunes with you and he's listened to me and understood me and consoled me, because he's also a lost soul who's thirsty for company like mine…He is, for me, an obsession…He represents security, normalcy and everything that's desirable. You represent everything I've left behind. He makes me feel special, he's mine, something just for me, for me, for me, something you can't screw up, something you aren't capable of influencing. And I'll have children with him, you'll see. And they'll be kids that will speak English and I'll never tell them anything about Cuba, there's no such thing as Cuba!"

She then went up to him, boldly, and told him with an arrogant gesture:

"Yes, I don't have any scruples, I don't have the slightest consideration for you. And if it goes bad with him, then I don't care. At thirty-five years old I've rediscovered my sexuality, my tremendous potential attraction for men. I know how to seduce them just by looking at them, I know how to make them feel uneasy, I know how to make them see that I'm looking for them, I have men I could catch and put right here, between my legs. Yes, don't give me that idiotic look like you don't know how the world works, I'm willing to use my sexuality *against you* to put you down, humiliate you, so I can be an independent and valuable human being."

Then Mireya, like a wild animal, threw herself upon him and hit him in the face. He retreated, blinded, but he quickly hit her back.

"I'm going to be happy, dammittttt," she screamed, brokenheartedly. "Goodbye, goodbye to the Island of Cundeamor!"

"Mireya, please," he begged.

She turned around and her face was distorted by the hatred and crying.

"What do you want?"

"Don't leave. Without you I'm just a sculptor."

"And with me what the hell were you, Nicotiano?"

"A man," he said.

Mireya turned around and ran out of the studio. Nicotiano then lay down on the lobster with the oversized claws and said, full of pain: "But I love you so much, Mireya…What happened, what happened…"

And he crouched down and curled up, his body crumpling, such as it was. Nicotiano started to cry, and for a while he wasn't able to think about anything. He tried to remember the causes, the invectives, the structure of revenge, the frustration, the resentment or failure, but he didn't remember anything concretely, he wasn't able to articulate one single thought. The pressure he felt in his chest and throat was such that he thought at one point he was going to die. That's how death should be, a dark red weight in the head, a whirlwind of anxiety and an impossibility of existing. A paralysis. He stayed like that for a long time, all contorted and crying without even being able to breath, and when he looked up he discovered, like someone who snaps out of an illusion only to go into a spell, Mireya's white panties on the table where they had made love. Was it a hallucination, a product of his anguish? No. There they were Mireya's panties. Nicotiano felt destroyed. Could she have done that out of treachery, to torment him even more, to torment him to death? Nicotiano got up and went over to that beloved little undergarment, but he didn't dare touch it; he leaned over the lingerie with a wounded tenderness and the gesture of a child smelling a flower. And he kissed the warmth reminiscent of that intimacy, the tenuous and delicious odor, he knew so well, so indescribable, of the woman who had been an adult all of her life, she, Mireya, his Mireya, the little life that was intimately happy in his exile, in his uprooting, his shit, his nothing, his dying, his emptiness, just like she had said. In reality, she was the only woman in his life, the symbol of his only moments of true happiness since he left Cuba, and now he understood: as in all decisive things, understanding came too late.

When Mireya left the studio, she had a horrible headache and felt sick. It was as if she just got off a dizzying carrousel that had scrambled her insides. She didn't know it, but the whole time she and Nicotiano were inside, Kafka stood on guard at the studio door to make sure no one walked in unexpectedly. When she saw the dog with his melancholy eyes, she crouched for a moment and hugged him, giving him a kiss. Kafka didn't say anything.

"Goodbye, Kafka," she whispered, and it was as if she were saying goodbye to Nicotiano one more time.

Skirting the pool again to enter the house and gather her most important belongings, she heard Guarapito's voice call her name, and he approached her like a hurricane. Just like that he was at her side, yelling:

"You whore! I just found out about everything at a restaurant on Ocean Drive. I'm going to tell Nicotiano so he'll stab you to death. Bitch!" Guarapito was as elegant as always. He wore a pair of light linen pants, beach moccasins, a butter-colored linen jacket and a Dior shirt. black sunglasses and a Panama hat. On his chest hung a thick Virgin of Charity medallion. Emerging from his hat was his eternal pony tail. Mireya liked Guarapito. He was the most jovial, the least complicated of the bunch. He was a little slow, but he didn't take anything seriously if he wasn't forced to, and Mireya liked that; this contrasted with Nicotiano, for whom everything had a dark background, multiple interpretations that only he could make out, and indecipherable meanings that plunged him into tormented thoughts.

Guarapito spent a lot of money on clothes without ever overcoming his gangster-pimp look. But in truth he was Mireya's only friend in the Crabb Company. Bartolo was withdrawn, incommunicative and fairly stupid; Sikitrake was simple and respectful but like Nicotiano he was too serious. For a split second Mireya felt the urge to throw herself into Guarapito's arms and to be consoled by that man-child. But she couldn't do it because now he was shaking her with tears in his eyes, going on:

"Bitch, you're a bitch and I loved you so much, Mireya, you're worse than a whore! Because a whore puts out for money."

Mireya was struggling to try to get away, but Guarapito suddenly released her.

"Get out of here, dammit, nobody's making you stay. Go on, get out. I don't even want to touch a woman like you."

As if his own words hurt him too much, Guarapito clenched his fists and covered his eyes.

"It's as if a sister of mine had died. To do this to Nicotiano! In spite of his defects and all of his crap, he's the most honorable, the most decent part of all this, the most truly human, the most helpful, oh Mireya…leave, get out of here, you have no shame."

Guarapito turned away and Mireya, letting out a blood-curdling scream, pushed him violently, shoving him into the pool with his linen jacket and Panama hat and moccasins and everything else. And I came running out and whisked Mireya inside the house, after yelling at the soaking wet Guarapito, strictly prohibiting him from bothering us.

"Come, my daughter, you need to calm down."

"Aunt Ula, you know everything, right?"

"Almost everything."

"I was planning on telling you today."

"Radio Big Lips beat you to it."

"Forgive me, forgive me."

"It's your life, Mireya. You will always have me here for you. Always on your side."

"I'm in love."

"Go for it, Mireya, if you're sure, more power to you."

"Fix me a drink, something strong, to give me strength."

I fixed her a Henry Morgan. Aged rum, Bailey's cream, cacao cream and ice. Mixed well. I served it to her in a champagne glass, sprinkled with more cinnamon, maybe too much. Mireya downed it.

"Help me gather my things, Aunt Ula."

"Whenever you want."

"This cinnamon is so delicious," and she began to sob quietly.

"The cinnamon," I said to distract her, "is a tonic and stimulant. Nero burned more cinnamon than all Arabia produced in one year."

"I'm going to miss you so, Aunt Ula…"

"Call whenever you can."

"Aunt Ula."

"What?"

"I love Nicotiano," and she cried in little spasms.

"I know, my daughter. Now I see it all so clearly."

"But I can't stand him."

"I can also see that now."

"It scares me, Aunt Ula."

Mireya burped.

"Drink up, drink up."

"I love him but I can't stand him. When I'm far away from him, I feel a kind of horrible emptiness all through my body and I can't do anything well. Being with this other man is the only thing that eases it. I want to be like everyone else, Aunt Ula…"

"I hope you get that. Just remember that not everyone can be like everyone else."

"That must be true for Nicotiano. That's why he repulses me."

"You've chosen a path. Stick to it. Forget Nicotiano and keep far away from here; why open up old wounds, why make him suffer more?"

"Nicotiano ruined my life."

"From an early age, Nicotiano was always threatened by a grim destiny. It's as if his future could only be a wind of adversity which will one day carry him away. I hope he can survive your absence."

"It'd be best if I just pack my suitcases and leave. I don't want Nicotiano to come in and start a scene."

"He won't come. While Guarapito was fighting with you, Nicotiano got in his car and left. I'm guessing he went to the beach, the ocean. I saw him carrying a book, a pencil and a bottle of rum. It's been a long time since he cast messages out to sea."

"To sea. Like somebody marooned?"

"I thought you knew. Whenever he suffered with any kind of pain, he would cast messages in bottles out to sea. I don't pay any attention to what he writes, nor do I have any idea who he sends them to. Letters to the past, maybe."

"Everything about Nicotiano is a goddamn letter to the past, Aunt Ula."

"Do you know when was the last time he set a message out to sea?"

"I'm not interested in his eccentricities."

"It was when the doctors were finally certain that you couldn't have kids. He moped around for a while, didn't sleep, barely swallowed his food."

"My insides are on fire, Aunt Ula. You'll see: my so-called sterility was just a psychic defect. With my new love, I'll have lots of kids. I have to root myself in reality, I can't keep living in the imaginary age of Nicotiano. Miami is my environment and I accept it; I've had enough of all the verbal diarrhea about Castro and Cuba, enough of criticizing life in exile and dreaming about a return that's just an illusion."

"Go ahead, Mireya."

"And you'll see that Nicotiano won't miss me. He'll find another woman just like that."

"I really hope so."

"You hope so, Aunt Ula?"

"You've deceived him and left him. I'm not being critical of you, but you know full well you can't be at Mass and ring out the bells at the same time. Nicotiano truly frightens me. He loves you too much."

"Well, it's been quite a number of years since he's shown me. Let him go screw himself now. Let him die for me if he really cares."

"Now that you're leaving, Nicotiano is the only thing I have left."

"That's not true. You'll always have a star that lights the way for you. And if you don't have one, you'll make the heavens build one, just for you. Don't I know my Aunt Ulalume!"

"Do you love your new companion a lot?"

"He gave me the strength to break away from you all and to become an independent woman. I can be sincere with you…sexually, Nicotiano does more for me than he does. As much as I try to light him up, he is…a very bland man, it's like trying to set fire to something that's wet. But…"

"But?"

"But with him I feel like I mean something. It's not like with Nicotiano, who already seems to have everything. It's a game, Aunt Ulalume, it's an obsession that gives me a great feeling of security."

We went up to the room and packed a couple of suitcases with the bare essentials. Cocorioco would bring the rest.

"Just leave, my girl."

"Don't call me 'girl'; I'm Mireya."

Just as she was about to get into the car, Kafka appeared.

"It looks like he wants to say goodbye to you, Mireya."

The dog approached her. And in his mouth be brought her that intimate and tiny undergarment that Mireya had left on the table in the last act of love with Nicotiano!

"Remember, Aunt Ulalume, don't ever call me 'girl' again: I'm Mireya, goddammit. I'm Mireya!"

Hetkinen and Guarapito…

"I think we should respect Nicotiano. We all have the right to feel despair and express our pain according to our own idiosyncrasies."

"Bah. Despair my white mammies, Hetkinen, that's nothing but an utter and incomprehensible weakness in an incredible guy like Nicotiano. What's this going around, all weepy and suffering? What he ought to do is just say to hell with her."

"Guarapito, you have to mock everything. And you know what Ulalume thinks of choteo, *of mockery: it's great for making life more tolerable, but also for cutting others down to size and repressing the ones who dare to have a dissenting opinion. Poking fun at everything tends to smother authentic expressions of feeling or thought. I take the regenerating capacity of suffering very seriously.*

"Because you're a Finn."

"You hide behind a mask of indifference. But I can assure you, Guarapito, that anguish can do miracles to a man."

"And to women, Hetkinen. Miracles of shame and whoring around."

"You speak as if you were an immaculate man."

"In Cuba, lots of men kill their wives if they screw around on them."

"It's the same in Finland and other places, because spite and jealous rage have no homeland."

"But since you people are so cold, you're more quiet and crazy on the inside. We're just crazy on the outside."

"Yeah, I know lots of men who get worked up, their minds and souls clouded by booze, one night suddenly go out to the forest and hang themselves from some fir tree."

"Hetkinen, I always thought that forests in Finland were overrun with poor bastards found hanging with their tongues sticking out. But in Cuba nobody hangs themself over some ungrateful wretch. I remember, back when I was a child, a neighbor of mine whose wife suddenly left him for another man. He knew she would come back, since they had a small boy; the woman just got up and left with a truck driver from some other town and the whole neighborhood was left in suspense. What would happen if she came back? At about the time she left him, the abandoned husband started sharpening his machete *every day. The people knew what was going on: the man would get up early, eat, send the kid off to school, and before going to work, he would sharpen his* machete *with painstaking precision. Everybody knew it and talked about it, but nobody did anything. It was like it was a storm that forms and suddenly rages and no one can avoid it. The man would come home from work, apparently calm, down half a bottle of rum and keep sharpening his* machete. *One morning she showed up and said: 'I've come to see our boy.' I still remember, see how it makes my hair stand on end, I still remember the pool of blood in the living room, the blood splattered all over the walls and the woman's head on a chair, right where she stood."*

"Nicotiano's not the type to sharpen his revenge."

"No, not him. But who's to say, Hetkinen, that she's not one of the ones who keep sharpening revenge for years, only to finally plunge it into his back?"

- Seven -

*F*or a moment Betty Boop didn't know what to do with her victory. Burruchaga was definitely out of her life and she had hoisted the flag of her dignity up high, but now the worst was ahead, maybe even an inevitable descent into annihilation. How she would like to have been named Oblivion, Solitude, or just Misery. But despite the overwhelming sensation of irreality, she was Betty and she would have to do something with her life. She lay sprawled out in bed in her apartment and felt like a fish spoiling in the heat.

"Betty, honey," she said to herself sweetly, "you can't just lie here and rot like a fish." She sat up and looked for the list that set down her post-El Regreso, post-Burruchaga, post-Fuñío, post-Castro and post-everything destiny. And Betty Boop started to make decisions.

She packed some clothes, shoes and dresser items. She called the police and reported Fuñío missing. She answered all their questions clearly and with aplomb. When they asked her for her address and telephone number, she quickly flipped through the Yellow Pages and gave the address for Waldorf Towers: 860 Ocean Drive. She took a long shower, put on a dress with sober, yet happy, colors and headed off to Mr. Kupiec's store on Washington Ave. On the way she picked up *The Miami Herald*, something she never did, and anxiously scanned the news stories, since a vague hope had flashed through her mind: what if Fidel Castro had been toppled the night before and Cuba dawned the next morning free and sovereign? And what if what had happened to Ceaucescu had happened to Castro, if he had leaned against a wall, the one on the Malecón maybe, and PANG, PANG, PANG, to hell with Communism in the Caribbean? That would have cast at least a little light on her destiny. In the little revolution of a post-Fidel Cuba she would have found a little hole to hide in. Who knows if thanks to the gastronomic experience she had gained in El Regreso, they might make her manager of a McDonalds upon her return, in Havana, in Camagüey or in Matanzas? But Fidel was like a *macao*, you had to shake it out of its shell, and the *Herald* didn't have any more news than the never-ending bitter squabbling between the groups opposing exile, every one of which attributed to themselves the most transcendental contributions in the fight to liberate Cuba from Communism.

Betty stopped. What had she seen in the newspaper? A familiar face...She turned back through the pages and found the picture of a good looking woman with friendly, warm smile and sure look.

"Good Lord, it's Ulalume!"

It was me. They'd done an interview with me about the plans and maneuverings of the Cuban American Transaction, which had planned to seize the Island of Cundeamor, kick us out and turn it into an emporium of casinos and hotels. The headlines read: MRS. ULULUME INSISTS THAT CRABB COMPANY WILL NEVER LEAVE ISLAND OF CUNDEAMOR.

Betty skimmed the interview.

Oh, look how pretty Ula is," she said, standing full of admiration in the middle of the sidewalk on Washington Ave. "She helped me out so much in the beginning, when we first got here, and she was a lot better off than we were, money-wise...We became friends, ate out together, talked and laughed...Later she made her way in life, while I retreated and began my descent into the caves of ruin..."

And she got the idea to come look for me and ask me for help one more time, but her exaggerated pride kept her from doing so. What? Show me her failure, her poor, pre-indigent state?

She kept going until she reached Mr. Kupiec's tiny shop.

The storekeeper was asleep in his wicker chair, with a volume of yellowing pages resting in his lap; in front of him was a large cup of half-drunk tea. His legs were crossed on an enormous, ancient, peeling writing desk that had outlived its usefulness, just like everything else in his store: there were rusted metal objects, such as knives, scissors, tools, locks, machetes, keys. He had a ton of musical instruments, most of them useless: mandolins without strings, trombones stained as if they had herpes, and several violins whose cases looked like the caskets of mummified children. A group of nine double-bass players formed a cornered audience of fat, puckered-mouth old men who squinted at Betty. Leaning against one of them, a graceful *balalaika* inlaid with mother of pearl looked like a poor girl seeking protection and affection. Betty saw the compasses of an undefined north and a pile of Jewish candelabras that branched out like a small leafless bushes. And the radios, shabby and nostalgic, of varnished wood and large bulbs like Christmas ornaments, were from the days Betty was small and her father would listen to Radio Reloj. There were also plenty of pots, kerosene stoves and lanterns, as well as quite a bit of silverware that looked ready to serve a dinner of ghosts. The piles of dolls, with their limbs severed, like right after a massacre, half-bald, their heads stove in, gloomy, with the whites of their eyes showing, felt oppressive to Betty. In a display window fashioned of cloudy glass were religious scenes and little statues, Saint Barbara, the Virgin of Charity, Jesus Christ crucified, martyred and bloodied in all sizes, to the point of nausea. The junk was piled high in an unhealthy atmosphere full of cobwebs, with scorpions probably in the drawers crammed with stethoscopes and binoculars, glass eyes and old shoes, and Betty felt frightened to be there all alone. Standing before the sweaty man who was snoring like a tractor, she felt almost like another second-hand object. Betty studied the title of the book the man held between his legs: *The Holy Bible.*

"Good afternoon, Mr. Kupiec."

The man stopped his labored snoring and quickly became alert.

"What can I do for you?"

Betty was direct:

"A deal: I'll sell you all my worldly possessions."

Kupiec didn't answer. He lay the book on the desk and studied her with widened eyes that were too sly for his pale, ghastly fat face; it was a look that lingered too long on an area somewhere between Betty Boop's knees and breasts.

"Everything?"

"Everything that's got a price," she responded and then looked down.

"Everything has a price, ma'am; the only thing without a price is the emotional price of something." Kupiec stood up. He was short, fifty-something, and with a considerable gut. His hair was reddish and was mussed in a tangle that Betty thought looked attractive but that probably stank. But no, reconsidered Betty, looking at it close-up it wasn't dirty, despite the store's sordid atmosphere, and there was something about his mouth that she liked. Without knowing why, Betty got the idea that Mr. Kupiec was a gentleman used to politely lying.

"Do you own a lot of valuable things, Señora?"

The last word he pronounced in Spanish.

Betty tried to concentrate, to give him the impression that she was a serene woman who knew what she was doing.

"You're a little nervous." The shopkeeper found her out.

"I think...that I do own a lot of valuable things."

"Emotional, or cash value?"

"Come over to my place," she responded sharply, "and buy whatever interests you."

Mr. Kupiec proceeded to lock up his hole-in-the-wall with reflex movements and furrows of skepticism, as if realizing that it all wasn't worth it, but that just the same he was doing it to help her out since she was so interested. They left in Kupiec's truck, and on the way there he said he thought he'd seen her before, yes, maybe in his store, didn't she buy some object once, or maybe he was mistaken? No, he wasn't mistaken; Betty had picked up the second-hand statues for her altar at his place. But she didn't say anything.

When they reached her apartment, Kupiec pulled out a little notebook and started jotting things down in a somewhat distracted manner as he walked around the room, with the air of a student taking notes in a museum. Finally, with a long sigh, Kupiec plopped down in Fuñío's armchair. He looked at Betty wearily and, like someone expressing condolences, said:

"Ma'am, I can give you $200 for all this junk."

Betty Boop let out a little scream, and then right after that, a real scream, which she stifled with one hand, but Kupiec wasn't fazed. When she did manage to get a word out, she said:

"Extorter...You're a goddamn thief. That handout for all this? My bed, my furniture, my decorations, my electrical appliances?"

"I'm sorry, ma'am, but your decorations are only a few chipped vases and a couple of quite ridiculous little plaster figurines. The plants don't count; I can't keep them in the store, because they'll wither and die."

"You're a heartless man, a greedy shopkeeper and a userer of the worst kind."

"Your 'electrical appliances', ma'am, are simply an old blender and a toaster. The radio and television are so worthless that you'd have to pay someone just to take them off your hands."

Betty swallowed and said nothing. She had had vain illusions. The money Kupiec offered was enough to spend at most two days at the Waldorf, which would undo her plans: to get rid of everything she owned and with that money live for a time, as long as possible, in the hotel. When she ran out of money, she would either throw herself into the sea some night and kill herself, or hook up with the homeless woman and vanish from Miami without a trace.

The proof of being a loser in life suddenly overwhelmed her self-esteem. Now there were no two 'buts' about it: after all those years of exile, this was what she was worth: $200. All those years of struggling every day and longing for inaccessible or lost things, to end up at a liquidation price.

"If Castro would just fall, at least I'd have some sort of chance!"

"Pardon me, ma'am? I didn't hear you."

Betty sat down on her bed and began to cry. Holding her rage inside, but also feeling embarrassed and impotent. Kupiec let her cry a little bit. And he took advantage of that pause in business to review his notes. Maybe he had been too generous...Two hundred dollars?

Betty stopped crying and looked at him as if she were about to strangle him. But she didn't strangle him; in one move she unbuttoned her blouse and unleashed, before Mr. Kupiec's astonished eyes, the breasts and appetizing dark nipples of a mature woman. Then she waited, without blinking, tempting and suffocating, until Mr. Kupiec's eyes began to turn greedy. "One thousand dollars for everything," she said. "Listen good: for everything I own."

"Everything, ma'am?"

Betty raised her breasts in a gesture of depraved offering. With poorly contained greed, Kupiec's incredulously brushed a hand across one of her nipples. His voice quavered and his mouth slowly closed in on that blurred rose.

"A thousand for everything in this apartment," the shopkeeper proposed, sucking away, "and for everything on this body once during the day for a couple of months."

"A thousand now," she replied, pretending to moan, "and twenty every time for a month."

"A thousand now," he bargained, reaching out to grasp her buttocks and caress her steaming bush, "and ten bucks every time," at this point he took his mouth off her nipple, because she couldn't understand what he was saying, "for a month."

"You behave, Kupiec, and I'll give you a lot for free. Love me a little and protect me, but now you get undressed while I cover the saints' eyes."

Betty covered the altar with a white sheet, so her beloved saints would not witness the desecration of her body. Unfortunately in all the rush and confusion, Saint Lazarus was still partly uncovered and thus had to watch, like a peeping Tom against his will, the awkward act that had nothing to do with love. Once they finished, however, Betty felt a kind of affection for Kupiec. The shopkeeper had come quickly and roughly, with the whistling of a locomotive and growls of a bulldozer, without pleasuring her in the slightest. But something about him inspired a tenderness in her, a kind of irrefutable helplessness that was secretly like her own.

Betty suggested that they shower together, since she loved to frolic, all lathered up as the water came down, but she saw that her new lover, customer and buyer of all her worldly goods had fallen into a deep sleep. The man was lying in bed like a deflated parachute, and Betty didn't bother trying to revive him. He didn't have an ugly body, but he did have very little energy in it. Betty searched his pockets. The cheapskate had only five dollars in his wallet, and Betty took one. She also found a picture of Kupiec, who looked slightly uglier than now because he had been younger. In another pocket she found a handkerchief, luckily clean, and even a little perfumed. Betty stashed the spoils in her bra.

And she awoke him with kisses. Kupiec didn't understand how a whore could be capable of such a display of affection, but with great relish he stayed in bed, on the receiving end of those intimate and free, almost genuinely loving caresses, caresses not included in any of the contract clauses establishing the limits of their relationship, since he felt he deserved special treatment. Kupiec thought that if a whore treated him with so much tenderness, practically bordering on passion, it was most certainly because his way of screwing her had been exceptional. Kupiec then left and was gone for so long that Betty began to fear that he had betrayed her. But in the end he returned with two men who wordlessly hauled away all of Betty's belongings on their backs, saints included. When the apartment was completely empty, it was dark out. Betty then took out a couple of candles she had in a bag. Kupiec, without knowing why, had bought a few Michelobs, which they drank while sitting on the floor, each of them in their respective corner. Betty lighted the candles in the twilight, placing them in the center of the room.

"Why are you lighting candles if you're moving out of here?"

"You light candles to strengthen your faith. When life mistreats us, it's beneficial to light candles; when we fall into the abyss of vice or perdition and long for redemption; when we are betrayed or when we have betrayed, because betrayal is always degrading. When night falls and the solitude is colder, it's good to light candles so their little flames seem like one of existence's forms of support."

"What you have just said is beautiful," Kupiec said, slightly lethargic from the beer. Then he sat watching the tenuous dancing of the little flames and kept a liturgical silence. If this woman wasn't a whore, then she was half-crazy; if she wasn't crazy...

"Look at the candle colors, Kupiec. Each of them has a specific meaning. The rose color is the symbol of the woman, that is, me. Green is hope, that is, you. The red candle is the symbol of burning desire and the white is the symbol of purity. The yellow candle is humility, but it's also the candle of the Virgin of Charity, the Patron Saint of Cuba. The Woman of honey and sweets, guardian of the sea and resolver of all amorous conflicts. It's also not by chance that I have lighted the white, red, and blue candles (the blue is a tribute to the sky) separately, since those are the colors of the Cuban flag. That also inspires faith amid all the pain."

Kupiec felt a little bewitched. The Michelobs, the rosary of tender ravings to which Betty's voice seemed to be praying in the half-darkness and the magical guttering of the candles made him lethargic and happy.

"Cubans are a difficult stock of people," he said. You and we Jews are alike, at least in our crazy nationalism."

"Where's my first thousand bucks?" Betty inquired.

Without snapping out of his state of beatitude, Kupiec started to laugh. He pulled out a roll of brand-new, one could even say starched bills, to Betty an amazing sight, and he gave it all to her. Betty had never seen a thousand dollars at once in somebody's hand.

"Count them," Kupiec said.

"No need to, sweetie. I trust you."

Betty put the money aside and gave Kupiec a long kiss. They made love on the floor, this time with a little more humanity. Kupiec didn't even think that it was free this time, since he knew he had those favors coming.

It wasn't hard to reserve a room at the Waldorf. When she made the reservation, Betty acted like a woman of the world. She paid three days in advance. Cash.

"We'll see how it goes," and she moved in.

The Waldorf was a small two-floor hotel, quite ugly on the inside, but cozy enough. It had recently been restored and had, like so many other buildings in the area, a kind of 1930's nostalgia air about it. At the beginning of the 80's, before the utilitarian modernism of the Art Deco District underwent a renaissance, the hotel was practically in ruins, on the verge of toppling over, with its crumbling facade and comical round tower, like a neon mini-lighthouse on the corner of 8th and Ocean Drive. But now, after a face-lift, it was charming, at least to

Betty. In reality, she could have picked any hotel in the Deco District, small wonders of architecture scattered along Collins Avenue, Washington, Pennsylvania, Euclid, Meridian, Jefferson and Michigan; she nibbled at them all, thinking that to stay in any one of them would have been like moving into a cake. On her solitary walks (always in hope of unexpectedly finding Fuñío) Betty would come across hotels, either on Spanish Way or on Lincoln Road, that were practically edible, pastel-colored pastries, with infinite detail in meringue-colored plaster. Fat little skylights and comical cornices, sea horses and dolphins playing a pleasant game of confectioner's geometry under the bright sun. But the Waldorf was unique for its little tower-mini-lighthouse, lit up at night like a youthful blue-neon ribbon that Betty Boop found quite moving.

She slept poorly that first night. The next day Betty opened the window and shouted out to the sea (to Cuba) that she still wouldn't give up. To the north, the sky had grown sick. "Water, it's going to rain," she thought, "and you, pretty girl, have a lot to do."

Betty stripped. In the center of the bed she placed the dollar bill, picture and handkerchief she had stolen from Kupiec, and took out a yellow candle as an offering to Ochún, with five rusty nails she had stolen from a drawer in Kupiec's store. Then she took out an old photo of her with Fuñío and tore it in half. She tossed the image of Fuñío into the toilet, and flushed as if afraid to get her hands dirty. Then she went back over to the bed. She knelt and, right under her sex, placed her own image next to Kupiec's. She nailed the five nails into the handkerchief she had stolen, tore the dollar into five pieces and then put everything together, sprinkled it with five drops of her habitual perfume, plus five drops of her Perfume of the Seven Males. As if inserting a penis inside her, Betty slowly lowered her body until she covered everything with her bare genitals. Next she lit the yellow candle in offering to Ochún. She stayed like that for a while, eyes closed, like a hen sitting on an egg. The candle wax burned her hand, and the nails felt cold, with one practically sticking inside her vagina. Betty raised the candle even higher and, with her eyes still closed, spoke with devotion:

"Just as this candle burns, I want his heart to burn with love FOR ME. Let there be no road that does not come straight TO ME. Let him not have any dream at night in which I DO NOT APPEAR. Let him not have one erection that I DO NOT PROVOKE. Let him drink MY BODY in the clear liquid of his Michelobs and in the amber of his tea. It will be mine and only mine against all omens and even against his will."

Once she had repeated this five times, which is the sacred number of the Ochún-Virgin of Charity, she tied the handkerchief, nails and pictures with a yellow ribbon, and placed the little package in her suitcase, snugly wrapped in her panties.

"You're screwed, Kupiec," she said in a defiant tone. "You'll be tied to me for the rest of your days."

It began to thunder outside and Betty, still naked, looked out the window. Flashes of lightning were striking the sea; the horizon was out of sight and Betty both shuddered and felt happy at those favorable signs. There was no doubt that the storm was Ochún's categorical answer: Kupiec was hers.

The downpour was one of sustained violence and it wasn't cold; the coconut palms on Ocean Drive looked like they would lose all their fronds. Streams of water filled the street and the cars were moving like boats.

"Flood Miami Beach, my little Virgin Mary!" Betty invoked. From the window, she could make out somebody moving forward with difficulty under a multi-colored umbrella. Betty thought the storm was going to blow the umbrella away, sending it up to the swollen sky. The rain was like an enormous mosquito netting that blurred everything, but Betty recognized that umbrella. "Shit, it's Bag Lady."

Without a second thought, she got dressed and went out to find her. When she caught up, Betty, who was now drenched, shouted:

"Dear friend! I have money, look! Now we can have fun."

"Did you kill him? Did you really decapitate him with the razor?"

"No, honey, just a ketchupy demise." And Betty suggested that they go up to her hotel room, change out of their clothes and get a bite to eat.

"They won't let me into the hotel," Bag Lady said.

"You just rest easy," Betty Boop responded firmly. "I can have any visitor up to my room I see fit. That's why I'm paying ninety bucks a night. You just stay with me. I want you to take a bath, put on some perfume, and get into clean clothes. One of my dresses should do the trick."

The man at the reception desk made an authoritative gesture to keep Bag Lady from coming into the hotel, but Betty pulled out a ten dollar bill like someone drawing a sword. She smiled affably and the man hesitated a bit, but took the bribe, shrugged and both women went upstairs.

"But don't go leaving those bags of shit in the room," the young man said.

"You gave him a Hamilton!" Bag Lady exclaimed, as if that were some sort of catastrophe. "A whole Hamilton!"

Bag Lady took a bath. Betty watched the layers of grime as they slowly broke down under the soap and water, and then she scrubbed her back and gave her deodorant and perfume, and also saw in all its magnificence the King Cobra revolver that Bag Lady always carried with her.

By the time they were both ready, the weather had cleared. Betty used all her grace and eloquence to convince the panhandler to put on a clean dress. She finally agreed, and Betty then saw that Bag Lady was an attractive woman, with curvy hips, well-formed shoulders and a youthful look, despite her indecipherable age. But there was one problem: now that she didn't have all those layers of clothing on, Bag Lady had no satisfactory way to hide the Colt King Cobra. Betty insisted that she leave it in the hotel, but the panhandler staunchly refused. In the end, she stuck it under her blouse as well as she could. They went to what they thought was the most high-class restaurant. They were already seated at a table when they thought of something quite unpleasant. Apparently they knew Bag Lady and, despite her new look, a rude white waiter told them:

"Please leave. We don't serve panhandlers here."

To Betty Boop's total amazement, Bag Lady stood up and said:

"In 1787, we the people of the United States, in order to form a more perfect union, establish justice, insure domestic tranquility, provide for the common defense, promote the general welfare, and secure the blessings of liberty to ourselves and our posterity, do ordain and establish this Constitution for the United States of America, which states that no state shall approve or enact any legislation that limits the rights or privileges of the citizens of the United States, nor shall any person be deprived of his liberty or property, nor can anyone be refused the same protection under the law."

And then she added:

"In God we trust.!"

The waiter stood there paralyzed, as did Betty. And they were served their meal. Poor service, but the women ate and drank as much as they pleased. Betty gladly paid. Afterwards, they sat for a while on a bench in Lumus Park.

"You should have been a lawyer, Lady."

They laughed easily.

"I like being your friend, Cuban woman."

They were suddenly surrounded by a small gang of youths. Their gestures were arrogant and their looks were aggressive and cold. The one who seemed to be the leader said to Bag Lady:"Hey, nigger, sell me that pea-shooter you got under your blouse. I'll buy it off you right now."

"If you don't sell it to us, we'll take it off you anyway, and you'll lose, just like in war."

The thugs formed a circle around them. Betty, who wasn't used to these scenes, was terrified and didn't dare blink.

"What'll it be, lady, what'll it be…"

"You don't back off, I'll fill y'all with bullets right this second," Bag Lady threatened with the King Cobra in her hand.

The kids had a little fun with her. They looked as though they were going to get closer and made obscene gestures at Bag Lady.

"Don't be so sneaky, nigger."

"Hey, where'dya leave those bags?"

"Bag Lady from Ocean Drive is getting civilized, gentlemen."

"We had no idea she had such a pretty and cheap pea shooter…"

The woman cocked the revolver, and the thugs, reluctantly, began to back away.

"Devils," Betty muttered, weak with fear.

Then the women sat together for a long time without saying a word, looking out at the calm of the sea after the rain.

"The world is a shit hole," one of them said.

"People don't have any scruples," the other reflected. "Anyone is capable of truly causing pain if they think they can get ahead."

"Exactly: trample, squash the head of your fellow man to get ahead."

Betty looked at her watch. She had just a few minutes to get to her daily engagement with Kupiec, and she wanted to maintain a kind of order to their encounters. That was, after all, her daily bread. She made plans to meet Bag Lady right there, in Lumus Park, at about nine o'clock.

Betty was conscious that her tone of voice was growing more and more affectionate when she spoke with Kupiec. When she wasn't with him, a vague longing would make her feel unhappy.

That afternoon, after making love, and while Kupiec was taking his mini post-coital siesta, Betty checked out the back room of the shop and saw that it resembled living quarters. When he awoke, she asked:

"Are you married, Kupiec?"

"A confirmed bachelor."

"Then why don't you take me home? At this point you should realize that I'm not exactly a prostitute, nor that the only thing I want from you are your handouts."

"I live here, Betty."

"Here, in this dump? Then you really still need me: a woman who could add some order and affection to your life. Pretty curtains, tablecloths, flowers, cleanliness and light. You can't live your whole life like a rat in this dump."

"I'm used to it."

"Starting right now we're going to meet somewhere else, to screw somewhere that's got more décor. A motel, for example. And if you decide to live with me, buy a little house. You'll see how pretty I could make it. And I'll teach you how to make *ajiaco* stew and black beans.

"A motel? A house? That's all very expensive, Betty"

"Don't be so cheap, Kupiec. How many lives do you think you're going to live? Take advantage of what you have left, look, it's the only thing you've got left. Everyone needs love and attention. If you don't do anything with your life, it won't do anything for you, either."

For one, Betty was willing to do everything possible to have her sexual relationships not lapse into an automatism and inertia. It wasn't good for her to have Kupiec get bored, but above all she didn't want to grow bored. Immediately after sex Kupiec always fell asleep and Betty began to accept that fact as inevitable. But once he was awake, she waited for him to rest a little and then, with strokes that were deeper and even a little vicious, she stimulated him and coaxed out an ejaculation, this time an almost loving one.

"Kupiec, I've discovered that you have a collection of Bibles."

"The Bible is a strange book."

"A sacred book."

"Strange; it's got all these nonsensical things in it. For example, there's History's first great drunken binge, which was Noah's. Do you know how old Noah was when Jehovah told him to build the ark? 600 years old. And when he died, he was 950."

Betty was taken with the image of 600-year-old Noah at the helm of an ark placidly floating upon an everlasting ocean in the company of the all the little animals he had, and would have, on board.

"You're not going to have Noah's longevity, Kupiec, nor are you going to build any ark, nor is Jehovah going to give you any kind of mission. So you have to marry me, I'm the ark of your life. Come out of that labyrinth of old junk and live the human life that I can offer you."

"You're indoctrinating me. I've always been alone. I'm a loner and that's how I'll finish my days."

"You think I'm a whore." Betty said this without the slightest trace of pathos.

"I don't care so much about that," replied Kupiec. "In the Bible, whores were always worshiped when serving the Elected People."

"You don't say! I always suspected that in biblical times the world was a real shithole."

"Take for example, Rahab, a public woman. She lived in the city of Jerecho, which was settled by the Israelites. Joshua sent two explorers to do reconnaisance on the terrain before laying siege to the city, and Rehab helped them, hiding them out in her house, thus betraying her own people in favor of the Jews. When the Israelites took the city, Rahab was rewarded."

"What kind of reward did they give her?"

"They respected her life."

"Wow. What generosity."

"The Bible is full of treachery and cruelties."

"Just like life."

"The more I read the Bible, Betty, the more I'm convinced that it's a poetic and propaganistic pamphlet."

"You're such a beast, Kupiec...I never imagined that I would fall for an atheist. You don't even believe in the mother that gave birth to you."

"You mean that the Bible gave birth to me."

Betty made a gesture of moral indignation:

"We all descend from Adam," she said.

With his eyes closed, Kupiec smiled and remained silent. He turned back and suddenly planted a kiss on Betty Bop's cheek, which was still flushed with love. It was an almost voluntary movement and without any apparent importance; Kupiec might have done it without realizing it or meaning to do it. But that kiss penetrated Betty Boop further than Kupiec's penis, which was surely a significantly proportioned organ.

She didn't really seem to do anything. She didn't return the kiss, didn't caress him, she didn't even dare move.

Finally she said:

"Tell me about other important women in the Scriptures."

"Judith and Delilah. The Bible glorifies the first for the same reason it condemns the second. Both are thieves and murderers in their own right. The difference is that Judith used her betrayal against an enemy of the Hebrews, Holofernes, whereas Delilah used it against Samson, an Israelite. Judith is a heroine, whereas Delilah has come to personify the pernicious influence that many women hold over men. As you can see, I'm not a beast, but my hobby is reading the Book of Books and I'm convinced that the Bible is a very tendentious document."

Kupiec said this with flagrant pride at being so sharp, and since Betty knew that to conquer a man the first thing one must give him the illusion that everything he says is transcendental; she goaded him on so that he would feel even more important:

"Kupiec, tell me about a biblical woman who was valiant, but not one who was scheming or despicable.

"Hmmmmm...Let me think..."

"Don't you mean that we're the origin of all plagues and Heaven and Earth's calamities."

"Look, Betty, if we set aside the story of Eve and the temptation of the Garden of Good and Evil..."

"As far as I know," Betty interrupted, "in the Garden of Good and Evil there was just Evil, Evil and more Evil."

"You women, for example, are to blame for the Great Flood."

"The Great Flood! Shit, now I see why you don't want to get married."

"It so happens that in Genesis, the book compiled by Moses in the Sinai Desert in 1513 B.C., we are told how all of God's angels abandon their heavenly abodes to come down, in sin, to fornicate with the daughters of men, who seemed pretty and attractive to them."

Betty sighed.

"Out of that shameful union," Kupiec continued, "unauthorized by God, were born a pair of terrible and huge creatures called Nefilim, which means "Wreckers." Given the state of things in the world, what with all the violence and iniquity, God gave very precise instructions to Noah, since the Flood was an inevitable fact..."

"Well if the angels all came down to screw," Betty Boop objected, "it was their free will; nobody forced them to abandon Eden, and we women are innocent of their horniness."

"It's just that Heaven must be horribly tedious, Betty; up there nothing ever goes on and eternal happiness is so boring. For life to be worth living, you have to take risks."

He was going on about this when I showed up in Kupiec's store. He was so cheap that he didn't even close it when he was with Betty, just so he wouldn't miss the extra chance at making another sale.

Guarapito and Maribarbola went in first and checked the place out. Then I entered and called out:

"Kupiec! It's me, Aunt Ulalume. Come out, I have to talk to you."

Kupiec grew so nervous that Betty thought he was going to have a heart attack. His face turned brown and his belly trembled. The shopkeeper quickly got dressed, and left. Betty stayed quiet, feeling like she wanted to turn to stone, die, come back to life and fly out of there like a bat.

"Aunt Ulalume in Kupiec's place!"

She had a burning desire to go out and greet her old friend, but her embarrassment stopped her. She tried to calm herself down and decided to listen to what they were saying.

"Tell me, Aunt Ulalume, what can I do for you? Your loyal servant is here for you."

"Kupiec, I'll get right to it. In the ten years I've known you, we've done business and I consider you a good friend; sometimes you've supplied me with some of the materials Nicotiano needs for his sculptures."

"Of course, it's my pleasure! Like when you needed Jewish headstones to turn into crabs…"

"We've always gotten along well. And I appreciate it. That's why I've come to give you a warning."

Kupiec turned pale. Betty, in her hiding place, did, too.

"Kupiec, man comes a long way by knowing his weaknesses and needs more than by knowing his means and abilities. Kupiec, open that Bible that fascinates you so much and look up: Ecclesiastics, 12-16. Read."

"Be aware and watch after yourself," Kupiec recited, "because disgrace surrounds you."

"I don't get it, Aunt Ulalume."

"Don't play dumb, Kupiec. How much money did you make on that drug shipment?"

Kupiec crumbled. "About eight hundred thousand dollars so far, Aunt Ulalume."

"Death surrounds you, Kupiec."

Betty, shocked in her hiding place (eight hundred thousand dollars!), misstepped, made a noise behind the door and Guarapito and Sikitrake both drew their guns. "Who the hell's there?" shouted Guarapito, ready to shoot.

"Whoever it is, come on out of there, with your hands held high," Sikitrake coldly ordered.

Kupiec started to whimper.

"It's a woman, Aunt Ulalume, a woman…helpless and unarmed."

Guarapito, with the movement of a well-trained cop, went in and searched with his gun held out.

"It's true," he said coming out, "a fat, stark-naked woman and nobody else."

A fat woman who felt ashamed and panicked, one might add, since Betty was ready to die of anguish. She felt vulgar and robbed of all dignity, like a street dog. Buck-naked and in the back room of a shopkeeper! I lowered my voice and Betty couldn't hear me anymore.

"Kupiec: oddly enough, the information that they're going to murder you came to the Crabb Company. They want to take you out of the loop. You know too much; they've used you for their purposes and now they don't need you anymore."

"Sons of bitches. What should I do, Aunt Ulalume?"

"Disappear. Go abroad. But before you go, can you get me another shipment of headstones?"

"If they're Jewish, they'll be very hard to get quickly."

"Steal them right here in Miami; not a lot, they can be dead Cubans. I want to give them to my nephew Nicotiano as a gift. He's going through a very difficult marriage crisis right now, he's very depressed and hardly sculpts anymore. Let's see if those headstones don't inspire him."

"Give me three days. And then I'll disappear from Miami."

"Good luck, Kupiec."

"Thanks, Aunt Ulalume, I owe you my life. The headstones are on me."

"Take care."

As I was leaving, I came back to say:

"And hey, Kupiec, get yourself a woman and make her love you, old man, hook up with her and learn to love life more. You can't go on living the rest of your days clutching on to whores."

Betty Boop did hear that part clearly.

Kupiec was breathless when he went in to see Betty. To her complete surprise, he hugged her and started crying. She watched him cry without really knowing why he was crying. Finally she asked him:

"Who's that woman and those thugs?"

"Friends," he snorted, "just friends."

"Where does that woman live, Kupiec?"

"On the Island of Cundeamor."

"But where's that? In Miami? There's no place around here with that name."

"No," he responded. "But she lives there."

Later they spent a long time stretched out in bed, not caressing each other, but lying very close, as if they were afraid to separate. Then Betty thought about the time and her appointment with Bag Lady. As a way of saying goodbye, she kissed him on the mouth and again on the forehead. Kupiec took out the money to pay her for her services, as stated in the contract, but Betty, with a small, yet immensely sad smile, refused it.

"That's enough, Kupiec. Save that for the whores who lend you their services. You don't have to pay me anymore. Even if I die of hunger, I don't want to take one red cent from you."

And she left with the impression that Kupiac would be left in a bad way, abandoned and miserable.

It was already getting late, but before heading to Lumus Park to see her friend, Betty went up to the Waldorf and took a lavish shower with lots and lots of soap. Curiously, that was the only time she was disgusted to have Kupiec's semen between her legs, and she scrubbed and rinsed until it hurt. She wanted to tell Bag Lady everything: about her whoring, and that she was finished forever.

It was already dark out and the restaurants and cafes were bustling. Betty thought she would be able to sit out on some terrace and have a couple of drinks with the money she had left, maybe even get something to eat.

"Nobody lives 950 years," she mumbled.

On a bench in Lumus Park, she saw Bag Lady's umbrella, open under the starry night as if she were protecting herself from the full moon.

"Lady," she called out happily.

But her friend didn't stir, because she couldn't. When Betty approached her, she saw that under the umbrella her friend's head was thrown back and hung over the back of the bench, her throat slashed deeply ear-to-ear, with several tendons hanging out and coagulated in a foamy, half-hard red. The blood that covered the clothes Betty had lent her was of a darker shade, black, almost like the light from the moon. One of Lady's eyes was open, and the other was kind of half-cocked, looking straight up. Betty backed up and retched, but she didn't throw up, nor did she scream. She walked away like an automaton, zigzagging, in circles, staggering along as if she were drunk.

There was a moment when Betty Boop, almost without realizing it, got in a cab. There was no way to tell if she had been wandering through the streets of Miami Beach for hours, days or weeks. She wasn't conscious of her body and she wasn't hungry, hot or cold.

"Where to, ma'am?" the taxi driver, a Cuban mulatto about her, asked her.

"To the Island of Cundeamor, please."

"But that island doesn't exist, my love…," the taxi driver replied with a hint of sadness at her ragged look and sad appearance.

"No, it doesn't exist," she replied wearily. "But take me there anyway."

Kupiec by himself, deserted and drunk.

"Where are you, my dear Betty?" How can I bear the ostracism, the guilty conscience and persecution? What am I without you? Just a simple wandering Jew!"

"You never know what you have until you lose everything you have forever."

"I thought you were a whore, Betty."

"There are no whores; just heartbroken women."

"And unhappy men, Betty."

"Fuck off, Kupiec."

"I'm not alone. You're with me."

"Oh yeah? And where are my kisses, my warmth, affection, which made you feel safe from all danger and cruelty, even your own?"

"Don't torture yourself, Betty…You didn't want me to tell the story about a biblical woman who wasn't traitorous or evil? Well then listen to what the destiny of Esther was…"

"Esther…what a beautiful name."

"It's a Hebrew name that means "Star of Venus." Beautiful young Esther was Jewish and was married to Ahasuerus, who was the King of Persia…Following her stepfather's advice, Esther kept her Jewish identity hidden like an inviolable secret.

"What happened to Esther, Kupiec?"

"At the instigation of an influential man in the King's favor, the total extermination of all the Jews in the Kingdom was decreed."

"What crimes were they guilty of, Kupiec?"

"It was said that they were a people who lived totally isolated, always in open or veiled opposition to all the other peoples…in accordance to the King's laws, the Jews observed a kind of life that was

deemed hostile to the King's interests and that's why they were a dangerous lot who impeded the Kingdom's good order..."

"That description, Kupiec, reminds me of the Cuban people, who always were, just as they are today, daringly and stubbornly in opposition, either openly or veiled, to any Power threatening their pride as a nation..."

The King then ordered each one of his satraps, governors and subordinates of the 127 provinces from India to Ethiopia, to violently kill every Jew: young and old, women and children, all in one day, and said that their belongings should be sacked and pillaged."

"So Esther must have run the same risk as well..."

"Her stepfather asked her to intercede before the King and beg him to save the Jews."

"I too would have done the same thing for the Cubans. But I'm not married to the President of the United States of America, who's the only one to have satraps and governors in the 127 provinces..."

"But there were inviolable laws that Esther had to respect...Whoever entered the royal enclosure without being summoned would pay for that daring with their life. Desperate, Esther reminded her stepfather of this, but he was insistent: if she didn't intercede, and if the Jews were spared thanks to other reasons, she would be sacrificed in dishonor."

"Poor woman. Poor women. If Esther did intervene, the King would kill her; if she didn't do anything, her own people would condemn her...It's always the worst for us, and then, to top it off, we're held responsible for the Great Flood."

"Esther went before the King, Betty...Twice she fainted, but she mustered up the courage to ask for clemency: she revealed her dangerous secret and said that the people she belonged to were going to be exterminated and the King listened to her, and all was well. A royal edict was sent to the 127 provinces, from India to Ethiopia, and the King's satraps, governors and subordinates refrained from wiping out the Jews."

"Oh, Kupiec if this were in my hands, or in any other part of my body, I would be capable of going before Fidel Castro, before Congress in this country, or even before Satan himself, and interceding if it were necessary to spare 10 million Cubans from extermination!"

"Come back, Betty, can't you see that without you I'm losing the little life I have left."

"You don't understand the value of what you have, until you suddenly lose it forever."

- Eight -

Nicotiano realized that if he finished what was left in the bottle of rum, he would pass out. A couple more drops and he would be unable to drive. He was now driving too fast, headed for Biscayne Boulevard, northbound. Even when he wasn't drunk, sometimes the same thing would happen: to get to a specific place in Miami he had to go round and round, like a top, since he was unable to orient himself. It was surprising that after so many years he kept getting lost in that city laid out in grids, so easily structured in memory. In truth, as Mireya had said so well, Nicotiano refused to accept that it was his city, that he lived there and that is where he would probably one day die.

When he crossed the long bridge surrounded by turquoise water, thick and hot like soup, festooned with floating seaweed, which separated the Island of Cundeamor from other successive islands, Nicotiano no longer had any idea what he was doing, and when he finally did, he found himself in Flagler instead of Miami Beach, which is where he wanted to go. He turned in the direction of Coral Gables and then began senselessly driving in circles. He followed the ongoing traffic or turned at any corner. Suddenly he found himself in Coconut Grove, surrounded by poor blacks who looked at him with indifference, disdain or rancor. He got onto the Dixie Highway and sped northbound. At the top of Brickell he turned left for some reason. Without wanting to, he found himself on 7th Street. He pulled into a gas station. As he was being waited on, he swigged from the bottle again.

"I'm going to crash," he mumbled. "A head-on collision and to hell with it all."

He felt sick. He wasn't used to drinking so much. Near the gas station, Maribarbola, who had followed Nicotiano all through his erratic itinerary, had parked his car without Nicotiano noticing.

The gas station attendant said to Nicotiano:

"Hey, my friend, you're stinking drunk. It'd be best if you took a bus or taxi to wherever it is you're going. A little advice from a Cuban."

"Thanks. Did you come over on the Mariel boat lift?"

The young man felt hurt. That word, Mariel, which refers to the refugees who arrived together in Miami in 1980 from the Port of El Mariel, contained a subtle charge of disdain that separated the exiled Cubans into a "before" and an "after" Mariel and meant: the ones who came before are better; the ones that came after are poor bastards.

"Don't screw around, boy," he told him sweetly, "Yeah, I came from El Mariel, but I'm not a crook, or a drug addict, or a fag, or a pimp, or some petty thief. We're all nephews of the same grandmother. Don't you agree?"

"Nephews of the same grandmother... You're right. I came here when I was very young. Besides, I lived a few years in Spain."

"You can tell by your accent that you came here as a tyke. You must have spent a pile of years here in Miami."

"Tyke, pile of years." It was a way of speaking that strummed intimate fibers of his memory.

"In Cuba I was going to be an engineer," the young man said. "I studied in CUJAE. Here I'm going to become a car salesman."

"I truly don't know what CUJAE is."

"It's in Havana: José Antonio Echevarría University College. They teach all kinds of engineering there."

"How can I get rid of this buzz?"

"My friend, you're more innocent than the Anglos. With a *colada*, man, drink a *colada* with a Cuban coffee and you'll be as good as new."

Nicotiano paid, leaving him a generous tip. The young man kept looking at him a little nervously, like he wanted to say something embarrassing but didn't dare. Nicotiano picked up on it. Finally the young man asked:

"Hey, man, are you high, or did you take some other drug? Because *colada* won't work on that.

"No," Nicotiano responded. "I'm drunk, that's all. Why?"

"Your eyes. They're red as hell."

"I've been crying, that's all."

The young man became serious.

"Somebody die?"

"My wife left me for somebody else."

"Oh shit," he said, identifying all too well with Nicotiano's pain. "That's worse, a lot worse."

"Where can you get a *colada*?" He thought about getting one in Salsipuedes, over on Calle Ocho. But on one of his senseless spins around the city, he spotted a liquor store not too far from the Miami River and he went inside. From a distance, Maribarbola followed him carefully.

Nicotiano didn't know what he was looking for. More alcohol was out of the question.

The woman at the cash register was black. She was reading a book and interrupted her reading to eyeball the apparent customer, just to make sure he didn't rip something off. The establishment was sordid and ugly, like practically everything else in that area near to the river. The sculptor roamed aimlessly among the shelves of bottles like someone who wandered into a museum by accident. Finally he approached the cash register. He stood in front of the woman and looked into her eyes.

"What do you want?" she said.

"I honestly don't know," Nicotiano replied, and without meaning to, and unable to hold back, he started crying.

The girl watched him, not trusting him in the slightest.

"If you feel sick, go see a doctor," she said rudely.

"I'm sorry," Nicotiano said, trying to control himself, and he emphasized: "Sorry."

"No sweat."

She kept looking at him. She had a gun under the counter; in the few weeks she had been there, she'd been robbed eight times. The weapon was to defend herself, not the money in the register. What did the stranger want?

"Don't be afraid. I'm a ruined man."

"I can tell. Go see a doctor."

"I had a wife who was like the air I breathe. And she left me for another man."

"That can happen to anyone. Don't go killing yourself just because of that."

And she smiled weakly.

"Thanks for smiling, you don't know how much I appreciate that."

"It's nothing."

Her hands were delicate, dark on the backside, light in the palms.

"You have very pretty hands."

"Thanks."

"I'm pretty crushed inside."

"I can tell."

"You've never suffered anything similar?"

"I've suffered."

"Yeah, there's something in your appearance...People who haven't suffered don't interest me. I honestly don't know why I'm telling you all this."

"Just try to take it easy."

"Forgive me if I seem ridiculous."

"I think you're really depressed. Try to do something pleasant."

"Together. Couldn't we do something nice together?"

"I don't know who you are, and you don't know who I am."

"I'm Nicotiano, a sculptor from the Island of Cundeamor."

"There's no such place as that island, sir."

Nicotiano took out a handkerchief and dried his eyes.

"Well then, I invite you to come and see it for yourself. You have to meet my Aunt Ulalume, and see my studio of sculptures. I sculpt crabs out of marble, granite, alabaster...In fact, I invite you to come fishing with me, or to take a ride on my boat, *El Villalona.*

Could he be crazy?

"You're Cuban, right?"

"Yes; I mean, I was born in Cuba...My Aunt got me out of there when I was barely a kid. Do you work here all the time?"

"I'm a student."

"What do you study?"

"Medicine. Only one more year before I graduate. Now I'm going through the procedures and saving money to take a trip to Cuba."

Nicotiano stood there dumbfounded. He was laughing and crying at the same time.

"What you are is drunk. Go home and get some sleep."

There was almost an intimacy in the young woman's voice.

"Sure, Sure! I'm drunk but you give me great joy..."

"Everything's hard in Cuba, especially after the collapse of the socialist...there's no oil, there's such a scarcity of food. But they say that the people hold on with nobility and joy...Or with resignation and fear, who knows...In any case, I like Cubans over there better than the ones here. I don't know if I'm idealizing them."

"I have faith that Cuba will save itself," Nicotiano said in one of those lucid moments that drunks sometime experience. "Other countries would like to see Cuba auctioned off, and want the subordination of Cuban peoples' irreplaceable interests, within a unipolar international situation, with This Country as Big Boss who nobody dares to contradict. I don't know whether you are aware of it, ma'am, but since the start of the century, Cuba's only enemies from within have been the ignorant, anti-national and economistic bourgeoisie, and internationally, the interests representing This Country. I'm skipping over the way Cuba will save itself as a nation, since communism does not solve the peoples' problems, either. My hope is that everything won't end in a bloodbath."

"I see you're not just another *gusano*."

"I'm just a single man."

"I see."

"Would you accept an invitation to come to the Island of Cundeamor some day?"

She smiled kindly, and her eyes showed open sympathy for the man, who was crying and laughing like a child. But she shook her head.

"I have other customers. Time for you to leave, please," she said courteously.

Nicotiano stepped away from the register to let the other customers pass, but he kept staring at her with a mixture of abandonment and desire. She had thick lips, beautifully formed, painted in a tasteful shade of red; her teeth were smallish; very white and uneven in a way that made her even more beautiful. Two other people were waiting in line to check out.

"Bye," he said.

"Bye," and she smiled again.

'Thanks," and he still didn't leave.

"Get some sleep; it'll do you some good," and another smile chopped through the sculptor's desperation.

The Salsipuedes was a small bar on our property. When Hetkinen and I bought it, it was called El Mojito, but I changed the name. For the longest time it was leased to a friend named Chucho Garsiendía, who ran the place with his daughter, Pájara Pinta. Chucho was a bit of a crook, but he paid his rent on time until one day, after a killer lunch full of tons of pork, he keeled over, dead of a heart attack. It was no secret to us that Chucho had turned the Salispuedes into a den of iniquity where riff-raff, petty criminals and arms and drug dealers would meet, a situation that didn't get any better when his daughter ran the place alone. But Pájara would hear all kinds of secrets of the Latin underworld there, very valuable information that Hetkinen could systematically learn from the young woman. In this way, El Salsipuedes was a source of income and also a source of information for the Crabb

Company. In addition, there was an unchanging clientele of old retired Cubans, people of humble extraction, the Poor Old Guard of the Cuba of Yesteryear, who would while away the day drinking beer (always putting it on the tab), and playing dominos without caring much that around them, more or less illegal activities were being conducted.

Nicotiano went in and took a seat at the bar. The Salsipuedes could use a total remodeling, but it was still clean enough for man to enjoy a beer without having to worry about the glass. An enormous painting of the Sacred Heart of Jesus, ghostly illuminated with lamps, and a couple of vases full of white gladiolas dominated the whole place. Four old-timers were playing dominos, all of them dressed in tee-shirts and sweating bullets. Nicotiano heard them discussing how best to go about toppling Castro. One was saying how the Armed Revolutionary Forces would turn against Fidel, deliver a withering coup d'etat and put a bullet in him. Another one said that the most practical solution would be for Fidel (whose father, after all, was a Galician immigrant who made a fortune in Cuba) to seek asylum in the Spanish Embassy in Havana, from where they would send him to some small forgotten town in Galicia so he could spend his final years of his pernicious life carrying on the revolution among those savages. The third man, the only one of the four who was thin, bordering on cadaverous, was chattering on, not letting the other ones finish their harangues: Raúl Castro, Raúl Castro, he repeated, is definitely blood-thirsty, you'll definitely have to kill him first. The fourth player, who spoke slowly, with a voice the wad of tobacco in his mouth made nasal, completed the reasoning with a calm estimate:

"Once Both of Them are off the map, after getting rid of some 700,000 more communists on the whole island, it'll be ready for us to once again construct a democratic future once again."

"What a wonderful surprise," Pájara Pinta said. "Nicotiano coming home! Happy are these eyes that see you."

Pájara was about thirty years old, the widow of a Cuban who came over on the Mariel boat lift and one day disappeared, only to be found a week later floating in Indian Creek with seven bullet holes in the back and his hands chopped off. A month later his hands turned up at the door of the Salsipuedes, still half-frozen.

Pájara Pinta was incredibly beautiful and had the reputation of being a gossip and quick to open her legs to anyone who fancied her. Before, Nicotiano had hardly even paid attention to her. Immersed in the world of his sculptures, the Crabb Company and Mireya, he had not had eyes for other women, despite all the ones who chased after him. That's why Pájara's mouth dropped when after she asked him what he'd like, Nicotiano replied:

"A *colada* and to give you a kiss, Pájara Rica."

When she got over her surprise, she grew animated.

"Wait, I'll put on some music," was her response and the place filled with the piano and bubbling rhythm of bongo beats, with saxophones in melodic layers that came in one after the other like currents of water with different colors and, finally, with the whole orchestra and its height of metals leading into the sassy chorus and seductive voice of Benny Moré floating over the cascade of colored water:

> *¡Castellano, qué rico and qué bueno baila usted!*
> *¡Cosa buena, mira cómo baila y usted no lo ve!*
> *Decían que yo no venía, ¡y aquí usted me ve!*

Pájara began to sway there behind the bar: not to dance; to move her hips without speaking, looking at Nicotiano, while she fixed two stiff *mojitos* with rum and too much mint for the size of the glasses.

"I asked for a *colada* and a kiss, not a *mojito*."

"Shut up and drink," she said with an irresistible authority.

"According to Aunt Ulalume, mint is an anti-spasmodic, anti-dismenorreica and anti-hypochondriac..."

She started laughing.

"Cheers!" she said. "And what else?"

"An anaphrodisiac."

"What's that?"

"It diminishes sexual appetite, lessens an excessive desire to enjoy sensual pleasures."

"So I did good by putting a lot of mint in the *mojito*. That way we won't kill each other right away. Cheers."

"I love you, Pájara."

"Liar; you need me."

"I like you, Pájara."

"That I do know for sure. Just swear it's not talk."

"I swear on Aunt Ulalume."

She became alarmed and knocked on the wood of the bar.

"Don't be cruel, kiddo! How can you swear on the person who loves you most in the world? Don't you see that you can cause her irreparable harm?"

With a single finger, Nicotiano traced her neckline without ever touching her breasts.

"Did Mireya leave you yet?"

"You knew she was seeing somebody else?'

"Even the light posts knew about it, Nicotiano," and she also caressed his face with one finger.

"I'm in bad shape, Pájara, real bad shape."

"You feel bad, but you'll get over it. Because you're also rich, really rich, you're a very attractive man, Nico, not handsome, but, yes, mysterious, half-crazy and your skin gives off an intense manliness. Your despair won't take that away from you; quite the contrary, you're now sending out the desire to let yourself go free, seek excitement, and that makes you even more interesting. Think about that when you're suffering. The Mireyas who want to sleep and share their life with a man like you are a dime a dozen. If she wanted someone else, well then, to hell with her."

She pulled herself up onto the counter and kissed him.

"You were always untouchable, Nicotiano," now she caressed the thick hair on his forearms. "Well, I don't know how to put this, just that you're not for me. You and Mireya, seen from afar...look, I just don't know how she's managed to mess this up, because you two were made for each other."

"But everything ends. Trees die, so do sadness and joy."

"True," she sighed. "Everything can go to hell in a day."

"Close the bar, Pájara," he begged.

"You're damn right, I'm going to close up. And you can do whatever you want with me."

Politely, but very firmly, Pájara threw out the old domino players. It wasn't hard; El Salsipuedes was unpredictable and, come what may, nobody would ask embarrassing questions.

They made intense love. It was as if Nicotiano didn't ever want to come out of her. Not out of that liquor inside of her that burned his hardened sex with contractions that were almost kisses, almost hickeys, to the *son* of the undulations of the young woman's delicious hips. Pájara had always desired Nicotiano and now it seemed like a dream to possess him. To have him inside. To have him all to herself in that prolonged moment in the universe. To give him pleasure. To trap him. "To screw him my way," she thought. She kissed him all over and well, she dug her teeth into the sculptor's broad shoulders and sucked his fingers while he, now outside of himself, fit himself inside her with the impetus of someone who wanted to stave off death.

Then she fixed him a strong coffee *colada*. Nicotiano looked at the young woman's body with lust and admiration, and he felt grateful. That woman had made him human again, he thought. Real. A flesh and blood man.

"It's too hot in here to keep making love."

"You love her a lot, don't you?"

He nodded.

"Nicotiano, you're too much for me. I don't want to fall in love with you."

"I want to fall in love with you. At this moment, you're everything to me. You're affectionate and fresh, Pájara."

"At this moment. But what about in the next moment?"

"You're capable of feeling nice things. Nobody is too good for you."

Pájara Pinta felt that something was tying her up and then snapped at a point right between her breasts. No male had ever told her that: that she, Pájara, the whore, the cheap blow job queen, the pervert easy to seduce with glances, the vulgar waitress of the Salsipuedes, was capable of feeling nice things. And nobody was too good for her.

Her eyes flooded with tears, and she repeated:

"Oh, Nicotiano, I don't want to fall in love with you!"

He remained silent.

"Nicotiano," she guessed, "Mireya had to have been really confused, or very worked up, the poor thing, to leave you for that asshole."

It was if someone had plunged an ice pick into him.

Nicotiano leapt up in the folding bed in which they were lying and said:

"Pájara, do you know who the guy is?"

She grew frightened.

"You don't know yet? Nobody's told you?"

"Tell me who he is."

Her voice trembled. Her unforgivable indiscretion! There was something terrifying in Nicotiano's look.

"Nico, don't go doing anything stupid…"

"Who the hell is it?"

"Nicotiano, you don't have any right to disgrace yourself over anyone…"

He began dressing like a man being chased by a ghost.

"I want you to tell me who he is, Pájara!"

"He's the owner of South Gallery."

"I'm leaving."

"Are you going to kill him, Nicotiano? Oh Dear God, I have such a big mouth!"

He stopped.

"That son of a bitch...And I've even displayed my sculptures there. Do you know him?"

"Yeah and he's a nobody. I've slept with him several times and he doesn't do anything, he doesn't know anything, he screws like a fifteen-year-old kid."

Maribarbola was staking out the place from outside. This was par for the course since work for the Crabb Company usually consisted of the endless tedium of the stake-out. However, now it was different. Now it was his brother. And what would happen if in his madness he committed a crime, or hurt himself?

The most important task, Hetkinen would say, is to bear the monotony, check things out, spy, sniff around, wait things out, lie in wait, observe and pick up on the smallest details. How many times had Maribarbola spent more than 12 hours straight staking out a house, a car, a supermarket or a window! Or sometimes, simply, a telephone booth, a trash can or a pack of cigarettes somebody tossed aside, carelessly, at a bus stop. In that art of vigilance, spying and lying in wait, Maribarbola was the Crabb Company's best men. Guarapito, on the other hand, was a disaster. He got impatient, talked incessantly, always had to go take a leak, couldn't stave off hunger, fell asleep, wanted to listen to music, bitched about how staking somebody out made him feel constipated. Sikitrake was more composed and stoic, while Bartolo was silent, awake and obedient, his only defect being his constantly drinking coffee. Hetkinen would say: "the qualities we need are: to make quick decisions, have a strong resistance to physical and psychological mistreatment, and have a great mental agility, not to mention being proficient in firearms, personal defense and technical matters." The areas of the Crabb Company's operations were sordid and varied: private investigations, discreet protection, stake-out service and information (absolutely guaranteed), Infidelities and Questionable Conduct (total discretion and incontrovertible proof), Quick-strike Operations, Transport and protection of funds...

When Maribarbola saw that his brother was heading for the South Gallery, he realized that Pájara had let the cat out of the bag and he was prepared to intervene in time to avoid a disaster. This time the sculptor didn't drive in circles; he parked the car quickly and poorly in front of the art gallery and stormed in like a cyclone. Maribarbola couldn't quite see whether Nicotiano, as he got out of his car, had grabbed the gun, which according to our rules he was obligated to carry concealed under the seat.

The man was in his office. Nicotiano moved like a flash past the secretary, who recognized him and stuttered in admiration: "Mr. Nicotiano..." And suddenly he found himself standing before the lover of his Mireya.

The man, recovering from his surprise, defended himself:

"She's tired of you, that's not my fault. You two have gone your separate ways and I fancy the girl quite a bit."

"Quite a bit..." Nicotiano repeated, his eyes like two embers.

"There's nothing to do, Nicotiano! Besides, let me tell you she chased after me and covered me with her desire and affection and it was she, for the most part, who seduced me. I'm no therapist, she came to me with a violent load of resentment against you...fed up with her situation. But let's be friends, patch things up in a civilized fashion...At the start I told her: "Mireya, don't fall in love with me, look, this is just a game..."

The only thing Nicotiano managed to get out was:

"And to think that I've shown my crab sculptures here...Did you know I respected you? Not as a friend, but as a professional, I don't know, as an acquaintance in this crummy city. A game...now I can see that you're a cynic and a lowlife. But she's too much of a woman for you. You can't be with her because intellectually, you're a dwarf. And sexually, you're an even bigger dwarf. For all of my spite, I pity you."

And he turned to leave.

"Nicotiano!" the gallery owner screamed.

The sculptor stopped and turned half-way around.

"Too much of a woman for you, dwarf," he repeated with disgust.

Almost at the door, Nicotiano saw a basket of fruit on a little table surrounded by armchairs there was a basket of fruit. They looked very ripe, and Nicotiano, swiftly, grabbed a wrinkled, almost rotten *papayita*, suddenly whirled around, and as if he were a pitcher who was angry at just losing his no-hitter, smacked the man right in the face.

"She's mine, oh great artist!" Nicotiano yelled over his shoulder as the man cleaned off his face, removing a seed from his eye.

"I took her away from you so easy and you are the dwarf! A couple of little glances, a little bit of flirting and lickety split I had her right here, take a look, sucking what I have here!"

By the time the man said this, Nicotiano, luckily, was already in his car. Neither of the men noticed that Maribarbola had been hiding behind the office door all that time, poised to intervene, with the secretary frozen and her mouth covered to avoid a scene.

What Nicotiano really needed was a writer's ability to put words together, but now he was reduced to writing a note he would cast into the sea currents, and that's why as he drove he was mentally repeating what he would write:

> Dear friend:
> A stage of my life has ended. An incomprehensible blindness caused me not to pick up on Mireya's true state beforehand. Her dissatisfaction. Her unhappiness. The damaging consequences of her sterility. The obsessive work has been a substitute for a country that I don't have, and that made me stop seeing her. She, who was the parcel of terra firme upon which my cretivity and productivity rested. Now, to begin yet again.

The beach was almost deserted. Next to a cabana not too far off, he could make out a group of people, maybe a whole family, grandparents, uncles, kids. They spoke with lots of jumping around, grandiose gestures, loud laughter. The ocean was a deep indigo color and almost at dead calm. The waves reached the sand like tired kisses. Nicotiano sat on the sand and wrote: "Dear friend", reproducing a version of what he had been thinking. He stuck the piece of paper inside the rum bottle, capped it tight and, without taking off his shoes or rolling up his pants, waded into the water up to his waist and threw the bottle as far as he could into the ocean.

He looked at the horizon and started to cry again.

Without his noticing it, two kids sneaked up on him. The older one was skinny, his hair cropped close, almost shaved, and he wore a pair of glasses with really thick lenses. The other kid was rounder, shorter, with lots of curly hair.

"Look," the younger one said. "A crying man."

"Yeah," the oldest one verified matter-of-factly. "he's come to cry at the ocean."

"His mom must have died," the youngest one conjectured.

Nicotiano turned around and the kids seemed like a mirage to him.

"It wasn't my mother who died," he said. "It's my wife."

"That must be almost the same thing, no?" asked the one with the thick glasses.

A red and white plane passed over the beach, moving slowly to the naked eye, barely advancing, looking for the airport. The three of them looked up.

"Look," one of the boys said. "Nothing like a shark."

"Planes can't swim," the other one corrected. "They fly."

"Yeah, they swim, swim in the sky."

"What did you throw in the ocean, sir?"

"A bottle. Look, it shines in the sun."

"With a message inside, like someone who's shipwrecked?"

"Yes," the sculptor said. "You can be on land and still be ship-wrecked."

Nicotiano came out of the water.

"You are both Cuban, right?"

"We were born here," the youngest one informed him seriously.

"But we're still Cubans," the one in glasses said. "Some here, some over there."

And pulling something out of his pocket, he added:

"Look, I'll give you this: a snail."

Nicotiano studied it. It was the size of a *mamey* seed, but had a clean and thick orange color, with some tiny brown streaks and fanciful lines in a yellowish shade. Towards the inside of the spirals, the orange became brighter. On the outside, the snail had pure white alkaline formations.

"That snail will bring you good luck."

And saying this, they ran off.

Nicotiano clutched the little snail and put it in his pocket.

In the liquor store, there was another clerk, a wan-looking woman with barely any lower teeth. Next to her at the register was a fat man, sound asleep. Nicotiano didn't ask any questions. He continued on his way, planning to return to the Island of Cundeamor, but he went to over to Calle Ocho and parked. Guayacán Restorán. Calibarién Supermarket. Antojitos Jewelry. Ayestarán Parking Lot. He turned on the radio and WQBA ("The Most Cuban"), then WRHC ("The Blue Station") and another station, but they all said the same thing: the fall of Castro was imminent, "...next Christmas Eve...in Havana!" Professors in the University of Florida, the announcer said, were a bunch of "liberaloids, lefterds, protocommunistst traitors and abjects who scoff at the idea of a Free Cuba..." On Union Radio, he heard something about the Island of Cundeamor, a high-ranking official from the Cuban American Transaction said that there was only one house left on the island, "inhabited by a famous security company and a Cuban sculptor who..." Nicotiano turned the radio off and thought he should get something to eat, but he couldn't think of any place. He really wasn't sure if he was even hungry. He felt a sudden urge to find the girl from the liquor store, but the clues he had were so scant that even Hitkenen himself would have had problems tracking her down.

Then he thought he absolutely had to see Mireya, hear her arguments again and then shoot them down. Or just to give her a kiss, even it was just on the forehead, or maybe even on the lips. Or maybe to kill her. But he was certain that all of this was absurd. Come on: she was in love with someone else, someone he thought was just a nobody, a pencil pusher, a nothing with a lower case "n". But that too was absurd, as well as a weak construction he had invented just to go on living. Because if that guy didn't have charm, he would not have swept her off her feet. Of course that dwarf from the gallery, at least to Mireya, was charming, a nice guy, and a cloud of sadness and jealousy enveloped Nicotiano. He saw Mireya passionately screwing her lover, heard her moaning as the guy was sticking it to her hard, and he thought he would explode in an anguish that felt like one painful stab after another, right in the middle of his chest.

As he was driving, again at a high speed, he stuck his hand in the pocket of his soaking-wet pants to clutch the little snail the kids had given him. "This snail will bring you luck," he mentally repeated, but the little snail wasn't in his pocket. He pulled the car over. He went through all his pockets, his shirt, searched the seat and under the seat, searched the whole car like a man possessed, and then went through all of his pockets again. But it wasn't there. It wasn't there!

He felt like puking, and couldn't hold back. He threw open the door and vilely puked in the street. He wiped his mouth off with a handkerchief, which luckily was wet with salt water, and left it on the pavement along with the steaming vomit.

Then he knew that the only thing he had left inside was a smothering sadness. He tried to hum a Silvio Rodríguez song that went: "I don't know why I'm crying, why I'm dying", but he couldn't even remember the words.

He stopped by the Salsipuedes and picked up Pájara Pinta.

Me and Doublestein

"Ula, why's this island called the Island of Cundeamor?"

"That really delicate climbing plant you see over there, covering part of the pergola, the wrought-iron gate and the fence, that's cundeamor. *Here it's also called Wild Balsam Apple, in Brazil it's called* Meloa de San Caetano *and in Latin it's called* Momordica

Charantia."

"*I don't see anything so special about it.*"

"*It's a wild plant, and, as you can see, a climbing plant. In Cuba it grows on fences of patios, in fields and on farms. My house in Cuba had lots of* cundeamor, *whose fruits attracted* zorzales *and* sinsontes *and lots of other kinds of birds.*"

"*It's a worthless plant; it looks more like a weed and its flowers are not as pretty as you say.*"

"*They're simple little flowers, a yellow shade that a little sun makes more pronounced. Take a good look at the fruits of the* cundeamor, *Double. They're yellow and indehiscent, that's why you have to open them this way, to release the seeds...*"

"*They're red.*"

"*Yes, bright red. And they're quite sweet...Here, taste them...*"

"*No way, Ulalume! Get that wild fruit away from me.*"

"*In Cuba, the kids in the countryside eat them like sweets, and the Chinese would fix a delicious dish with the tender cooked fruits of the* cundeamor."

"*I'm not some Chinaman living in Cuba.*"

"*The* cundeamor *has multiple properties: it is, for example, a vermicide...*"

"*Disgusting.*"

"*It's an anti-helminthic. It fights against all kinds of worms and parasites.*"

"*Well then we'll have to mass produce that drink and pass it out in Miami, to see if we can do away with the parasitical Cuban-American 'worms'.*"

"*Cooking the* cundeamor, *with a couple of pieces of bell leaves, can expel tricocefalos worms...*"

"*The Miami Cuban American gusano worms are all a headless kind.*"

"*Try to contain the envy you have toward all us Cubans, and swallow your prejudices. Fidel coined that term of "Gusanera," or wormy, as a blanket term denigrating all of us who left his socialist paradise. Without a doubt, there are true "worms" in Miami, but all of us aren't.*"

"*We have to cook the* cundeamor *for all of them.*"

"*The* cundeamor *reestablishes women's menstrual fluid; it's good for liver stones and cures rashes, eczema and herpes.*"

"*Who knew that such a sickly plant could have so many qualities? It's like you Cubans: climbing everywhere and, who knows, maybe even a little poisonous, despite the sweetness of the seeds.*"

"*You can use everything from the* cundeamor: *its leaves, fruits, stems, roots...but what I haven't said yet is that it can also be harmful.*"

"*You see? Like you Cubans.*"

"*The* cundeamor *has hypnotizing powers, or produces a reduction in strength and, according to the dosage, even deep depression.*"

"*And you wanted me to eat those little seeds!*"

"*The seeds are good, silly; however, juice taken from the inside of the fruit is a powerful drastic purgative, capable of making you throw up even your dark soul, which must be getting corrupted in one of the sewers of your Yankee organism.*"

"*Ugh! the tropics sure do produce freaks.*"

"*Do you know, Double honey, why this island is called the Island of Cundeamor?*"

"*Well, I at least have an idea.*"

"*And finally, I can tell you that a famous biologist lists the cundeamor among plants that are 'doubtful or questionable'.*"

"*C'mon, Ula, let's talk business.*"

- Nine -

*T*he loss of Mireya's company, coupled with Nicotiano's crazy reaction, had left me adrift. To see him suffering aimlessly, without any appetite or getting any sleep kept me in a constant state of vertigo, that goddamned feeling of impotence. I also lost my appetite and ordered Maribarbola to keep his eyes on Nicotiano. To follow him everywhere! To top it off, Mireya didn't even call me. Was her resentment that bitter? She could at least drop by, how are you, Aunt Ulalume, I don't want to ever hear anything about Nicotiano, but you, how can live without me, how are you, have you missed me? Who's handing all the paperwork at the Crabb Company? But nothing. It was if all the years of intimacy and daily contact had disappeared.

That's when Betty Boop arrived.

Betty was a blast of fresh air that dissipated the grim air of all my troubles. The poor thing arrived looking unwell, her nerves shot, all alone in the world and without a penny to her name. Shame consumed her: the frustration of "not having accomplished anything in exile, only failure after failure."

"I won't be a burden," she told me resolutely. "Help me out for a month or two, give me a home, a bed and one meal per day. After a few months I'll get a job and be on my way."

But I treated her like a queen. I made her rest, I fed her well, we went out together and had a good time, I bought her nice, decent clothes. Betty wasn't a woman who could stand feeling dependent, and I didn't try to convince her to stay and live permanently on the Island of Cundeamor. But I did do everything possible to make her to feel better and to get her to stay for at least a year.

Betty Boop's presence rejuvenated me. During long evenings drinking wine from Rioja or frozen daiquiris, next to the pool or by on shores of the bay, Betty told me about her terrible descent into hell and some other odd tobacco she smoked with me. We cried together, howled with laughter, swam until we were both exhausted. Sometimes, to the song of dawn, we would go down to Miami Beach and skinny dip. But so as to not to call attention to us, just in case some Jew boarder had gotten up early in their beach hotel to go for a swim, we would enter the ocean in our bikinis. But once we were in the water we would strip like two naughty little girls, receive the wet caresses of the early morning water. We were sometimes the object of a different kind of unexpected caresses. As we placidly floated in the fresh and transparent water, with the landscapes of pastel-colored hotels before us, a huge school of gray mullets surrounded us, playful, thrashing about, chaotic like children rushing out of school, brushing past our naked bodies with their fins and their hard bodies, slipping away without harming us in the slightest. The mornings in the ocean were splendid, and if a squall was coming, the sky would then divide in half, black on one side and bright on the other, with both of us swimming in the quiet before the storm. The distant ships floated between darkness and brilliance, as if in a pond of mercury.

Our high living standard gave Betty a bit of an inferiority complex. When she saw our library, she was dazzled. Our collection of Cuban paintings from all periods left her impressed; she didn't know who was who or what was what, but the beauty of the images and my explanations stoked her curiosity.

"You're a learned woman," she said to me; "I'm a superstitious ass. This city is full of asses, and you all are the exception."

As she was searching for her own path in life, Betty started taking private classes in "general culture." Since there was no television to watch in our house, Betty started reading novels, and little by little she made it a habit to read a newspaper or magazine every day. In *The Miami Herald*, she found the ad for classes in "general culture." The teacher was a mulatto who'd just arrived from Cuba, handsome and learned, and Betty would have fallen in love with him if he hadn't been queer. Just a few days after starting her classes, she said to me:

"To improve my vocabulary, my teacher recommended that I buy a dictionary of pseudonyms."

"Don't you mean synonyms, Betty?"

I paid for her classes, and it was a real pleasure to do so, since Betty, after all the hard knocks she'd suffered, deserved the best in the world. She also picked up singing. She decided she was a "lyrical soprano" and in the late afternoons we would sing Cuban *danzones*. She had a profound respect for Hetkinen:

"What a great man you've got, Ula."

"I had to find him at the end of the world, Betty."

And I told her what I could about my husband. I say "what I could" because Hetkinen's life is tinged with unconfessable events.

"He comes from a family of farmers who lived in a mythical forest in Carelia; when he was young he left for Helsinki, where he became a cop whose sole job was to plan and put into action, with as much impunity as possible, a master plan to round up some capital. After numerous and careful preparations, down to the last detail, he and another associate knocked over an armored car. The other thief went to Australia with his share of the loot and Hetkinen took his money, crossed the Swiss border and hid out for a while in Haparanda. His disguise was perfect and he had a fake passport. That's where I met him.

"Haparanda," Betty said surprised. "That sounds kind of like that dance, the *parranda*."

"But it isn't; Haparanda is a sleepy town, a few streets, nothing festive about it at all, they have a bitter white winter, year round. And in the summertime, they say there are clouds of mosquitoes that come down from the Laplander glacial regions and blanket the midnight sun. But I don't know about that, since I was there only for one memorable winter. Nicotiano and I passed through, since every winter sculptors from every country in the world meet there, just to sculpt in ice. Nicotiano was fascinated with the idea of producing the most ephemeral and fragile of works of art, an ice sculpture: a dazzling, transparent, gigantic ice crab. Hitkenen was holed up in the hotel, disguised, armed, on the lam, flushed with cash and, as I already told you, carrying fake papers. At first glance we fell in love and I smuggled him into the Miami dream.

"Ula," Betty responded, "when you say 'the Miami dream' what I see is really a nightmare."

If Betty hadn't come into my life at that precise moment, I think I would have gone crazy. Nicotiano continued to suffer deeply, and I barely saw him. He refused to talk to me, had completely abandoned his sculptures and the guys all said it was impossible to have a coherent conversation with him. What little I knew about him was what Maribarbola told me, that he couldn't always keep an eye on him since he had his work for the Company. I anxiously awaited the supply of headstones with the names and epitaphs in Spanish that I had put Kupiec in charge of getting, but he was running behind and I began to fear that maybe they'd bumped him off. One day they'd find his body tangled up in the mangroves that grew along McArthur, or maybe riddled with holes in his junk store. Betty spoke of him both fondly and with spite, and didn't want to see him.

"I want to keep going," she would say. "Better alone than in bad company."

"Go on," I spurred, "go on."

Betty and I agreed to organize a dinner party, invite some people from the Island of Cundeamor to eat, drink and gab. Guarapito and Cocorioco would be in charge of the food. Poor Cocorioco had reacted to Nicotiano's anguish pretty calmly, but he was very worried and the responsibility of a huge feast would distract him. Besides, he had a permanent toothache, but of course you could forget about his going to see a dentist.

Like two teenagers, Betty and I shaved off our eyebrows to paint new ones on and achieve, as she would say, 'the desired effect.' Both of us were convinced that we were aging in the most pleasant way possible.

But there was something Betty didn't dare tell me. She was happy on the Island of Cundeamor, she felt appreciated and from the first moment all of us treated her like a member of our family, but she felt a need, like a crater in her heart and I noticed it. Finally she confessed:

"Oh, Ula, what I need at my age is a man who will show me affection and who will love me."

And she told me that with the help of her teacher of "general culture" she had written a classified ad that she planned to run in the newspaper. The text went like this:

> WANTED: a gentleman (divorced or legally a widower) who has all the following characteristics: 1) physical appearance: pleasant to look at and to touch (not too thick or fussy). 2) Age: approximately between 45 and 60. 3) Race: doesn't matter in the slightest; nor does nationality or skin color. Also: very good cultural and social level, even tempered, healthy, decisive, of refined morals, sincere, and sleeps well. And, above all, he must like and care about marriage. The PETITIONER is a widow of an elevated social status, without any economic or family problems, distinguished, sensitive, hard-working and faithful.

I liked it. It sounded like Betty, with her special mix of dreams and truths, desires and realities. I urged her to publish that classified ad as soon as possible, and I realized I could do the same to find an appropriate young girl with whom to replace Mireya, to handle the paperwork at the Crabb Company and who could also help me with the book about Nicotiano and the Island of Cundeamor that I was going to write. After many changes, my text was finally ready:

> Looking for a single or married woman no older than 35 who, whether ugly or not, white, pretty, black, rich or poor, has all the following requirements: she has to be able to keep secrets; have a perfect knowledge, oral and written, of Spanish. She has to have a clear understanding of friendship and honor. She must be able to handle secretarial duties. We offer extra salary benefits. Those interested will be submitted to a rigorous selection interview.

We decided to mail the classifieds so they would run in the Sunday edition of the *Herald*. Then, all that was left to do was to wait.

One day, Mireya finally called.

"How good it is to hear your voice," I said to her.

"Don't hate me, Aunt Ulalume."

"I love you, my dear, tell me how you're doing."

"I don't want to see Nicotiano for ever and ever, amen. But you...Do you miss me?"

"A lot. All the time. You will always be my Mireya. But now that you no longer live here...Couldn't you stop speaking so formally to me?"

"I don't want to. You are too strong a personality. And I always need to keep a certain distance."

"To keep me under control?"

"So you wouldn't overwhelm me with your care and affection. How's he doing?"

"He?"

"He."

"Quite well," I lied.

"I don't believe you, Aunt Ulalume. I know he's suffering like crazy about me."

"Does the new light of your life love you?"

"He's put me on a pedestal. For now we're living in my mom's house."

"How come?"

"Well…There's another woman, one he's got to get rid of…"

"I see."

"If you want, tell him I called. And that I am happy, to put it simply."

"I'll tell him," I lied again.

"I've found my roots. Now I know who I am."

And she hung up. She hung up!

Doublestein came to see me one afternoon. I welcomed him openly, since I enjoyed his company. I wanted to propose a business and talk about our projects.

Doublestein had the waspiest voice of all the Anglos living in Dade County. His Spanish was cute; amazingly, he got all the subjunctives right, and his rrrrrs were quite human. He wasn't just anybody: Double was my friend and, in addition, my main business associate in the commercialization of Nicotiano's sculptures. Without him, we would probably be up to our ears in crabs on the Island of Cundeamor, victims of Nicotiano's overproduction.

Double was an efficient art dealer, an eclectic collector and he was intelligent. He ran galleries in Boston, New York, San Francisco and Miami. His network across the country was impressive. Double was a kind of refined knave, a fox at auctions and an investor who was always on the mark. His specialties included old paintings, nineteenth century European paintings, impressionist and post-impressionist paintings, modern painting and sculpture, contemporary art in general, continental European ceramics, Chinese ceramics, English silver and, to a lesser extent, French furniture. Double was absolutely convinced that Nicotiano's crabs would be worth millions, if the subtleties of marketing were applied to them.

Betty didn't like Doublestein. Hitkinen didn't like him either, and Kafka couldn't stand the sight of him. Kafka's grudge against him was mysterious and also somewhat embarrassing. More than once, Kafka had ripped Doublestein's pants to shreds. What was strange is that he never hurt him, just terrorized him. With respect to Hetkinen, it was normal for him to dislike Doublestein: my husband still retained the harshness, rustic quality and self-absorption of a Finnish farmer. Double, on the other hand, was worldly and communicative, with the refined and somewhat affected behavior of born winners, those who never had to start from scratch. I didn't like Doublestein as a man. I civilized Hetkinen. I would have had to decivilize Double to be able to enjoy him. And, nevertheless, you had to admit that he was attractive. Old without hiding it, always tan, neither soft nor muscular, his chest covered with curly gray hair, and on his face and neck he had those kinds of wrinkles that on men look more attractive than ugly.

He came dressed in white, a Montecristo cigar in the corner of his smile. He greeted Hetkinen and Betty, who was reading under the umbrellas.

"You should have named the dog Marx and the cat Kafka," was the first thing he said.

Hetkinen had taken the day off and was leafing through the newspaper. I know he was listening closely to Double's words. Betty had learned to make my husband's favorite drink, the *koskencoco*, and brought out three on a small tray. The *koskencoco* was composed of Koskenkorva vodka, fresh coconut water, full of crushed ice, Malibu and a very drops of Cointreau, all of it mixed well.

We got down to business. In Italy, Doublestein had sold a small series of alabaster crabs for $60,000. We cheered, and I saw that Betty was speechless when she heard that figure. The other matter that our art dealer and friend wanted to review were the preparations for Nicotiano's grand opening.

"We have to sell your nephew in the Personality Market of Art. It's time to put him through the Celebrity Machinery. Nicotiano can't keep being the "invisible genius." That's a waste and an absurd whim: we're not living in the Sinai desert."

A plump fly turned in the radiant light and its fat ass perched upon the edge of Doublestein's glass. Hetkinen observed it and I noticed of his evil satisfaction. A plane flew low and made a sound like it was at war.

"It's an Eastern DC-10," Double said. "Here the unpleasant sounds come from the sky, not from the ground."

"Such is the Island of Cundeamor."

Double discovered the stupid fly, and it shocked him. He then took the Montecristo cigar from his mouth and spoke with visionary grace:

"I've promised collectors and investors that Nicotiano's going to emerge, once and for all, from the pseudoanonymity in which he so stubbornly remains. That is, we're going to take him out of that anonymity. We're going to sell his face and words. A concise essay on his work, as well as an interview, will come out in *Art in America* magazine. And in *Playboy*, with a pair of really hot-looking blondes, posing completely naked on a black granite crab. We shall open eight exhibitions simultaneously in eight different cities. Nicotiano will give interviews, sign autographs, attend the charity balls of the Artistic World.

Your nephew can eventually become one of the Greats of our time."

As we were talking, Betty and Hetkinen, drowsy, sipped from their *koskenkocos*. Kafka was looking at us from the *arecas*.

"Where's Marx?" Doublestein said.

"Sleeping in some quiet corner."

As if an invocation, a lizard darted past us and Double made a disgusted face. But before he finished, Marx burst onto the scene and nabbed the lizard with his bare teeth. Wagging his head, and making the reptile's body twist convulsively, Marx impassively wandered off into the weeds.

"That's disgusting," Doublestein shouted.

"Double, do you hate all animals?"

"Of all the animals, I can only stand women."

"Thanks a lot," I said, without looking at him. "Lizards, just like roaches, crabs, crickets, fish and vane men, make up our culture."

"Name just one insect that doesn't make up 'your culture.'"

"Art dealers," I responded, looking at him.

"When all is said and done," Doublestein said acting normal, going back to the object of his visit, "all artists long for fame and universal recognition of their talents."

Kafka was coming our way, but I didn't feel like telling him to leave Doublestein alone.

"Who's going to write the articles for *Art in America* and the other magazines?"

"Friends of mine; newyorquinos, some New York Puerto Ricans, with proven professionalism. By the way, where's Maribarbola?"

"Busy," was my answer.

Kafka brushed past the dealer's legs.

"Help!" Doublestein shouted, but Kafka ignored his panic. He wandered over to Hitkinen and nipped his hand. My husband sat up and said:

"Something's wrong."

Another plane flew through the sky of the Island of Cundeamor, and then we heard the first gunshots. It was automatic gunfire, short bursts, dangerously close. We sought protection inside. Doublestein wanted to hide in the basement and Hetkinen didn't take too long to figure out what was going on: from his terrace roof, Mr. McIntire had begun a fierce battle against a PanAm jet, which luckily was moving away.

"They're going to have to lock him up in a nuthouse," Hetkinen said. "Don't go outside, he could get the idea to open fire on us."

McIntire kept firing at the clouds, the sea, and at nothing. And as he shot, he swore incomprehensibly.

"He's lost his mind," Betty said.

"He's going to kill us all!" Doublestein whined.

At the front gate, the dogs Gotero and Montaver announced by barking that somebody was approaching. It was Mrs. McIntire, of all people!

She was trembling, walking with difficulty, crying in stuttering bursts and one of her eyes was the color of a ripe plum that had been nibbled by a big-beaked bird.

"He hit me, he threatened me with his rifle," she raved. "He's going to destroy us, he can shoot me, but just leave me alone, leave me alone!"

Double served scotch to everyone.

"Help me, Mrs. Ulalume, for the love of God!"

"Oh, you poor thing," Betty Boop said, and she gave her a hug. "She's a bundle of nerves."

McIntire's shooting didn't die down. Police sirens could be heard. We were in the bright living room on the first floor.

"So many books," Mrs. McIntire said blowing her nose. "Look at all the beautiful paintings…"

And she kept crying and sipping her whiskey while in Betty Boop's arms. The police sirens had already reached the Island of Cundeamor. Outside, the shooting took on the intensity of a battle field. Weapons of all kinds and calibers were thundering, screams could be heard and somebody, over a bullhorn, commanded McIntire to surrender. Then a couple moments of silence. Then some stray shots. Then nothing.

Mrs. McIntire, still hugging Betty as if she had known her all her life, told us she regretted not having been friends with me for so long. She spoke to me about "the danger that hovered over the Island of Cundeamor," since they would force us out through blackmail and other lesser pressure tactics.

"And *they* are so powerful, they don't have a cent, but they have political influence…We're done for," she said." They harassed my husband, cut off his credit, boycotted our business…"

"Who's *they*?"

"A Cuban American organization…Millionaires…They're the ones who will run Cuba once Castro falls. They're a combination political party, business consortium and mafia…They've hounded my husband, threatened him and you all won't be spared…They're relentless in their machinations and they are truly set on taking over the Island of Cundeamor...I'm leaving for Tampa," she added, resigned and totally scatter-brained,"to my eldest son's house."

Hetkinen came in behind Kafka and two cops.

"I don't want to make any statement," Mrs. McIntire shouted and grabbed hold of Betty.

"Ma'am," said a police officer, a little tense, "come with me; I'm sorry to have to be the one to give you the bad news."

The woman squeezed Betty as hard as she could and buried her face between her breasts.

"Calm down, please," the cop emphasized, "I'm asking you to please come with me."

We all remained quiet. Hetkinen looked at me and in that instant, I read everything in his eyes, mysterious like the lakes of Carelia.

In all of our years as neighbors on the Island of Cundeamor, this was the first and last time Mrs. McIntire came over to visit. Her husband, without leaving the terrace roof, had gotten his head blown clean off.

Me and Mireya (on the phone)

"In my relationship with Nicotiano, I was always the one out of favor."

"I made the mistake of not gauging the extent of your frustration."

"That's enough, Aunt Ululame! That was his mistake, not yours."

"I thought your duties and responsibilities as our secretary released you from feeling like a subordinate."

"Nicotiano took my voluntary servitude for granted. But I quickly figured everything out: for him it was the fame and everyone's adulation. For me, it was self-sacrifice, giving myself over, obedience and a place in the darkest part."

"The pain of that uncertainty grows from the fact that you can't have kids..."

"Think about that, Aunt Ululame; in our culture we don't even have a clear term to designate a woman who can't have kids...Sterile, am I sterile?"

"Don't torture yourself, Mireya...Keep on the right path and look for something that resembles happiness. Don't keep going back to what you're missing, keep what's good for you and move forward..."

"Advice, advice! My mom makes me sick. She says that's what I

get for being a whore; that if I could not keep a man as noble as Nicotiano, then no other man will ever love me in my life; she says I have a complex, that I think I'm more important than I am; that 'she' doesn't deserve 'this', that I'm ungrateful; that I don't act like a Cuban; that I've got a lot of nerve; that that's one more time I've shown I don't love my parents; that the last thing one should lose in life is one's sense of shame; that such things would not happened in Cuba and that I should ask God to let her die...I feel so low, Aunt Ulalume..."

"Why don't we get together, Mireya? I know it's not possible here, but at some restaurant, for example."

"They must be saying horible things about me on the Island of Cundeamor."

"To speak badly of you, in my presence, they would have to kill me first. Curiously enough, it's not Nicotiano who considers you the most sinful of all evils."

"Nicotiano loves me."

"It's a very damaged love."

"I understand him."

"Are you happy, Mireya?"

"I feel like the keeper of my body."

"Have you given it to someone who's worth it?"

"At least it's someone I chose, me, me with my own free will."

"I wish you luck, my daughter."

"Don't call me your daughter. Aunt Ulalume...I'm afraid."

"Afraid of what?"

"To return like a dog, drooling and with my tail between my legs."

"As far as I'm concerned, your dignity is intact."

"If I came back, how would Nicotiano receive me?"

"Life is a dynamic flux, my daughter. You throw a rock into the ocean and it sinks. You throw a cork in the ocean and the currents sweep it away. You throw a ball against a wall and it bounces back. You bite your tongue and it bleeds...Events change people and I suspect that Nicotiano..."

"I don't care. It was just a question, that's all."

- Ten -

*P*ájara Pinta started it by sticking out her tongue. But she did so with so many attempted penetrations and reptile-like contractions, followed by retreating maneuvers so astute and slow that Nicotiano didn't feel the caresses in his mouth, but in an area that stretched from his pelvis down to the base of his penis, and from there, in radiations of high tide, to his glands.

"What a delicious tongue you have," he whispered.

"The better to lick you with."

"What a pretty and warm mouth you have."

"The better to swallow you with."

"What big teeth you have."

"The better to bite you with."

"What a spoiled child's voice you have."

"The better to lie to you with."

"What thick black hair you have."

"The better to ensnare you with."

"What round buttocks you have."

"That's so you can enjoy them, my love…"

They were in the Salsipuedes again, naked on the folding bed in the back room and swamped in oppressive heat.

"We're melting in sweat," Nicotiano said, startling a fly on his bellybutton.

"We're melting in love!" Pájara Pinta said. "Like two love shavings near the fire!" And the fly landed on one of her nipples. She didn't shoo it away. She watched how the insect greedily rubbed its legs together and then its head, but it tickled her and she frightened it with a swipe.

Outside, Maribarbola had made a decision: it was bad enough to chase after Nicotiano like a fool; what he had to do now was intercept him and bring him down from his cloud. His brother had been with Pájara in all kinds of motels, in little beach hotels, in the Omni, in the Grand Bay Hotel and lots of others, without him ever losing his trail. Most disturbing were his encounters in the Salsipuedes. Pájara would shamelessly close the bar to open her legs. Just the fact of being in the Salsipuedes, completely naked, unarmed and making love like a saint, could end up being dangerous for Nicotiano. There were surely drugs there, shady deals going down and nefarious payback arrangements being planned.

The sun began to set in Miami, and Maribarbola, always confined to his car, got a call from Guarapito, who was doing shots with Sikitrake.

"Get Nicotiano to come to Bay Side," he said, "to see if he can stop his fantasies. What he needs is a distraction. Here there's a swinging orchestra playing next to the ocean, females of all sizes and colors, and the scene is hopping."

Sikitrake, as always, was honest:

"Mireya's here with that guy. Eating, drinking, and having a good time. The bitch is really drunk. Bring Nicotiano so he'll feel better, if you think that's wise. We'll wait for you here, we've got a table reserved."

"I'll do what I can," was Maribarbola's response. "Don't leave."

Inside the Salsipuedes, Pájara had whipped up mammoth daiquiris, which she served in two glasses that looked like crystal buckets.

"You exaggerate everything," Nicotiano said.

A roach, which judging by its erratic movements, looked drunk or half-poisoned, had climbed up the folding bed and approached Nicotiano's naked body. Pájara quashed it with a shoe.

"Humping in the Salsipuedes," she said, "is like being in the third world. Don't you think?"

Nicotiano began to laugh. It was true: the walls had cracks, the refrigerator could have been one from some dumpy *cantina* in Lima or Bogota, and out on the patio there were chili and banana trees, several hens and a trash pile composed of rickety stools and old coca cola and beer boxes, among which thrived thickets of grass.

"Miami is the third world, Pájara."

Nicotiano lighted a cigarette.

"I hardly smoke anymore," he apologized. "But with the daiquiri…"

"You don't feel smoked, Nicotiano?" And she caressed his penis, which was still flooded with her lubrications. "Because I've smoked everything I've ever wanted to…"

"Yes, Pájara," he conceded. "You've taken all the smoke you wanted right out of me."

The young woman's breasts were truly sumptuous. Her nipples, now distended, were still slobbery from Nicotiano's saliva. He squeezed them with hands opened wide to envelop those masses.

"You've practically given me back my sleep, Pájara. Since Mireya left me, I'm incapable of sleeping alone."

"Just love me all over, my sweet, and don't think about Mireya anymore."

"That huge daiquiri really did the trick on you."

"It's our creole-inebriated-refreshing frost."

"Pájara drank from her daiquiri with her eyes half-closed and she said, pensively:

"Hey, Nicotiano, you know so much…Why is something called 'creole'?"

He also sipped from the creole frost while a roach, this one considerably more sober and agile, climbed the wall towards the ceiling.

"Creole is a term," he explained, "that was used in Cuba to differentiate slaves born on the island from those that came over from Africa, or 'Nation blacks.' Then, by extension, it was applied to everything produced in Cuba, to music and sugar, to huts and tobacco, and finally, to all of us, who are mestizos and creoles."

"Hey, careful now; I'm pure white."

"Sorry, Pájara; we're grandchildren of two grandmothers: one white, the other black."

"I love being with you. Between rolls in the hay, a girl can talk about interesting stuff."

And she added:

"Oh, man, how I like you."

Nicotiano laughed again. Pájara observed that his laughter was almost childlike: jovial and absolutely innocent.

"I'd like to take a shower," Nicotiano said, exhaling clouds of smoke.

She got him off the folding bed and made him climb right into the kitchen sink, the same sink where she washed the glasses customers drank from. Pájara took out a hand shower with a hose, hooked it up to the faucet and started hosing herself down.

"This is the Salsipuedes shower."

"The Third World!" he exclaimed, dying of laughter.

"In this country, civilization begins north of Cape Canaveral."

Once they got dressed, they opened the bar.

"The night is young," Pájara sang to herself. "And it comes dressed in satin."

It was hard for Nicotiano to leave. As soon as he left Pájara, he was seized by an anguish that made him desperate. He didn't know where to go. And he was afraid of bed: it lay there like barbed wire, taut, thorny, rusty and without eyes to close and sleep. And he could hear the sounds of its entrails. It was if it had several hearts pounding away in his ears, eyes and mouth.

"Even though she may return," Pájara said, "and you're lazy enough to take her back, I ask you to keep seeing me. Secretly, however you want. I think I've fallen for you."

"Give me a coffee," he said and sat down at the bar. "Now that I'm leaving, sadness has gripped me again."

"It's almost our duty to be sad, Nicotiano. We're *tontihueca* and *siguatunga* people. We don't have any choice in the matter."

Nicotiano didn't understand anything.

"We're *casitroca* and *guatimberra* people," she went on. "We don't have any choice in the matter."

"What language is that, Pájara?"

She shrugged.

"We don't have any choice in the matter," was her response, and her eyes misted over. "We're *casitrocas, guatimberros, siguatungos* and *tontihuecos*. All that means is that we're made to suffer and enjoy without understanding where one begins and the other ends. And we're made for betrayal and vanity, for illusions and excess and love that makes no sense. I mean, we're so fucked but happy to be that way. Sheer *siguatungas!*"

"Oh, Pájara, I'm falling in love with you."

And he finally left the Salsipuedes. Maribarbola saw him leave, intercepted him and said:

"How are you, bro?"

"Were you watching me, Maribarbola?"

"My brother," Maribarbola said as he put his arm around him, "let's go get a drink over at Bay Side. Sikitrake and Guarapito are waiting for us."

"Those *guatimberros*," he said to himself, "*siguatungas* and *tontihuecos!*"

Maribarbola looked askance at him without saying anything.

Guarapito and Sikitrake were at a table right next to the dance floor and orchestra, practically next to the warm nighttime sea. The atmosphere was pleasant, there were people moving about, the food smelled delicious, and lights were competing with the moon's yellowish lamp.

"Full moon," Nicotiano said.

"Don't start watching the cloudscape," Guarapito said.

"What time does the band go on?" Maribarbola asked, trying to act normal.

"Soon, soon," Guarapito was rubbing his hands together. "And we'll all dance; just look at all the dazzling women here: asses for all tastes."

Mireya and her new love sat only a few tables away. But Nicotiano's gaze seemed stuck on the full moon.

"I'd like to sculpt the moon," he said, "and turn it into a crab."

"That's a great idea, my friend!" Guarapito gestured. "Then we can sell it to Satan for a mint."

"I don't know how to dance," Nicotiano lamented, lying; he knew how, but he was to shy too dance in public.

"Well, poor thing," Guarapito snapped. "And poor Maribarbola who can't dance either, unless he decides he's either female and dances with males, or he's male and he dances with females."

"Don't start," Maribarbola protested. Nicotiano didn't see Mireya, but she saw him from the moment he walked in, since she had already spotted Sikitrake and Guarapito. The ocean breeze, the jostling of the waiters, the clinking of glasses, the people with their happy bantering, and the company of his friends filled Nicotiano with a kind of peace of mind he hadn't felt recently except when he was inside Pájara Pinta. Nicotiano lit a cigar.

"It's been such a long since I've seen a moon so mysterious," he insisted.

"Nicotiano," Guarapito grumbled, "come on down from the moon."

And he added, in his most refined mocking little tone:

"Hey, look! Nicotiano lights his cigars like he was sucking on some turned-on chick's nipples."

And he lit a cigar for himself, with his lips mimicking the gross gestures of someone flamboyantly sucking a nipple.

"Well, I think," Maribarbola came back with a devastating calm, "that when you smoke cigars, you all do it like you were sucking some guy's dick."

Guarapito was shocked.

Sikitrake, who also had a cigar in his mouth, quickly took it out and looked at it suspiciously. With a look on his face that was either dreamy or goofy, Nicotiano blew smoke out at his mysterious full moon.

"But did you hear that unbelievable crap that little androgynous Mexican bastard said?" Guarapito was indignant. "How dare he call us cigar-smoking men a bunch of symbolic cocksuckers!"

"I'm hardly Mexican," Maribarola said scornfully. "At most, it was the place I was born, which I have no memory of. With respect to the comparison...I still say it's true. You guys smoke like you're sucking dick."

"But gentlemen, this is unacceptable! This little monkey has just offended all of our Hispanic culture, Christ, all of our concept of the world! From now on, you won't be able to smoke a cigar without being caught up in the complex that you're sucking somebody's cock."

"God's dick," Sikitrake softened; "smoking a cigar is like sucking the dick of God himself."

"Hey...That's surely why Fidel stopped smoking," Guarapito reflected. "That business about sucking God's prick must have been too much for his historical stature."

"Historical stature," Maribarbola repeated, like a deformed echo.

As if talking to the moon, Nicotiano then got wrapped up in a boring dissertation on tobacco. He said it was the afternoon of the 5th of November of 1492, or maybe the next day, when Columbus (that is, the world; such is how he put it) discovered what tobacco was. He said that Columbus, in Cuba, had sent two Jews from his crew, Luis de Torres and Rodrigo de Jerez, to set out on an exploration of the interior of the island. When they returned, his men brought back news of narcotic leaves; they probably had the pleasure of having smoked them. He said that the Spanish Inquisition had tortured Rodrigo de Jerez for blowing a diabolical aromatic smoke through his nostrils, and that King Jacob I of England demonstrated, scientifically, that the streams of gases with which Satan would torment his victims in Hell are identical to the fumes tobacco produces. Finally, he said that Pope Urban VII, in the 17th century, prohibited tobacco in all of its forms, but another Pope, Benedict XVIII, was a submissive lover of snuff and Sigmund Freud would smoke some twenty Cuban cigars a day, while Winston Churchill smoked more than fifteen.

Guarapito, who heard only the tail end of the monologue, said: "Look: so Cuban tobacco not only played a part in the discovery of psychoanalysis, but it helped win World War II."

"Right," said Maribarbola, incisively going into detail on the matter. "While Hitler was destroying all of Europe, Churchill was getting off sucking God's cock no less than fifteen times a day."

"That's why God helped him win the war," Sikitrake concluded.

"Come on, men, we're too condescending towards Maribarballs. To insinuate that we're a bunch of cocksuckers! An insolence of such a magnitude should not be left unpunished."

"You all are a bunch of *siguatungas* and *casitrocas*," Nicotiano mumbled, but nobody heard him.

At her table, Mireya was theatrically playing with her hair with both hands and lifting up her elbows. Her new lover had his back turned and hadn't noticed Nicotiano and friends; she shot him constant glances, sometimes side-long, but most of them were direct and defiant.

Maribarbola had an urge to go and sit down and chat with Mireya. They had been friends, very good friends, and he was still fond of her. Where was all that hostility coming from? All of this is unworthy of Mireya and Nicotiano, he thought.

Nicotiano called over the waiter and ordered a bottle of mezcal.

"That shit?" Guarapito grumbled. "I prefer rum, my boy."

"Oaxaca Mezcal, please," Nicotiano insisted. "A bottle of Red Worm."

Suddenly, Guarapito backed down. And what would happen if that party ended up like the party of *guatao*? And if Nicotiano did something stupid, like shoot Mireya, for example? Besides, they were there to avoid a catastrophe. After having thought of that, he still regretted the farce of bringing Nicotiano to Bay Side. Why make the poor boy suffer more? Because the mezcal thing wasn't one of Nicotiano's eccentricities, but a self-destructive act, to get completely shit-faced.

"Why don't we get out of here?" Guarapito proposed. "This place is a little boring, no?"

"We'll have none of that," Maribarbola shot back. "We'll stay here until the music starts."

The bottle came and they drank. Nicotiano drank without noticing that several feet away Mireya was shooting him quick, sardonic glances.

"Look," Guarapito said, with disgust. "The worm in the mezcal is alive."

"That's a purgative, man," Sikitrake answered.

"Maribarbola," Guarapito said annoyed, "You, who are neither a man or a woman, and as a result neutral, explain to us how a man can go nuts for a treacherous woman."

As an answer, Maribarbola looked out at the ocean.

On the stage there was some activity, microphones being moved around and instruments being tuned.

"Pardon me, Maribarbola," Guarapito continued, in a more offensive tone, "you can't know why a man goes crazy for a woman; you only know about crazy women who fall in love with other crazy women."

"Stop torturing Maribarbola," Sikitrake intervened. "Sometimes I think you're in love with him."

"Never," Guarapito screamed, "why does Doublestein kill me?"

"Who?!" Maribarbola shouted, and he grabbed Guarapito by the lapels.

"I think," Sikitrake said to smooth everything over, since it was clear Maribarbola was ready to explode, "that the solution to the mystery is the papaya. That's what drives us crazy. That's what we cannot share with anyone.

"It's true," Guarapito straightened his lapels, "the silky slice, that juicy miracle."

Nicotiano stopped looking at the moon. Drinking and smoking, he was only thinking about the way Mireya had given herself to her lover: where, what they'd said, how they'd caressed each other, who had undressed whom, whether she had whispered in his ear: fuck me, give me more, give all of it to me, if she had told him how much she hated Nicotiano, if the guy had made her moan and if he had given her multiple orgasms. Then he said:

"The poet and priest Ernesto Cardenal has written about the female's sex: 'that little bit of infinity.'"

"For that to come from a priest, "Guarapito said pithily, "ain't bad."

"The Nicaraguan poet says," Nicotiano went on, "that man learned to make fire by rubbing by imitating that rubbing. And in some place that's how the feminine sex is evoked: "Oh, tiny cosmos."

"How beautiful, my boy…" Sikitrake said slightly moved.

"I don't like it," Guarapito objected. "It's too sidereal…come on, it's like comparing the sweet stench of a *bollo* cake with Yuri Gagarin or with Jupiter."

"The Sweet Stench," Maribarbola mimicked in a sinister tone.

Guarapito launched into an attack:

"Maribarbola-Maripervert-Marifaggot-Maribitch-Maributch…what he would've wanted to be if he'd never gotten into the Crabb Company is to be an ambulance: they open him from behind and stick a

whole guy inside, only to have him fly out afterwards and go screaming down the streets."

"Guarapito," Nicotiano asked, "don't you get tired of corroding
my brother's liver?"

The impersonal music of the loudspeakers stopped and in the
nighttime air a kind of silence floated, flecked with trumpet sounds
and flute whistles, light pounding on the drums and laughter, glasses
clinking and silverware in action. Maribarbola saw that there was movement at Mireya's table. They were apparently involved in a dispute.

With a series of kettledrums, the rhythm of the *son* opened into
the marine night. A blocked up *gangarria* marked the rhythm that advanced in a growing swaying. It was Hansel and Raúl, those Cuban
voices of Miami, who were singing:

> *Déjalo que regrese*
> *Que ya no puede vivir sin ti*

"It's got a great rhythm," Sikitrake said.

"The man needs rhythm like he needs light," Guarapito said. "Isn't
that right, Maridyke- Marifag-Maribimbo-Maribombastic?"

"Guarapito," Maribarbola said unable to keep from laughing,
"knock it off. Look, the oven's not for bread sticks."

"Just think about it," Nicotiano continued reasoning, "all the vi-
tal functions are carried out rhythmically: the beating of the heart, the
circulation of blood, breathing, pulse."

"My pulse is like a *guaguanco*," Guarapito said, shaking his backside in his seat.

"And a woman's menstruation, and walking is pure rhythm…"

"It's true," Guarapito insisted, "the body works by dint of drum-
ming, trumpet sounds and choruses that sing without saying anything…"

> *Déjalo que regrese*
> *Que ya no puede vivir sin ti…*

"And screwing is the most rhythmic of all," Sikitrake concluded
victoriously.

The people were dancing happily. Some made delicate turns of
exquisite precision; others danced with inhibition, and everyone danced
sensually.

Yo creo que él se merece
Otra oportunidad...

The first song ended before Mireya could dance; the second song, a sugary and caressing melody didn't take long to get started. A wave of trumpets dragged an undertow of *guayos* and liquid drum beats, and the rhythm grew increasingly pleasant, a wave with more spume on its crests.

No se puede vivir así
No podemos seguir...

Nicotiano tossed back a repulsive mouthful of that liquor-fire, and the aftertaste of burnt wood or a live worm seemed to be appropriate for the occasion: Mireya was on the dance floor. At first he thought she was a mirage, produced by an excess of moonlight. But no; there was Mireya, dancing with her dream prince. The trumpets and *son* were now calling for the blood to heat up.

De repente
Tú te has vuelto insoportable
Me haces miserable
Y no sabes ni por qué...

Everyone was watching Nicotiano. He had the look of an idiot that would have been funny if the situation had not been so truly serious, at least for him. He sat there with his mouth half-open like a mongoloid eating ice cream and Guarapito pinched Maribarbola and asked him in a half-supplicating tone:
"Hey, Mari, don't you think it's about time we get out of here?"
"Do you think I'll have to kill her?" Nicotiano whispered, while gazing at the moon, and Guarapito and Nicotiano gave each other a look that said: "What do we do?"
A flute cut into the little breeze with the smell of liquor, deodorants and food, with an energy that spurred on the dancers.

Sin un momento de alegría
Sin un momento de placer...

Mireya danced with the grace of leaves blown by a wind. Nicotiano was watching her intensely. Every movement of her shoulders and waist accelerated the whirlpool of his anxiety. All of them saw how Nicotiano grew smaller before her eyes, not in a symbolic fashion, but physically and palpably he was shrinking, folding up, looking as though he were going to transform, to the beat of the music, into a wrung-out rag, not even useful for wiping up leftovers and stains on the table.

> *Que no se puede*
> *Ya no se puede*
> *No, no se debe*
> *Vivir así...*

"Unbelievable," Guarapito whispered in Sikitrake's direction, "as if she were the best woman the world. Nicotiano drives me crazy."

"Incredible," Siki agreed, "a guy worth so much, cowing to a skank like Mireya."

Then Maribarbola, much to Guarapito and Sikitrake's surprise, filled Nicotiano's glass with mezcal and said:

"Drink up, dammit, and do something."

Nicotiano didn't react.

"Drink it, goddammit!"

Nicotiano obeyed like a baby.

"It tastes like mud," he said.

"Then drink it, drink the mud," Maribarbola insisted, with the same decision in his voice as when he was on some dangerous mission and would turn into someone else altogether, barking out orders, acting with an inexorability that provoked an admiration, and even fear.

"The moon is laughing at me," Nicotiano said.

"She is the one making fun of you, kiddo," Guarapito said.

"Drink up," Maribarbola ordered.

The music was cajoling, and in the end Guarapito gave in to his hunting dog instincts:

"Look at how, she shakes her ass, gentlemen."

Sikitrake followed him in a stinging, wounding counterpoint:

"She's swinging her hips around and sticking to him with her back turned with a real sexiness so the guy can enjoy her buttocks to the rhythm of the *son*."

"They're practically screwing while they're dancing."

"The truth is, she's beaming."

"See how that thoughtless bitch looks over here?"

Mireya seemed absolutely in control of the situation. Her pelvis gyrated, provocatively. Her partner didn't move much, his steps were unsure, a bit rigid and out of rhythm, which only accentuated the rhythmic-lascivious style of the woman.

"Let's go, men," Guarapito said, as if about to leave. "Nicotiano doesn't deserve this show."

Nicotiano then squeezed his eyes shut and, when he opened them, the moon wasn't looking at him anymore. In the midst of his vertigo, he was afraid that he would start bawling. His fears were well founded, since a rush of a stinging liquid flooded his nose and eyes.

"Look how they're rubbing against each other."

"Man learned to start a fire from *that* kind of rubbing."

"Oh, tiny cosmos!"

"Attention ladies and gentlemen! The frustrated wife of a great sculptor looks for dick on the street corner!"

Maribarbola, who had barely tasted the mezcal, was about to throw up. Seeing things coldly, all Mireya did was dance, neither more nor less depravedly than the other girls there. She was having a good time with her new love, that was all. Nicotiano downed the mezcal that was left in his glass and murmured:

"Tastes like blood."

The three of them tensed, but when Nicotiano leapt to the dance floor, none of the three stopped him. Tripping over tables and staggering among the couples, Nicotiano caught up to them, grabbed Mireya by the waist without her or the man having enough time to react, carried her with his lean, yet solid sculptor arms and, making his way through the surprised dancers, noisily tossing Mireya into the nighttime sea.

The orchestra kept playing, Hansel and Raúl made an ironic quip about the "nocturnal swimmer" and the party kept its course with even more gusto as Mireya's new companion took a swing at Nicotiano, who despite being drunk, dodged the blows with surpassingly efficient movements, proof of the training Hetkinen had given him. It was a mystery, but also fortunate, that Nicotiano didn't hit him. Guarapito burst in on the scene and pretended to be a plainclothes cop: he took Nicotiano, into custody, pushing him all the while, for creating a public disturbance. But a couple of real security guards, employed by Bay Side, came in to restore peace, and Sikitraki, with a display worthy of the worst crime shows on T.V., flashed a fake badge as he shouted:

"Vice! Nobody move!"

And they left the place in a dramatic fashion. Like a third-rate thug, Nicotiano was shoved head first into the Crabb Company's bullet-proof van, and with a squeal of tires and guffaws that Nicotiano didn't hear, they took off for the Island of Cundeamor.

When they arrived, I had already been brought up to speed. Mireya, out of her mind, had called: the man had left her soaking wet at her mother's house and had taken off in a rage. He accused her of pretending to have a good time with him, "dancing with tremendous self-confidence," while what she was really doing was "making Nicotiano jealous." He had called her a fraud, an unstable woman who couldn't be trusted.

It was as if on that night we had all decided to turn into complete idiots.

"Cuban conflicts always end in the sea," Guarapito declared.

"You have to leave that girl alone," I told my nephew as he recovered by eating a big plate of goat meat in tomato and pepper sauce.

"If she's at her mom's house," he reflected after a long silence, while drinking coffee that was too strong at that hour, "and if the guy left in a rage, then I'm going to see her. She might need me."

"Is this boy dense?" Guarapito asked himself incredulously.

"Nicotiano, go to bed and don't be ridiculous," Maribarbola practically implored him.

"Nothing's worth anything without Mireya," he responded. "Not my sculptures, not me, not any of you."

"We're going to bed," Sikitrake declared angrily.

"Yes," Guarapito answered. "This is almost farcical."

"I don't really care what you all think," Nicotiano replied in the tone of a rebellious teenager.

"You're going to ruin yourself, Nicotiano; don't overplay it."

"You already threw her into the water, my friend," Sikitrake intervened. "Now go to bed. You know that misfortune never comes alone. Like Guarapito says, if you keep it up, you're going to ruin your life."

"I can't, I can't sleep, I can't."

As if stung by a wasp, Guarapito went up to Nicotiano and grabbed him by the face with both hands, forcefully. He kept them there for a moment, looking hard into his eyes, as if he were trying to search out his friend's helplessness and obsession. It looked like he was going to kiss him. But what he did, abruptly, was strike Nicotiano across the forehead so hard that he collapsed onto the sofa, dazed.

"What you're looking for," Guarapito accused, "is to annihilate yourself. You've never loved life."

"It's true," Sikitrake stepped in with a tired voice, "you're a stranger in this world. You've never accepted that this is your life, your only life, here and now in Miami, and that you have to live it."

Nicotiano rubbed his bruised forehead.

"She was the country I never had; she was the woman of the life that I don't accept, and now I understand, she was even the daughter I never had."

"And so what?" argued Guarapito, by now exhausted. "None of us has a country and we all still enjoy this friggin' life as best we can. Women...there are thousands who would give you their best care, consideration and even many daughters."

"A woman is not a country, dammit!" Sikitrake, having lost patience, shouted out.

"I can't sleep," the sculptor said, and he rose. "My sadness won't let me sleep."

He knew that near the airport there was a restaurant called "The Fried Yucca of Exile," where a trio called Los Panchitos livened up the food.

"I'm going to hire Los Panchitos to serenade Mireya. I think she deserves to have it made up to her. I shouldn't have thrown her into the ocean, dressed up and all."

We all looked at each other in a grotesque silence.

The restaurant had a cover charge. A security guard stopped Nicotiano at the door and said he couldn't go in, but he immediately changed the man's mind when he slipped him a twenty dollar bill.

"I just want to talk to the musicians," Nicotiano said.

"OK, OK, but you can't stay."

The place was full of old, flabby faced, fat-assed women, accompanied by a bunch of languid old men, who were celebrating the birthday of an old-timer who looked like a mummy in a tee-shirt. A strange smell wafted through the room, something between lightly fried tomatoes, onion, garlic and peppers, and a mixture of stale fragrances from other eras of splendor and glory.

The old man's brood was numerous and had the air of important people, as usually happens in Miami. A man who had no land in Cuba had an illustrious last name; a man who had no political position in the Cuba of Yesteryear belonged to the Country Club in Havana, or at least won points conspiring against the tyranny of Fidel Castro. In this case, the human relic they were celebrating had been a close collaborator of Dr. Carlos Prío Socarrás, member of the Cuban Revolutionary (authentic) Party and last President of the Republic of Cuba.

"What kinds of songs do you want for the serenade?" the Panchito-leader asked.

Nicotiano didn't know what to answer.

"We have tunes for all occasions: reconciliatory, sarcastic, hurtful or emotionally moving. Other are revengeful or treacherous, designed to leave your loved one with a profound guilt trip."

Nicotiano didn't know that the art of the serenade was so complex.

"We also have," the musician added, "frivolous, sleep-inducing, mournful, shocking, lyrical songs…"

"You choose," and they agreed on a price for ten minutes of music.

They left for the house of Mireya's parents in Coral Gables, but on the way Nicotiano began to have second thoughts. His drunkenness had begun to wear off with the goat in tomato and pepper sauce and coffee, and he started to feel ridiculous. However, the intense affection he felt for Mireya propelled him to continue.

When they arrived it was almost two in the morning. It was brisk outside and the cavernous *jaguey* trees exuded a wild odor. The crickets had their own serenade organized. The Panchitos took their places under Mireya's window and began with a guitar solo; the maracas caressed the mellifluous harmony of the accompaniment.

> *Tanto tiempo disfrutamos de este amor*
> *Nuestras almas se acercaron tanto así*
> *Que yo guardo tu sabor*
> *Pero tú llevas también*
> *Sabor a mí…*

Nicotiano thought: "Come out, dammit, come out and see me." But nothing happened. The music was especially pretty in the verdant quiet of the night. The Panchitos were now singing:

> *Lloraré, llorarás*
> *sin poder prescindir del ayer*
> *que es una obsesión…*

Inside the house, Mireya turned restlessly in bed. When the first chords of music rose to her window, she was deep in a nightmare filled with blood and water: she dreamed she was in labor and she pushed down, pushed down furiously on a table in Nicotiano's workshop, cared for by dark spectral crabs. But although she felt terrible, overwhelming labor contractions and gushed out water and blood, she could not give birth, could not give birth. Mireya rose from bed, walked to the window and had to pinch herself to see whether she was still dreaming. Nicotiano was out there, serenading her! In the bathroom she filled a pail with water. At first she thought about adding caustic soda to it, or at least detergent. But finally, almost without thinking, she poured a whole bottle of her favorite perfume into the water.

"This will burn him a lot more than a caustic soda," she thought.

Below her, the music continued to strum the velvet night. Near the *malanga* shrubs a beautiful stand of papaya grew, and Nicotiano pretended to dance with it. From above, the papaya tree in the darkness resembled a woman with long hair, and the hanging papaya fruit looked like large dusky beasts.

> *Estela de espuma se queda*
> *Como rastro de mi triste adiós*
> *Y mi alma agobiada se lleva*
> *Tu imagen, que en ella grabó...*

Mireya opened the window and let herself be seen. Somewhere a dog began to bark. The Panchitos were quite a pathetic sight; faintly visible in the light, phantasmagoric and with their faces tilted up like images from medieval paintings.

But Mireya felt moved. So Nicotiano had gone to such extremes!

> *Adiós...mi perfumada flor...*
> *Adiós, me voy con mi cantar...*
> *Las olas del inmenso mar*
> *Recojan mis penas de amor...*

"That's enough!" she screamed, and she poured perfumed water on them.

The Panchitos took off running, trying in vain to protect their instruments. They all were drenched and perfumed.

"And now get out of my life!" screamed the woman, adding an exclamation point to her sentence by furiously slamming shut her window.

Maribarbola, incredulous and sad, had witnessed the bizarre scene from his car. And his suspicions were right: Nicotiano didn't return to the Island of Cundeamor, nor did he pick up Pájara Pinta, but headed straight for the Liquor Store, looking for the young black girl who had stolen his heart.

And that night she was there.

The streets were deserted and the woman, all alone in the place, looked vulnerable and exposed to the uncertainties of the Miami night, but at the same time she seemed confident. This time the conversation was much more friendly, almost affectionate. Nicotiano noticed that she spontaneously perked up when she saw him.

"Did it rain?" she asked, looking at his drenched clothes. A radiant smile spread across her face.

"I serenaded my ex-wife," Nicotiano said straightforwardly. "A farewell serenade, because now I know I'm going to tear her from my soul. And as you can see, she threw water on me."

He said this with a nice gesture and a smile that was almost like a request for an apology.

"But you smell like flowers," she said, and her pretty smile opened even more.

He shrugged.

"I smell like her."

"Maybe your ex-wife isn't as sure of having torn you from her soul..."

"Now I don't care. I still love her, but I have to keep moving on, living, I can't die over that woman."

Now she was the one who shrugged.

"My name's Mary," she said.

"Do you remember my name?"

"Nicotiano. The Island of Cundeamor. Those are names you can't forget."

And another smile, which wreaked havoc on Nicotiano's nervous system.

"I like your smile a lot, Mary."

"Please, don't also give me a serenade. What are you going to buy?"

"Nothing. I just came to see you."

She looked down.

"When are you going to Cuba?" he asked.

"As soon as I can."

"When are you coming to the Island of Cundeamor?"

"Whenever you want."

And she said this with another voice, a more serious one and looking straight at him. Nicotiano felt a little weak, quite weak in the legs.

"First thing tomorrow," he managed to respond and he went up to her. "You shouldn't work here at night."

"I know. It's dangerous. But you have to live. I don't live on no Island of Cundeamor. I live in Liberty City."

"Come live with me," Nicotiano grabbed her by the hand and, so she couldn't avoid him, kissed it.

"You live where you can," she replied, without pulling her hand away.

Nicotiano leaned over the counter and they kissed.

"Buy something," she said with a kind of sadness, as if she wanted to erase the kiss, but Nicotiano was euphoric. He went over to the shelves and randomly began grabbing bottles.

From the car Maribarbola saw a young man go into the establishment and he immediately turned off the windshield wipers. He instinctively kept a few traits in mind to describe the man: white, light brown straight blond hair, a red checkered shirt untucked, in his twenties, overweight, white sneakers. Maybe it was the air of a hounded man who thought somebody spotted him, the nervous way he eyeballed both sides of the street before going inside; in any case, Maribarbola was on his guard. He felt the slight shiver on the back of his neck and the same impersonal and cold serenity, like a dagger stored in the freezer, which would overcome him whenever he faced the immediate possibility of violence. While Nicotiano, whose back was to Mary, was filling a basket with bottles, the young man pulled out a heavy, stainless steel .45 pistol, and Maribarbola saw through the half-open window, and several feet away, how the man was aiming the gun at the employee. At the same time, Maribarbola, without getting out of the car, pulled out his huge Colt Python .357 Magnum and aimed it at the armed attacker, resting it against the window, totally relaxed, concentrated and motionless.

What happened inside the store was dizzying. Nicotiano unwisely ordered the thief to leave, the young man turned and pointed the gun at him, perhaps to frighten him, or simply to shoot him, and Maribarbola, not waiting a single second and thanking God for not having Nicotiano in his line of fire, pulled the trigger twice.

Without even screaming, the young man crashed against the shelves full of Bacardi rum, causing an avalanche of bottles. Mary took cover under the counter and Nicotiano, following the teachings of Hetkinen that had become automatic, kicked the hand of the wounded man, since the young attacker, victim of pain and panic, clutched his thigh with one hand and with the other moved the pistol without managing to squeeze off a shot. Nictotiano's kick sent the gun flying into a stack of 7-Up bottles that exploded with a fizzing sound. The young man was now crying out horribly and lay in a growing pool of blood, asking for help and howling, saying something about his mother, calling out for her in a voice that grew weaker. Nicotiano, who couldn't look at blood without fainting, recovered from his first wave of nausea and overcame his fainting spell. The man needed help. He took off his belt and was already applying a tourniquet to the wound when Maribarbola came into the place, seized the weapon, a Colt Delta Gold Cup, brand new, and he tightened the tourniquet on the young man since now the blood flow was more of a gush. At that point, Nicotiano was dazed and lay face down, with his face buried in the robber's blood. Mary, convinced that both men had been hit by fire, ducked behind the counter and grabbed her gun, but she was too terrified to shoot at Maribarbola.

"Ma'am, come on out," Maribarbola said with an unworldly calm, without even looking up at her, "I'm Nicotiano's brother and he's wounded; you're out of danger now."

"They're dead!" she screamed. "They're dead!"

"Calm down and call an ambulance."

Maribarbola worked on the young man's wound. She came out from hiding and said, overcoming the shaking of her hands:

"Leave me alone, I'm a med student and I have some experience. My God! One of the bullets must have gone through the femur, and I'm afraid the femoral artery. He's bleeding to death."

Mary called an ambulance and the police, but not until examining Nicotiano and convincing herself that he was not wounded. She then started to cry.

"How awful," she sobbed, "how awful."

"Don't say that this guy tried to knock the place over; just say he came in running away from something and that a stranger, who joined in on the chase, gunned him down from outside..."

"Get out of here, leave...Take Nicotiano with you!"

"Look," and he showed her the robber's arms, "they're filled with holes. He's a drug addict, and drugs force you...Well, do whatever you think."

"Get out of here!"

Without looking at her, Maribarbola picked up his brother. Mary then said:

"Look how bloody Nicotiano is! Tell him to call me, please. But not here, tell him to call me at home."

"Does he have your number?" Maribarbola asked dryly.

She became exasperated, looked around, searching for something, and her hands started shaking again.

"I can't find anything to write with!"

"Tell me your number twice; I never forget anything."

She told him. Three times, but not slowly. Maribarbola didn't forget.

The tourniquet had staunched the thief's hemorrhage. Maribarbola left with Nicotiano on his back and Mary saw how the bittersweet Miami night swallowed them up in one gulp. Maribarbola thought his brother wore a sickening smell of Mireya's perfume, alcohol and someone else's blood.

Guarapito y Sikitrake...

"What do you think about Alma Rosa, Guarapito?"

"She's a sweet little melon-melon-melon. Look at her, sunbathing next to Aunt Ulalume, with that stupendous rack, and that tiny bikini. Black looks good on her, since she's so pale."

"It's the whiteness she brought from the dark clouds and cold of Madrid. The bright sun of Miami is going to first make her red, then brown."

"A little female to suck every little thing on, from her big toe all the way up to her ear lobes."

"But she doesn't even look at us."

"It's too bad Aunt Ulalume hired a dyke. With Maribarbola, we've already got our hands full, don't you think."

"Hey, Guarapito, you can't live without picking on Maribarbola, can you? It doesn't bother you to insult him all the time?"

"He-She is the only faggot freak I would give up my life for. But don't get me wrong: I'd give it to him as a man."

"Guarapito, listen good, I'm serious now: I've caught Alma Rosa Contreras shooting little glances at your ponytail..."

"Don't be a dick, Sikitrake! Don't get my hopes up, see, you're giving me palpitations...What I do think is that she's halfway mixed up with Nicotiano."

"Don't believe it; he's so stupidly in love with his black girl that he doesn't have eyes for another woman. And to Alma, Nicotiano is nothing more than a museum piece."

"I would gladly shag Alma Rrrrosa Contrrrrrreeeeras, even though she munches fuzz to her heart's content."

"That's strange, bro, I always imagined lesbians as human trolls,

*with their flat feet and herpes-wracked bodies, all of them asthmatic
and with saggy tits."*
    "And fat, with yellow teeth, and a voice like a circus trombone."
    "Alma Rosa is the Prohibited God."
    "She ignores us with a hilarious majesty."
    "Sometimes I think that she likes guys too. Bisexual, you know..."
    "Well, then ask her out."
    "Shit! She inspires a strange respect in me."
    "That bitch. It's almost like your respect for Maribarbola, right?"

- *Eleven* -

*I*t didn't take long for Betty and me to start receiving a flood of letters in response to our classified ads. All the men who responded struck Betty as despotic, crude, vacuous, pompous, adventurous, or presumptuous. As for me, I couldn't tell, either. No one girl seemed sufficiently reliable, moldable, modest or qualified. I found all of them fickle, lacking any critical spirit and without the slightest trace of humanist education. The responses didn't speak of young people with their own personalities, but of puppets of publicity, fashion, with vain ambitions and mirages of the time. Of the piles of letters we got, we selected only a few for interviews; Betty, for obvious reasons, had higher standards for the men's responses and didn't want to meet more than two of them, both of whom she rejected flat-out. We went to all the meetings together, to lift our spirits, to give each other support and sound advice.

But in the end there was a letter that impressed me the most with its terseness and the emotional turmoil it expressed. Behind the note I could sense a depressed conscience, but one that was sure of itself:

> *I'm a woman who fulfills almost all the requirements you request; you too, ma'am, seem to have all the characteristics of somebody with whom I could perhaps could establish a frank and close partnership. Having put behind me several difficult-to-forget painful episodes, I don't have anything to live for. Try me out to see if I might be of some use to you.*

Without hesitating, I called the number she gave me, and it turned out to be, I immediately discovered, the number of a dumpy beach hotel. I dared to make the author of that letter the object of an exceptional privilege: I invited her to the Island of Cundeamor.

I would have preferred to do the interview on board the *Villalona*; there we would have had more privacy, a feeling more pure than being all alone in the world, floating out there in the sea. But at the last minute Bartolo had gone out "on a party" with his family, supposedly out to the keys or to go fishing, and the *Villalona* wasn't available. That's why Betty and I met the candidate in the library. We poured a couple of glasses of sherry and the girl said:

"I prefer something stronger; I'm nervous."

From the beginning, I was glad she recognized her nervousness, which you certainly couldn't detect. She asked for a rum on the rocks and I got right to the point:

"Miss, I should tell you that the job I'm looking to fill..."

"Really," she interrupted, "you needn't call me Miss...If it's not too much trouble, you can call me by my name from now on."

"What is your name?"

"Alma Rosa Contreras."

"Sounds like the name of some heroine on a Mexican soap opera," Betty said, and the girl laughed.

"Well," I went on, "the job I want to hire you for might be rather tedious, but the compensation is quite generous. As for my questions, just remember that there are no stupid questions, just stupid answers. Respond to whichever ones you want and pass on the rest.

"Anything you say."

"What Betty said was right; your name has a ring of failed loves, undeserved failures and repressed cries."

"If you say so."

"Do you have any children?"

"One. A son."

"Make sure you raise him as if he was the center of the world; that's the cause of unhappiness in the majority of men."

"And you, do you have any children?"

"Today I'm the one doing the asking. No, I've never had any; I have a nephew, Nicotiano, who's a sculptor and whom you'll meet very soon, and I have an adopted son, Maribarbola. They're my whole life."

"I'm sorry, but no one is ever somebody's whole life."

"Do you believe in God?"

"No."

"You've never felt the need to believe in something that transcends you?"

"Sure, lots of times."

"What does the word *friendship* mean to you?"

"The word itself, nothing. Friendship, on the other hand, means sincerity in all circumstances and a will to achieve maximum loyalty."

"Do your parents live in Miami?"

"No, in Madrid."

"Oh, in Madrid!" exclaimed Betty, who was now beginning to like the girl, "The Gran Vía, the Prado Museum, Las Ramblas!"

"Las Ramblas, ma'am, is not in Madrid."

"How is your relationship with your mother?"

"Absolutely terrible."

"And with your father?"

"Complicated...Look, ma'am," the young woman said taking over the conversation. "I'm trying to get my life in order. Get settled, provide for my son's education. In Madrid I worked at a language academy. I taught English. There I fell in love with an Argeline, who was a French teacher, and I had a child with him. Just like that, no marriage or anything. Truth of the matter was that I barely knew him. Then my mom kicked me out of the house...with the cowardly acquiescence of my old man who, despite everything, I still adore. My boy is mulatto, a mix of Saracen and Cuban..."

"He must be so pretty!" Betty interjected. "A gorgeous child."

"My situation in Madrid became...difficult."

"Unbearable."

"I suddenly lost my job. The Argeline was also unemployed and then he took off for Paris by himself, without even asking me. He left me a little note on the table: 'Don't come looking for me; best of luck.'"

The young woman paused and Betty took her hand, sweetly.

"They brought me from Cuba to Miami when I was only six, so I'm bilingual. Now that I'm going through this crisis, I've come back. I have a widowed aunt here who's going to look after my son while I'm at work. But as soon as I save up a little money, I'm going back to Madrid. I can't live my whole life here. Do you understand, ma'am?"

"Don't call me ma'am; call me Aunt Ula."

"OK, Aunt Ula."

"Do you know how to use a computer?"

"Yes."

"Accounting?"

"No."

"Marketing?"

"Nope."

"Office Administration?"

"Uh-uh"

"Shorthand?"

"Not at all."

"Cuban History?"

"Quite a bit."

"That's very important. Why did the Argeline leave?"

"He was a coward."

"What is it to be a Cuban woman?"

"I honestly don't know; a destiny like any other...maybe a special way of dreaming and failing."

"Which Cuban patriots and intellectuals attended the burial of Father Felix Varela when he died in Havana in 1851, that is, the same year José Marti was born?"

"Oh, Aunt Ula, what a pedantic question," Betty Boop protested." Let's not wear the girl out with that boring stuff, look how much she's suffered already!..."

"The venerable Father Varela, 'the man who taught us Cubans how to think', didn't die in Havana, but here in Florida, in absolute poverty, in Saint Augustine. And it wasn't in '51, but in 1853, that is, the year Martí was born. In 1911, if I remember correctly, his remains were moved to Cuba. Today they lie, if I'm not mistaken, in the University of Havana."

"See there, Ula, that's so you'll learn to respect youth!"

"In this house, which will also be yours and your place of work, there are lots of attractive (and above all seductive and shameless) men, constantly coming and going. Do you like men a lot? Are you capable of controlling your attractions?"

"I'm not attracted by men at all; ever since the Argeline, I've only liked women."

"You have very good taste, dear," Betty Boop uttered with her head high and without letting go of the young woman's hand.

"Do you eat everything?"

"Everything, but frugally."

"You can tell by the size of your breasts," Betty Boop inserted, "that you could stand to stand a little more meat on them."

"What's your greatest virtue?"

"Perseverance."

"What are your defects?"

"I don't know how to dance. I sometimes cry without really knowing why. I'm unpleasant to everybody when I get my period, and I hate it when people boss me around."

"Alma Rosa, take this $1,000 advance."

"But Aunt Ula…"

"You're hired. We'll start tomorrow."

"But you still haven't explained what my job consists of."

"Writing some letters, organizing documents, auditing accounts from time to time, manning the phone, being my good friend, keeping secrets and, perhaps, transcribing a book, a kind of novel I'm going to dictate, about my nephew, my friends, Miami and this house.

"A book. Who will it be against?"

"What do you mean by who will it be against? I don't get the question."

"Oh Aunt Ula, don't be so naïve; you know very well that everything written in Miami is always written against somebody."

"I hadn't thought about that."

We toasted, hugged each other, chatted on until late, and then I invited her to attend Cocrioco and Gurapito's dinner.

Nicotiano began dating Mary and his wounds began to heal. He still slept poorly, but he stopped drinking like a fish, started eating better and went back to sculpting. For now, his relationship was platonic, though not by choice, since she didn't trust him and resisted sleeping with him. Mary's reluctance made Nicotiano really respect and admire her, since he could tell she wanted to, that she desired him with a burning you could almost smell in the air that separated them. And she also felt in her entire body that he was crazy about her. But she didn't give in to him, nor did he force her to.

One afternoon Nicotiano decided to go to Salispuedes to end it, once and for all, with Pájara Pinta. The only person in the Salsipuedes was Bartolo, who was drinking a coffee.

Bartolo was dodgy, a little nervous, but Nicotiano didn't notice. He said something about how Hetkinen always gave him the Crabb Company's most boring jobs, and that by taking it easy on the *Villalona* he could regain his strength and concentration. Bartolo drank only half his coffee and left.

"Pájara," Nicotiano proposed, "let's go get a drink somewhere. I have to talk to you."

"Hold on, my sweet, I have to get dressed."

Nicotiano waited for her out in the car. How could he tell her he didn't want to see her any more, that for him their little fling was over? Most of all, he didn't want to hurt her. He couldn't say he loved her, but he did feel strong affection for her. Their encounters created an amorous sparring and a game of delicate eroticism, open and direct, and in that little game she had grown closer to him, enveloping him in her charm and immediacy. Nicotiano was nervous. Simply put, he had no experience in these matters and didn't know what to do. Just cynically tell her that everything was fine, that he wasn't interested in her anymore? He turned on the radio. A few heavenly organ strains made him think about church and he was right, since a sweet and deep voice floated over the current of the organ:

> *I believe in God and I believe in Cuba, my country,*
> *And in its presence in the soul of its children.*
> *I believe in the races of the Cuban Nation,*
> *Clinging to the rocks of its national heroes.*
> *I believe in its spirit of independence,*
> *Forged in jungles and in cities.*
> *I believe in the triangular wound of their flag,*
> *And the white purity of its solitary star.*
> *I believe in the bones of its dead...*

Nicotiano quickly changed the station.

> *Trust in the unbeatable To Cuba Inc.! The safest package shipping to Cuba, money, clothes, medicine and knickknacks with absolute security and guarantee! Home delivery all over the island, no extra charge, if you include a package of Pilon coffee we won't charge for that delivery. Trust in To Cuba Inc.!*

He turned off the radio. Out on the sidewalk in front he a saw a man drinking some coffee while seated on his motor scooter. He was wearing a filthy torn hat and his skin was tanned, also filthy, and to Nicotiano he looked like a pimp from Cuba who acted like and thought he was still in his native land. On the rack of the scooter sat a coke crate full of legumes. The man left on his little scooter (which was a pink shade, hand-painted by himself, almost the same color as beach hotels), and without knowing why, Nicotiano felt a little more alone. Pájara was really "getting dressed" and Nicotiano looked around: old Cubans shambled past as if looking for time lost among the places that sold *batido* shakes and coffee, the sun beat down making everything blacker and whiter, the Three Bunny Bakery, El Morro Jeweler, Mike Gonzalez Fantasy Garden—Flowers for all occasions—The sweetest thing is a flower!"

That bizarre name then came to mind, that name which for many was pleasant, Sagüesera, but which for others had unpleasant connotations: *gusanera*...Wasn't that nickname, more than a portmanteaux of the words "South" and "West", a self-defaming expression with which Miami Cubans punish and denigrate themselves as a *human group*? South West...South Westera...the teeming presence of Cubans...Sagüesera.

He turned on the radio again and closed his eyes:

La mejor cantina de Miami y la más abundante, catering service to your home in aluminum containers, *la comida más sana y buena, igualita que la que usted cocina en su casa*, frijoles negros—black bean soup, *mariquitas*—Plantain Chips, *Picadillo a la criolla*—Ground Beef Creole...

What was he doing in that place and at that moment in his life? What was behind those façades, was there anything else on Calle Ocho but façades like the ones in some low budget movie? All of Miami, Miami itself, weren't they living façades? What was behind the façade? Pájara was approaching and Nicotiano asked himself what would come from all that obsession, when Cubans could freely return to their island. And he asked himself what Pájara, and he himself would be like if they had stayed in Cuba.

As always, Nicotiano was sad, but now even more so, since he hadn't found a way to tell Pájara that what little had brought them together no longer existed. It would be best not to complicate things. "Pájara, you've given me so much affection. But I don't want to be with you anymore..."

Since she wanted to eat, they went to Versalles, which was close by. Pájara had put on a phosphorescent green mini-skirt that went with her earrings, a couple of really thick rings. Her mini-skirt was so tight that she could barely walk.

The Versalles was bustling. Nicotiano was about to say: "And to think that in this restaurant they plotted the assassination of Orlando Letelier, Salvador Allende's Minister...", but he didn't have time to. They had barely sat down when Nicotiano saw that Mireya, who was at a nearby table, was coming towards them without even looking at them. So as not to call attention to herself, Mireya sat down next to them with a calmness that left Nicotiano puzzled, and she spoke with a stifled rage and an enigmatic gleam in her beautiful eyes:

"So you've sunk to this, Nicotiano? This girl is a skank and you're a fool twice over. Or maybe you didn't know that she's Bartolo's bitch?"

And she turned halfway around, leaving Nicotiano poisoned and

Pájara utterly devastated and defeated.

"Is that true, Pájara?"

She answered between sobs:

"Oh, I'm so ashamed, dammit. I sound like some whore."

Nicotiano felt a sharp pain in his gut and the pressing urge to crap. He went to the bathroom, but as soon as he opened the door a great blow to his belly nearly sent him head first into the john, knocking the wind out of him. Then, like a machine, he let fly with several haymakers that left his surprised attacker sprawled out on the floor in the men's room. These were terrible and overwhelming movements, absolutely unworthy of an artist, but it was what Hetkinen used to say: violent movements have to be triggered automatically, in an inexorable way, and without the slightest bit of reflection.

His attacker was Mireya's new companion, who coincidentally was in the bathroom, duly taking advantage of the young woman's cruel maneuver. When he saw Nicotiano come in, he inflicted a few quick blows to get revenge for the humiliating beating he took to his face and the way he made a fool of himself in Bay Side. When Nicotiano left the bathroom, the man was still writhing in pain.

"You fool," he managed to call out, but Nicotiano didn't hit him again. He exited the restaurant enraged, planning to leave by himself.

But Pájara was in the car.

"Sorry," she implored in a low tone of voice, without looking at him, "just give me a chance."

"It's over," he said. "I don't hold anything against you. You've been nice to me. Thanks for everything."

"I was with him first; then you showed up...At first I didn't dare tell you the truth...Then it didn't seem such a bad thing to have you both...The two of you are so different...I sound like some whore."

"I don't care. Get out, please."

"But now I know I don't love Bartolo, I love you!"

Pájara looked as if she was about to go into convulsions. She writhed in her seat, started mumbling curse words and started banging her head against the window, loudly, and the sound echoed throughout the car.

"Never before," she stopped banging her head, "did I have a better man than you. And now I miss you miserably! I'm a disgusting screw-up, oh dear Saint Barbara, let me faint and keep me stiff right here!"

Nicotiano closed his eyes and felt completely disoriented. What was life? What was it to be a couple? What was love like on the inside, what good was sex? Maybe everybody understood these things and not him? So then everybody had to screw everybody else to feel real, important, loved and up to their full potential? Pájara was crying and her eye make-up had muddied her whole face.

"Love me, Nicotiano! Everybody makes mistakes in life..."

"Pájara, please, go on making them without me."

"Next to you, Bartolo is a pig." And she began to bang her head again.

"I'm in love with another woman."

It was like pressing a button. She stopped crying and banging her head, tried to wipe away the make-up grime her tears had made and spoke with a pride that stopped being prideful, and was now pathetic.

"But if you want to come back, you know where you can find me. You're the best I've ever had, Nicotiano, you're truly a humane person, you're a man who've I've not seen, nor who I will ever see in this shithole, Miami. Leave me, I deserve it. But you are leaving me a complete wreck.

No sooner had she said "complete wreck" than Pájara gave him a quick kiss on the shoulder, as if she feared he would reject her, and she got out of the car. Nicotiano felt a pain in his belly, similar to the pain from the blows he took in the restaurant bathroom, but it was steadily rising up into his chest and throat. He saw how Mireya and her new companion were moving away in the distance. They were holding hands and arguing. He also noticed how Pájara's miniskirt, incapable of containing the girl's bountiful wonders, had split and now exactly half her ass was practically hanging out. The same half he had kissed and sucked until it was almost left purple.

"A complete wreck," he repeated, and for the first time since Mireya left him for someone else, he felt an irresistible urge to sleep. To sleep and not dream about anything.

During dinner there was both good and bad news. The best news was that our Cocorioco, urged on by Guarapito's goodness, had finally gone to see a dentist.

"They fixed all my teeth," the old man said, "like they were parts of some rusted-out engine. I'm rejuvenated. Can't you tell?"

"First I had to kidnap him at gunpoint," Guarapito exaggerated. "Then I had put him under general anesthesia."

The other good news was that Betty had gotten a letter that left her excited and longing. The note went like this:

*I am a gentleman of very pure feelings, but of a dissi-
pated past, who therefore wishes, remorsefully, to
reconstruct his life in the company of a woman who
cannot be anyone else but you. Hounded by destiny,
I'm am going far away from this degrading city. I
invite you to be my companion for life.*

I confess that I too was impressed by that text, for its precision
and for the almost desperate desire it expressed for a new life.

"Ula," Betty told me, a little embarrassed, "I took the liberty of
sending a note to this gentleman, inviting him to dinner, since I don't
dare wait one more second. I'm overwhelmed by the desire to meet
him!"

The idea seemed splendid to me.

"Our house is your house," I responded.

Out under the pergola, on the damp bed of plantain leaves, was
the table with lobster salad that Guarapito had prepared. The entree
would be stuffed red snapper, Cocorioco's specialty. The snappers he
bought were truly opulent, a splendorous pink color, and each one
flashed its black mole as a mark of Caribbean distinction.

Nobody had ever made stuffed red snapper with Cocorioco's flair.
He needed hours to scale the fish and season them with crushed garlic,
white pepper, salt, basil leaves and lemon juice. He would then gar-
nish them with thin slices of purple onion and green and red chilies.
Then he would let them soak in that marinade for a few hours. In the
meantime, in a big casserole, shrimp, crab and lobster shell, a spicy
batter simmered, mixed with slices of ham and more garlic and chilies. Finally, he prepared lightly fried onion and tomatoes and stirred
them into the mixture of ham and shrimp, leaving it all to soak for a
while in a bath of dry sherry, either Tío Pepe or La Ina brand. Once
cooled, that became the stuffing for each snapper, which Cocrioco
would bake only a few moments before they were served.

"Oh!" exclaimed Doublestein, who was the first to arrive, "the
power of that *sabor cubano* is making me dizzy. I think I need a
drink."

The bartender for the cocktail hour was my husband; afterwards,
everybody served themselves whatever they wanted. For a waitress,
we had Florinda, who was really my long-time dry cleaner. She and
her husband had a dry cleaning business in Sagüesera, and Florinda
came in once a week, picked up my dirty clothes and brought back
whatever she had already cleaned and ironed. In addition to the Crabb

Company boys, she was the only person who had her own key to freely enter the house, and she was the only being in the outside world whom the dogs, even Kafka, would let pass without barking at her or tearing her to pieces.

Bartolo and Sikitrake were outside, working, and would not be able to attend the feast. Guarapito was shining like a star in the night, with his little pony tail and spectacular red linen jacket, red silk shirt and black leather belt, shiny like the leather of his shoes. The feminine star was Alma Rosa Contreras, who wore a dress soberly printed in black and white, that emphasized her hips and buttocks, with a sensual low-cut collar that provoked the following remark from Betty:

"I was wrong about Alma Rosa's breasts. The girl is very well-endowed."

"Betty," I told her, "you have a sick fixation with your own breasts, and those of others."

"All of us women have that obsession, because we know men obsess about them."

"How are you doing, Guarapito?" said Doublestein, who came in wearing a loose lightweight shirt.

"Doing great," the young man responded, "we have no country, but we can still screw."

"Ugh," Doublestein said with disdain, "that's all you think about."

"And what is 'that', Mr. Double?" Guarapito responded sarcastically.

"Cuba and sex."

"That is what makes the world stay in our Solar System: national pride, screwing and surplus value."

"Hey, boy," Doublestein said, pleasantly surprised, "that bit about the Solar System and surplus value isn't half-bad, you know?"

Maribarbola and Alma Rosa immediately became friends. Maribarbola showed her every last nook and cranny in the house, the trees, the most interesting flowers in the garden (she loved the big ones, the majestic *malanga* shrubs), Nicotiano's studio (she was impressed), and throughout the whole evening they stayed together, laughing and talking. Guarapito made a few bullfighting feints toward my new secretary and friend, lazy amorous comments, moving in closer and pulling back, little glances and some flirting, but his every effort seemed pathetic and failed. Betty finally went up to him and whispered:

"Guarapito, there's nothing here for you: Alma prefers us women."

He raised a hand to his heart:

"She's a dyke? The pain...what envy I have for the weaker sex, capable of stirring lust in that sweetie!"

My guest of honor was Curro Pérez, an old friend who had me worried because he was an alcoholic; he would have long spells where he didn't do anything except lock himself up inside and drink. To top it off, he was diabetic, and not long ago Hetkinen had saved his life by pure chance. My husband had to question him about a fact in an investigation concerning a certain Miami political group and found him in his apartment, semi-conscious, a victim of excess of alcohol and lack of food.

Curro Pérez was a tragic case. If he had been more astute, bold and impertinent, he would have been able to live like a king in the Miami dream: Curro had been a member of Assault Brigade 2506, that is, he was a veteran of the historic invasion of the 1961 Bay of Pigs. That page in his life was enough to make a prosperous career in any Miami business, but he had not cashed in on it, not exactly regretting what he had done, but distancing himself from the other veterans and making certain declarations that brought him general repudiation. When I saw him arrive, I felt saddened; he was skinny and wan, had an infected rash behind his ears and his whole being radiated needed, self-destruction and a precarious condition. You could tell he had really tried to make himself look presentable, but his polyester pants and faded pullover sweater gave him the look of a kid from an orphanage.

Pérez went up to my husband and requested his welcome drink with a gentlemanly air:

"Give me a rum on the gilded, foamless crested waves that crash against the rocks of sunset…"

"Just a minute, Curro," Hetkinen responded. "First speak to Aunt Ulalume."

I told him that if he kept getting drunk, he was going to die, and that if he didn't take the money I was offering him, so he could eat three hot squares a day, I was going to take back my friendship forever. On several occasions he had rejected the economic help I sent along with Guarapito, and that's why now, without giving him time to react, I stuck three hundred dollars in his pocket.

"Don't drink them," I admonished. "Eat heartily and stop neglecting your insulin."

Nicotiano showed up with Mary, who was stunning. She was wearing a dress with little red flowers printed on white, in such a way that her firmly curved body beautifully showed through. Nicotiano introduced her to all of us from a little far off, almost hastily (it was she who didn't want to stay for long since she felt out of place) and Guarapito whispered to Maribarbola:

"Holy Mother of Mary! Next to that Afro-American beauty, Mireya's a skank."

"She's lucky she's got the Cuban," Alma Rosa Contreras joked, looking slyly at Guarapito, who didn't find her joke funny.

I took Mary aside, carefully introduced her to Kafka as a new member of the brood and told her:

"I want you to know that our home is yours. Nicotiano has talked a lot about you. It sounds like he loves you, but you'd know that better than me. From now on, you can come and go here whenever you please: I am your friend. And if you want to come here and live with us, you can do it as soon as tomorrow. And, I'd really prefer it if you called me, affectionately, Aunt Ululame."

"Thank you so much, Aunt Ululame, I'll keep everything you've told me in mind."

They ate some salad and they were about to say goodbye when Doublestein accosted Nicotiano. Totally ignoring Mary, he put his arm around Nicotiano's shoulders and said:

"We're going to turn you into The Sculptor of the End of the Century."

"Allow me to introduce you to my future wife."

"Oh, very good to meet you...You look divine in that dress."

"Thank you."

"I need blocks of Red Dragon and Little Red Coral granite," Nicotiano said, "and some Travertino marble. Let's see if they can get me some marble that resembles the Cuban marbles: *Siboney Gray*, *Orchid Sierra*, *Sand Pine*..."

"Please take notes, miss," Double ordered Alma Rosa Contreras, but she cut him off:

"We're having a party tonight, Mr. Doublestein. Tomorrow I'll get together with Nicotiano and write down everything he requests."

"They're going to launch you," Guarapito said, "like some NASA rocket."

"Yeah," Nicotiano smiled; "then I'll spend all of eternity going around and around through the sidereal space of the history of art like an immortal moron."

"What good did it do for Van Gogh to die anonymously and in poverty?" Doublestein asked rhetorically. "How could poor Vincent ever have imagined that his sublime Sunflowers were predestined to make a mint and to adorn the walls of the Yasuda Japanese Insurance Company?"

"Become a millionaire, Nicotiano" Guarapito toasted, "so we can buy a medieval castle in Europe!"

"I propose," Nicotiano said with a too serious face, "that Maribarbola take my place, that he stand up, that he become an art forger, a magnificent impostor."

"I don't have anything against that," Maribarbola joked.

"I have to think about it." Doublstein said with a pensive air, and Nicotiano, who felt like leaving with Mary, said:

"Who designed the reliefs of the Ninive Palace, what was the Etruscan sculptor's name who left us Cerveteri's portentous sarcophagus, made out of terracotta? Who laid the little stones in the Pompayan mosaics, who painted the Bonampak frescos? And the Olmec heads of San Lorenzo and La Venta, who chiseled them?"

"But, my dear Nicotiano," Doublestein objected, "back then the Museum of Modern Art didn't exist, nor did Sotheby's auction house. So just forget about that eccentricity: soon a Newyorrican essayist will come to see your studio and talk to *you*, not to Maribarbola. You're the artist and with that we can put an end to your fantasies."

"What a shame," Guarapito bitterly lamented, "the career of the memorable sculptress Maribarbola was the most ephemeral in the history of art."

Mary and Nicotiano quickly said their farewells and went into the house.

"They're head over heels in love," Betty said.

"They're going to screw," Guarapito said.

"Don't be so crass," Betty Boop protested.

"We'll have little *mulatos*," Guarapito prophesized.

When Mr. Doublestein found out that Curro Pérez was a veteran of the Bay of Pigs invasion, he latched on to him like a barnacle.

"I wouldn't want to talk about my experiences as a mercenary of freedom," Curro said sarcastically.

But after downing a couple of glasses of rum on the gilded, crested, frothless waves that break against sunset (which was just aged rum with ice and soda), Curro Pérez started singing a song that everybody already knew:

"You contemptible Yankees, you immoral, despicable opportunists recruited us, trained us, fed us, enrolled us and financed us; you gave us the weapons and ammunition, you planned everything, and you sent us to fight a battle that was already lost. You and your lineage of sons of bitches!"

Doublestein grew frightened.

"Don't say *you*, please...I'm innocent."

"OK. It was the CIA and your country's government. And today, more than thirty years after that debacle, this country's Armed Forces refused to recognize our indisputable condition as veterans of the North American army."

There was rancor in Curro Pérez's voice.

"Just maybe we didn't carry North American arms? Just maybe North American officials didn't train us and didn't move us about in This Country's Army Transport Units?

"Fix yourself some more salad, Curro," Cocrioco ordered him kindly.

"This country's First Lady," Doublestein argued with his index finger in the air, "who was then Jacqueline Kennedy, called you all heroes."

"She just didn't know us. That was here in Miami, in the Orange Bowl stadium on September 29, 1962. I was there. Kennedy was vacationing in Palm Beach and organized an impressive act to review the defeated troops, more than six thousand young men who were recruited from among the young. Jacqueline went with him. In that solemn act, before some fifty thousand spectators, a member of the 2506 Brigade Squad handed Kennedy a Cuban flag, which had supposedly flown at the command headquarters of Playa Girón and had been spared from the hands of the Communists. Kennedy took the flag and said: "I can assure all of you that this flag will be returned to the Brigade in a Free Havana!" But what Kennedy didn't know was that the asshole who gave him the flag had deserted on April 19 at 14:00 hours without giving the order to retreat, or even letting the more than 400 soldiers still fighting on Playa Girón and San Blas know that he had done so. Nor did Kennedy know that the famous flag hadn't been at any goddamn headquarters, but had been crudely and quickly fashioned the day before in some house in Sagüesera. And I'll tell you that I saw it, the triangle came out bad and the points of the star were uneven. As you can see, Doublestein, the Kennedys didn't have the slightest damn idea what had happened."

"And what did happen?" Doublestein inquired.

"Well, in February 1961 I was screwing around in Miami, on the way to New York, where my parents were. And every time I met up with a relative or friend of mine, they would ask: "And you, you bum, hasn't the CIA recruited you yet to take part in the invasion?" It was like a carnival and gave the impression that all of my friends had already enlisted. It was said that the militias in Cuba were on the verge of turning on Fidel and that everything would go to hell."

As the freedom fighter was telling us other things, Sikitraki and Bartolo arrived, but only to speak to Hetkinen for a bit. Before leaving again, Bartolo approached me:

"Aunt Ulalume, can I take the *Villalona* out again this weekend?"

"You practically live on the yacht," I replied with a smile.

Without my noticing it, Doublestein, ignoring Curro's state of health, fixed him a homicidal amount of rum.

"And what happened next? You, Señor Curro, are a historic personage."

"Then I enlisted and they transferred me to a top secret camp, and from there they transported us by plane to Guatemala. The military training camp was buried deep in a site we called Garrapatenango, since it was full of *garrapata* parasites that tormented us, those little bastards."

"The military advisors, were they Guatemalans or Cubans?"

"Bah, they were Americans. Our officer's name was John and we called him John Wayne. I had a blast: shooting, marching, eating three squares. What I didn't like was the getting up at the crack of dawn, which I was allergic to."

"But you were diabetic…Wasn't it kind of foolish to go off and fight a war?"

"But they told us that in Cuba they weren't going to put up any resistance…They swore to us that the miserable peasants would unite with us immediately. Just imagine the magnitude of the fraud, that they gave us two uniforms, one for combat, the other for the parade, since our plans were: disembark, be cheered on by the Cuban people and head directly to Havana, where we would march victoriously in a parade before the eyes of the world…Look, I feel proud about being the only diabetic soldier in the history of This Country's army."

"I suspect, in some symbolic way, that you are insinuating that the Assault Brigade 2506 was an army of diabetics."

The ex-mercenary shrugged and a little smile flew across his lips.

"It wouldn't be strange," he said. "All of our national problems were, in one form or another, always related to sugar."

"And you insist," Doublestein continued, in order to goad him on, "that you're a veteran of our army."

"I am. Even though they don't recognize it, I am. In the Bay of Pigs, I risked my life for This Country. And those sons of bitches don't want to recognize it by awarding me the standard pension I deserve.

Who knows if they'll posthumously recognize my deeds?"

The succulent odor of the red snapper could have raised the dead.

"So, you landed in Playa Girón…"

"Nothing like it. I fell into the hell called Horquitas. There I fell from the beautiful skies of Cuba."

"Oh, so you're a parachutist."

"That time I was, and then never again. Just imagine that the only training they gave us was "the five points of contact" when you fall to earth, and we rehearsed by dropping only a barrel."

"You're kidding…"

"No, no, a barrel. And my descent into Horquitas was my first and last. Suffice it to say, I fractured my leg, and that's what saved my skin. A few peasant militiamen took me prisoner; of course they treated me quite well, and that's the whole story of my glory. And I'd put on the parade jacket just so I wouldn't waste time!"

Just when it was almost time for dessert, Betty approached me, upset and sad:

"Ula, the gentleman who sent the letter didn't arrive. You think he might have gotten lost looking for The Island of Cundeamor?"

Just then the dogs at the front gate began barking. Hetkinen and Guarapito went to see who it was. When they returned, they went over to Betty, and I immediately understood that something strange was going on, since Guarapito was cracking up.

"There's a man outside," my husband said, "who asked me to give this note to a widow of an elevated social level, without economic or family problems, distinguished, sensitive, hard-working and loyal. That woman must be you, no, Betty?"

"One and the same," she proudly responded, and she suddenly became a basket case at the prospect of meeting the man who just might be the man of her life.

"Let him in," I told him.

And when Guarapito entered with him, I nearly died of utter happiness.

"Look, Ula!" Betty exclaimed and she showed me the man as if he were a laurel wreath, "The distinguished gentleman whose answer impressed me so much… is none other than Kupiec!"

And she added:

"My Kupiec!"

Betty was shaking with happiness, she jumped and did a little waltz, fluttered among the invitees and delivered kisses while Kupiec, in a collar shirt and tie, looked like a little kid with a meringue pastry in his hand, about to take the first bite.

"First thing tomorrow we're going to Mexico," Kupiec announced, "to begin our lives. I've bought a huge house with a pool and maids and lots of horses, cows and lots of land near Vera Cruz: a mansion worthy of my wife Betty."

(I knew that was a tall tale, a deft and necessary maneuver of disinformation by Kupiec so that the drug dealers hounding him wouldn't ever find him. Kupiec's plan, which he developed with my help, was the following: first, he would spend a year on an estate in Santa Cruz de Tenerife, in the Valle de la Orotava, with Teide as the lofty guardian of their lives; they would then travel a little through Poland, Kupiec's native country, for he longed to see the river banks of the Vistula in Torun, and the black waves of the Baltic in Gdansk, Gdinia and Sopot. Then, finally, they would really leave for Mexico, to a house Kupiec had described, one that wasn't in Vera Cruz, but in Chiapas).

"I'll know how to make you happy," Betty Boop promised.

"And I'll know how to make you happy, Betty," he responded, and they kissed to cheers and applause.

"My dear friend," Kupiec told me with the gravity of one who begins an important letter, "if I hadn't been born Jewish, the only thing I would have wished for is to have been born Cuban."

"They look like a soap opera couple," Maribarbola whispered in Alma Rosa's ear.

"These things only happen in the Miami stew," she responded with a conspiratorial smile.

We all joyfully toasted, except for the mercenary Curro Pérez, who had fallen deeply asleep in his seat.

"Mexico is a traditional refuge for North American turncoats," Doublestein commented in a nasty tone, although softly, so as not to spoil the party.

As soon as she was able, Betty broke away from her Kupiec, to whom she seemed tied by an invisible rope, and she said in my ear:

"The spell I put on him works, Ula, isn't that marvelous? My little Virgin Mary never fails me."

I told her yes, it was something out of a novel, and that Kupiec surely wanted, more than anything, to construct a peaceful life with her, without all the scams or robbery or danger.

"He has more than enough money," I told her, "you'll learn how to manage it for him."

"Oh, Ula," Betty Boop said, with sincere emotion, "this is like the American Dream…"

What Betty didn't know was that I was behind that miracle. From the first time I read the letter in response to our ad, Betty noticed the correction of the Spanish used by the sender, and she even made some comment to me on the matter. Well, the fact is, was that Kupiec didn't write the note, I did. Because when I saw how low Betty's spirits were after not finding a husband, and her desperate need to find her own way, independent of me and the Island of Cundeamor, and at the same time, after hearing Kupiec's lament about the hard-scrabble life he lived outside of Miami in the most withering, fugitive and stateless solitude, I dedicated myself to testing the terrain and seeing whether Kupiec could be a good man for Betty. It didn't take long for me to find out that he was: Kupiec corroborated for me what I had suspected, that is, that he loved her, and was certainly head over heels in love with her. A true transformation had taken place in that knave's heart. "I have bitter regrets," he confessed to me; "Betty Boop didn't act like a whore, but was a desperate woman."

"And you're not a wretched and despicable buyer of bodies," I lectured, "but a sorry case who has to learn the value of responsible and loving female company."

So once I was sure that everything would turn out fine, I proceeded to use my talents as a go-between and showed him her note from the newspaper, as if I had come across it by accident. He took the bait, wanted to answer "to challenge destiny" and I penned his response. As soon as Kupiec heard my translation, he approved it, full of hope, and I saw once more how he truly wanted to get together with our Betty.

Surrounded by the coffee, cappuccinos, *bonitatillo* with coco, pumpkin pie, *guayaba* sweets with cream cheese, *villaclareño* puddings, vanilla ice cream with mango marmalade, *señoritas* cigars, cognac and the other liquors and fresh fruit from the conversation, all of which Florinda the dry cleaner served on Andalucian china, Curro Pérez suddenly awoke and resumed his story:

"Damn, those militiamen could shoot! I enlisted in the offices of the Democratic Revolutionary Front, which back then was on 27th Avenue and 10th Street in Sagüesera. The pittance was $175 a month, which I thought was reasonable, if you took into account that it was all a pack of lies. I thought the following way: to be a patriot forever is good; and if they pay you to be on the other side, that's even better. When we finally left for our great destiny of landing in Cuba, Tachito Somoza came to see us off at the docks. I remember he told us: "Let 'em have it good, goddammit."

Doublestein took advantage of the ex-mercenary's erratic moment of wakefulness and served him, on the sly, a superhuman glass of cognac.

"What's this?" the ex-soldier asked, and tossed back half the drink.

"It's grapefruit juice," Doublestein answered politely. "And what else happened during the Bay of Pigs?"

"It so happens that as the afternoon of that April 18, 1961 drew to a close, all of us invaders were already decimated and gone to hell. Our glorious bosses requested, with large moans, that This Country intervene in the conflict with the mammoth power of their Armed Forces. Just imagine what this band of heroes our leaders would be; that the Brigade Corps, composed of 45 members (one of whom was the joker who gave the fake flag to Kennedy) was the only unit that didn't suffer casualties. On the 19th, they were putting up a ferocious fight at Playa Larga and Playa Girón. The historical truth is" and he gestured expansively with the glass of grapefruit juice, "that both sides fought valiantly there. Until our people, now without any leadership or morale, or help from the wretched Yankees, began fleeing in all directions for the swamps of Zapata. And as for me..."

"Go on, go on," Double urged. "This is fascinating. Drink up, drink more juice, slake your thirst."

"I don't how, if it was on the back of one of my fellow men, I don't know, I ended up on swampy ground with my broken leg. They left me there and it was there, panic-stricken or in shock, or simply from the lack of insulin I had lost along with my backpack, I quietly passed out. When I awoke, there was a dead man lying next to me. It was a militiaman with his guts hanging out."

At this point in his story, Curro Pérez paused as he always did, took a long drink of cognac and began weeping remorsefully. As he sobbed, his disastrous condition grew more evident.

To Doublestein it seemed unnecessary for his nation's army to squander hours of red tape and money to provide a pension for that human relic.

"And we were surrounded by crabs!" he exclaimed, wiping off snot with his napkin. "Oh, Mother of Mercy, those crabs...They were eating out the eyes of the dead man, right in front of me, Mr. Double, not his guts, but his eyes, and it was a miracle they didn't eat mine out, too! Do you understand? They were eating his eyes, the sickening little whites of the dead man's eyes with his teeth..."

Instinctively, Doublestein moved away from the man and made a gesture that substituted for the smile he imagined making with his old devilish mouth. He then excused himself:

"I'm sorry, Señor Curro, but I have to go the men's room."

And as Curro Pérez was falling asleep again, Cocorioco and Florinda both put him to bed in one of the rooms we had reserved for drop-in guests. Now in bed, as I injected his insulin, the poor, betrayed, and American pension-less mercenary started raving, his eyes rolling:

"They didn't shatter my goddamn leg, they shattered my destiny. To hell with everything!"

As this was going on, during the dinner under the stars and planes, in the bed that had been Nicotiano and Mireya's lay Mary, naked, iridescent and wet, with her beautiful thighs of glowing splendor completely shaved. As Nicotiano was caressing her breasts, softly pinching her nipples with both hands, his mouth was lost in the enchantment of the thick black bush of the young girl's sex. Grabbing hold of his head, she was moaning in a sweet plaintive murmuring that was and was not, as if that moist caress, persistent and so delicate, would vanquish her beyond all modesty. They made love with a delight that sometimes became almost violent and which never seemed to end. They paused at last, entwined, turned soft and flooded in the secretions of love, now united by the most intimate act that could unite man and women.

She told him that in 1984, she had spent a few months in Nicaragua, right in the middle of war, as a volunteer nurse. Her studies in medicine, quite advanced but interrupted due to lack of funds, allowed her to be useful in a town close to Jinotega, a poor hamlet you could get to by traversing mountains and rivers and uncrossable roads, which were a couple of muddy streets the rain had turned into swamps, where pigs would wallow. Hills bounded the town, farmers were trained in the use of weapons to fight against the 'contras', and she, along with a Swedish nurse from Luleå (who always had diarrhea, but who would never give in to any hardship) vaccinated the children in the area, taught the farmers to diversify their nourishment and, on more than one occasion, made their medical services available to the young men wounded in combat. In Jinotega, in Matagalpa and in Managua, Mary's story continued, as she had met many Cubans and Nicotiano, jealous, imagined with certainty that she must have had a relationship with some "Cuban from over there." Mary refused to move into the Island of Cundeamor; there were three of them in an apartment in Liberty City: her mother (who had a kidney condition) and a younger brother whom she didn't want to leave alone.

But as she passionately kissed Nicotiano, she confessed that she was in love with him, that she never thought she was capable of falling in love with someone white, least of all a Cuban from Miami, but she was, love was strange; a marvelous struggle and many wonderful and affectionate feelings for him bubbled inside her, and even though he was a fool she wanted to have him always at her side, because when she was away from him she felt a kind of burning in her breast that made her feel uneasy and unhappy. Nicotiano told her that the same thing happened to him, that she restored his ability to sleep and his confidence in life. Using lots of descriptions of the sea and night and magic of the dawn he convinced her to go out with him on the *Villalona*, to spend a couple of days in the solitude of the sea or on some deserted beach, fishing and making love or just dreaming about nonsense, and she hugged him as tight as she could and told him yes, that she would love to have him to herself and make him hers in the vastness of the sea, but that they would have to take a couple of kilos of seasick pills with them.

Outside the immense and starry night was still warm and with the aroma of stuffed snapper, belches of cognac and pumpkin pudding, refreshingly tempered by the mangrove and salt breezes under a sky sprinkled with warm, bright stars, and a noisy plane here and there that reminded us of poor McIntire. The brand-new couple, Kupiec and Betty, were kissing like two teenagers when Sikitrake called, highly irritated, urgently asking to speak to Hetkinen. In a dark place in Miami, he and Bartolo had received the load of headstones "acquired" by Kupiec from a couple of straw men.

"Sikitrake has some disturbing news," Hetki told me and he passed me the receiver.

"Aunt Ulu," Sikitrake said to me, dryly, "break an egg on the face of that moron, Kupiec. Among the headstones that those third-rate burglars he hired ripped off from Weldon Park Cemetery was the headstone of Doctor Carlos Prío Socarrás, ex-president of Cuba."

Nicotiano and Bartolo...

"Bartolo, is it true you're going out with Pájara Pinta?"
"Who?"
"With that girl at the Salsipuedes."
"I don't get it, Nicotiano; you've never been a man to gossip."
"Answer me."

"Well, if you're so interested...frankly, yes."

"But you're married and have kids."

"And what's that got to do with anything, Nicotiano?"

"It's all hypocrisy and despicable. I've been with her, too."

"Don't start, brother, I couldn't care less. Pájara isn't worth it."

"So then neither you nor I are worth anything. I think she was in love with me."

"Don't be ridiculous, Nicotiano! Pájara just doesn't fall in love with anybody; that woman doesn't know how to go bed alone"

"I don't think I know how to go to bed alone either, Bartolo."

"Pájara is looking for dick, Nicotiano."

"I don't buy that. I don't know, I get the feeling she's looking for something else, somebody to look after her, for real..."

"Don't be so naïve. Look, Nicotiano: to grow up you have to learn to betray. If you're loyal, they'll deceive you, they'll step on you. And if you won't betray others, you'll back down, you won't get ahead in life, because you don't learn. Tell me, man, one single thing that isn't based on betrayal: business, love, revolution itself, how many betrayals don't lock you up, how much scum is not behind the sublime orders? And exile...what's become of the Cubans in this city since 1960? A nest of snakes. Every man for himself. Everyone stepping on everyone without morals, or without showing mercy. You can't keep your nose clean in a world that doesn't float in the blue sky, but instead wallows in shit."

"Pájara also has feelings of affection that are real; she also has the right to have people respect and love her."

"So?"

"We're the ones who debase her."

"Fine, brother: you try to save her and you'll see how you'll get crucified. Is it my fault that Pájara opens her legs to the first man who courts her and gives her a little attention? What value does she herself give to her sex? Mireya, your beloved and adored Mireya, was she a worthy female? Mireya screwed you over because she lost respect for you, because she stopped seeing and appreciating your worth. For women, men who screw any woman behind their backs are exciting, interesting, worth conquering. People covet the things other people want to have, and women even more so. That is how the world is. You were never unfaithful to Mireya, that is, you never made her feel that others coveted you."

"You speak of human beings as if they were things, objects that depend on the laws of the free market."

"You know more about the mysteries of slabs of rock than about hard and dirty everyday life. There is also a market of human flesh, my brother, and a market of personality."

"I don't know what to think, Bartolo."

"If you don't betray, you become stagnant."

- Twelve -

*K*upiec and Betty's departure was sad and mysterious. In order to
avoid Miami International Airport, which is a nest of narks, drug dealers and knaves, they left for New York by car one night amid heavy
thunder showers. They would spend a few days holed up in a little
hotel in Manhattan. From there they would go to Boston, since Kupiec
wanted to say goodbye to his grandmother. Then, finally, they would
vanish by way of Canada for the bucolic overseas destination in the
Valley of Orotava, waiting for the final destination of Mexico. Betty
was crying her eyes out, and Kupiec was also quite upset. The theft of Prío
Socarrás's headstone had thrown the whole exile community into a
state of exuberance, and poor Kupiec was thoroughly embarrassed.
The reward for finding the guilty party already had several prices and
various organizations announced substantial rewards to whoever found
the stolen headstone. On the radio, television and in the press, the little
revolution took on more and more apocalyptic dimensions. "My Kupiec,"
Betty would say smugly, "has sent exile into a state of emergency."

"I was never this ineffective before," he lamented. "Oh, Aunt
Ula, how I've disappointed you! If only I could help you get out of this
mess!"

"We're not going to ruin our friendship," I consoled him, "over
the tombstone of a shameless bastard."

And they left.

Hetkinen called an emergency meeting to make a decision on the
blasted presidential headstone. What was he going to do with it? Let
Nicotiano turn it into a crab, so the doctor's epitaph would indelibly
remain on the carapace in the form of an ad or trademark? Return it
through a third party and get the best reward, announced by none other
than our enemies at the Cuban American Transaction? Sikitrake and
Maribarbola weren't present at the meeting, since they were off on

some highly delicate and discreet investigation concerning the presumed existence of a dangerous traitor within the Crabb Company; all signs pointed to Bartolo, but we still didn't have anything in the way of proof. Despite certain evidence to the contrary, we all refused to believe that he was capable of betraying us.

I spoke in the following way:

"Friends: that vicious uproar over the theft of the headstone of ex-president Prío Socarrás blaring across over Cuban radio stations in Miami is so venomous, with such embarrassing degrees of vulgarity and patriotic virulence that it would have to provoked the general disgust of the listeners of any civilized country. The climate of collective hysteria that's been whipped up could spell disaster for us."

At this point, Hetkinen took over. He took out a tape recording and said:

"I beg you all to listen to this recording, just as an example:

"May all the suffering Cuban exile community," a speaker pleaded emotionally, "come together like a single man consumed with patriotic fervor and take a fierce but collective step forward to the front to contribute, beyond petty party or ideological interests, even one dollar, ten dollars, a hundred dollars to the civic campaign for the greater glory of Dr. Carlos Prío, the last President democratically elected in our Republic, whose remains came to rest in peace in this hospitable land of Miami, until those hands dirty with already weakened and dying International Communism, in cahoots with pre-Fidel elements secretly operating in the bosom of our community, profaned his tomb to dishonor all Cubans from Yesterday and Today. This ignominious affront will be unceremoniously punished! That's why we ask you, Cubans with heart, to please contribute one, ten, hundred dollars to the campaign…"

"May God take us when we are free of sin," Cocorioco said.

"Some day, psychologists will have to clear up the mystery," Alma Rosa Contreras said, "of how a bunch of radio stations and a few ignorant charlatan announcers have managed, decade after decade, to keep practically the whole entire Miami Cuban community in a permanent state of hypnosis. Doesn't that idiot's bullshit make you all want to throw up?"

"It makes me want to go down to the station," Guarapito said, "and kick whoever that is in the face, knocking their teeth out, making their gums swell up. That way they won't be able to talk shit for a few days."

"Carlos Prío Socarrás," I informed them, "was born in 1903 and died in 1977. He was President of Cuba from '48 to '52."

"Yes," Cocorioco said nostalgically and a little bit of shame, as if he were talking about dirty things against his will, "Prío was a bit of a phony, but I voted for him anyway. On the 13th of March, 1952, Batista and his military uprising toppled him."

"Whew, what a republic that was," Alma Rosa Contreras sighed.

"I'd like to make a crab out of that headstone," Nicotiano said.

"A leprous crab," Guarapito proposed. "Hey, do you know whether there are leprous crabs?"

"It would be unfair, my son," Cocorioco practically begged. "Don't say things like that, please. Prío had his good points. He even conspired to overthrow the tyrant Machado in the sad decade of the 30's...He wasn't so bad."

Then Bartolo, who had just returned from sea in the *Villalona*, spoke up:

"The tyrant Machado, whose nickname was "The Dumb Ass with Claws" is buried in the same cemetery, Woodlawn Park Cemetery on Calle Ocho."

"Two Cuban head of states in the same cemetery?" Hetkinen said truly surprised.

"So it seems," Bartolo continued, "and Anastasio Somoza also lies here, only his grave is no longer marked. When it was, it was defaced with graffiti insults. They had to make it unmarked."

"The Grave of the unknown tyrant," Nicotiano coined.

"Miami is a scrapheap of politicians," Hetkinen reflected and then he said:

"I asked Doublestein what value Prío's headstone would have if it was turned into a crab, and he answered: 'If we're able to hide it for sensible amount of time, I could sell it to a Cuban collector for a fortune...'"

Cocorioco then made a magnificent proposal:

"If Nicotiano really gets it into his head to use that stone, I'll respect him for it; we could submerge the presidential crab-headstone into the sea, where Nico and I have already sunk several giant crabs, so coral formations, sponge, barnacles and that stony coral that makes crabs even more mysterious will cover them."

"It's true," Nicotiano assured. "The effect they cause after having been put in the sea for awhile is spectacular. And the idea wasn't mine, but Cocorioco's."

"I've always said Cocorioco is a genius," Guarapito said, and he gave the following information: "A hooded man came on t.v. and insisted that, as a reformed agent for Security of the Cuban State here in

Miami, he knew that the whereabouts of Dr. Prío's tombstone would never be known, since it had been transported by submarine to Cuba to be pulverized with an iron hammer right in the Havana Palace of the Conventions, in the presence of the Castro brothers."

Nicotiano and Alma Rosa started laughing at the same time. It had been so long since we'd seen my nephew's unbridled and warm laughter! And Alma Rosa whispered in Nicotiano's ear: "The submarine was yellow, I'm sure."

Guarapito continued:

"As if somebody had hit a button on some magical machine, suddenly all kinds of knickknacks and wares with Carlos Prío as the object of veneration began to be sold: curtains, sweaters with his image, hats, pens, and candies that say in colored letters: 'Viva Carlos Prío,' towels, bedspreads, gold or imitation gold medallions, and even bathrobes and balloons with Dr. Prío Socarrón. Wasting no time, a small café in Sagüesera is specializing in the production of chocolate shavings, *boniatillos* and sponge cakes that say: "Prío-Prío". And everywhere there were little plastic and plaster statues that reproduce the stolen headstone, in miniature."

"May God have mercy on us," Cocorioco said, making the sign of the cross, as if that embarrassment were all his fault.

"All that's missing," Guarapito concluded, "is for them to sell condoms with Don Carlos Prío Socarrás's face on them."

"Let's put an end to this shit," I proposed.

"Gentlemen," Cocorioco interceded without much enthusiasm, "that man was a senator of the Republic by the time he was thirty-seven...Shouldn't we honor his memory somewhat? After all, you shouldn't speak ill of the dead."

"Carlos Prío is not dead," Guarapito said with his hand over his heart and his eyes half-closed. "He lives in the purest part of the soul of the Fatherland."

"If it were up to me," Alma Rosa said respectfully, "I would do what Aunt Ula proposes: pulverize that crap."

"Or turn it into a crab," Nicotiano said.

Hetkinen then spoke up:

"As you all know, we are now absolutely alone on the Island of Cundeamor. Since McIntire's suicide, the Cuban American Transaction is now the owner and mistress of our island. The Transaction has announced that thanks to the investigations they financed, the 'best private eyes of This Country have found the stolen headstone, which will be restored to its place in a solemn and televised ceremony this very afternoon'. What they have done is simply to send a fake of the original headstone."

"How dare those bastards!"

A wave of astonishment left us all speechless. Hetkinen continued:

"I propose that at the same time of the "solemn act of return" we carry out another "solemn and televised act," to return the true headstone to the police, so we can make the Transaction look ridiculous and take advantage of the situation to irrefutably demonstrate the investigative effectiveness of our Crabb Company.

"I'm so sick of being Cuban," Cocorioco exclaimed.

"Oh, man," Guarapito said, hitting his forehead. "In the Renaissance, Hetkinen would have been called Machiavellian. Hetki, how do you say Machiavellian in Finnish?"

"Hetki," I said, "come on, we're going to rain on Transaction's parade."

Alma Rosa feverishly rubbed her hands together and Nicotiano said:

"What a shame; one less crab."

"May God have mercy on us." Cocorioco made the sign of the cross again.

What happened next was dizzying and wild, and is now on record in the Miami police files and the Telemundo channel archives. While the headstone was being returned to its place, in a patriotic ceremony, with a stone faked as fast as possible at the expense of Cuban American Transaction, the Crabb Company (except for Nicotiano, who was waiting for Mary to head out to sea in the *Villalona*), Alma Rosa and I headed to the cemetery. We got there, by the way, accompanied by two policemen and by reporters from all the accredited radio and television stations in Miami. These events, by virtue of their importance to the Cuban community, were going into the homes of television viewers at the same instant at which they were taking place. The Directors of Woodlawn Park Cemetery publicly confirmed that our headstone was the genuine one, with the help of two of Dr Prío's heirs, who, luckily for us, for reasons that only they knew, abhorred Transaction.

Once more, the devastating impact of television in modern societies was proven. Just like that, Transaction was scandalized and humiliated. All radio campaigns ended, and the sale of articles with the image of the ex-President plummeted.

Telemundo did a quickie interview with Hetkinen and me.

"Suffice it to say, dear viewers," the interviewer commented, "that the scandal of the presidential headstone stolen from Woodlawn Park

Cemetery has taken on historic proportions. Questions were coming fast and furious in an improbable carnival of enigmas, but right here in our studio for an exclusive interview with Telemundo we have Aunt Ulalume and master detective Mr. Hetkinen, who are the architects of the main achievement that led to the breakthrough of the horrifying event that's kept practically the whole Cuban exile community awake: finding the real tombstone of Dr. Carlos Prío, may he rest in peace. This was due to the Crabb Company's effective investigative operations and not the forgery which the Cuban American Transaction, incomprehensibly, endeavored to undertake."

Here there was a pause for commercials: detergents, dentures and Coca Cola (you can't beat the feeling), chalets near the blue ocean and Juicy Fruit gum (It's a pack full of sunshine), frozen french fries and Gillette blades, the best a man can get.

"Mrs. Ulalume," the interviewer resumed, "according to our sources, you're a Cuban woman of high standing here in Miami. You're a member of the Latin American Friends of the Museum of Science and Planetarium, you're a member of the Big Five Club and of the Hispanic Ladies Auxiliary, you belong to the League against Cancer and to the Friends of the Miami Dade Public Library...Mrs. Ulalume, was Prío a good president?"

"Prío was shaped in the forge of Grau San Martín, his predecessor in the Public Presidency. Grau, who I knew personally, was a refined man in his manner and had the gift of gab, and physically, he was slender, a fencer. Grau never got married. It was rumored that he had high class prostitutes, but I can't entirely be sure of that...What I do know is that Grau was the typical deadly mosquito; in his private life as well as in politics, he knew how to play the game to perfection. He was also a weak and unpredictable man. He let himself be bossed around by his sister-in-law, Doña Paulina, who was the real Executive Power of the Government during Professor Grau San Martín's tenure.

"So, Prío was the political heir to Grau."

"When Grau came to power, he divvied up governmental posts among his cronies. For example, the stupid gorilla who had been his bodyguard became the Chief of Police overnight. He gave the Public Works post to his brother Joseíto, or Pepe, San Martín, who was an architect. All across Havana, little José then began building the only thing he knew about, that is, small plazas, and the town gave him the nickname "Pepe Plaza." And all of this in a country that needed jails, hospitals, or schools for kids in the countryside..."

At this point the interviewer grew nervous and interrupted me:

"What were Grau's political slogans?"

"There will be treats for everyone."

"What? I didn't catch that, Mrs. Ulalume. That was Grau's main political slogan?"

"Yes sir, that's how things were in Cuba; Grau's other slogan was "Cubanness is love.""

"So, Mrs. Ulalume, for you it's important to know who Grau was to understand who Prío was."

"Exactly. Did you know that it was during Grau's presidency that the "Mystery of the National Capitol Diamond" happened? I'll tell you about it in two words. It just so happens that in the National Capitol of Havana there's been, since 1928, a huge bronze statue. It's a statue of a majestic, chubby female, disproportionate like everything made in Cuba in the name of the Fatherland. Now, in front of her, in a marble, gold and bronze tabernacle, was a diamond that marked point zero from which all roads, highways and paths of the country originated. One day in March of 1946, it was discovered that the jewel was missing. It was immediately clear that the thieves must have enjoyed absolute impunity, since the setting of the jewel was solidly built. Nothing more was ever heard about the Capitol Diamond until some fifteen months later when the press spokesman of the Presidential Palace announced, without further explanation, that the stolen jewel had surfaced, wrapped in a paper cone, on the table of the President, Ramón Grau San Martín."

"Well, ma'am, moving now to Prío, the figure…What was his political project?"

"'I want to be a cordial President.'"

"That's how Dr. Carlos Prío explained his political desires?"

"That's right."

"But let's not forget that Prío built the Orient and Villas Universities…In 1952, only Venezuela had a higher gross national product than Cuba…Let us also not forget that it was Prío who made possible the establishment of the National Bank of Cuba…And that Harry Truman bestowed upon Carlos Prío Socarrás the glorious U.S. Legion of Merit medal."

"Well, I don't know if you remember that that medal was also given in Washington to Fulgencio Batista, who defeated Prío in a coup d'etat and tyrannized Cuba and murdered thousands of Cubans…"

"Let's stick to the subject, Ma'am…"

"Unfortunately, when Prío became President, he placed his family members in the most important posts in his Administration. For example, he turned his brother Antonio, who had no qualifications of any kind, into the Department of Property. That deal was so shady that people called that Department "The cave of Ali Baba and his Forty Thieves" It was, young man, an atmosphere of black market, pillaging, robbery, disorder and defrauding the National Treasury. And when Batista fought to the finish in March 1952, Prío didn't offer any resistance, because who would risk his life for him? Cons, thugs, corrupt politicians and pimps? Carlos Prío Socarrás cordially filled his suitcases with millions of dollars, sought asylum in an embassy and he ended up here."

"This has been a very personal opinion of Mrs. Ulalume which Telemundo does not necessarily share, of course, but which we respect. Now, in conclusion, a few questions for Mr. Hetkinen. What can you tell us about the investigations that led to locating the real presidential headstone?"

The camera focused on my husband's cold but almost tender, gray eyes.

"The Crabb Company is distinguished by its utter professionalism and its absolute discretion. From the moment we found out that the tombstone of an ex-president of Cuba had been cruelly pilfered, Aunt Ula asked us to do everything possible to find it, even though Prío had been a ...shall we say...typical politician of that epoch. We then mobilized all of our resources, which are inexhaustible, and at the end of a couple of days we found a clue that, with a little perseverance, led us to success without shedding a drop of blood."

"Mr. Hetkinen, could you clear up the detail about how it was established, with absolute certainty, that the real tombstone was the Crabb Company's and not Transaction's?"

"By the epitaph," Hetkinen responded. "The stolen headstone had carried on it the following inscription: "Carlos Prío Socarrás, 1903-1977." And underneath: "Member of the University Student Board of Directors of 1930". Only later did they add that Prío had been president from '48 to '52. So the frauds from Transaction, a veritable bunch of hacks, forgot all about the Student Board of Directors of 1930 part. The rest is easy to deduce."

"Mr. Hetkinen, what do you think about the behavior of Cuban American Transaction trying to pull off the unbelievable fraud of returning a fake headstone?"

"That organization, I suppose, is made up of people of unimpeachable decency. But their unhealthy patriotic fervor, as well as their proclivity for confusing the History of Cuba with their private business, leads them to excesses that border on delinquency and, as in this case, the ridiculous."

"The whole town of Miami knows that you've refused to accept the handsome rewards that…"

"I'm sorry, sir; we don't do business with the honor of an entire people."

"Thank you so much."

When we left the Telelmundo studio, there were two small, but rowdy groups of angry Cubans protesting outside. One group was thundering invectives against me, saying that I had sold out my country, that I was a Fidelista in disguise and a commie. The other group was equally aggressive, but their message was the opposite. As soon as they saw me, they began cheering and singing as they passed in a conga line:

> *¡Ya los gusanos no tiene cueva*
> *porque la tía se las tapó*
> *se las tapó*
> *se las tapó*
> *Porque la tía se las tapó!*

"I admire you, Aunt Ula," Alma Rosa Contreras said to me and she gave me a hug. "I feel satisfied and victorious."

But when we got to the Island of Cundeamor, we found Marx decapitated; the cat's head was nailed to one of the iron arrows on the front gate, right above the sign that said:

DANGER!
BEWARE OF OUR DOGS' OPINIONS

They had singed one of its eyes with a lit cigarette and its body, half-skinned, had been tossed inside the gate, and Kafka had to intervene to keep Gotero and Montaver from divvying up the remains. Kafka wasn't able to go after the murderers; according to Cocrioco, who was the only one in the house, it all happened quickly, since the perpetrators came on motorcycle, committing the act without even getting off the bike. They had chopped off Marx's hind legs; three days later we got a macabre little package in the mail.

As a result of these sordid events, Alma Rosa became sick; she barely ate and for almost a week she didn't leave the Island of Cundeamor since she had to stay in bed, in a weakened state, vomiting at all hours. Nicotiano and Maribarbola brought her son to the island so they could see one another. The boy would swim in the pool or play with Kafka (and with Nicotiano, who showed an interest in the boy, which surprised us all and which kept him absorbed for hours on end), and then they would take him back home.

Marx's burial ceremony was simple and emotional. I said a few words of farewell and on his grave, which was located in the shade of one of my *jaguey* trees, we left a marble cross with his name baroquely wrought by Nicotiano and Cocrioco. In a tiny crystal vase I kept a fresh bouquet of flowers.

Hetkinen ordered a redoubling of surveillance on the Island of Cundeamor, since we feared for Kafka's life most of all. On some parts of the island there were already cranes and excavators; however, the house that had once been the McIntires' was still standing. A feeling of anxiety seized me, but I couldn't tell anyone. The dark certainty that we would have to leave the Island of Cundeamor was growing inside me.

It was then that Alma Rosa and I began writing this book.

One morning I went out to the yard, having jumped out of bed without even brushing my teeth, barefoot, to enjoy, as always, the clean massage of the wet grass, and as I was caressing my avocados and taking in the aroma of my herbs, I felt an overwhelming depression that practically paralyzed me. I felt in all the liquids and tissues of my body that until this moment my life had unfolded like an insignificant document, with light, destiny and the years deteriorating more and more rapidly. What would become of us if we had to leave that island?

They were all still asleep, even dear Kafka. The only thing stirring was Florinda the laundry lady, who had come this morning (much earlier, incidentally, than usual) to take the dirty laundry and deliver the clothes she had already washed and pressed. I went inside and walked into the kitchen to make a strong cup of coffee, to see if I could get myself going.

What I didn't know was that Florinda was hiding in wait for me in a corner. When I came in, she walked up right behind me. She was trembling despite having drunk a half glass of rum already, this early, and for the sole purpose of getting up the nerve to commit a crime. Florinda raised her right hand, in which she brandished a poisonous syringe she had brought, wrapped in a plastic bag. Her legs wobbled a bit, but she fought and managed to stay on her feet. She also overcame a fit of vertigo, which almost knocked her to the floor. She then squeezed the needle and raised it even higher, as if to jam it in with more savage force. But I was wearing the Saint Barbara from Waikiki house robe, and Florinda felt the saint's gaze focused on her, dazzling her, accusing her of being a traitorous and murderous swine. I made a slight movement and turned to the side, without noticing the presence of my premeditated aggressor; Saint Barbara was now looking out of the corner of her eyes at Florinda, who was unable to carry out her treachery, but also incapable of lowering the syringe and repenting. As I stirred sugar into my coffee, and some milk to thicken it a bit, my shoulder blades moved slightly and Saint Barbara made a gesture that showed incrimination, deception and disgust. Florinda began crying behind my back, with the syringe still held high.

I turned around and Florinda let go of the needle, which fell onto my bare feet, cutting the big toe of my left foot. The poor woman then collapsed in a chair, completely broken and shamed. Moaning like a little girl who'd just been orphaned, Florinda explained her actions:

Two strangers had gone to see her at the dry cleaners; getting down to business, they offered her ten thousand dollars for my murder. At first she refused; then they threatened her dry cleaning business: it would be better if she reconsidered, the crime would be perfect since the tip of the needle would hold a poison, and the slightest touch to any part of the body would be lethal. After all, they had the means to destroy her stinking dry cleaners, legal means as well as financial and commercial means, and the job to take me out was so easy to pull off that it didn't make any sense for her to refuse the reward.

"In these lean times..." they told her.

Seeing that the needle had scratched me, (it had stuck me next to my toenail), Florinda thought my days were numbered. I also thought they were, and I prepared to leave this life in a more or less dignified manner. But the small wound didn't even get infected, and further analysis of the needle showed that the bit about the poison was a lie; the needle was clean: they had set up poor Florinda, and they had planned a terrible death for me.

"Who would have guessed," Maribarbola said later, "that Saint Barbara from Waikiki would save your life?"

Despite everything we could do, it was impossible for us to protect Florinda. When we thought they would leave her alone, one afternoon a car ran her over on Collins Avenue, killing her instantly. The guilty party fled and the crime remained unsolved. We had a wake for her at Woodlawn Park Cemetery and buried her a few feet from Dr.

Carlos Prío Socarrás's grave and not far from the anonymous vault of Anastasio Somoza.

Amid the atmosphere of threats and sadness, Nicotiano entered a period of extraordinary creativity. Mary's love had suffused him with new energies and he returned to his sculptures with a gusto that greatly satisfied Doublestein and Cocrioco. One afternoon when the sky was overcast with gray, almost greenish clouds, and with reddish sparkles along the edges, Cocorioco and Nicotiano were polishing a sculpture that seemed to be what it wasn't, but which represented something that the eye tried to discover there but couldn't.

"What I'm polishing here,' Cocorioco warned, "isn't a crab, or some other crap, but the belly of a woman, and this is her bellybutton and here's her crotch, and behind that are the bulges of her buttocks, nice and even, of course..."

"The body of a woman," Nicotiano explained, "grows before you as she disrobes. In terms of feeling, a woman's nudity gives the sensation of infinity. The front of a woman, her mouth, her neck...are regions where you can get lost if you're not careful. Especially when women speak, when they tell you things while they're naked."

"My son, I've never heard you speak like that. It must be love that..."

"Her breasts, for example, appeal to the weakest and most intimate part of us men, perhaps the purest part, since they represent our desire to feel secure, both boys and grown men, protected and turned on, strong and helpless. And then all those hollows they expose us to, those soft curves, those blizzards and slopes, those bulges, as you put so well..."

"All of that's so very pretty, my boy, but what the hell does that have to do with our crabs?"

"Cocorioco, I honestly have no idea."

"It's better that way; the day you find out, you won't be able to create another crab."

"And if I stopped sculpting, Cocorioco, what would you do?"

"I'll go to that dock in the Keys where there's a cement marker that says: 90 miles to Cuba, throw myself into the sea and start swimming until I can't go any further and can't turn back."

An hour, or perhaps more, went by without anyone saying anything. Outside, the downpour was torrential and the gusts of wind had lost any notion of decency.

"Cocorioco," Nicotiano said at last, "I've fallen in love with a black girl."

"I'm glad, son. Because if you'd fallen for some green or albino woman, and whenever she became as nice and good as Mary, I would have been happy, just the same."

Just then, the arrival of the New Yorker essayist Doublestein had sent to visit and interview Nicotiano interrupted them. Cocorioco was furious.

"We're working!" he blurted out. "Have the decency to keep out."

"Are you the sculptor?" the essayist inquired without saying hello to anyone. He was tall and slim, had a cloud of fresh dandruff on the collar of his wet jacket and he squinted. But his expression was frank and warm, and if you ignored the streak of vanity that infused every one of his gestures, you could, without any great effort, repress the urge to smack him.

"No," Nicotiano responded. "This gentleman and I are mere assistants. The artist is out."

"It's a shame you came here for fun," Cocorioco lamented. "With all this rain…"

"Such is life in the tropics," the New Yorker replied. "Sad."

The essayist paid by Doublestein took out a little book and began to wander, mouth agape, among the sculptures. He fingered the crabs, measured them by extending his arms and comparing some of them with others.

Finally, he said:

"I'm fascinated. You really have to be a Spic to get into doing this kind of stuff. I've always said: it's backwardness, cretinism, underdevelopment and brutality that engenders true art. We and the Europeans are sated, sterile and paralyzed from so much well-being, so much culture, so much progress. We no longer invent, we just take delight in our own mental excrement. This is creation! Only a city as mindless as Miami could give the world works of this magnitude. This is…" and at this point he began to scribble down in his little book what he was saying, "hallucinatory precision of the immoral sediment of the popular culture, both insular and ashore, in all of its intellectual poverty, though coming from an uprooted and solitary genius, ripped from a visceral capacity to organically relate the vegetal with the erotic and the animal with the oneric in crosshatchings of morphologies of subtle insinuations, the likes of whose horrific, monstrous beauty we haven't seen since the surrealists…But now I have to leave," he interrupted. "I shall come and interview the master another day. Adiós, señores!"

And this last part he said in a high-flown, effeminate Spanish.

Nicotiano and Alma Rosa...

"*Doublestein wants to make you a star...*"

"*He's caught my aunt's madness and has lost his sense of proportion. I'm not a great sculptor.*"

"*I don't know; what I can assure you is that your crabs have a tremendous ability to amaze. They're a little like you: incomprehensible.*"

"*Alma, are you flattering me?*"

"*You're a sad man, Nicotiano.*"

"*Doublestein would like me to be a businessman as well as a sculptor. Every now and then he talks to me about Tiziano, who was the first painter to understand the importance of circulating his images internationally. Tiziano had at his disposal a propaganda machine like no other artist of his time could ever dream of having; he was a master with the guts of a businessman who served his clients, such as the Church, the Pope, the sovereigns, in an almost "modern" fashion, and he was immensely rich. I'm not Tiziano, Alma, I'm Nicotiano.*"

"*I'd like to let you in on a secret.*"

"*Me? Why me, Alma?*"

"*I don't know, maybe it's that being with you...with you nothing embarrasses me.*"

"*Nothing?'*

"*I don't think there's anything, Nicotiano.*"

"*You're a sad young girl, Alma.*"

"*It's not a big secret...Aunt Ula and I are writing a novel about the Island of Cundeamor.*"

"*A book about all of this? That's sheer folly. By its very nature, it'll be a chaotic and untruthful book ...So, that was the secret?*"

"*There are other secrets, Nicotiano, that I could reveal; but they're even sadder and more foolish.*"

"*Alma, with you nothing embarrasses me, either.*"

"*Nothing?*"

- *Thirteen* -

And the sea opened up before them.

Mary had never seen Miami from the ocean, and sitting next to Nicotiano at the wheel, she gleamed under the sun that blinded her. Miami was flattened and full of greenness. Even the ugly downtown skyscrapers, which always gave off an oppressive feeling of impersonality, of violence practically, made her feel tender and nostalgic as they grew smaller like abandoned giants, until they turned into a mirage of glass and concrete in the shimmering sea.

Mary thought a bit about those feelings of affection mixed with repulsion; Miami was her place of birth, her hometown, but it was also the source of all of her humiliations. It was other people's city, not hers, not her brothers', not her friends'. A city of white people. What did she have to do with those downtown buildings, banks, and offices of Power? But she didn't say anything. She didn't want to poison the happiness of the trip, or the good bright weather that the little breeze made even more enjoyable, and she enjoyed the good will of her companion, because Nicotiano truly never passed up an occasion to show his love. Despite a thousand contradictory feelings, she felt comfortable with Nicotiano; it was an emotion like a stream of warm liquid through her body, making her feel warm, eager to give and receive a closeness, affection; she could almost say that despite all the evil in the world, she felt safe next to that white and noble Cuban she barely knew.

"Nicotiano, where's Cuba?"

"Cuba?"

"Yes; from here, if we wanted to go to Cuba, which direction would we have to head?"

Nicotiano didn't answer right away. He looked out at the absolute calm and the sky strewn with clouds, intensely white, and then looked at his companion's beautiful face, her lively eyes and her mouth, which captivated him.

"You're my mate," and as he gave that answer, for no reason at all, he seemed to be asking for a kiss.

She picked up on his request and he received the flavor of that tongue that made him feel like a man all the way to the tips of his hair.

"Cuba is everywhere," he said.

"Don't be silly. If we wanted to go to Cuba," she insisted, "where would we have to steer?"

And as she said this, she pointed to various directions at unknown points in the horizon:

"This way, over there, off that way?"

"To get to Cuba," he explained, "any other person would have to navigate exactly in that direction." And now he was the one pointing off into the horizon. "But if I'm the one who wants to go to Cuba, it doesn't matter where I steer the boat. I can go in any direction and I'll always get to Cuba, because Cuba is everywhere."

"Cuba is everywhere," she reflected. "...Just like Liberty City: anywhere I go, I'll never go anywhere else other than that goddamn black ghetto, Liberty City."

And she added:

"Did you know, Nicotiano, that in the tourist brochures they warn that people coming to Miami not to have anything to fear 'if they use common sense and avoid the streets of Liberty City, which is in the northeast part of the city, and is where the poorest, most drug- and crime-infested black community is located?' Did you know that surveys show that young people in Liberty City almost never swim in Miami Beach? And blacks in the city, for example, don't dare to try on clothes in the stores?"

Mary bit her lips, as if to stop talking. Nicotiano wanted to tell her: "Let's not let injustice separate us," but he looked at her without saying anything, and she, most likely, read his thoughts in that look, since what she did do was kiss him again, this time more insistently.

"It's impossible to picture the Miami at the end of last century," Nicotiano said steering the yacht with soft movements. He lit a cigar and admired Mary's iridescent body.

"You mean the Miami of Julia Tuttle," she remarked ironically, "of William Brickell and Henry Flagler."

"It was Flagler who built Miami's first hotel, the Royal Palm, which stood at the mouth of the river. Somebody described it as an oasis of civilization and luxury surrounded by savage Nature."

"Flagler made his fortune with John D. Rockefeller in Standard

Oil. It's said that it was Flagler who brought the train to Miami, extending the line to Key West…"

"The famous Overseas Railroad…"

"But the workforce was black, Nicotiano. Exploited and black. In the 1909 and 1910 hurricanes, which interrupted the work of extending the railroad to Key West by the devastating damage they caused, the majority of the victims were black."

As they navigated the wind of the boggy landscape of mangroves and channels that lead to Key West, Nicotiano tried to imagine the brutal work conditions of those laborers (most of whom surely were blacks, as Mary was saying) who made the Overseas Railroad a reality, with its long bridges anchored in murky depths of sand or corral reefs. Mary was looking at him now with a warm expression.

"Shall I fetch us some beers?" And she got them without waiting for an answer.

Among the scattered Keys, *lagunas* opened up that seemed to have been stagnant for thousands of years, a turquoise-colored soup which would turn from sapphire to a shade of creamy green, like liquid guacamole, depending on the fluctuations of the sands at the bottom, the brightness of the sun, or the water's salinity. They saw long bridges that linked the little islands, chalets scattered among the coco trees, small fishing ports where the bougainvillea was more red and the hibiscus more strident, the oleanders brighter and the tourists, seen from the sea under the shade of the flamboyant reds, seeming unreal, like little dolls in the solar salt residue.

They took their time sailing about, at times accompanied by other yachts, sometimes almost alone. Nicotiano steered the *Villalona* into a small archipelago of intensely green tiny islands populated with frigate birds, dropped anchor and encouraged Mary to fish. She hadn't gotten seasick at all and was drinking a gin and tonic, trying in vain, amid the laughter and protests, to imitate Nicotiano in fishing the *cuberetas*, whose quantity and voracity seemed inextinguishable. The crystal-clear water, festooned with long braids of olive-green algea moving errantly at sea, slowly ran between the small islands of wading mangrove, and Nicotiano was pulling out red and slender *cuberetas* one after another. Suddenly, Mary hooked a heavy and violent fish, which at first seemed to be either a dogfish or a moray eel, but she refused all help and struggled bravely with it. It turned out to be a wreck fish, more succulent and beautiful than all the fish Nicotiano had caught. In the shelter of the islands populated with seagulls and a pelican here and there, they cooked and devoured charcoal-grilled fish, garnished with only olive oil, lemon, salt and parsley, while they downed tall glasses of very dry chilled white wine.

Sometimes other, smaller yachts passed by, and the people aboard would look enviously at the splendor of the *Villalona*, and then react with surprise or sneer at the presence of a black woman and a white man on board.

"I don't why," Mary observed, "…but I get the impression that a light blue yacht has been following us from the moment we set sail from Miami."

Nicotiano didn't pay too much attention to her, and didn't even look at which yacht she was talking about. It would turn out to be a costly mistake, but he simply felt too happy to allow any cause for worry to disturb the calm.

"Everybody comes here to fish and sightsee," he joked, and then he started the engine while Mary put on some coffee. She was fascinated by the luxury of the *Villalona*; when you went inside the yacht, it changed into an apartment with several rooms, with all the amenities you could think of, and she said something to that effect.

"According to Cocorioco," Nicotiano said, "ships are like women: they open up when you enter them. For Aunt Ulalume, the *Villalona* is her habitable island, her hometown in the ocean currents."

They were heading for the top of the Seven Miles Bridge, an amazing construction that connected the Piscon Keys with Bahía Honda, when Mary said again:

"I repeat: that yacht is either on the same course as we are, or doesn't want to lose sight of us."

Then, instead of remembering what Hetkinen always said, that is, in matters of tailing and staking out, repetition is a sign to take into account, Nicotiano gave a demonstration of what kind of ship the *Villalona* was. With an engine capable of reaching a top speed of more than 80 knots, by the time they reached the end of the Seven Miles Bridge, the yacht "that was on the same course" was so far back that they could barely even see it. And when they got to Key West, the supposed pursuer was just a memory.

In Key West, they docked and strolled around the city. They made the obligatory stop at Captain Tony's Saloon, formerly Ernest Hemingway Sloppy Joe's Bar, and Mary noticed that the fish hanging from the sign outside was a wrecker fish, the same kind she had caught earlier. After walking around the city a while, they noticed it was clean and like a toy city, fake and without any great interest for them. Nicotiano told Mary how important that citadel was for Cubans. Out of the 200 political clubs that José Martí founded to get support and funds for the independence of Cuba, 76 were in Florida and no fewer than 61 in Key West, where more than 3,000 Cubans resided at the end of 1890.

They raised anchor and Nicotiano set course for the Gulf of Mexico, towards an immense sun that was sinking, flaming, into a holocaust of melancholy clouds. It was already completely dark when Nicotiano put the yacht on automatic pilot, at its lowest speed, and they sat down to eat cold cuts with Riojo wine under the black and silky canopy of the tropic sky. Nicotiano perceived a deep sadness in Mary; they would talk, make love, have a good time, but there always remained a core of something in her that didn't go with happiness.

"Mary," he said, "Liberty City is here also, isn't it?"

"All of this seems too foreign," she responded. "It's like somebody else was living it, and not me."

They were now heading deeper into the waters of the Gulf of Mexico, without any fixed course. The waves at night were quiet and powerful; they were all alone in the universe and Mary told him about her stay in Nicaragua and her affection for that little country torn apart by the war of North American pillage and by the calamities of the revolution. Nicotiano didn't dare ask questions that made her reveal certain details, but when she told him that she had met some Cubans, especially a Cuban who was a dentist but that the circumstances of the war had forced him to work even as a surgeon at times, he realized she was talking about an affair and without thinking twice he said:

"I'm not going to let you go to Cuba by yourself."

She took it as a joke and kept talking about those fast-talking Cubans who adjusted to anything: lack of food, diarrhea, sharpshooters, and insect bites, and despite all that, worked twenty-four straight hours without sleep then played the drums, and with their eyes covered, would assemble or disassemble a machine gun. Nicotiano's jealousy began to grow. He imagined that Cuban as a handsome, spirited and combative mulatto, one of the sons of the revolution like those who would never again exist in the post Cold War world. He imagined that the mulatto dentist had danced with her, like Nicotiano would never be able to do, and all in an environment of solidarity and rough times that had surely drawn them close together.

"That's why you want to go to Cuba," he said angrily, "to look for your dentist."

"I had the sad privilege," she defended, "of seeing how the revolution slowly destroyed itself; now I want to see how the Revolution in Cuba will go to hell, or how they'll save what can be saved."

"Was he mulatto?" he ventured to ask her.

"Yes, almost black."

"I'm also mixed," Nicotiano said; "no Cuban is all white, and I must have a black grandmother somewhere."

Then he said:

"I want you to marry me, Mary."

"Not too long ago, you were still sobbing like crazy over the woman who left you…Maybe the most important woman in your life…Don't you ever think about her now?"

"Please…"

And without using even one pious lie to win her over, he explained just how much Mireya had meant to him: for all of his adult life. She had been the emotional base of his existence, but the inconsiderate and painful way she had treated him awoke him from his slumber, and now it seemed to him impossible to live with her again. Something had broken forever between him and Mireya.

"Relationships between humans," he said, "most of all relationships of love, are neither eternal nor static and we didn't know how to grow together. The years separated us and, as a result, made us strange to one another. Everything changes…"

And he added, shrugging:

"Some day life will end as well."

The wine sweetened the kiss and gave a pent-up spirit to the excited lassitude of their bodies. For the first time, she sucked the sex of that man, savoring it, as if she wanted to make it hers forever. For Mary that caress was the most intimate one she could offer, her tongue wrapped around that hardness, and she had been saving it for the moment in which the desire to offer it came out from the deepest part of her heart. That's why it was an act of tenderness and ardent sweetness. She had received with impetuous gratefulness of Nicotiano's anxious mouth in her own sex, and now he returned the caress with all the desire he was feeling. For Nicotiano, who hadn't had lots of experiences with women in bed, it seemed he could only compare Mary with Mireya and never with Pájara Pinta; that was love, dammit, this was something as deep as the dark sea they were afloat on, this wasn't just attraction, which deep down was always common; nor was it crude sex for sex's sake. Mary then grabbed hold of Nicotiano's member with both hands, like a scepter, and first kissed it several times before guiding it inside her under the obsessive opalescence of the tropical firmament. Nicotiano entered her with his eyes closed, completely entranced by a tenderness he hadn't felt since he was back with Mireya, and he felt like a fish that enters an underwater palace never to come out again.

Afterwards they were more awake than ever and Nicotiano, absorbed in happy and feverish activity, did something incomprehensible to Mary. He picked up a piece of paper, wrote out a few lines on it with a felt-tip pen, put the rolled up paper in the last bottle of wine they'd drunk, corked it tight, and, without any explanation, hurled it into nothingness, because the pitch-darkness in which they were rocking was a synonym of Nothingness.

"You've thrown a message out to sea, like a shipwrecked sailor?"

"It's a message of hope," Nicotiano said.

"And you want it to reach Cuba, I suppose."

"Yes; I want it to go everywhere. You know what the message says."

She caressed his face.

"That you love me," she guessed and received a tropical shower of kisses, hickeys, hugs and generous caresses.

"You're like a kid," she said.

He then wanted to give her a surprise. "Close your eyes," he told her, and when she opened them he was comically holding a machine gun in his hands.

He explained to her that the *Villalona* was, in reality, a small arsenal, since the yacht was used for "certain missions" of the Crabb Company, and before the young woman's stunned eyes, Nicotiano unloaded the weapon, covered his eyes and in several minutes blindly reloaded it.

"It's the same kind of machine gun that the boys in Nicaragua had," she said, without daring to touch it.

"It's an AK-47, a small jewel. Because of its efficiency, simplicity and its high output of firepower, the AK is the most frequently used assault weapon in modern times. A Russian tank designer, Kalashnikov, designed it. According to what Hetkinen told us, Kalashnikov ended up wounded during WWII, I think, at the battle of Briansk. From that moment on, he dedicated himself to the war industry. In 1959, the Russians brought out a lighter and an even better AK, the AKM. There are four of these on the *Villalona*, in addition to two .50 caliber machine guns hidden in compartments under the bow and stern. Compared to the North American M-16, which is a magnificent weapon, the AK is easier to handle and repair and, in some points, superior as an assault weapon."

"Look," and he pulled out the .50 caliber from the stern, a machine gun attached to a bipod with a long, slender and shiny barrel, "it's a Barrett. They call it a Licht-Fifty Model 82 A-1. Those are the boxes with the magazines."

"How much does a weapon like that cost, Nicotiano?"

"Six thousand dollars, give or take."

To Mary it seemed like an aberration that a man so sensitive and extraordinarily soft of character would know so much about those artifacts of death.

"And why did you faint that day when Maribarbola wounded the robber?"

"Because I can't stand to see blood," he said with a smile. "I've suffered from that weakness ever since I was a kid."

"I'd say it was virtue; nobody should ever see blood without fainting."

A pleasant lethargy was inviting them to get into bed when Mary while looking port, discovered a strange luminous ball passing by at a relative distance. It was a luxury liner in the pitch dark of the Gulf that looked like a meringue cake with lots of little neon lights. She picked up the powerful binoculars and saw people dancing and eating, men in tail coats and women in elegant evening dresses being served by waiters who poured champagne, bowing in slow motion, all the while a phantasmagoric orchestra of musicians in ties played, she imagined, beautiful waltzes with trumpets and violins. To her the instruments were mute until that oceanic vision, distant like a drunken dream, slowly faded in the darkness of the sea.

Then once again the concave solitude of the deep sky, upon the terrible solitude of the depths of a sea which, with the slow breathing of the waves, only hinted at its presence: not a trace of light in any part of the darkness, except for the phosphorescent sprinkle of the Tropic of Cancer constellations. And the moon, the huge bright moon, now with a power to enchant, tracing a hot path of pink-grey reflections onto the undulating landscape of the black, slow and foamless waves.

Nicotiano gave into drowsiness, let the *Villalona* drift and lay down to sleep. Restless and fascinated by that astral landscape that seemed from another world, Mary stayed awake a while longer. Then she curled up next to Nicotiano, totally surrendering to her sleepiness, but without understanding how they could spend the whole night like that, floating in the vastness of the sea like a cork in the darkness, at the mercy of the currents and winds and all the dangers of the nighttime sea. Mary felt a combination of fear and security. She didn't have the slightest idea what risks and dangers might threaten them, but there must be some, for a boat alone in the immensity…But Nicotiano inspired confidence and she hugged him, as if to assure herself that he would never leave her alone, not even while she was asleep.

Thinking about that, she fell asleep, until the sharp whistle of the *Villalona's* communication machine woke them both at the crack of dawn.

It was Hetkinen. With the terseness he habitually used to relay catastrophic news, Hetkinen informed them that there was, most likely, some 150 kilos of pure heroin on board the *Villalona*.

"What?"

"Heroin; it's Bartolo's stuff."

For a while, Bartolo had spent time slipping drugs into Miami, in cahoots with a group of drug traffickers and in flagrant betrayal of the Crabb Company. With the pretext of taking his family out to sea, he had used the *Villalona*, which was a "clean" ship, for his shameless illegal trafficking. Bartolo had stolen a shipment from his buddies and it was now stashed on the yacht. He made up a story of having to get rid of the goods at sea, due to the danger of being searched by a Coast Guard anti-drug unit.

"And how do you know all that, Hetkinen?"

"Bartolo buckled under pressure. He confessed everything to Sikitrake and Guarapito. Bartolo knew that the group suspected he was lying, and that the goods were either on the Island of Cundeamor, or was still on board the *Villalona*. Needless to say, Bartolo has been kicked out of the Crabb Company and, as of this very moment, is a dead man. The dealers are only waiting to find out what happened to the cargo."

"What do I do, Hetkinen?"

"We know they're looking for you at sea.

"Oh, shit."

"Listen up: search the boat; if you find drugs, immediately throw everything overboard and get back here as soon as the weather permits. Under no circumstance should you let any boat approach you. I repeat: not one boat. Ready the machine guns and don't skimp on the ammo. Don't let Mary come out. You already know where the hand grenades are, I think there are two boxes of missiles. Be careful."

"Holy shit," Nicotiano said, and for a few moments he couldn't do anything. When he told Mary what was going on, she said:

"You see, Nicotiano? Liberty City is everywhere."

Bartolo hadn't even tried to hide the goods. The packages were in the cupboards. It was difficult for Mary to coordinate her movements. She didn't know whether to hide or jump into the ocean, and she couldn't collect her thoughts. What trap had she fallen into? What was true and what was a lie in that version of events? What was the Crabb Company, really? Who was Hetkinen, a member of the secret police, a professional criminal, an assassin? And that nice, though mysterious woman everybody called "Aunt Ula?" It never occurred to her that Nicotiano, a sincere and gentle young man, would dedicate himself to trafficking drugs…

Nicotiano fixed their location and set a course for Miami, full speed ahead. Mary kept scanning the morning horizon with the binoculars, while Nicotiano didn't take his sight off a point that was coming closer on the radar screen. They hadn't had any breakfast; their speed across an ocean with certain kinds of waves produced a movement of an insistent knocking in the *Villalona* that stirred Mary's insides.

After an hour, they realized that their idyllic jaunt out at sea had turned into life or death. A yacht was heading towards them. It was light blue.

"It's the same boat!" Mary said, in terror. "The one I told you was following us!"

"They lost our trail in Key West; they didn't think that we'd dock."

Nicotiano shut off the engine, and Mary was furious, almost hysterical. She screamed that they should flee, that they would be slaughtered like pigs without anyone ever finding out, without anyone to help them in the solitude of those waters, but Nicotiano violently hugged her and spoke to her in a voice that frightened her, the voice of a man without scruples and not the voice of her Nicotiano-boy, of her naïve Nicotiano, capable of crying for the love of a woman.

"Get down below in the cabin, hide and let me take care of this. I don't want to see you up here."

She didn't pay attention to him, but she managed to calm herself. She saw how Nicotiano pulled out a grenade launcher and a box of ammo that looked frighteningly like small rockets or bombs. Mary made out something that looked like a man, maybe two, holding large weapons on the yacht that was approaching. Then, incredibly, after taking out the two Barrettas, Nicotiano aimed the *Villalona* full speed at the presumably hostile boat, setting it on automatic pilot in that direction. From the window of the steering wheel he aimed the grenade launcher and fired the first shot, which kicked up a geyser of water some forty-five feet to the left of the yacht, now dangerously close. Concentrating, wordlessly, Nicotiano kept firing the grenades one by one, in such way that the explosions detonated closer and closer to the yacht, from which now came the fire of at least four M-16. Nicotiano then managed to place a grenade so close to the rear bow that the yacht suddenly changed course to avoid being hit directly. The *Villalona* kept closing in intrepidly, aggressively; the gun shots were taking out the windows and sides of the *Villalona* when Nicotiano went out to the bow and began shooting wildly, without letting up, maintaining a volume of fire that practically destroyed the boat pursuing them and totally silenced the return fire. Nicotiano, who was in a trance, then changed course at full speed, putting distance between the two ships, all the while firing away with the rear machine gun until he emptied the magazine.

The ship didn't dare follow them.

"That's that," Nicotiano said angrily, his mouth full of a foul taste, and he began to shake, unable to control himself, and then he urinated in his shorts and threw up over the side of the boat before Mary managed to calm him down by hugging him and giving him the shot of rum he asked for. Of course he promptly threw it up. So "the hero of the *Villalona*," as Gurapito, dying of laughter, would later call him, was now crapping in his pants.

Hetkinen, Maribarbola and Sikitrake had gone to sea in a rented yacht, made radio contact and found Nicotiano several miles east of Key West. Together they were safe from danger.

The episode left Nicotiano in such a bad way that for three straight days he was unable to hold down any food. He barely got out of bed and Mary had to stay on the Island of Cundeamor to give him some tenderness and care for him with her knowledge as a nurse, as if she were treating a baby with serious stomach disorders.

"How's the hero of the *Villalona* doing?" Gurapito asked amiably.

Only three days later someone murdered Bartolo in the Salsipuedes. He was drinking a beer when a man came in and asked:

"Do you think we're a bunch of schmucks?"

And he shot him with a .357 Magnum, right in the face. Bartolo toppled over, blood streaming out of his mouth and ears, and Pájara Pinta, screaming, cried out:

"Call an ambulance, he's alive, he's still alive!"

Bartolo's right leg was twitching in the last spasm of death, and that sad gesture made poor Pájara think that there was still hope for Bartolo, amid the horror and her hysteria. But when the killer, who had calmly stepped back without making the slightest effort to hide, heard Pájara howling"...he's alive, he's still alive," he turned back around, much to the shock of the few customers that afternoon in the Salispuedes, and finished Bartolo off with a shot to the temple.

"You think we're a bunch of schmucks?"

Those were the last words the killer repeated before leaving, taking his time, like someone who avoids needless sweating when walking.

Me and Alma Rosa

"It's better that Betty hasn't been here. So she won't find out about Nicotiano's terrible death."

"She's your best friend, Aunt Ula, and you could have used her comfort."

"That's true. But let her be happy."

"Aunt Ula...don't cry anymore, I beg you."

"I'm so lucky to have you near me, Alma Rosa!"

"Aunt Ula..."

"Give me more rum, dammit, I'm going to get drunk."

"Aunt Ula, calm down; now that this semi-novel has been written, it needs a title."

"They killed him like an animal and I couldn't do anything to stop it."

"Look how completely calm the bay is, Aunt Ula...the blue-green of the water, the sun coming up...What a strange sensation. It's as if nothing ever happened."

"What do the dearly departed take with them, Alma?"

"A bunch of living things, Aunt Ula."

"And they leave other things in their place. Living things, dead things."

"Nicotiano leaves his scupltures..."

"Leftovers, dammit, rags!"

"You're Aunt Ulalume...You never back down from any fight...You've been an astute, noble, loyal friend and like a mother not only to Nicotiano, but to each of the men in the Crabb Company...Your only defeat has been Nicotiano's death."

"What a huge loss, my dear! It won't fit into the years we have left to live."

"Now...I'm almost sure that you've done good by writing this book. While Nicotiano was still with us it seemed absurd, the foolish whim of an aunt, proud of her nephew."

"Foolish? Really? I remember what you said to me: Aunt Ula,

Miami doesn't deserve a novel."

"Now, to be honest with you, I don't even know if Nicotiano deserved this parodic joke of a novel. Maybe he was worthy of something else."

"Not only does our Nicotiano deserve this book, such as it is; you also deserve it, and Betty and Maribarbola, and Hetkinen and the boys, and Bag Lady...and Mireya and Mary also deserve it. Even I do, as a witness of the reality of the Island of Cundeamor...

"But wait, you said...our Nicotiano? Alma, I always thought you were absolutely indifferent.

"There are things you don't know, Aunt Ula...c'mon, let's finish this book once and for all. It's going to be hard to finish the last chapter.

"In truth, you've written this novel."

"The words are yours. That's your voice recorded on those tapes. The only thing I've done is transcribe them onto that stack of paper. That's all."

"What is it I don't know, Alma Rosa, what are you hiding from me? And why do you cry so much, my daughter, for me, or maybe for Nicotiano? Fix me another rum."

"It makes me want to go back to my mother."

"As much as you want, you can never go back to your mom."

"To my mother's belly. It makes me want to take her clothes off, push her onto the bed, open her legs and shove myself violently inside, through her vagina."

"Honey, don't say awful things like that. We can't lose our minds."

"And make her hold me again in her goddamn womb for nine months, so she'll give birth to me dead. That's it: give birth to me stillborn."

"My God, we're crying like two orphans, and you're ranting horribly. Why do you say that?"

"Because sometimes I regret having been born...like now, ever since Nicotiano died."

"Alma Rosa, did you and Nicotiano..."

"For a while now...Nicotiano and I were involved."

"Did you sleep with him?"

"Lots of times."

"And all the while he was falling for Mary! But honey, you aren't..."

"Lesbian? No; I lied so Guarapito and Sikitrake would leave me alone, since I didn't come to the Island of Cundeamor to complicate *my life with sexual affairs. But as soon as I met Nicotiano...Let's finish it now, Aunt Ula; we have to give it a title."*

"Whatever you want. The Miami Dream, *for example. I don't really care."*

"That's not half bad. Miami is the Cuban dream, dreamt by the American dream."

"Take that out, forget it, come up with something else."

"The Cuban dream wiped out the American dream. It made it superstitious, ostentatious and loud-mouthed, it made it coarser than it already is."

"Another title, let's find another title, and fix me more rum."

"The Miami dream made the American dream more pathetic, vulgar, fanatical and lurid. Why is that you always feel that Miami doesn't belong to you, that you can't belong to this mirage, either?"

"Because Miami is the image of something that no longer exists."

"But how can someone feel love for this shit? And do we always want to come back to the Miami dream?"

"To make us spend nine months inside it, and then for it to give birth to us stillborn."

"Like in all dreams, Aunt Ula, you can't tell you're dreaming until you wake up. It's dangerous to wake up from the Miami dream."

"Nicotiano woke up dead."

"Give me some more rum, Aunt Ula."

"Let's come up with another title. How about something like Pages for the Sea?

"For the sea?"

"Yes. For the sea. Now, Alma, I calmed down and you're still crying."

"Aunt Ula, I want to ask you for a favor: let me choose the title of this book."

"Fine, my daughter, let it be so. But once the last chapter is finished and before forever leaving this house and island, which I have neither the strength nor reason to defend, help me put the pages of the fragments that make up this novel into dozens of bottles."

"To cast them out to sea, like the shipwrecked sailors do?"

"So the sea will take them away, as well as it can, everywhere or nowhere."

- Fourteen -

*T*he day before he was murdered, Mary said to Nicotiano:

"I don't know if you knew, but today is the Calle Ocho Festival."

"No, honestly, I didn't know that," he responded.

"I've never gone, either out of prejudice or because of a thousand mental blocks. If it wouldn't bother you, let's go together. I want to see what it's all about."

Nicotiano loved the idea. Guarapito had invited him once and Mireya did, too, but he never wanted to deal with the crowds. That's why we were all somewhat taken aback that Mary had so easily persuaded him, and before they left, Hetkinen told him:

"Be careful out there, Nicotiano; that incident with Bartolo and those goddamn drugs could still have consequences."

"Don't take your eyes off Nicotiano and Mary," I warned Maribarbola; "Stick to them wherever they go."

Calle Ocho was unrecognizable. Mary thought the scene was more worthy of a city like Rio de Janeiro or Havana than Miami, and the area showed how much the presence of her black brothers had been eclipsed by Latinos, above all in the tremendous Cuban influence. As soon as he set foot there, Nicotiano associated the open air festive atmosphere with the carnivals of his childhood in Villalona.

Tens of thousands of sweaty, eager people thronged Calle Ocho from Fourth Ave., on up to 27th in Sagüesera, in a stretch of colorful, deafening hustle and bustle and unbridled jubilation. Robust smells of fried onion and beef, *churros* and fried fish, alcohol and *empanadas*, *tamales* and croquettes, thickened in a *salsa* of collective sweat, seasoned with the most strident of colognes and indiscreet of deodorants.

No fewer than seventy-eight platforms, each with a different orchestra, provided the entertainment for that fiesta, whose colors, frenzy and disproportion, made it unique. There were Latinos from every country, and the music, food and delirious hip-shaking united them in a frenzy which in Mary's eyes bordered on hysteria but which, clearly, made them feel alive, that they belonged to an undefinable, yet vibrant race, maybe making them feel even more real than they felt during their normal work day. Despite the insurmountable differences in social status, political affiliation, skin color and national origin, that festive atmosphere leveled them, made them anonymous, lumped them into with one single human wave looking to get drunk, be unruly and celebrate. The contagious rhythms of the Mexican *corridos*, Dominican *merengues*, Colombian *cumbias*, *sambas*, calypsos, *lambadas* and all sonorous links of the Cuban *son*, which in commercial terms was called *salsa*, brought together thousands upon thousands of thronging dancers who moved from one stage to the next, all caught up in the same delirium. It was as if you should have taken part in that precious occasion right down to the last drop and with an intensity that would exclude any inhibition.

On a corner was a group of Cubans, both white and black, clad in shirts with frills and huge pink, yellow and blue ruffles on the sleeves, playing a *guaguancó* that stood out with its high tide of drums and harpsichords, in spite of all the surrounding noise. A gaunt woman with bleached, thinning hair, whose age was beyond estimates, though she was very close to a century old, was swinging her hips in sensual steps and with her eyes rolled back as if the *guaguancó* were possessing her with its lascivious swing. Everyone had formed a circle and the agile old woman, with the mood of a dreaming teenager, moved lewdly about, opening and closing her legs, waving her skinny arms riddled with the madness of the century, and you couldn't tell if she was going to levitate with the rhythm or if she would collapse in a trance, vanquished by her own happiness. The old woman was now gently placing one hand on her temple as she moved her waist in a circle and made her shoulders lightly shake to the *son*, which now seemed almost vegetable, from the drums, whose obsessive flow of refined, ritual, repetitive pounding seemed to loosen the old woman's joints. Her other hand, which gave the impression of having lots of fingers, all of them skinny and fly-away, like fringe, sketched arabesques in the congested *salsa* of the air. Suddenly, there was a change in rhythm, the wave became more insistent and the drums were pulled out of shape, provoking a shaking in the old woman's little body:

Anabacoa coa coa
Anabacoa coa coa

Que you me voy a Guanabacoa...
Patikimbombo, patikimbó
Arroz con picadillo, yucá
Sal de la cueva, majá
Que yo me voy a Guanabacoa...

Amid the festive fervor, a man ran from one side to the other, as if a scorpion had stung him, holding up a sign and shouting: *Cuba without Fidel Castro, Cuba without Fidel Castro*! Mary and Nicotiano, under the attentive eyes of Maribarbola, passed by a place where there were a couple of tables adorned with Cuban flags, and some groups called "Center for Cuban Democracy" was collecting signatures calling for a plebiscite in Havana. A man bathed in sweat, but that's not why he loosened his tie, and who, with the help of a bullhorn, was shouting out more stridently than Celia Cruz's voice, haranguing the drunk and parading crowd, which he ignored, and he went on: Gather around ladies and gentlemen, support the civic company of all decent and patriotic patriots for the celebration of a plebiscite that would return freedom to our Cuban island!

The political competition, on the other hand, had been masquerading as a carnival, but it was just as carnivalized despite the sweet, rhythmic and gastronomic melodies of the Festival. The Cuban American Transaction, always diligent, had set up a platform surrounded with tables flamboyantly mantled with the glorious Cuban flag. On the platform was a crusty group of old men whose age ranged from 75 and 79 years old and who constituted "the purest nucleus of Cubans affected by the expropriations of Communism on the island", according to another activist shouting, emulating in verbal flourishes through a bullhorn to his closest neighbor while explaining the content of the lists which, like long Egyptian scrolls, were on the table: everything that had been a possession before 1959 in Cuba: real estate, land or any kind of property, must immediately be written down on the lists, so whenever Fidel Castro falls and a Department of Misappropriated Property, overseen by Transaction, goes into action, all of the old property would be legally returned. The activist interviewed the lot of living remains one by one; they could barely stand on the platform, with one of them bitterly complaining that "there in the province of Pinar del Río," in the place where there was once his residence and his "little lands," was now a big school for handicapped students.

"What am I going to do with those installations," the old man complained, almost inaudibly due to the loops and flourishes of the flute solo coming from the nearby band.

Not far from all the politicking was the platform of a religious group, no less inspired and frenetic, who were selling tee-shirts, hats, balloons and shorts with the unfathomable inscription written on them:

CHRIST HAS RESERVED A PLACE FOR YOU
IN THE OASIS OF TRUE HAPPINESS!

Then Mary, dying of laughter, asked herself what place would be the most appealing to the blessed in that "oasis", whether under a co-conut tree, as in all the travel agency ads, or alongside one of God's streams. Nicotiano told her there was no sense worrying about it, since the best places would already be reserved for those who could afford a first class ticket, or even a round trip one. But their laughter was covered over by the pitch of the music, all the jostling, the roasted pig, all the tramping about and asses shaking in the heat, which was first perfumed, then revolting. Then they saw a group of not fewer than two hundred young people pushing their way through like a school of strange fish, handing out religious posters, carrying huge cardboard signs that covered their chests and backs. In a few gothic-like letters inked in a golden phosphorescence, the signs proclaimed:

CHRIST LOVES CALLE OCHO

A conga line swept through, and the school of religious fish scattered. It was a group of blacks in white tee-shirts with red bandanas around their necks and they were playing base drums made by hand and four trumpets, two trombones and drums slung from the waist. The rhythm they were pounding out with their march was irrepressible, roaring and dissonant, though irresistible like a hit of narcotizing smoke, dragging Nicotiano and Mary along for a good distance without them being able, or wanting, to separate from that dazzling scene. Amid the human wave, a group of tourists, which judging by the solar peeling of their noses and by the ruddy cramping of their dancing efforts to the rigor of the conga, were probably Scandinavians, perhaps led there by some tourist guidebook from the hotels in Fort Lauderdale or Miami Beach. They were trying to maintain a minimum of decency in all the pawing and clumping together of that lawless party, all the while nibbling on *tamales*, and the conga line whirled around them like a cyclone of music and whipped up participants. The trumpets blared away and the chorus irresistibly bellowed: Ay…Malembe, la Sagüesera ni se rinde ni se vende…¡Malembe!

Suddenly, as if somebody had opened a curtain of an impossible dream, on the corner of 14th Ave., they saw a swarm of kids pulling on bright-colored ribbons of a creole piñata in the form a huge *yaray* hat, three stories high and 30 feet wide. Endless sweets, toys and balloons spilled out of the piñata and the happy throng of kids would have absorbed the attention of the couple if Nicotiano hadn't discovered that there on the corner, undaunted and light like a float that the tide brings and takes, oblivious to himself and the crowd thanks to the drunkenness that threatened to knock him to the ground, was the ex-member of the expeditionary force of the glorious Assault Brigade 2506, the semi-parachute jumping diabetic Curro Pérez. Curro was holding up signs which were very similar to the ones the religious group had, but more of a home-made creation; they were hanging like a sandwich over his chest and back and said, in uneven letters painted in water-color:

WE MERCENARIES
OF THE BAY OF PIGS
DESERVE
A PENSION
AS REGULAR SOLDIERS
IN THE UNITED STATES
ARMED FORCES,
GODDAMMIT!

"If it weren't for the fact that he was so drunk," Nicotiano lamented, "and for the fact that he looks crazy, I would have split Curro's poor head open."

It was quite an accurate observation, since every so often somebody would pass by and deliver a blow to the once brave and admired mercenary, as if he were just a homeless kid who never bothered to learn anything in school. Nicotiano tried to take Curro with him so that the drunk could sleep it off on the Island of Cundeamor, but he could barely establish contact with him.

"I'm exercising," the great ex-mercenary belched out and explained grandiloquently without recognizing Nicotiano, "my sacred democratic rights, goddammit!"

And he stood there on the corner, stubborn and pathetic: beached, like the rusted-out, hole-riddled skeleton of a landing boat on the solitary beach of the treacherous ruins of the era he was forced to live in, all the while the happy crowd jostled him and, between all the insulting jokes, splashed him with Budweiser or rum.

"Don't drown," somebody shouted and they pushed him down.

The Queen of the Festival was Celia Cruz. Despite the fact that Mary was getting tired and wanted to leave, Nicotiano made her stay for a minute to see Celia, that natural force of Cuban earth and sun, the syncopated booming voice of that collection of islands beneath the wind. Celia was singing with the Tito Puente Orchestra and they were paying tribute to the "Barbarian of Rhythm," Benny Moré. The huge crowd was electrified and jammed together in front of the stage where Celia and Tito performed, and it was impossible to get through. This was where Maribarbola lost them.

Until that moment he had followed them without any real problems, despite the human whirlpool they moved through. But suddenly Maribarbola found himself face to face with a betrayal he had never thought of: practically right in front of him, dressed in white pants and a shirt with multi-colored hibiscus design, wearing black pimp-like glasses just so the son of a bitch wouldn't be recognized, was Doublestein; he was also wearing a little party hat in an attempt to blend in with the Latin atmosphere of the Festival. He was hanging all over a young boy, who was bending over as he danced, snaking his body like a belly dancer. Sometimes they would stop dancing and, completely ignoring to the stares and shouts of "Hey, you crazy bitches, go somewhere where it's dark," they would give each other little amusing kisses and whirl about gaily using the music as camouflage for their embraces. The delicate little boy-snake was scarfing down bread with roasted pork. Maribarbola, who knew how to control his emotions and hold back his aggressiveness in order to direct it completely against a chosen target, could not hold back this time, not his emotions nor his hands. A couple near him was making their way through the crowd, each one carrying a plate of codfish croquettes, and Maribarbola, so quickly that the couple didn't have time to react, snatched the croquettes and, without saying a word, stepped in front of Doublestein and his delicate companion and proceeded to smear the croquettes into both of their faces. The de-croquetted couple was about to protest, maybe even throw a punch, but seeing Maribarbola use the croquettes so quickly and stealthily, they roared with laughter: "Hey, men, look how the fags have been creamed!," all the while Celia Cruz was ruining the spell of her Caribbean style as she sang "When I Left Cuba." Then Maribarbola ripped off Doublestein's sun glasses, threw them to the litter-strewn ground and aimed a closed-fist punch perfectly designed to split an eye open and give him a shiner with the look of those bowls of black bean stew that sometimes goes cold on a table because nobody liked it. The ensuing confusion was like a separate small crowd in the center of the ongoing movement and noise of the street party. The little queen was trembling like a tree in a strong wind and Doublestein passed out, after asking Maribarbola for a thousand pardons, but Maribarbola didn't hear him, since he had already elbowed his way through the crowd, trying in vain to locate Mary and Nicotiano.

The next day, Nicotiano, happy and full of energy, left Mary in bed and got up at dawn to work on his sculptures. Speechless from so many impressions, he didn't know if he had dreamt everything or if he had really been diving down into that pond of madness. It would be about nine or ten that morning when Mary, having bathed and eaten breakfast, went into the studio and said she was going home. Nicotiano would pick her up that night to go out to eat at a nice restaurant.

They would never see that dinner.

At exactly two that afternoon, Mireya arrived at the Island of Cundeamor.

She refused to go inside and didn't want to talk to me; she asked for a moment with Nicotiano and waited for him at the front gate. He was immersed in his work and become very nervous when he found out that Mireya had come to see him. Mireya, speak with me? First, whether out of pride or fear, he felt like refusing to see her.

"Get out of here and go ask her what she wants, boy," Cocrioco ventured to say, "after all, she was your wife for all those years…"

Nicotiano lighted a Cohiba, that fine Cuban cigar, perhaps one of the best cigars in the world (Hetkinen had gotten them from the elements that had sneaked past the economic embargo against Cuba), and, puffing away to mitigate his emotional confusion, he headed towards the front gate.

Mireya didn't look well at all; she had lost weight, but not in a good way; she had large circles under her eyes and wrinkles that Nicotiano didn't remember. Upon seeing her, he thought that he himself probably had the same destroyed look.

"You've aged, Nicotiano," she said, without saying hello.

"Yes, Mireya, when you left, I spent a lot of time not sleeping, practically not living. You don't age little by little, but in fits and starts.

"That's right," she said in a whisper, "…in fits and starts."

Then she said:

"Only you all are left on the Island of Cundeamor."

"Aunt Ula doesn't want to move. You know how she is. But in the long run, we'll have to give everything up to Transaction."

"Nicotiano…" There was a dense sadness in the young woman's voice; it sounded as if the words would get caught in her throat before she could pronounce them. And when she talked she didn't look at him, but kept her eyes fixed on the palm trees that flanked the main driveway to the house.

"Nicotiano…"

He did look at her: Mireya, his Mireya, seemed almost smaller, crumpled inside and out. Again: that was life? What he had lived before, what was that? His Mireya seemed strange to him, at the same time she felt very close, and the unreal, foreign palm trees that lined the road leading to the house in which they had been happy.

"Were we happy, Mireya?"

"Of course we were, but we always make mistakes, I lost sight of what I had, your enormous value, the value of your love, and I threw it all away…Nicotiano…I suffered a lot, I know you have, too. I've treated you badly, I've humiliated you, I've trampled on your manhood, I'm aware of all that…But I've come to understand that you're the only thing I have. I've felt happy with you, really, you're the only one I've truly felt happy with in my whole stinking life…."

"That's enough, Mireya, don't put yourself down: you loved somebody else, and that's all. I've already gotten used to that horror, it's all right to poke at old wounds. Tell me now, please, what do you want?"

"To come back, Nicotiano," and she looked up from the leaves of the palm tree and stared at the radiant sky, as if she were swallowing back a fit of crying. He was unable to come up with an answer and she looked directly at him. She wasn't crying; she was torn up on the inside.

"It's too late, Mireya."

"It's like I've smashed into the ground, Nicotiano. From the top of a tree, from a goddamn balloon. I feel like I've been deflated, overvalued everything that wasn't you or me…What am I without you? Nothing, dammit, nothing: You've been the best part of my life…I know I mean a lot to you…As for that other man…it was an attraction, I don't know, I fell in love with him like a school girl, but deep down I didn't love him, deep down I knew there was nothing for me…As for falling in love, there's nothing left, it's over, that man is dead and buried. Because I want you to know that he didn't give me anything, not in terms of sex or on a more general human plane, nothing, we barely had anything to talk about…"

"That's enough, Mireya, I don't accept that. You gave him your body and he used it however he wanted and, you also got pleasure from his body. None of what you're saying makes sense. Because for me the most important thing is not what he gave you or stopped giving you, but what you were looking for in him, and what you gave him."

"Nothing, I didn't give him anything...Nicotiano, that man is a sack of yams, making love with him was like...like screwing a fried egg."

He smiled, somberly, almost because he had to, but she did not smile.

"The important thing isn't any of that," she continued in a labored voice, "but the causes. This has been a total identity crisis. I'm a woman who can't have children, Nicotiano!" And she started to cry.

"Frustrated for a thousand reasons," she added. "You weren't present in my life; Cocorioco and those stone crabs were more real to you then I was. And when you leave someone alone...emotionally alone...she looks for something else, an escape valve, someone to tell her problems to, to look for perspective and to run away from the situation we had created at home, a way of life that was unbearable...Let's adopt a child, Nicotiano...I'm desperate to have a child, even if it isn't mine, even though I can't have it inside of me for nine months and go through labor pains. Let Hetkinen steal it from wherever and give it to us, I know he can do it, let him buy it, a baby, you ask Aunt Ula and she'll tell Hetkinen and that's that...Oh, let me come back, Nicotiano, I beg you, accept my love, let's sit down and talk and try to create a new life, more for both of us, to do things to satisfy you and me both, not just sculptures, the Crabb Company, please, we have our whole lives ahead of us."

"You've hurt me in a way, Mireya, that makes any kind of reconciliation impossible."

"Hit me then, slap me, smash my face, do whatever you want with me, choke me, put out an eye, smack me around...What do you want, for me to eat dirt, drag my tongue down the street? He didn't give me anything, even if you don't believe me, that's the way it is; but at home you didn't give me anything either...To you I was a ghost, I was worthless, to be discarded. So...it was act of desperation. He made me feel excited, the tension of the forbidden and the feeling that it was an act of freedom, something I could do by myself, behind your back, against your will...In some way, that made me feel bigger inside, but at the same time it covered me in disgrace. Not for what will they say, I couldn't care less, but for my integrity, Nicotiano, because that guy is a cynic and isn't worth spit."

"I'm in love with another woman."

Mireya's eyes gleamed like a switchblade somebody flicked open.

"Who?"

"A girl from Liberty City. We're going to get married, we're going to take a trip to Cuba. We're getting the papers in order...We're going to have children."

"You're in love with a black girl from Liberty City? You're going to have children with her?"

"That's right."

"Nicotiano, that doesn't make sense, it's a mirage...it's cruel revenge against me. Look at me, dammit, look at me and tell me the truth: don't you still love me?"

He answered her with all the sincerity he could muster:

"Yes, Mireya, it feels like I still love you a great deal. And I think I'll still love you, as long as you live."

Mireya didn't let him talk anymore. She hugged him and covered him with kisses on his neck, head, chest, eyes and finally she violently covered his mouth with hers. He made a feeble attempt to pull away, but, without stopping her kisses, she begged him not to reject her, to accept her remorse and her love.

This was the scene Mary saw from her car.

She had rushed over to tell Nicotiano what was going on in Liberty City, but seeing him kissing another woman, she parked at a distance. A white woman. A Cuban woman. Probably his wife. The woman he had serenaded.

A day earlier, while they were having fun at the Calle Ocho Festival, three cops of Cuban descent had killed a black businessman in Liberty City while trying to take him down to jail. One of the cops implicated was Johnny Rodriguez, the officer who came to the Island of Cundeamor to investigate the mystery of McIntire's shots. A wave of protest was then unleashed in the whole black community in Miami and now the violence had intensified: vandalism, shots, deaths, and injuries, looting, cars burning in the streets, battles between the police and blacks looking for justice for the brutal homicide.

Nicotiano saw Mary's car as she threw it into reverse, swerved full speed and disappeared in a flash. Mireya saw her as well.

"It's her, isn't it? It's her, dammit!"

For a moment, Nicotiano stood paralyzed, with Mireya hanging off his neck and kissing him harder. Life, such was the life of adults: always difficult. Because now he was a grown man, no? He had come out from the imaginary time of his childhood, late and worse for wear, and love presents itself with a double-edged sword, sharp even at the handle. Or maybe he was still the boy sculptor, incapable of understanding the complications of passion. In any case, love was an eternal misunderstanding. You can forget what's inside you, cough too loud and explode. You fall asleep, wake up a little sleepy, light a cigarette without realizing it. Anything that one might do, it is said, as well-intentioned as it might have seemed, would end up hurting *someone* terribly. But maybe there weren't any happy people in the world. What were happy people like? Because life without love, without giving himself over to a woman, was impossible, at least he didn't see a way to make it through life.

"Mary, Mary!" he shouted.

He had to shove Mireya aside to get her off him.

"Where are you going, Nicotiano, tell me where you're going!" she shouted.

He turned back.

"Everywhere," he said, in a voice that scared Mireya; "Everywhere."

Mireya came inside and we hugged each other. She told me a thousand incoherent things about her failure and her determination to go back to Nicotiano, before she told me what had happened and gave me the information that left my body stone-cold: Nicotiano had taken off after Mary. I was worried with fear and impotence, because it couldn't have happened on a more fateful day: Hetkinen, Maribarbola and Sikitrake were away from Miami, in Tampa, guarding a transfer of bank funds. I had heard about the uproar in Liberty City, which had now spread to places downtown and to Coconut Grove. The situation was so explosive that it was almost a civil war. After the brutal injustice committed by the police of Cuban descent, all the frustrations of the black community come to a head, like a monster unleashed.

As he drove, Nicotiano thought, in blind rage, that the vortex of that tornado affecting his life had a name: betrayal.

"Betrayal is like fire in the same way that it's like marble: inside them, life is impossible."

However, for some reason, which apparently no one had to understand, just accept, everyone was always willing to betray others. That execrable willingness existed in all beings, and it only required certain conditions to appear, unscrupulous: Mireya, the ex-mercenary Curro Pérez and the men who put him in that mess, Pájara Pinta, Bartolo, all the Cuban exiles, he himself. It was if human beings didn't care about betrayal; sure, that was the lesson, that deep down things like fakery, felony, treachery, infidelity and intrigue were, for humans, like grass for beasts and ever since the beginning of time everyone had always betrayed everyone. Cain will always continue to murder his brother Abel, everywhere. Loyalty and consideration were unusual things, even fidelity to the person we love most: all of that was nonsense! His childlike naivete, from the imaginary time over in Cuba, in his place of birth, when an unforgettable friend would be capable of any sacrifice for the sake of friendship. That was so far, far away; he had become an adult, finally dammit, finally; he had not only matured, but he had aged, and maturing meant learning how to betray others.

"I'm not going to throw any more bottles with messages into the ocean."

Nicotiano bypassed the barrier set up by police, who had fired off tear gas to make their way through, and he entered Liberty City on foot, trying to reach Mary's house, ask for forgiveness and explain what had happened.

The streets were ablaze. Everywhere he could hear gunshots, at times in volleys. Hordes of black citizens ravaged everything they found in their path, and Nicotiano thought: "They're pariahs in their own country, a country capable of the most colossal and criminal waste, with the goal of putting a man on the moon, or of toppling a government on the other side of the sea, but incapable of providing even a minimally dignified life to their dark-skinned sons." As he was running through the gas, his mouth and nose covered with his shirt, which he had taken off, he thought that blacks in Miami had nothing to lose except their indignity, and he wanted to join them in their rebellion and destruction.

But Nicotiano wasn't black; Nicotiano was Cuban, maybe black and white in his heart, but not in his skin, and death was roaming the streets. At that moment, without asking why, the sculptor absurdly searched his pockets for the small snail which the children had given him at the beach that day he had cast the next to last bottle to sea, and when he didn't find it he felt the same despair that overtook him when he discovered he had lost it.

Two men grabbed him by the hair and threw him against a wall. When they threw him again, Nicotiano tried to explain, convince them that he was one of them, that they should let him go, that his girlfriend lived nearby and that he identified with their struggle, their insanity, their fury, but they attacked him and Nicotiano had to put up a fight by dealing them a couple of belly blows. A third man leapt on him from behind and pushed him out towards the street, where two young guys, kids practically, savagely struck him in the head with a couple of steel belaying pins.

Nicotiano staggered bleeding profusely, managing to still splutter please, that he wasn't an enemy, or maybe he mumbled Mary's name, but another savage blow to the head made his brains leap out and that's when the exile, doomed man and sculptor collapsed in a heap, his whole body shaking from a convulsion in his extremities that didn't end until a large Chevy ran right over him.

He remained there for a few hours, forgotten, bleeding to death next to an overturned and burning truck, until a gang, loaded down with loot that included appliances, food and clothes, passed right by him, fleeing the police, who were moving in to restore order. And then a man, who somehow found a bouquet of multi-colored flowers among the things he had stolen, made a quick stop so he wouldn't fall behind, pulled a white rose out from the bouquet, and put it into the gruesomely disfigured mouth of Nicotiano's corpse.

Alma Rosa and I

"You look a little more rested. There was a moment when I thought the pain would destroy you."

"I'll never be the same again. But our first order of business is to not let it kill us."

"What's going to happen now, Aunt Ula?"

"We're going to leave the island at the mercy of the Cuban American Transaction and move to Spain, which after all is the Motherland. Hetkinen, Cocrioco and the boys will find a big house in the hills of Málaga, near the countryside and the sea. According to Cocrioco, Cundeamor would grow very well there. We'll invest our money in Cuba. In a joint venture with a Spanish company and the government of Fidel Castro, we'll build a five-star hotel on the beach of Villalona."

"But Aunt Ula, people will be outraged, and with good reason, whenever they see you, a gusana *who made a fortune in exile while the people of Villalona remained poor and subjected to the most horrible deprivations for not having wanted to abandon the Revolution."*

"If somebody says that to me, I'll just tell them: "They said I wouldn't come, but here I am!"

"What are you going to call your hotel?"

"*Maybe Hotel Salsipuedes.*"

"*But Aunt Ula, you can't call a five-star hotel that.*"

"*Anything's possible on an island.*"

"*And what are you going to do with the dogs?*"

"*Gotero and Montavar will spend the rest of their days at a board-ing kennel.*"

"*And Kafka?*"

"*He'll go wherever we go, since he's eternal.*"

"*And the sculptures Nicotiano left behind?*"

"*We've donated most of them to the National Museum of Cuba. Since that insane North American blockade impedes doing even these kinds of things, we made an agreement with Cuban authorities and sent the crabs by sea, with the help of old man Santiago and as the biggest of secrets.*"

"*I wonder what will happen to us Cubans, Aunt Ula.*"

"*We'll fight and keep quiet. Times are bad for prophecies.*"

"*In Cuba people suffer and keep quiet; outside we bounce about like those bottles in the water. Look, Aunt Ula, how the segments of our novel are disappearing among the waves. Look how the sun reflects its light on the bottles.*"

"*The current's taking them away. They're scraps of our lives.*"

"*Aunt Ula, you were happy in Miami, right?*"

"*Not in Miami; on the Island of Cundeamor. But a diminished happiness is more harmful than the worst of sorrows.*"

"*Aunt Ula...Will you take me with you? I want to share your destiny.*"

"*You're welcome to come, Alma.*"

"*There's still one bottle left, but we've already sent the whole book out to sea. Should I throw out the empty bottle?*"

"*No. Get some clean paper, copy this last conversation, and write down what I'm going to dictate to you. This will be my last message from this side of the ocean.*"

"*Whatever you say, Aunt Ula.*"

Malmö, 1989-1992